THE SCAR

THE SCAR

Frank Kippax

COLLINS
8 Grafton Street, London W1
1990

William Collins Sons & Co. Ltd
London · Glasgow · Sydney · Auckland
Toronto · Johannesburg

First published in Great Britain by William Collins 1990

BRITISH LIBRARY CATALOGUING IN PUBLICATION DATA

Kippax, Frank
The scar.
I. Title
823'.914 [F]

ISBN 0-00-232231-5

Photoset in Linotron Trump Medieval by
Rowland Phototypesetting Ltd
Bury St Edmunds, Suffolk
Printed and bound in Great Britain by
William Collins Sons & Co. Ltd, Glasgow

FOR PETER AND RITA

ONE

'What I can't see,' said Paddy Collins, 'is what he gets out of life. I mean, for Christ's sake. The Porsche's never run. It's lying there, bleeding rotting. I mean, a Porsche, in a street like this, I ask you. And it's never moved, in two months to my certain knowledge. It's got a flat, front near side. What's he *got* it for?'

The fat man did not reply. He looked at the Porsche, though, because it was something for his eyes to do. Not something different – the men had been in the street for three hours now. Three hours and seventeen minutes, to be precise. He eased his buttocks on the driver's seat. They ached.

'Your arse killing you, as well?' said Collins. 'It's ironic, isn't it? We're in a bleeding Lada, with our arses wearing off, watching a prat with a Porsche he never drives. Jesus Christ, the *irony*. A bleeding Russian car. The *irony*.'

The fat man belched, quietly. He looked up and down the road, as he was meant to do from time to time, registering no change. A swirl of litter picked itself up a hundred yards away and dashed towards them. After a moment, though, it dropped back to the pavement. The gust, when it reached the Lada, shook it momentarily.

'Still,' said Collins. 'I suppose we'd look a bit conspicuous in a Porsche, wouldn't we? Even more conspicuous. Although what two grown men are doing in a bleeding car for hours on end in this dump's a mystery to me. It's a good job there's no one with any brains to see us, isn't it? I mean, if two blokes in a Lada sat in my road for three hours, I'd call the cops. Ridiculous.'

He gave a bark of laughter. He turned his face to the fat man. The fat man gave him a brief smile, as if apologising for his silence. He sucked his teeth.

'I'm bored,' he said. 'News time.'

Paddy Collins turned the radio on, and they listened in silence for a while. For the third day running the main news was the jail siege, somewhere North of the Border, somewhere where the savages ran around in skirts, and that was just the men. According to the reporter, there was snow on the ground up there. Snow on the ground, and snow on the roof where sixty-seven prisoners were standing, dressed in overalls and blankets. Collins shivered involuntarily.

'Mad,' he said. 'Fucking insane. They ought to bring back hanging, didn't they? As a blessed relief. Or transportation, to a warmer clime.'

The fat man sucked his teeth. He did it several times a minute, and most of his colleagues were driven mad by it. It made routine surveillance hell. Paddy Collins was indifferent. He did not even notice.

'That's what they're complaining about,' said the fat man. 'One of the things. Some of the precious darlings have been sent across the Border, haven't they? Dispersed to English jails. So their loved ones can't afford to visit them. Prats. Next it'll be because the porridge is too lumpy.'

'Do you know that one?' asked Paddy Collins. 'About the monastery? With the vow of silence? Apparently, there's one monk, see—'

'Yeah,' said the fat man. 'I do. Look. Black tart. Jesus, she don't live down here.'

The street, not far north from London's heart, was an eyesore. It was built in yellow-grey London brick, and the houses had not had a red cent spent on them since eighteen ninety-five, when they had been finished. It had been by-passed by the yuppie revolution. The prices explosion had never happened. It was a throwback.

Black women passed along it in plenty. In fact, more than half the people who had passed the watching men had been black women. Most of them had children in buggies, and all of them were poorly dressed. Like the Asians and the whites, whom Paddy Collins – his name and ancestry of no significance that he remembered – categorised as feckless bleeding Micks. The street breathed poverty.

Not so this woman. As she swung confidently along the dirty pavement towards them, the two men in the car eased their backs and stretched their legs, and watched. Collins leaned forward and switched the radio off. He twiddled a knob on the dashboard, and a red light came on. A small computer bleep sounded.

'We'll get a picture for the record,' he said. 'Jesus, wouldn't you just love to screw the arse off that?'

The woman, tall and elegant in slim black skirt and short white jacket, approached without apparently registering them. Why should she, indeed? Among the sad array of old and seedy motor cars along the gutter, only the Porsche was vaguely out of place, despite its filthy paintwork and dilapidated air. The Lada looked at home. Even if she had glanced at it, however, she would not have noticed that the rusty aerial was swivelling in its socket. The metal button on its top was only normal size, despite the camera lens inside it. Her features, as they were photographed, were firm, relaxed, and beautiful.

'One for the album,' said Paddy Collins, with satisfaction. Then: 'Jesus. I don't believe it!'

The fat man grinned at him.

'You can't see what he gets out of life, eh cock? There's things I'd rather do than drive a Porsche, any time.'

'Yeah,' said Paddy Collins. 'But how does he *do* it, that's what I'd like to know. How does the bastard *do* it?'

The tall and lovely black woman was at the top of the steps, her finger on the bell. After a moment or two, the door opened. Andrew Forbes, thirty-nine and scruffy, blinked at her in the daylight. The camera in the aerial blinked simultaneously. Two perfect mugshots, in one frame . . .

The coal in the small iron stove dropped gently, making hardly a sound. It was enough to wake Sarah Williams, although the man beside her did not stir. She looked at his back, the shoulder covered in fine blonde hair, and smiled. Despite the stove, the air inside the narrowboat had a raw edge to it, still, so she carefully took the corner of the multi-coloured counterpane. As she began to draw it up, to cover him, he awoke.

'Oh. Sorry. I was trying to keep you warm.'

Michael Masters grinned. He was lying on his front, and as he rolled over, to see her better, the counterpane moved too, wrapping itself round him, slipping across the bed, across Sarah, and into the small gap between them. Sarah, naked, laughed.

'So much for my act of kindness. Thanks!'

Masters, lying on his side now, facing her, lifted the covers and shook his shoulders to free them. Sarah moved her body into his as the counterpane was wrapped back over her. She felt his penis hardening against her stomach, immediately.

'Michael, you're an animal! Not again?'

Their eyes were close. They had to squint to see each other. They were smiling happily, relaxed.

'Not really. Just an old man's whim. Although come to think

of it, perhaps I ought to. They probably don't have girls like you in jail.'

He said it with a laugh, but Sarah's face clouded. She did not like it, not even as a joke.

'Shut up, darling,' she said. 'Please.'

Sarah closed her eyes, and Michael began to stroke her hair, gazing across her shoulder, across the cabin of the narrowboat, and into the cold grey sky. The branches of a tree were visible, already showing buds. They were shaking in the bitter, gusty wind.

'I'm not going to a proper prison,' he said, quietly. 'Six months, that's all. In Ford Open. For God's sake, it'll be nicer than being at home, in some ways. No bloody kids and dogs, for starters.'

'So it's nice then, is it?' said Sarah, after a tiny, timed, pause. 'Being at home?'

Unseen by her, Masters rolled his eyes slightly. He patted her bare backside, in the warmth of the bed. He squeezed.

'You know what I mean, Thing,' he said. 'Nicer than being outside. John says I can have anything I want. Booze, books, bloody caviare on toast if I want it. It'll be a rest cure.'

She kept her eyes tight closed.

'And no you,' he said. He began to stroke her bottom, letting his fingers dip between her thighs into the warm, wet matted fur. 'Think of that. My balls'll be like hand grenades. Count to five and I'll go off like a bomb!'

Sarah laughed, despite herself. She pushed him in the chest, swinging her legs out from underneath the counterpane, her bare toes feeling delicately for the floor.

'Later,' she said. 'I'm not ready yet. I need a pee and a gin. Cover that thing up. Disgusting.'

Michael Masters did so, making a little boy face.

'Not so much tonic this time, Thing,' he said. 'And put some coal on the stove, eh? Make yourself useful.'

Sarah Williams stood facing him. She was five feet four, black-haired, and magnificent.

'You're a cheeky sod,' she said. 'I shan't miss you at all. Not in the slightest.'

Masters dropped onto his back, studying the smoke-darkened wood of the deckhead.

'I'll be out in under four months,' he said. 'If I'm a good boy. Wouldn't it be nice if I could say I was in for the full six? I wonder if she'd believe me? Wouldn't that be nice?'

Sarah, framed in the doorway between the cabin and the lavatory, did not smile. Inside, she was completely hollow . . .

On the ground at Buckie, on the southern shoreline of the Moray Firth, Rosanna Nixon was the last of the press contingent to seek the warmth of Eliot's Bar. Her nose was red, her eyes were running, and her hands were knots of pain. Still she stood there, huddled by a wall, as the shadows lengthened and the sun from time to time lighted the rolling white horses before disappearing behind another racing cloud.

She had been there a day now, since relieving a sick colleague, during which time she had filed two stories back to Glasgow, and nothing – absolutely nothing – had happened. The wind had howled across the firth from the north and east, there had been occasional flurries of snow, and she had stood and stared at Buckie Jail. It was, she had decided, the most extraordinary, the most terrible, sight she had ever seen, and also the most frustrating. It rose black and square from the green fields on the cliff top, stark granite against the pale, cloud-flecked sky, and it had an air of ancient malice, of malevolence about it. It was designed to take in human beings, and grind them down, and break their spirits, it was a crushing mill. And nobody, no one at all, seemed to give a damn.

As the light drained slowly from the sky, and the western hills turned from dark green to black, Rosanna tried – and failed again – to drag her eyes from the men who refused to be crushed. Blinking away the tears of exposure, she tried to count the small dark shapes among the chimney stacks, whom, all day, the police had photographed obsessively. According to the Scottish Office, they were thugs and murderers and worse, who had gone up to escape retribution after rioting and injuring eleven prison officers. Their banners told a different story: of violence and sadism, a cruel regime and cold indifference to complaints, of prisoners cut off from all human company, and others sent to England, where no relatives could afford to go to visit them. They wanted an inquiry.

When Rosanna finally went into the back room at Eliot's, an ironic cheer rose from the team of pressmen. She was known to many of the Glasgow crew as young, and inexperienced, and a graduate entry to the profession. She was quiet and a trifle superior, and she had Bleeding Heart written all over her. In her heavy coat and boots, her woollen hat pulled down so far it almost touched her dripping nose, she did not even look worth trying to get to bed. Some of her colleagues, not inaptly, referred to her as the Mouse. She put her own hand into her pocket to buy a drink.

Later, though, when they'd got a few big ones inside them, they were friendlier. This involved mocking her unmercifully, but in a jocular way, about her absurd belief that the Buckie Jail siege mattered, or that anybody really cared.

'Forget it, hen, God's sake!' yelled a man called Angus. 'They bastards up there are just thickarses. The government'll see them freeze or starve to death before they lift a finger. Damn right too.'

'How is it right?' yelled Rosanna. She had to yell because the bar was full, and everyone was drinking whisky, in full-throated cry. 'They've been brutalised! Conditions in Buckie are appalling!'

Those who were near enough to hear her, yelped with laughter. There were prison officers in Eliot's now, their shifts at the barricades over. Policemen, too. Many of the journalists were chatting to them, happily, hoping to pick their brains for usable quotes and bankable opinions.

'Tell that crap to them lads!' roared Angus. 'If you dare! Those men on the roof are animals. You're wet behind the ears!'

Sandy Hamilton, slightly younger and less drunk, decided it was time to be nice. With four large Grouse inside him, and a pint or two of lager, he felt fairly irresistible. His eyes were wet with lust.

'I'm on your side, darling!' he shouted. 'The trouble is, the British government. The *English* government, should I say? Know what I mean?'

He moved in on her, rather unsteadily, trying to cut Angus out. Much to Rosanna's astonishment, the older man became proprietorial, taking her – none too gently – by the upper arm.

'Hey hey, laddie,' he warned. 'I saw her first. Back off.'

Rosanna jerked her arm free, spilling half her whisky. Both men immediately tried to buy another for her, and she in turn tried to attach herself to a different group. Luckily, it was getting late.

'Hi,' she said, to a photographer she knew. 'Look, what's the plan for keeping watch tonight? Or is there a rota system?'

He focused on her, after several seconds.

'Rota? What for?'

'Well,' said Rosanna. 'I only arrived today, so . . . Well, what if something happens? In the night?'

He blinked, apparently having difficulty maintaining her in view. Then he gestured round the room. It was bursting. Half the prison officers in Scotland seemed to be there.

'There's nothing happening tonight, Doll,' he said. 'You have my personal word for it. It's fixed.' He stopped, and his eyes glazed slightly. Then they cleared. They brightened, and he lumbered forward. Rosanna knew the signs too well.

'Unless,' he slurred, 'we have a little happening of our own?'

As Rosanna pushed her way to the door, she heard men talk about her. Her beloved and esteemed colleagues.

'Aye, Rosanna. Rosanna Nixon. She's a graduate, know what I mean?'

'I surely do. Knows fuck all and full of bullshit. She dresses something different, eh!'

'So she does. She's called the Mouse. Nice little pair of tits, though.'

'Aye.'

To her distress, Rosanna discovered she could see the roof of Buckie Jail from her hotel bedroom. She stood at the window for several hours, on and off, watching the huddled black shapes, picked out sometimes as moonlight slid behind the chimney stacks. The fringes of their kingdom were illuminated constantly, and harshly, by mobile batteries of electric lamps.

One of the men she watched, although she did not know it then, was called Jimmy McGregor.

Donald Sinclair's arrival in Buckie, like his departure from London, had gone unnoticed, just as he'd intended. He had flown from Heathrow to Aberdeen, alone, and taken a taxi the fifty-odd miles to the cold, bleak little town. The driver was not surprised at the extravagance involved, assuming he was a pressman. A pretty miserable one, however, for unlike most reporters he would not talk about the siege at all. In fact, after several conversational gambits had been rebuffed, the driver lapsed into silence and the passenger closed his eyes to the stark landscapes and appeared to go to sleep.

He had not slept, however. Although there was nothing more he could do to affect the outcome of the operation – except perhaps abort it – it was a matter of total, absorbing interest to him. It was his plan, and his alone, and if it came off he was made. By the time he got his first glimpse of the jail, as the car rounded a coast road bend, he was in an odd state. The startling vision, black granite against the wild, clean sky, made his stomach lurch. Before, he had seen it only on TV.

'Stop,' he said. 'Isn't that amazing?'

The driver was probably more amazed by the sudden decision to communicate. He liked to talk, especially on long trips, and he was resentful. He came to an ungracious halt.

'When we get closer,' he said, 'you'll see the cabaret. If the government had any sense, they'd bomb the place.' He gave a grunt of laughter. 'Some hopes of that. They ought to send the SAS in, and do the job. Who'd mourn them? Shoot the scum.'

The fare had reverted to type, apparently. He did not answer. In the mirror, the driver glanced at the face staring at the jail, its expression rapt. He banged the car into bottom, and moved off harshly. Probably a nut, he thought. Probably on the side of the madmen on the roof. He looks like a psychiatrist.

The siege at Buckie was the third in Scotland in as many months, and 'bombing the place', if the taxi driver had but known it, had damn nearly been considered as an option. In Whitehall it was generally felt – if not said aloud – that Scotland was another country, and the inmates of its prisons were a breed of semi-savage wildmen. But it was spring now, and the fear was that as the weather warmed up, the infection would spread across the Border. The rumbling discontent in England's prisons was real enough, and in many ways the conditions and the overcrowding were even worse. The Scottish example, the frequently recurring protests on the roof, the hostage-taking, the cries of 'brutality' and 'repression', the demands for an inquiry – they were a danger and a running sore. The Prime Minister, finally, had cried enough. In eight short months two men had failed to solve the problem and had seen their hopes of higher office and political advancement crumble. Another man was hanging on by the skin of his teeth. And then there was Sinclair.

As he paid off the disgruntled driver, as he checked into the small and unobtrusive Fox Hotel, pre-booked in the name of Philip Swift, Donald Sinclair savoured the continuing collision of emotions in his brain and belly. It was a high-risk game he was playing, and he loved high risks. The reality of the jail, its almost medieval air of brooding cruelty, had been the perfect touch. It was a fitting setting for a dangerous game.

Like most successful politicians, Sinclair was an opportunist. Although home affairs had always been his area of special interest and although he had watched the deteriorating situation in the prisons with great interest, he had made no overt moves to get involved. He had known the first junior minister to lose his head over the problem quite well, and he had picked his brains – while quietly expressing sympathy over drinks – so that he might avoid the same mistakes if his chance should ever come. When the second man had gone Sinclair had begun to do some pretty in-depth thinking and research, and also to make his interest known to the Home Secretary, Sir Gerald Turner. But when Turner had asked if he might like to be actively considered for the bed of nails, Sinclair had demurred.

'Quite honestly,' he had told the older man, 'I'm not sure if I'm ready for it. The way I see it, the problem's impossible in England, and in Scotland ten times worse. It needs a genius. The wisdom of Solomon.' He paused, then grinned, engagingly. 'I'm working on it, though. I'll tell you when I've found the answer!'

It was a bold joke, and they both laughed. In the event, the post of Under Secretary, Home Office (Prisons) had gone to a pale and ineffectual lawyer-politician called Cyril Richardson, the greyness of whose suits exactly matched the greyness of his mind. Donald Sinclair was well satisfied at that, because he did not think Richardson would survive another major crisis. By the time the Buckie siege blew up, nine weeks later, he had completed his research, and formed his strategy. When Cyril Richardson collapsed from nervous exhaustion shortly before he was due to face questions in the House, Sinclair judged the time was ripe. He picked up his office telephone and spoke to Sir Gerald's secretary. Two hours later the men were face to face.

Gerald Turner was a comfortable man, and for a minister of the Crown, a rather civilised one. He had been Home Secretary for five years, five years in which the crime rate had soared and the number of people behind bars had inexorably risen, and he had survived. He had his own views on the questions of law, and crime, and punishment, which would have surprised a very large number of people if he had ever expressed them publicly. But at the annual party conference he always made the right noises, and he was able to listen with apparent sympathy and concern when the question of a return to hanging raised its – to him – dreary and irrelevant head. He spent many peaceful hours sailing his Nicholson 32 in the pleasant waters of the Channel with his wife Elizabeth, a process which somehow gave him strength to view with equanimity a job he basically found distasteful. When

Sinclair offered him a solution, he was prepared to give him undivided attention.

'Firstly,' he said, when the preliminaries were over and both men were seated in comfortable chairs with cups of coffee, 'firstly, Donald, are you proposing a solution just to Buckie, or to everything?'

Donald Sinclair smiled. He took it as a reference back to his joke about Solomon. Then he allowed a serious look to settle on his face.

'I'm not completely a fool,' he replied. 'I honestly believe I can sort out Buckie, given luck and back-up. If I can – if I do – who knows what might not happen? I think I can do it so well, I think it will be such a concrete solution, that the Scottish problem might cool off. The copy-cat effect might lose momentum. And if that proves so . . . well, with a bit of luck the summer in England might be bearable.'

The Home Secretary sipped his coffee.

'You're not thinking of the SAS?' he asked quietly. 'Because if you are, Donald, forget it. We've had enough gung ho military solutions in the last few years to last a lifetime. We've kept the lid on pretty well, as you know. But one more inquest, one more documentary, one more arrest attempt that turns into a . . . well, let's just say it's no longer on.'

Sinclair nodded.

'I'm afraid I agree, rather,' he said. 'I sometimes wonder how long the myth of infallible brilliance can last in the face of so many botched-up jobs. But no, I wasn't thinking of an SAS solution anyway. Any fool could send the Army in and clear the siege up inside twenty minutes. But the TV and the press are there already. Apart from the visible brutality aspect, the overkill effect, it strikes me there's another danger there, a very real one. Even if they pulled it off successfully, the prisoners somehow share the glory, don't they? If you need the hardmen to clear them out, presumably they're the hardmen too. That's how they'd see it, anyway, and the gutter press as well, in all probability. But . . .' He paused, significantly. 'But I'm quite surprised the PM. . . ?'

It was a question, which Gerald Turner's smile acknowledged, then dismissed.

'I am the Secretary of State,' he said. 'That's all you need to worry about at present, isn't it? I'll grant you this: a lot of rules are already being bent or broken at the moment, because the PM wants a solution, once and for all, and, as you've guessed, the PM is for boldness. In theory, this whole Scottish problem should be handled by the Scottish Office and the Scottish Secretary, as you know. It hasn't been, as you also know, because results are needed, results by any means. If I give you permission to stick your oar in too, you'll be stepping on a lot of corns. If you fail, Donald, I can promise you the knives are out. So good it's got to be. Bloody good.'

Now, musing at the open door of the drinks fridge in his Buckie room, Donald Sinclair felt the apprehension level rise slightly, enough to outweigh the excitement. The plan was good, and simple, and almost foolproof. Gerald Turner had been most impressed and had generously said so. But of course, the military were involved, they had to be in some capacity unless he was going to go in himself, alone. A small team of soldiers – not the SAS – a handful of selected civil servants, the governor of the jail. What Sinclair feared was the potential that a minor cock-up, a slight mistake, could precipitate a disaster.

He glanced at the miniature bottle of malt whisky in his hand, then twisted his wrist to reveal the face of the slim platinum watch. It had been a present, although only he knew it, from Gerald Turner's daughter Carole, who had once been his mistress. Sinclair's eyes registered the watch, not just the time, and his brain registered the irony. What would his chances have been if Sir Gerald had ever worked out that particular truth? The tiny flutter of apprehension, irrationally, increased.

'I'm scared,' said Donald Sinclair, and he laughed. 'I'm bloody terrified.'

As he said it, the fear slid rapidly away, exorcised. But Sinclair, having felt it, knew its potential. Firmly, he replaced the miniature Laphroaig and closed the little fridge. Later he would drink champagne, perhaps. He laughed again. Or fall into the gutter with a pint of meths . . .

Up on the roof of Buckie Jail, nobody had spoken for more than an hour. The routine had become so crippling, the cold so intense, that in the night hours the men entered a state approaching coma. They remained in their normal groupings – men who liked each other, or at least shared lives – but human contact became nominal, irrelevant. Not that their night was dark. From the heart of blackness at the centre, by the chimneys, they stared out, if they stared at all, at intense, white, painful light.

For all Jimmy McGregor knew, straining his eyes into the harsh electric barrier, there could be anything out there. There could be soldiers with high-powered rifles, there could be a commando of paras ready to scale the walls, there could be a division of Russian bloody tanks. He and his fellow prisoners had been up so long, had talked, and argued, and fantasised so long, that if the Kraken itself had awoken and peeped through the arc lights he would not have been surprised. They had burst out of the prison, smashed ceilings and slates and joists, in a white-hot rage that had been months maturing. In the last three days, it had been chilled from their very marrows. It was being frozen out of them.

Jimmy McGregor's job in all this, because many of the prisoners were too feckless, too enraged, to really care, was to watch a two-foot hole through which the empire might strike back. He sat at it now, his back to an angle of stone, his legs dangling into the darkened roofspace below, and let the thoughts of that empire warm him, momentarily, with the warmth of hatred. The rage he could remember, but not with any vividness any more: that part had truly frozen with his body. But the hatred was always there, like pus in an abscessed tooth, to be sucked and savoured. It was his sustenance. He was prepared, when it came down to it, to stay on the roof until he froze to death, or hell froze over.

A shape detached itself from the shadow of a chimney stack. Tall and thin, in blue denim and a woollen scarf. It came to Jimmy, stooped, and sat beside him. For several minutes nothing was said. When he did speak, his voice was hoarse and cracked. Francis Leadbitter was sixty-two years old.

'How are you feeling now, Jimmy?' he asked, without wishing for or waiting for an answer. 'I feel terrible myself, I've never felt worse in the whole of my life. If I don't get some proper food inside me soon, I think I'll vomit till I'm inside out. There's some of the lads, ye ken, who think we should go down. There's some of them that think enough's enough. I telled them. I said if you fancy a damn good kicking to help your stomach ache, that's the thing to do, OK? Toe-cap porridge, that's the story, right? What do you think, son?'

McGregor felt appalling, his mouth like lukewarm slime and his stomach aching, constantly. There were spots before his eyes, dancing, which had been there for thirty or forty hours, and made him dizzy when he stood. But he forced himself to respond.

'Shut up maundering, you daft old twat,' he said, almost affectionately. 'Nobody's going down there, sick or no. I telled them yesterday, and so did Porter and McBride. When it comes daylight I'll tell them again, OK? No one's going down.'

Leadbitter nodded, both pleased and satisfied. In his eyes, morale was cracking. But if McGregor thought he could hold it, fair enough. McGregor was a ringleader, a man who wouldn't take seconds from anybody, a hero. He was also the brother of Angus McGregor, universally accepted as the hardest man in all of Scotland's jails, the Animal.

'It's no me that's whining, by the way,' the old man said. 'I've sunbathed in worse than this. But some of the loons . . .' He looked at Jimmy sideways. 'You must admit, son, it's blistering cold.'

McGregor touched the soreness round his mouth and eyes. It was cold. Their hard luck, wasn't it? A cold snap in the middle of spring, winds enough to freeze a brass monkey. In the last three days even the wildest of the wildmen had begun to think half-longingly of their nice warm cells. It was cold.

'Listen, Grandad,' he said. 'You tell the soft lads. Every bugger's seeing us, even down in London. They're watching us, in the freezing fucking weather, doing nothing bad, just standing round like Eskimos to make our point, all right? The only way the government can end this, you tell 'em, is to send the troops in – and they can't. Because the telly's there, OK? And if they shoot us on the telly, they've blown it. You tell them.'

The old man grinned. He made an obscene gesture, to an imaginary camera. Like Jimmy, like all the others, he believed.

Sixty feet below him, the last of twenty armed men took up their positions. E-block, where they had been assembled, was still full of filth and debris from the start of the outbreak. Its devastated state might serve as evidence, or make good news pictures when the trouble was resolved. It was full of debris, but empty of prisoners. Those who were not on the roof were in their cells, knowing less about what was happening in the building than anybody else in Britain. For the moment, indeed, most of them were asleep. Nobody in the know wanted them awake until the next half-hour was done. Why play with fire?

The officer in charge, a major called Carl Edwards, had briefed his men carefully, and in detail. They were elite troops, and neither they nor he particularly relished this task in bleakest Scotland. In joint briefings with the prison officer back-up squad, they had not been much impressed. Racism aside – they were all English – they found the warders unambiguously violent in their attitudes towards the prisoners, and full of resentment that the soldiers were to go in first, and have the fun, as they saw it. They told the English, in no uncertain terms, that the rooftop men were savages, and should have been treated as such – by them, their natural masters.

Major Edwards, when the prison officers had been redeployed next door, had said nothing controversial. But his facial expressions were famous to his men, and the sneering curl of his lip and raising of the eyebrows was a classic.

'Contrary to what those chaps believe,' he said, 'we are going in to prevent trouble, or contain it, not foment it. As I told you earlier, we will be deploying certain techniques that the boys with the billyclubs are not privy to. Instructions from on high. What it all adds up to is that the men up there will listen to reason, and be docile, and will be ready to come down like lambs. The psychiatrists have guaranteed it. Any questions?'

'Do you believe that, sir? I mean, I've never met a docile haggis-shagger. And if the *psychiatrists* say so . . .'

There was a ripple of laughter. Major Edwards smiled at the burly soldier who had spoken.

'Stranger things have happened, Higgs. Let us wait and see.' He glanced at his watch. 'We move out in five minutes. Don't slip on any porridge.'

Donald Sinclair – once a journalist and now a politician – had assessed, as James McGregor had, the vigilance of the media. As the night hours had worn on he had retained his composure, felt it grow, in fact. He had relaxed, read a book, even managed to sleep a little, although not well. For the past thirty minutes he had been in the operations room, a hotel suite which overlooked the floodlit outline of the prison. He had been a quiet presence, standing unobtrusively by the curtained window. On balance, he could hardly see that anything could go wrong.

He turned back from the window now, letting the curtain fall. The colonel seated at the large oak table watched, expectantly. There were other soldiers next to him, and some civilians to one side.

'Right,' said Sinclair. 'According to my watch, there are four minutes left. I propose to leave you. You'll find me in my hotel room.'

The colonel's head jerked visibly, in surprise.

'I assure you, sir,' he said, 'you're more than welcome to stay. There won't be any . . . unpleasantness, or anything.'

Sinclair smiled.

'I sincerely hope there will not,' he replied. 'My intention is that not a drop of blood should be spilled, not a cheek scratched. But that is your task. I can only get in the way. Good morning.'

He nodded, and left, followed by his civil servants. The colonel glanced at his ADC.

'Rum fish. Bloody glad to see the back of him, however. More tact than most of his fellows. Are we set?'

'We are, sir. Two minutes to the off. And counting.'

'Streets?'

'No change. Practically empty. It'll be another hour before there's any movement there. We're watching.'

'Major Edwards?'

'In position under the roof. No problems.'

'Good. And the back-up?'

'Medicos standing by, prison officers deployed at every stairwell. Dining hall ready to receive and contain the prisoners. Oh, and Maxwell's team checked in. The lights are a hundred per cent again. They can blind them or black them out on signal.'

The colonel nodded.

'Good,' he repeated. 'Very good.'

At the appointed moment, the contingent of twenty stormed the roof of Buckie Jail to confront the sixty-seven prisoners. They had moved into their positions like wraiths, and the flinging up of grappling hooks and lightweight ladders came as a total shock to the frozen, huddled men, many of whom had been asleep. But by the time only four or five soldiers were through the broken roof, the prisoners were ready, their hands full of jagged slates, the holes surrounded. Unless the soldiers were going to open fire, to shoot them down like dogs . . . The prisoners glanced round at their companions fearfully, their breath blasting into the cold morning air with their sudden burst of vigour. Jimmy McGregor's heart was pumping. Should they charge? Should he give an order? A short, powerful man was facing him, his eyes bright through black face-paint. Should he jump on him?

The man shouted. It was an English voice, full and cultured. It was an officer.

'Stand!' he said. 'All of you! You must all surrender!'

No one was expected to obey. Major Edwards lifted his hand towards McGregor. He was holding what looked like a small tape recorder or a hand-lamp. The prisoners were expected to attack.

But the men on the rooftop were finished. They had had enough.

These were SAS, they thought, these were the killing squad. There was no noise, no movement forward. Even when three more soldiers slipped out onto the roof.

Major Edwards was wrong-footed. His orders were to immobilise three men in quick succession, then more if necessary. The psychiatrists, at all the briefings, had been adamant: morale would be low, the others would be horrified.

But they seemed horrified already, already they were immobilised. For several seconds he stared at James McGregor. For several seconds there was silence.

Then McGregor jumped. But not at Major Edwards, as predicted. With a strangled roar he sprinted for the parapet, tearing at the makeshift balaclava covering his mouth. He screamed, a violent, tearing bellow, first at the other prisoners, then, leaping onto the low surrounding wall, into the blinding lights below, to the hoped-for TV cameras hidden in the glare, to the outside world.

'Look out down there! Attack! Attack! The SAS!'

Suddenly he crumpled. His knees sagged, and he staggered, one hand reaching for a chimney stack, for support. The jumble of noises on the roof, the beginning of a hubbub from the other prisoners, stopped. A sob of wind buffeted them. McGregor swayed, and almost fell.

'Lights!' hissed Major Edwards to the operator beside him. 'For God's sake kill the lights!'

As the operator snapped the instruction into his tiny hand-held set, McGregor did fall. He opened his mouth and slurred one word: 'Bastards.' Then he pitched backwards off the parapet without another sound. The silent men heard his body hit the ground, quite clearly.

The world's press did not see him fall. The TV men and women were all in bed, in various hotels. Only Rosanna Nixon, standing at her window in her dressing gown, saw it happen, and she could hardly believe her eyes. She watched the man jump high onto the parapet, and wave his arms, and stagger. She saw him reach sideways, then turn his back to her in silhouette, and topple backwards, not at all dramatically. Before it truly registered, before she could make sense of it, the scene went black. After the stark white of the electric arcs, the dark was startling, total. But the image of the falling man seemed to pulsate, flashing black and white on her retina. Rosanna blinked, and shook her head, and stared. Then she ran for her shoes and coat.

By the time she reached the cordons, the protest – although she could not tell it – was over. The prisoners, bemused and silent, had shuffled down below to the cheery prison officers, their long wait done at last. The lights, strangely, had been switched back on, but from where Rosanna stood there was no one visible on the roof. If there was anyone on the ground she could not see him. They made sure of that.

Only the banners remained, a garish white in the reflected candlepower. 'INQUIRY NOW,' blared one of them. 'WE DEMAND.'

TWO

It was stuffy in the kitting room, and the five officers got into the protective clothing as quickly as they could. There was little talk, because it was too early in the morning, not yet dawn. Two of the men had been asleep when the order had come, and the others had been sitting in the rest room, comatose. It had been a very quiet night.

'What's it for, Gordon?' said one of the officers. He was struggling into a heavy blue chest protector, and turned for the straps to be tightened by his senior colleague.

'I should be told?' replied Gordon, sarcastically. 'The call came twenty minutes ago, and we copped for it, OK? Stuart – that goes the other way around, you prat. He'll pull your bollocks off.'

Stuart Saxty, across the room, pulled savagely at the abdomen shield. He had a splitting headache and a foul mouth.

'Bastard,' he muttered. 'He's even trouble when he's sleeping. Bastard.'

It took them nearly fifteen minutes to prepare themselves. As they put on the layers, they grew from normal-sized, if bulky, men to resemble something different, something alien. Last of all, they fitted the dark helmets, adjusting the straps carefully so that they could not slip even under the extremest pressure. They raised and lowered the toughened visors experimentally, then clipped them in the up position. Already they were sweating. It would be soon enough to lower them when crunchtime came.

Gordon Snell, the officer in charge, checked their equipment briefly. Then he indicated the stock of short, transparent shields and the rack of weighted sticks.

'Gloves first,' he said. 'The bastard bites, remember.'

As they walked along the quiet corridors, the men could feel their tired grumpiness begin to lift. In a couple of minutes there would be a real hullabaloo, a row enough to wake the dead. The sleeping prisoners, snug in their little nests, would hear it and respond. The peace would drain away. The tension would flood back. By breakfast time the place would be like the centre of an electric storm. All five officers had dry mouths and sweating palms.

The cell they wanted was at the end of a wide, garishly floodlit corridor, through three sets of steel, multi-locked doors. Outside it, they smiled nervously at each other, and fixed their visors down. Gordon Snell checked each man in turn, rapidly and carefully, for exposed flesh or loose straps. When his gear had also been checked, he prepared the keys. When ready, he opened the spyhole in the door, almost stealthily.

Because Angus John McGregor was such a violent man, the authorities deemed it necessary to keep a light burning in his cell for twenty-four hours every day. Because Angus John McGregor objected to this treatment, which he understood to be illegal, he had taken to living naked in the cell. Because he was insane – the prison officers thought – he also refused to use a bucket or a lavatory, but smeared his faeces on his body. The residue went on the walls and ceiling, and the smash-proof glass that hid the lightbulb. McGregor's rationale was this: if he was covered in shit, and if he bit and spat and scratched at anyone who might come near him, he would not be beaten quite so much. After all, he might – with luck – have Aids, or hepatitis.

He was wrong about the beating. Finding him asleep, Snell unlocked the door with practised speed and stepped sideways as the four armoured aliens swept in. McGregor was halfway to his feet when the first night-stick struck him, and before he could make a recovery he was knocked into the corner of the tiny room under a battery of blows and kicks. Saxty, who had slipped in a pool of liquid filth and messed his glove completely, rammed it in a rage into the bleeding mouth. It was over very quickly, and with remarkably little noise. Five minutes later McGregor, only barely conscious, was bundled into the back of an armoured van with a pile of blankets and a soft plastic bottle of water, to begin his journey south.

In the kitting room, the five officers carefully removed their gear. They would strip completely naked, and most of the gear would be destroyed. It was an expensive business. Their mood swung dangerously between elation and despair.

'Where's he going to, that's what I'd like to know,' said one of them. 'The driver said across the Border. To England.'

'Who cares?' replied another. 'Anywhere can't be far enough.'

Gordon Snell exhaled tiredly.

'Look on the bright side,' he said. 'He's gone. What's more, we didn't wake the place up. No one even heard a thing. Think of the aggro that's prevented.'

They nodded, smiling and muttering in agreement. Stuart Saxty kicked his bloodied helmet towards the sluice.

'He got a nice wee farewell kicking, too,' he said, with satisfaction. 'The Animal. Never a truer nickname, eh? A fucking animal.'

They could all agree with that.

At 8.15 that morning, Donald Sinclair paused for breakfast. As he drank black coffee and chewed some toast at the ridiculous little writing table in his room, his eyes ranged yet again over the computer-printed details of Angus John McGregor's history. Thirty-four years old, ex-gangland hitman, cold-blooded murderer of four. Since the age of seventeen had spent eleven years in prison, and was now serving a recommended minimum of thirty-five. His record of violence inside jail had been appalling. Sixteen officers attacked, one almost blinded, one part-castrated. Three had been invalided from the service, and it was a standing order that he was never to be approached in units numbering less than three. His only known relative was James Malcolm McGregor, twenty-three, who was in fact the only human being McGregor Senior had ever shown any interest in. There was, indeed, according to the brief, a close bond between them. And this was the man, thought Sinclair bitterly, that the morons had to kill. James Malcolm McGregor, aged twenty-three, deceased. When the Animal found out, God in heaven alone knew what would happen.

Sinclair looked at his watch, momentarily wishing he could sleep. When he had heard the news in the early hours, when he had digested the full import of the disaster, he had had to crush incipient panic. His had been the plan, and the military had wrecked it for him. But he could still win, if he kept a grip. For a moment, he had been tempted to ring Sir Gerald Turner, to ask his advice and thereby, subtly, to implicate him by association. But Sinclair knew that there was a better way of retaining the Home Secretary's support. He would get himself clear first, alone, then share the glory with Turner, not the blame. It was a gamble, and he'd bring it off.

Firstly, Donald Sinclair had spoken to Christian Fortyne, the civil servant who had preceded him to Buckie as his aide. Fortyne was a cold man, not a friend, but his brain was excellent and his nerve unshakeable. Sinclair, not wishing to talk to anybody face-to-face until he had the situation entirely in command, had instructed him by phone, although their rooms were only yards apart.

'The operation on the ground,' he said, 'was under the control of a Major Edwards. I don't know the protocol on this, but I want his head. No. I want his bollocks. On a plate.'

There was a slight pause, which Sinclair could imagine was filled with well-bred distaste at his coarseness. Then Fortyne said: 'Fried or boiled?' Sinclair laughed, gratefully.

'Any way you choose,' he replied. 'But I mean it. I want him broken. And this McGregor, the older one. I want him out of Scotland. I want him kept in solitary confinement, and I want him moved today. Now. Is that possible?'

A longer pause. Then: 'To England. That is difficult. The Scottish Office—'

'Give me a number. I'll ring . . .'

He tailed off. Fortyne, intelligent to a fault, picked up the thought. Politically, they'd be treading on yet more corns.

'I see what you mean,' he said. 'Far better if . . . just for the moment. Look – leave it with me. I'll call you back in ten minutes.'

'Good man. And then – the other thing.'

Fortyne's chuckle was dry.

'On a plate,' he said. 'Devilled.'

When he had finished his breakfast, Donald Sinclair ran himself a deep bath and climbed wearily into it. He lay for some minutes on his back, his head tilted at an angle so that his scalp was immersed and only his eyes, nose and mouth were clear. He tried to still his brain, to slow it down at least, so that it would be ready for one last burst of sustained thought before he caught his plane to London in a couple of hours. Slowly, he felt the tension drain away.

By the time he had dried himself and dressed, he was confident he had it. He called Fortyne to his room and he ordered himself a car to take him to the airport, as Philip Swift once more. He instructed the tall, watchful civil servant to announce a press conference for 10.15 a.m., and told him how he expected it to go. Fortyne listened intently, nodding from time to time.

'But you'll be back in England,' he said. 'It seems a pity, in one way, that you can't put in an appearance. The shock effect would ensure great coverage. The mastermind behind the Buckie triumph.'

Sinclair examined the closed, clever face for any hint of irony, but found none. He smiled the briefest of smiles.

'What triumph? The ending of a Scottish jail siege in sixteen hours without the US Cavalry? When McGregor's death does leak out my role might not seem so brilliant, might it?'

Fortyne's look was quizzical.

'Maybe a mystery then, to help make sure it doesn't leak?' he said. 'They love a mystery, don't they? I think I might feed in a shadowy figure in the background, a master puppeteer pulling hidden strings. Deniable, naturally, but it would serve to keep their minds off other things.'

Sinclair, who had served his time in newspapers and TV, began to warm to Fortyne. He suspected he might be a very useful ally indeed. The ploy was excellent.

'I'll leave that up to you,' he said. 'I'm going to trust you on this, Fortyne. One hundred per cent. But the bottom line is, for the moment, no Army, no death – and no me. I'm sorry to have to ask you to do this, but I honestly believe that if the facts emerge immediately the results could be disastrous. I can't imagine what might happen. Frightening.'

Fortyne pushed his spectacles up the bridge of his nose with a tiny smile. Again there was no trace of irony apparent in his face.

'Fatal,' he said, drily. 'It will be a pleasure to ensure that nothing untoward should happen. You shouldn't imagine that I want to stay up here in Siberia a moment longer than I have to, by the way. I hope to follow you to London very shortly. Perhaps if you rang me when you got back to your office? I could bring you up to date.'

In the aeroplane, Sinclair thought of Fortyne for some little time before he drifted into sleep. If everything went to plan and his own promotion came, he might be a damn good man to have as his right hand. A damn good man indeed.

Inside the basement kitchen, the elegant black woman was completely out of place. Her handmade grey kid boots alone were worth more than all the furniture, and the bright colours of her skirt were startling against the backdrop of brown linoleum and sagging yellow paper on the walls. Opposite her, across a table that was festooned with dirty crockery, an open bottle of milk and a coffee-stained *Observer* three weeks out of date, Andrew Forbes was more at home. He wore an off-white shirt over crumpled trousers and he had not shaved. He also had a hangover.

'So that's it, then?' he said. 'You're going. And I still don't have the foggiest why you came.'

Alice Grogan gazed levelly at him for a few moments before replying. She was very beautiful, with high cheekbones and a haughty, contemptuous mouth. She did not smile.

'Don't play stupid, Andrew. It doesn't suit you. I told you most of it yesterday. I came to you because you're straight. Clean. I came back because nobody followed me when I left.'

Forbes laughed. His pale, battered face became alive and attractive. He was amused.

'Jesus,' he said. 'I'm only a dirt-digger. Not even the Mets would bother to spy on this place. But how come you fixed on me? Who gave you my name?'

She twitched her lip. Some day I'll make her smile, thought Andrew Forbes. I'd like that.

'Why do men always assume women need telling things? I've been in London two months. I've read the papers. Seen your pieces. I figured you must have the contacts.'

Forbes nodded. It was a pretty roundabout way of getting information across, but she might be on the level. She'd told him yesterday she couldn't approach the police directly because she didn't trust them. His job, as he figured it, was to pass things on to someone in authority who was not a crook. He smiled to himself. Some cynical lady.

'I'm flattered,' he said, 'but I'm disappointed, naturally. I thought maybe you'd come back because you couldn't stay away. You wanted my body. You wanted to share my life.'

Alice almost smiled. Her eyes took in the dank basement, the cluttered surfaces, the dirty cooker. It was bachelordom grown rank.

'Andrew,' she said, 'are you crazy? Yesterday I gave you times and places. I came back with the name. That's important. You better pass it on.'

He sensed that she had become nervous. He had noticed it earlier, when she had first brought up the name. She had seemed to find it hard to say, as though it frightened her. Alice reached across the table and fiddled a cigarette from a pack. She lit it and inhaled. As she leaned back the green-painted kitchen chair creaked. She jumped. She was nervous.

'Charles Lister,' said Andrew Forbes, deliberately. 'You must hate him, Alice. I wonder what he did to you.'

The chair creaked again as Alice Grogan leaned forward. She

blew smoke out in a level stream, the cigarette held near her eye. She looked at him unblinkingly.

'Pass,' she said.

Forbes picked up a mug. It was a quarter full of cold black instant coffee. He glanced at the cooker, then away. No point in offering her a cup, he had tried before. Something about his housekeeping. Soon she would get up and go, and he'd probably never see her again. That would not do.

'All right,' he said. 'We'll try the English way. Whatever you think of Charles Lister, what about me? All jokes apart.'

She flicked ash onto the table. There were maybe five draws left. She looked at the lighted end.

'All jokes apart,' she said, 'you've got – I hope – good contacts. I needed that. I need it.'

'Fine. It's as good as done. And what about the . . . Look, what I'm trying to say is . . .'

'Will I screw you?'

'Yes.'

Slowly, Alice Grogan reached across and stubbed her cigarette out on a plate. She reached her bag up from the floor, checked the contents, snapped it shut. She stood.

'All jokes apart,' she said, 'you really are quite cute. So that would be a pity, wouldn't it?'

'What?'

She smiled a tight small smile and turned towards the stairs.

'What's your history, Andy? Why do you live like this? Ain't you got a woman?'

'Widower. I've got a few. Nothing special.'

She stopped, her hand on the newel knob.

'Widower,' she said. 'That's bad. And I'm a gangman's woman. Ex. If I screwed you, Andy, you'd be screwed for good. Dead. Charlie's like that. I'm mortuary meat.'

There was a coldness in her that chilled him. She was comfortless, but she needed comforting. She was unapproachable, but he wanted to approach. He made a clumsy move forward, but stopped in time.

'Give me a number,' he said. 'No, I know you won't do that, no phone. Let's meet somewhere, let's leave it for a while, see what happens over Lister. This stuff you've given me. I mean . . .'

He meant, but did not say, that if all went well – if any of it was true, indeed – Charles Lister would soon be neutralised. He'd be off the story for a long long time.

'Anyway,' he said, as Alice Grogan began to climb the stairs to street-door level. 'You've got a classic arse!'

She turned towards him smiling at last, very nearly laughing. It did not last for long, but his stomach shifted. Pleasure and excitement.

'I sometimes go to the Shaw Theatre,' she said. 'Looking at the exhibitions in the entrance hall, you know? Say Friday?'

'Do you?' said Andrew Forbes. 'That's pretty weird.'

'Of course I don't, you tramp!' she said. The brightness was back in her eyes. 'Jesus, Andrew, don't play hard to get!'

'Friday.'

'Well.' She moved another two steps upward. 'Well, how long will it . . . ? Yeah. Maybe Friday, who can tell? Or maybe the Friday after.'

He let her go then, on the high. He let her make her own way to the street and slam the door. He lit the gas underneath the saucepan he used as a kettle, and he had a little fantasy about the long legs and the pink inside her mouth.

'Christ,' he said out loud. 'I'll have to change the duvet cover. I'll buy a new one.'

But first of all, he'd have to contact Peter Jackson. Of Her Majesty's Customs and Excise. Today.

Outside in the road, Paddy Collins and the fat man watched Alice Grogan slam the door and clatter down the steps. From their car – today a blue Ford Escort, twelve years old – they noted the small smile on her lips as she reached the pavement.

'There she goes,' said Paddy. 'I bet she can hardly walk. I dreamed about her last night, you know that? I nearly had to fuck the bleeding wife.'

'That's terrible,' said the fat man. 'We should be on a bonus.'

'Did you know?' said Paddy. 'They got an ident through. She's an American. Alice something. No wonder she looks so good, eh? Not like the black-rag tarts round here. Class.'

The fat man sucked his teeth.

'Anything on her?'

'How should I know? We're only infantry, aren't we? I mean, no one tells us nothing, do they?'

As the woman reached the corner of the street, an old Fiat pulled away from the kerb fifty yards in front of the Escort.

'She must be someone though, it stands to reason,' went on Paddy. 'Or else she wouldn't have gone near that scruffy little prat. Or else we wouldn't have her on the files, more to the point.'

'Hang about!' said his companion. 'That car!'

The Fiat was at the junction. It was turning right, in the direction the woman had taken. The fat man was wheezing.

'Bastards! It's one of ours!'

Paddy Collins watched the Fiat disappear with a grunt of disgust.

'Put a tail on her and no bugger tells us. The bleeding infantry.'

They slumped back into their seats, disconsolate. There was no more action from Andrew Forbes' house, before or behind the peeling, cracked front door. They had another four hours to do, and more. Four hours to develop their piles and indigestion. Meanwhile, Andrew Forbes was probably sleeping off his sexual excesses with the black, and someone else was following her slinky, swaying backside along the streets. It wasn't that other people got all the good luck. It was more that they got none of it . . .

Three hours after the press conference, Rosanna Nixon was the only journalist left in Buckie. Even the fact that the pubs were open was not enough, for once, to detain the media circus. They had their story, and they had their pictures. The priority was to get to Glasgow and give them to the waiting world. The smarter of them, although they were well satisfied with their officially sanctioned interviews and photographs of smashed-up cells, were also itching to follow up the mystery. They figured that the clues dropped at the conference, unintentionally they imagined, might be enough for a canny political correspondent to come up with a name. Who knew, they might even wangle a flight to London to run him to earth themselves.

Christian Fortyne had controlled the show, with a pair of assistants to display the quickly assembled visuals and move the essential little coloured symbols across the diagrams. One of the assistants – the best-looking woman in Fortyne's team – also unconsciously displayed quite a lot of leg whenever she was required to reach the top part of the easel-board. Although it never occurred to her, Fortyne had thought of everything.

He ran quickly and easily through the briefing, emphasising the total lack of force, and the total lack of injury. The only damage, he said, was that which the prisoners had done on the original rampage. The governor had agreed to allow them into

E-wing later that morning for a photo-opportunity, and one agency man would be allowed to photograph the damaged roof, photographs which would be pooled for everyone.

He knew it would not be long before someone asked who had been in charge, and he was right. Fortyne adjusted his spectacles and smiled.

'I am afraid we are not at liberty to disclose that information at present,' he said. 'I can say, however, that the government's determination to stamp out this kind of outrage – especially in Scotland's prisons – is absolute. The ending of this particular siege, I can say, was the result of an entirely new strategy which involved neither firearms, force, nor indeed any military intervention whatsoever. The man in ultimate control—'

He stopped, allowing a flicker of self-doubt to cross his face. He looked down at a sheaf of notes, and coughed.

'What I should have said,' he continued, 'is that the junior minister. No. If you'll excuse me, ladies and gentlemen, we'd better leave it there.'

There was a barrage of excited questions. One of the better briefed provided Fortyne with his next lead.

'But surely,' the reporter asked, 'isn't the junior minister Cyril Richardson? Isn't he in hospital?'

Fortyne, reluctantly, had to acknowledge that Mr Richardson was, indeed, in hospital. He also admitted, under pressure, that in such a crisis it was entirely understandable that delegation of responsibility would be probably inevitable. And no, the Scottish Secretary – although it was ultimately, he supposed . . . Fortyne stopped once more, consulted his notes rather desperately, tried another tack, then refused to be drawn any further on the subject. It was masterly.

In the lull, Rosanna Nixon took her opportunity.

'You said,' she began, hesitantly. 'You said that nobody was hurt. In any way. Is that true?'

There was a murmur of embarrassment from around the sumptuous, panelled room. What was the Wee Mouse on about? Everybody knew there'd have been some broken heads, obviously. Everybody knew the waiting officers would hardly have kissed the prisoners and tucked them into bed. But there were rules in these things, and Rosanna did not know them. It was a pointless question, rudely put.

The civil servant acknowledged the implicit insult. He looked down his long, disdainful nose at the woman, noting her isolation from her colleagues. His tones were Etonian: self-confident, relaxed, dripping with contempt.

'My dear young lady,' he said. 'So comprehensive a statement is unthinkable, I'm afraid. There were sixty-seven men on Buckie roof, many of whom are habitually violent, many of whom hate and resent all forms of authority. So far, we have no detailed picture of their behaviour and mien, as they were redeployed. But it would be surprising, I suppose, if there had been no incidents at all. Certainly, if any prison officers were attacked they would have employed only the bare minimum of force necessary to restrain their attackers. I have no reports, however, even of that, nor indeed of any officers injured. Yes?'

He raised a languid hand to indicate another questioner. But the woman would not finish.

'Did a prisoner fall from the roof?' she said.

Rosanna, nervous as she was, had rather expected her question to cause a storm. Even saying it, to her, felt rather as a bombshell might. Her stomach had constricted, her throat was painful, and her hands were aching fists. The civil servant's expression, however, did not change, not so much as by a flicker. And all around her, she heard her colleagues groaning. Her face began to burn.

'What an extraordinary question,' said Christian Fortyne. 'Why do you ask?'

She forced her dry mouth open.

'I saw it,' she said. 'From my hotel window. I saw a man fall off.'

The room was silent. Outside, the wind moaned. Fortyne, outwardly calm, gave himself time to think. Not long enough, though, for his silence to lend credence to her statement.

'Well well,' he said. 'What time was this? Can you remember?'

It was a superb stroke of deliberate patronisation. The faintest hint of a smile was on his lips. It paid off.

'About four o'clock. Just afterwards. I didn't . . . I didn't have time to notice. I was too shocked.'

The silence broke. Her colleagues' contempt was almost palpable. Another woman journalist tittered. Fortyne allowed the atmosphere to mature.

'I'm afraid that's not much help, then,' he said. 'But as I know you men and women of the media are all professionals, I'll put it to the test. I appeal to you, individually and collectively. Has anybody else heard this tale? Can anybody tell me where it comes from?'

Someone shouted coarsely: 'From the bottom of a bottle!' There was a burst of laughter. But underneath it there was anger. Rosanna Nixon was showing them all up. It was reflecting on them badly. As professionals.

'Fine then,' said Fortyne, briskly. 'So let's get on. But I do feel bound to tell you something that I had intended to keep under wraps for operational reasons. The actual clearing of the roof, the removal of the men itself, took place in darkness. The lights had been switched off.'

There was another roar of laughter, longer this time, directed at Rosanna. When it died away, she knew better than to try to carry on. She gritted her teeth and studied a fixed point on the floor. She felt as though she'd been kicked in the stomach.

Back in her hotel room, sitting on the bed she'd hardly used, it took her a considerable act of will to pick up the telephone to call her office. In the early hours, she had phoned a memo onto her news editor's tape machine. Now she did not mention it, and to her surprise nor did Maurice Campbell. She outlined the press conference briefly and told him of the 'mystery politician'. It was done without excitement, listlessly.

'It's good,' said Maurice Campbell. 'Terrific. Shall I put you onto copy? Are you ready to spout?'

'Hey, give us a break! The conference finished fifteen minutes back. And anyway, what about . . . you know.'

Maurice chuckled.

'Ach, hell,' he said. 'The diving boy? We all have hallucinations, hen. Don't fret about it.'

'Listen, Maurice. If you think I was drunk . . .'

'I don't think anything, I'm saying nothing, lassie! Four o'clock in the morning, God's sake! I once rang the Pope! He was pissed as well! I'll bet you didnae raise it at the conference, eh? Nor did any bugger else!'

'I did raise it. I . . .'

Rosanna let it go. Between seeing the man fall and going to the conference, she had spent hours wondering what to do. Inexperienced as she was, she'd known that asking police or soldiers in the street would bring nothing but trouble, although after dawn she had tried to watch the gates a while. She had seen some men in jeans and sweaters getting into a truck behind the jail some forty minutes later, but she had not got near, and if they had significance it had eluded her.

The hotel bed was soft, and suddenly she longed to lie on it, to sleep. Maurice's voice, from the receiver in her hand, jolted her. God, but she was tired.

'Lassie? Are you still there?'

Rosanna stifled a huge yawn.

'I'll put the copy over, Maurice. Give me half an hour. Then there's the photo-call at the jail. Tam'll drive the pix across immediately, and I'll follow on, OK?'

'Good. But why not come back with Tam? You havenae got your motor with you, have you?'

'I want to do some digging,' said Rosanna. 'Follow up some thoughts.'

Maurice Campbell laughed richly down the telephone.

'Not on my payroll you don't,' he said. 'There'll be more life in a corpse's trousers than in Buckie today. It's over, hen. I want you back in Glasgow, right? Today.'

Rosanna made a brief farewell, too tired to argue, and put the phone down. She looked at her watch, reaching for her notebook.

She had a mental image of the man, falling from the parapet. Ungainly and shocking. The picture blurred. She was beginning to doubt that she had seen it, after all. She yawned. A staggering, racking yawn.

If she even mentioned it in her story, they would take it out. Nobody believed her, nobody even cared. It stood in the way of the real stuff, the defeated animals, the shy superman who had found a way at last to thwart the hardnuts but was too modest to have his picture in the paper. It would not be mentioned, so it did not happen.

That could not be right . . .

From late morning onwards, the coverage on radio, TV and then the evening papers became more and more laudatory. In newsrooms all over the kingdom – England as well as Scotland – a slow news day was gloriously transformed by speculative swoops, background pieces, and in-depth interviews. At 3.16 Sinclair's political adviser Judith Parker fielded the first query as to his part in the saga, and by 5 p.m. there were reporters and cameramen waiting hopefully all round the Palace of Westminster to catch a glimpse of him, while others staked out his home in Surrey and the London flat he hardly ever used.

Sinclair, who had spent an hour on the telephone to Christian Fortyne, was confident that it was safe to put his head above the parapet, but thought it would be tactically better to wait. Tonight they could speculate, tomorrow he could assess how much it would be politic to reveal. In any case, if anything did go wrong, it left another clear day of denial time.

While Judith, a brisk, intelligent woman with ambitions of her own, guarded the phone, Sinclair sat in a deep armchair and dozed. He was awoken early in the evening by a gentle shaking of his arm.

'Sir Gerald Turner,' mouthed Judith, handing him the phone. 'I thought you'd want to speak.'

Sir Gerald was brief, but generous. A brilliant piece of work, he said, which confirmed everything he'd believed about his protégé. Wonderful.

'Thank you,' said Donald Sinclair. 'Thanks indeed. But—'

The Home Secretary interrupted.

'The PM's delighted,' he said. 'Couldn't be more pleased. Between you and me, laddie, it's in the bag. Unofficially, the job's yours. What do you say to that?'

Sinclair made the appropriate noises, then he seized his chance. If Turner was going to claim him for a protégé indeed, why not? There ought to be a quid pro quo. He would use it to start as he intended to continue – with all guns blazing.

'Sir Gerald,' he said. 'Before it's announced – assuming it's confirmed – I'd like to do some things. Set some wheels in motion, a few balls rolling. Any chance?'

'If I knew what you wanted, I'd have a better idea,' replied Sir Gerald. 'But now's the time, now certainly is the time. Is it anything difficult?'

'Oh no,' replied Sinclair. 'For you, quite simple, I'd imagine. It's a political thing, though. Needs a heavyweight. Could I . . . ?'

'Come and see me? How about eight o'clock tonight? Better warn you though – Queen Anne's Gate is crawling with the press. How about my club? Get there unseen.'

Sinclair was amused. Cloak and dagger stuff. But Turner's club would do superbly. Some of the men he needed most would be there, for a certainty, in a very mellow mood what's more. It was perfection.

'Eight o'clock. Thanks indeed.'

'Nonsense, Donald. Once again, congratulations.'

It was two o'clock next morning before Sinclair reached his

flat. Not the one he rented a mile from the Palace of Westminster, which was still staked out by disconsolate reporters, but the three rooms he had owned for many years behind a block of shops in Stockwell, and which he called his safe house. It was not modern, it was not fashionable, but it was extremely secret. Even Sinclair's wife did not know of its existence. Totally exhausted, he tore his clothes off and fell into bed. He had had a very successful conclusion to a very successful day . . .

THREE

Charles Lister lay on the narrow bed in the dimness of the heavily curtained room, counting the telephone warbles.

Two sets of three, then hang up. One set of four, ditto. The warbles had now been going continuously for about fifteen seconds. When they stopped, there would be three more, then a break. When it rang again, he would pick it up. All the way from Florida, the calls were coming, a hell of a lot of button-punching. But when he answered, finally, they knew it would be him – and uncoerced. There were dollars hanging on this security. Sixty million dollars.

'Charlie,' said the voice from Florida. 'Is this you? I have a message from Mae. Come up and see me sometime.'

Crazy, thought Charles Lister. We don't even crack a smile. He completed the code.

'Owney says: "What's wrong with the rackets, anyway?"'

'Shit,' said the voice. 'The things we do for money. Listen, Chuck, trouble. This is the big one. This is serious.'

Charles Lister's stomach fluttered. Some hard man, he thought. But it had all been too easy, so far. He'd been expecting something.

'Shoot.'

'They've got a smell of you, OK? We spoke to Jean-Claude in Paris. Their men were teed up yesterday, moved out this morning. The Dutch guys met at Flushing, yeah? And the English end is definitely go. We think they're going to jump.'

Lister lay flat on his back. Try as he might to control it, his breath was coming faster.

'They don't know where I am. I've been in this hole less than thirty hours. No one could have tapped me, no one's seen me, I haven't moved.'

'Yeah. Alice is in London, isn't she?'

A flash of anger.

'Alice knows fuck all. She don't know where to find me, think I'm crazy? So what, Alice is in London?'

The voice was conciliatory.

'Yeah, so it's a mystery, OK? But the Customs men are going

to jump. OK, Chuck, maybe we got it wrong, OK? Maybe it's horseshit, maybe they're trying to scare you out, make *you* jump. That's up to you, OK? You're the brains.'

Lister did not reply. He was thinking.

'Listen, buddy,' said the voice. 'There's sixty thousand k out there on the ocean, right? You want we shouldn't tell you? You want to end up in some oldie English fucking jail, or something? If that ship turns up off the keys and you ain't there, we in the shit. Does that make sense? You gotta be here, Charlie. If them Customs bastards are moving in, you gotta *jump*.'

Still Charles Lister thought. His options were strictly limited. The job was not finished yet, there were ends to be tied up. But if the Customs teams were really on to him, he was in trouble. He was in trouble bad. Three times he had evaded them, in the past eight weeks. If they got him, they would watch him like a hawk. They'd move into his brain. They'd even have his shits for him.

'Listen,' he said. 'There's things I gotta do, in Europe. Or the ship don't even get there, in the first place. Like it or not, I'm going to have to take some risks.'

Now it was the turn of the telephone to stay silent. Lister allowed himself a smile. Sixty million bucks of risk. It wouldn't sound so good over the wire, would it?

'What sort of risks? Them bucks is—'

Lister cut him off.

'There ain't no bucks if I don't get the job sewn up, got that? I'm going to have to call some friends. An outfit.'

'An outfit! There ain't no outfit over there! You're on your own!'

'Listen, you said just now. I'm the brains, right? Just think about it. Just watch your mouth. There's an outfit.'

A pause. Lister could almost hear the cash register in the Florida brain. Another outfit? This could cost . . . He waited.

'OK, Chuck. We ain't arguing. You're on the ground. We all trust you, here.'

There was a small but significant edge to the voice. And the speech.

'Yeah, sure you do. Me too. A mutual trust society. Listen – I ain't chucking up that sort of money, am I? No way. Not for any consideration. Just don't ring again, OK? Not for any reason on earth. Until you hear from me. OK?'

'Sure. We understand.'

'Good. And thanks for the information. Save my life, save us all sixty thousand grand. Cool.'

'Sure.'

'And don't mess your pants, OK? If you hear I've been arrested. Got that?'

'Arrested! What the fuck? But—'

'Just hang in there. I mean it. Just don't do anything, right? Until you hear from me.'

'Jesus, Charlie!'

Charles Lister hung up. He looked round the cold, impersonal, badly furnished London room. He wished that he was back in Florida, in the sun.

He thought for a very long time. Then he pulled the telephone towards him and lifted the receiver.

In the heat of the courtroom, after the first two hours, Michael Masters found it difficult to stay awake. He was dressed sombrely, in a dark, double-breasted pinstripe suit, and his counsel, Sir Cyril France, had impressed it on him to be alert at all times, to concentrate, however difficult it was. The press gallery was full and he was being watched. There was a certain weariness, one knew, a certain tired cynicism about the sentence he would receive, and nothing in his body language should compound that cynicism.

The trouble was, for Masters, that he already knew the sentence, as did Sir Cyril, three other barristers in the court, and the judge. Even before the original trial had ended, seven months before, the verdict and the punishment had been hammered out behind locked doors. The judge, indeed, would probably have come to Michael Masters' 'farewell party' the night before if that would not have been quite beyond a joke. Masters, at the thought, covered a small grin with his hand and coughed guiltily in the dock. His own head was throbbing slightly from the alcohol he'd consumed. This dry-toned judgment he was meant to be listening to, this legal rigmarole that seemed set to last all day, would have been even more halting and stultified if Mr Justice Harper had been drunk the night before. Why the hell, thought Masters, can't he just dish out the sentence: two years imprisonment with eighteen months suspended, and a fine of £50,000. Or to put it another way – four months inside an open prison.

He let his mind wander lazily over the events of the night before. It had been a hell of a thrash, with almost as many reporters and cameramen cruising around the brightly lighted grounds of the lovely old manor house as there had been drunken yuppies cruising around the dimly lighted rooms seeking fresh champagne and debbie thighs to try and stroke or squeeze. The count of bright young City types had been just a shade too high, although there had been a solid groundbase of the genuine Establishment. The problem was the press. Everyone who arrived was snapped and harassed by the dogs of Wapping and the rest. So some invited guests had had to stay away.

The party, on the night before he was due to receive his sentence, was a typical Masters gesture. At thirty-eight, he was a millionaire a few times over, a handsome, fit, flamboyant man who invited envy from the gutter press in the same measure that the more serious papers hinted at unease. Most millionaires, most safe millionaires, were quiet, modest, reclusive men who had the good sense and the common decency to be old and decrepit and preferably sick. It was hard to be upset by Getty's millions, because he so clearly had not enjoyed them. And Armand Hammer? What reader of the yellow press had heard of Armand Hammer?

But everyone had heard of Michael Masters, and he revelled in it. He had a classic English country house with forty acres, he had a classic English wife chosen, plucked and married while her parents were still too busy looking down their aristocratic noses at him to notice she was pregnant, and he had two sons at Eton and a pack of hounds. He had never, it was his proud and constant boast, had a proper job.

Masters was a money man. His dealings in the City and on the world's exchanges were so complex that it had taken a team of eighteen lawyers more than two years to prepare the case against him. The Inland Revenue had had a hand, and the Customs and Excise, VAT Division, had spent thousands of man-hours working on him. His post-Big Bang activities had involved juggling inside knowledge of some of Europe's most successful companies, and in a positive spate of takeovers, Masters' name, or the names of several dozen small, obscure companies he controlled, could be detected. Ivan Boesky had named him, and three of his American associates had committed suicide. Nobody – not even the investigators – knew how much money he had clawed down during the period of the great chaos, but it did seem clear that he, alone among many, had actually made several million from the '87

Crash alone. He had studied maths to O-level at a Norwich comprehensive.

The party was noisy, but it was relatively restrained. Although Masters enjoyed the trappings of gentility – and now spoke with as Home Counties an accent as one could wish, when he wished to – he did regret the innate respectability of the English high-middle and upper classes. Even the yuppie boys, with their ridiculous little Porsches stacked three deep in the drive and their silly suits and ties, were careful in their drunkenness. They only insulted people of their own age – mainly women – and they threw up strictly in the lavatories or the shrubs outside. Masters stood in the doorway between two enormous rooms and watched the Fionas and their beaux swilling his vintage champagne and chattering noisily but *nicely*, and wished someone would shout, or rave or something. Perhaps he ought to invite a few of the press lads in. That would put the cat among the pigeons.

Two men in dinner jackets, with ruffed silk shirts, approached him. One was on champagne, the other gin. They were both quite drunk.

'It's an outrage,' said one of them. 'Michael, old chap, it's a fucking outrage. You ought to get a knighthood, not go to jail.'

The other one looked at his companion, aghast.

'Don't say that, you fool,' he said. 'Michael won't go to jail, will you, Michael? Don't be so bloody rude, David. You can't say a chap'll go to jail!'

Michael laughed, loudly. They might be prats, the very rich, but he did like them. Not protocol to mention jail!

'Of course I'll go to jail, Ben. Nothing more certain. Serves me bloody right, as well. You ought to join me. Purge your soul.'

'Oh God,' said David, blinking owlishly. 'Don't mention it, for Christ's sake. They ever latch onto me, and I'll be finished. Chuck away the key. I'd cut my throat. Have to. Don't mention it.'

'Jesus,' said Ben. 'I wish I had your courage, Michael. To make a joke of it like that. I wish I had your nerve.'

I wonder, thought Michael Masters, what they really think? Surely they're not as stupid as they act? Surely they know that half the population reckons the whole thing's rigged? One law for the rich, and one for everybody else? The whole process had fascinated him, ever since the Crash, the Guinness case, the Boesky revelations. In America, fair enough, men had gone to jail. Men had been bankrupted, ruined, punished till the pips bled, in half a hundred cases of insider trading, sweetheart deals, illegal concert parties. But that was America. They had a tradition there, they could deal with the corrupt – given luck – up to and including presidents. But this was Britain, the land where the buck never stops, where only the powerless were ever guilty. The roots of corruption, he had learned, went so deeply into the fabric, that it was a wonder anybody inside the charmed circle was ever blamed for anything. And indeed, the handful who had been convicted, who had gone to jail for more than token terms, had been small fry, very minor fish indeed. The big ones were given legal aid, were acquitted – then sued for millions the people who had dared to tell the truth about them.

'It's not a case of nerve, Ben,' he said. 'It's a case of lawyers. If I get more than probation and a knighthood, I'll sack the lot of them! Then I guess the gutter rags will crucify me, and say the judge was bent! You can't win, can you?'

Later, Michael had gone to his study and phoned Sarah Williams. She had been fighting tears when the phone rang, and the pleasure and elation in his tone did not help. She tried hard to control her own voice, but he picked up the misery.

'Thing!' he said. 'What's up? I love you, you know I love you.'

Oh God, he thought. Why do women want so much? Of all the good affairs he'd had in the last few years, that this should happen. That love should raise its head. Sarah did not cry. She read his voice completely.

'I'm sorry, Mike,' she said. 'How's the party? It's just the court tomorrow. What if it goes wrong?'

'It won't go wrong. I'm fed up telling you. Cyril says I can probably even smuggle you into Ford. Dressed up as a boy! How does that sound?'

Cinderella, as usual, wasn't at the ball, but Cinderella was a tough girl. She laughed.

'Maybe I could drive over now,' she said. 'I could meet you by the lake. You could fuck me up against the boatshed, couldn't you? Go back to your little wife and guests with your cock all nice and sticky.'

At this point, fortunately, Masters was brought back to his senses by the banging of a gavel. He was in the courtroom still, and he was being stared at by many eyes. He realised he had been dreaming, totally unconscious of his surroundings. He also had an urgent erection, which luckily nobody could see inside the dock. Unless he had been handling it?! She would have, too, he thought. She'd have had me up against the boathouse wall, even with the floodlights on and the Fleet Street insects running round. She was that sort of a woman.

Sir Cyril was signalling to him, angrily. Concentrate!

Mr Justice Harper put down his gavel. He regarded Masters balefully, over his half-moon spectacles. He continued from where he had clearly broken off.

'Given, as I was saying before I lost your interest Mister Masters, that there is an expectation that justice must be seen to be done, given that although the losses you sustained were undoubtedly enormous ones, and given the discomfort and embarrassment suffered by you and indeed your family – I feel that in the climate of the times, the sentence I must pass must be an exemplary one. There has been an air of unreality, for many people, in this case. An air of never-never land, of sums of money well beyond the grasp of normal minds, beyond the dreams of avarice. Many people have talked almost openly of double standards in the law, many commentators – sailing, I would say, very close to the brisk winds of contempt – have muttered darkly of friends in high places, of coteries, of arrogance . . .'

It slowly dawned on Michael Masters that something had gone wrong. Mr Justice Harper was using the wrong script. There had been a huge mistake. Furiously, he tried to attract the attention of his counsel. Sir Cyril France stared straight ahead. Frantically, he glanced around the room at the lawyers he had spoken with, had eaten food with, shared laughter. Grey-wigged heads examined papers carefully.

Five minutes later, Michael Masters, stunned, stood in the dock and watched the judge retire through the oaken door beside the seat of justice.

Four years. Four years imprisonment. Not in an open prison, not in Ford. In Bowscar Jail, in Staffordshire. A real jail. One of the fortresses. Michael Masters opened his mouth to shout at his counsel. But Sir Cyril France was ducking out of sight. Two court officers, recognising signs, moved smartly down the dock from either side of him and took his arms. Not rough, but firm.

'You can see him down below,' said one. 'Come on, get out of this. We'll get you a drink of tea.'

Masters turned his head towards the public gallery. His wife Barbara, a slender, dark-haired woman of thirty-four, was in the front row, her hands gripping the rail, her chin almost resting on it. Her clear grey eyes regarded him, from under fine brows. Her face held no expression.

Is it Sarah? thought Masters. Does she know? His wife's uncle was a judge. Two more were in the House of Lords.

Had she finally had enough?

If Donald Sinclair had been the most modest of all politicians, he could not have prevented the triumphs of this day. The bolder of the morning papers had named him as the mystery man of Buckie, by midday he had ousted Cyril Richardson officially as the junior minister for prisons, and by early afternoon the news that Michael Masters had been locked away for four whole years had swept the country. His first news conference was scheduled for 3.30 to give the evening papers a chance, the TV people enough time for constructing specials if they wanted to, and the dailies to do backgrounds, profiles of the hero and his dog, and shock features on the state of crisis in the country's jails.

Sir Gerald Turner visited him in the ante-room in Queen Anne's Gate where the make-up girl was putting the final dabs of powder on his cheeks and forehead.

'Nervous, Donald? You shouldn't be. Just remember what Velma Goodman always says: "Don't be afraid of lying – it's the truth we've got to fear"!'

He laughed with real pleasure at the joke, although Goodman, the Prime Minister's press secretary, would probably have meant it, every word.

'I still wish you'd agree to join me,' replied Sinclair. 'I'll feel pretty damned exposed with only Christian Fortyne to back me up. And any credit that's due should really be yours to start with.'

'Nonsense. My only wisdom in the matter was to give you your chance. You've put the prison question firmly on the map, and that's just where it should be. And I can tell you, my lad, it's bloody nice to have some good news for a change.'

An aide put her head around the door.

'Mr Sinclair? Could you be ready in two minutes? Mr Fortyne's all set. The media people are in and settled.'

'Sir Gerald,' said Donald Sinclair.

'Not another word. Good luck!'

Smiling, his broad, pleasant face genuinely warm, he left. You're too good to be a politician, Donald Sinclair thought. And much too good to be Home Secretary . . .

The press conference was a delight. With Fortyne ever ready at his elbow with facts and figures, with the obligatory pretty women – but cool, professional, businesslike – to hand out and explain the media packs, it went like clockwork. The atmosphere was friendly, the questioners radiated goodwill. For once, as Turner had pointed out, there was some good news about the prisons. For once, as well, there seemed to be a man in charge who knew his stuff, was bold, imaginative, and in control.

Firstly, would there be an inquiry into Buckie? No, said Sinclair earnestly, because there had already been three into the condition of the Scottish system in – how many months? Fortyne, efficiency personified, gave the answer. And do you know, said Sinclair, with an air of vague surprise, they all drew the same conclusion? Basically, the problem was the inmates, not the jails. A small body of desperately disruptive men who terrorised and bullied other inmates into actions they neither wanted nor approved of. There was no evidence of an overly oppressive regime, no bullying or brutality by the officers, just the wildmen. Well, the secure unit at Schotts had gone some way to meeting the challenge, and there were more of the same under active consideration. That, he thought, would probably solve the problem.

For most of them, that was fair enough. Nobody seemed to know, or care, that the inquiries had all been internal ones, and totally rejected by both prisoners and the outside bodies interested in reform. But one Scots voice asked: 'Is it enough though, Minister? Are you completely satisfied? Even given your brilliant stroke at Buckie?'

Sinclair coughed, modestly.

'There were more people involved in Buckie than just me,' he said. 'Don't anybody forget that, please. But no – I am not satisfied. Nor am I satisfied with the situation here, in England. Or in Wales.' He banged the table, gazing into the attentive faces. 'Make no mistake,' he said. 'The prison system in this country is a mess, a parlous mess. But I can promise you this, ladies and gentlemen: I am determined, personally determined, that things will get better very soon. That, I hope and think, is why I was entrusted with this job. And I shall succeed.'

In a small way, it was a sensation. A minister of state admitting that there was something wrong. An undercurrent of rare excitement was discernible. Sinclair went on, rapidly, to outline the bare bones of a strategy. A fact-finding mission around the prisons, an 'open door and listening ear' policy to the people in the know, the governors, the prison officers, yes – even the prisoners themselves. Then, perhaps, a tour of foreign systems, many of which, he readily admitted, made Britain's way look very out of date.

'At the moment,' he concluded, 'I am in the early stages. I am at the bottom rung. But I am not afraid to tell you that we need a new initiative, that something must be done. The failings in the prisons must be tackled, the tendency to sweep things underneath the carpet has to end. It is not a one-way process, I must emphasise. The problems of the criminals themselves must be addressed. Too many get away, too many receive sentences which at the very least do not deter them. Both aspects need attention. Already, as I am sure you will agree, there are straws in the wind. Ladies and gentlemen, I intend that wind to grow into a gale.'

Many of the assembled journalists were left floundering by the unaccustomed directness of it all. But the smarter ones homed in.

'These straws in the wind, minister? Is that a reference to the Masters case?'

Sinclair achieved a studiedly blank expression.

'I'm sorry. I don't quite understand.'

They thought he did. They were certain that he did. Someone near the back almost shouted: 'Everybody thought he'd get a token sentence. Six months maybe. Probation. But he's gone to Bowscar, hasn't he? Were you behind it, minister? Is that the straw in the wind?'

There was a hubbub of questioning. Sinclair waved his hand for silence.

'Ladies and gentlemen,' he said, 'I was not, repeat not, referring to a specific case. Are you suggesting I could – indeed I *should* – attempt to influence the judiciary? Even the Home Secretary would . . .' He permitted himself a small laugh. 'Let me put it this way. I certainly do not have any "clout" where their judicial lordships are concerned. The Home Secretary may have their ear, but I am certain nobody else does. In all this, indeed, I feel I cannot stress too frequently how indebted we all are to Sir Gerald Turner's statesmanship. For myself, I think a climate may have been set, that is all. I think the climate might be changing. I solved Buckie, yes, I will accept some credit there. And the climate may be changing. Those are the straws in the wind.'

Afterwards, he drank a cold beer in Fortyne's office. The civil servant, still cool, still detached, saluted him with his glass.

'Have you had any training?' asked the Old Etonian. 'Formally?'

'Why? Wasn't I all right?'

'One thing,' said Fortyne. 'You shouldn't have kept calling

them ladies and gentlemen. You weren't talking to them, remember. You were talking to the cameras. To the world, so to speak.'

'Oh. Good point. But on the whole . . . well, I was pretty pleased, weren't you?'

The civil servant put his glass of Beck's down on the green leather desk-top and removed his spectacles. He scratched his nose, then replaced them. Suddenly, his face cracked in a grin.

'If you're not careful,' he said, 'you'll end up as Prime Minister. You were bloody brilliant!'

It was late when Rosanna Nixon steered off the M8 into Glasgow and headed for Hyndland. She was so tired the streetlights flashed before her eyes, and when the traffic lights on Hillhead Road turned green she did not move off until a man behind her tooted angrily. Outside her flat in Kingsborough Gardens she parked the Renault with one wheel on the pavement, and fumbled clumsily for seconds before the key turned in her front-door lock. She slammed the door behind her and switched the light on. Silence and the smell of home. She wanted to go to bed.

As she made herself a drink and picked through her correspondence, Rosanna pondered dully on her failure as an investigative reporter. She had alienated her news editor and friend, she had blown a day of leave, she had driven hundreds of miles, and she had got nowhere. As Maurice Campbell had said the evening before, when she had insisted on driving back to Buckie even if it meant him sacking her: 'It's your time you'll be wasting, Doll, and that's fair enough. But you're throwing away credits, aren't you? I had hopes for you, despite the daft degree. Don't show me up to be a prat, eh hen?' She knew now what he had meant, she thought. She'd made herself a prat, and in Maurice's eyes that made him one as well. It was the game.

The flat was in a basement, and the bedroom, at the front, was huge and empty. The bed – a mattress on the floor with a quiet brown counterpane – looked like a lonely island on the polished boards. Beside it were a book, a box of tissues, a telephone and an alarm clock. The overhead light was operated by a pull-cord, dangling between the pillows. Rosanna pulled her clothes off briskly, leaving her tee-shirt on. In bed, with her feet getting warmer, she undid her bra and worked it out through one sleeve. She lay on her back, and balanced the hot milk in front of her chin, and watched the steam curling to the ceiling.

A failure. A hundred people spoken to (or dozens, anyway),

more and ever more embarrassing visits to the police, attempts to speak to warders at the gates. Rosanna had buttonholed women she thought had been among the silent watchers on the pavement during the siege, and been rebuffed. She had questioned hotel staff about their guest lists and been warned off. She had checked the nearest hospital, and the Sheriff's office, even the cemetery. And she had hung about the bar frequented by off-duty prison officers until she had been barred by the licensee with quite crude frankness. Everybody, it seemed, knew who she was and that she was snooping after something. In a small way, she became a laughing stock. That was part of the cause of the exhaustion.

As Rosanna drifted into sleep, the telephone rang. She picked the receiver up half-bemused. It was a man's voice. An English voice. Harsh, low and urgent.

'Is that Rosanna Nixon?'

'Yes. Who is that?'

'You don't need to know that. Let's say I'm one of the Mighty Shit Upon, shall we? The Army of the Damned.'

'I beg your pardon?' Rosanna sat up, with a jerk. 'Are you a soldier?'

'Shut your mouth and listen. I've got a name for you, right? Jimmy McGregor. James Malcolm. Mean anything to you?'

'No. Should it?'

'Hah! Some of us here would like it to. Some of us think we've been shit on once too often. Medals? You must be bloody joking! We heard you might be interested.'

'I am, I am!' she said. 'Is it . . . was it Buckie?'

'James Malcolm McGregor,' said the voice. The tone had changed, to satisfaction. 'You ask 'em if he's still alive. You ask 'em who fell off the roof. You make 'em have it.'

'McGregor,' repeated Rosanna. She was beside herself. 'Look, please, who are you? Can we meet? Did you say—'

The phone went down at the other end, and she shook her head, frustratedly. She slammed her own receiver down and jumped out of bed. She picked her clothes up, then dropped the dress and tights. She pulled her pants on, then a pair of jeans, from across the back of a chair. But she had nowhere to go.

'Oh fuck, fuck, fuck!' she said, aloud. 'I don't know what to do! Oh *fuck*!'

She picked up the phone, and began to dial Maurice Campbell's number. Then she put it down. She went for her contacts book, to ring the Home Office, London, a number she ought damn well to remember but she couldn't. Then she slung the notebook on the bed. She dragged her hand through her thick, short hair.

'What should I bloody do?' she said. 'James Malcolm McGregor. What should I do?'

She dropped onto her bed, banging her bottom hard through the mattress with the impact. She hugged her knees to her chest and rocked.

Eileen Pendlebury sat in her car and watched her father emerge through the wicket gate and walk towards her along the narrow service road to Bowscar Jail. It was almost midnight, but the road was garishly, almost blindingly, lighted, for security. In the orange glare Richard Pendlebury, her father and the prison's governor, looked smaller than his five feet ten, and stooped, and tired, and old.

Behind him, the prison wall was huge and surrealistic, stretching off interminably in its odd orange cocoon. The gates were so enormous that looking at them made Eileen shiver, despite the number of times she had waited for her father in front of them. They were old, and black, and solid, in a turreted mock-gothic gatehouse straight out of a nineteenth-century fantasy. Her father said they symbolised the prison service that he worked in, and perhaps the British character. He was not exactly happy in his work.

Eileen leaned across and opened the passenger door, as Pendlebury arrived. He bent and smiled at her, his eyes dark with fatigue.

'Sorry,' he said. 'I couldn't face the drive myself. I knew you wouldn't mind.'

Eileen smiled, and started up the engine without speaking. It was not all that far to home – twelve miles – and her father had set out for the jail at six that morning. The job had been ever more crucifying of late, and he came home when he could, to keep his sanity, he said. Very frequently these days, he was staying in his suite in Bowscar. He hated it.

Had her father wanted not to talk, she would have kept her silence. In fact, they had driven through the quiet Midlands mining village and out into the open countryside before either of them spoke. Then Pendlebury sighed.

'Eileen,' he said. 'If you go into government, I'll cut you off without a penny. If you go into the Home Office, I'll personally have you shot.'

She changed gear to negotiate a crossroads. Out on the trunk road, she opened up the engine. She did not bother to reply.

'I've spoken to a man today,' he said, 'who I would guess is as intelligent as you or I. He is serving thirty-five years for murder, and he rejoices in the nickname of the Animal.'

'I've heard of him,' said Eileen. 'A Glaswegian, isn't he? A sort of racial stereotype.'

'A sort of unexploded bomb,' rejoined her father. 'When I say I've spoken to him, I tell a lie. I'm being over-optimistic. I spoke to him, I tried to speak to him, he'd just arrived. He ignored me. I can't say I blame him. His lips were black and blue. I could hardly see his eyes.'

'God,' said Eileen. She waited, after that.

For many minutes, Pendlebury did not speak. He did not tell her that the man had been injected with Largactil, the liquid cosh, that he had been hardly capable of standing up, or that the receiving officers had tried to prevent the governor from seeing him. McGregor, according to his papers, had come from Long Lartin, and before that, Hull and Frankland. Since crossing into England, he had been constantly on the move. Pendlebury felt ashamed to be a part of it.

'Do you know what I've done with him?' he said, at last. 'On orders from on high? I've incarcerated him. He's in a strip cell. A cell with padded walls. To speak to no one, under any circumstances, except the staff. He's cut off from the world.'

He turned his long, intelligent face towards her. Eileen shot him a glance, then put her eyes back on the road. She reached across and touched his leg, a gesture of sympathy. Pendlebury had a vision of a big log fire quietly dying for the night, and a gigantic whisky. Eileen, he knew, would have arranged it.

'It's just another coffin nail,' he said. 'An unexploded bomb.'

Alice Grogan was thinking how secure she was when Charles Lister came to call. She had moved apartments yet again, she had teed up Andrew Forbes, and she was safe. The only people who knew where to find her tonight were—

The window broke with a burst of glass and a splintering crash as the frame was pushed inwards. Alice almost screamed, then gave up. No one would hear her, here. No one would come. Alice had been around.

She knew it was Charles Lister, although he wore a mask. A balaclava helmet, only more so, with two small eyeholes and a mouth. He looked like a rapist from a nasty magazine. It was Charlie.

'Hi, Chuck,' she said. 'I guess you dropped by to kill me.'

She was sitting up in bed, naked, and she got out of it, stood up, and faced him. She was very fine to look at, slim and muscular and full-breasted. She was panting, which enhanced the effect. Maybe it was a rapist, she thought wildly. Please God. Anything, so long it wasn't Lister.

But the man was not there for sex. He was there to kill. He pushed her violently back against the wall, beside the bed-head, and slid a long, thin-bladed knife up under her ribcage and deep into her heart. Alice felt it as a red-hot wire, followed by an electric shock. As he stepped backwards she fell onto her knees, then onto her face. She was moaning, gently.

'Oh Chuck,' she said. 'You didn't have to do that.'

She twitched, one time or two, then was still.

It had all been over in two minutes.

FOUR

The young man in the cheap dark trousers and the nylon anorak lifted his damp feet alternately, and wished the bus would come. He had been at Chorlton Street for forty minutes, and he was cold. Behind him, through the misted window of the cafeteria, he could see people drinking tea. When the bus came, he would have one. Then get off home to Withington, and his basement. He had a lot more machining to do if he was to keep to schedule.

When the single-decker did arrive, he watched the people getting off with little interest. He had been at the game so long that he could tell the ones who had been visiting the prison. They were women, they were poor, they had children, usually screaming. Today seven got off, their hair and clothes still damp despite the lateness of the bus's arrival in Manchester. So it was raining at Bowscar, as well.

The woman Peter Smith was waiting for was last off. Ahead of her she pushed two toddlers, and she was carrying a sleeping baby over her shoulder. Like her, the baby was ill-dressed, fat and pale. One of the toddlers was bawling, and the other had a runny nose. The driver, with as much sympathy as he could summon, tried to get them down the steps without disaster, and then pulled the folded buggy off behind him. He had no children of his own, but he unfolded the buggy in three quick movements. He had been on the prison run for eighteen months.

The woman's face was moonish and exhausted. She had made an attempt at make-up many hours ago, when she had set out on the monthly pilgrimage to see her man and keep their marriage and their hope alive, but the black around her eyes had run onto her cheeks from tears or rain. She was short-sighted. She gazed at Peter Smith for seconds before recognising him. She did not try to smile.

'Tea?' he said. And to one of the toddlers: 'You. Get in there before I smack your face, right?' The child, who knew Peter Smith and did not like him, went on playing with the rainwater sliding down a concrete pillar from the roof.

Inside, the woman sat at a red plastic table, spreading like a Buddha. The toddlers, unlooked-at, spread further to poke at people's bags, touch sandwiches, and stare. Peter Smith brought two cups of tea and, shivering, wrapped both hands around his own. He brought nothing for the children.

'Go all right?' he asked. 'No problems?'

'Mam!' screeched one of the toddlers. 'I want a drink! I want a drink, Mam!'

The woman reached down and smacked the child's legs, hard. A few people at tables nearby looked on, some rather shocked. But the place was filling up, as a Rapide from Birmingham had just disgorged. The child moved off, bubbling, and messed around the legs of travellers.

'Is it drugs?' she said, unexpectedly.

Peter Smith looked at her, his eyes narrowing in fear and anger.

'Shut your mouth,' he hissed. 'Do you want the cash or don't you?'

The fat, moonish face flinched. She nodded. She sipped her tea.

'Yeah,' she said, very quietly. 'I give it him. It cut my mouth. It was sharp. What was it?'

'Right!' said Peter Smith. 'That's it! You've had it, you have! That's the last bloody time!'

'No!' she said.

'Yes. And no cash, neither. You've bloody blown it, you big fat fucking cow.'

He began to stand, watching her reaction. She was terrified. He continued the movement until her mouth began to open. In a second she would bellow, which he did not want. At the last moment, he threw his weight forward onto both hands on the table top. He glared into her eyes.

'Listen,' he said. 'Get this straight. One more question, one more whinge, ever, and that's the lot. I told you at the start. It's not drugs, it's nothing bad. Your bloody husband sent you out a note, didn't he? I read it out to you. It's all right. It's helping them in there. Don't you want to help them?'

At the closest tables, people had looked at the couple, slightly curious. But the noise inside the café was phenomenal. Nobody could hear a word they said. Slowly, Peter Smith lowered himself into his seat. The woman sniffed. She drank her tea. When she next looked up, there was a brown envelope on the table between the man's hands. With a stubby, oil-stained finger, he pushed it across towards her.

'Twenty quid a go,' he said, almost kindly. 'It's a lot of cash for bugger all, isn't it? Just do yourself a favour and keep your bloody nose out of what don't concern you. I told you at the start-off, didn't I? No questions, and you get the cash. You cause me any trouble, and you'll be in the shit. You'll wish you'd never been born. There's a lot of nasty accidents can happen in a prison, aren't there? And outside.'

The fat woman's toddlers were coming back together, down an aisle. One of them was holding what appeared to be half a Danish pastry, that had been trodden on. The other's face was smeared with dirt. Peter Smith stood up.

'Just keep your bloody mouth shut, right? I'll be in touch.'

He turned and walked out. The damp air, after the cafeteria, was almost pleasant for a moment or two, almost a relief. But by the time he had walked to Piccadilly Gardens to catch his bus, his hair, neck and shoulders were soaked through. Back at his big, empty house, there would be nothing welcoming, no woman, no hot meal, no central heating. Just the basement, with his lathe and other tools. It was the barrel next, that would be a laugh, at least. How could she get that in? In a cigar tube, up her . . . ? He chuckled to himself. She could bangle in a howitzer.

After he had paid his fare, Peter Smith began to think. What if he machined it in two sections, that screwed into each other? It would mean an extra trip, but there were three women on the job. Shit, why had that fat cow started asking questions? Peter Smith did not like that. Maybe her next trip had better be her last.

In a way, he felt quite sorry for her. He remembered her face after he had mouthed his warning. Fat, pale and pathetic. You had to keep them frightened, though, didn't you? It was the only way.

There was far too much at stake to sod about . . .

By the time Michael Masters was required to go through the induction procedure at Bowscar Jail, he had had more than thirty hours to absorb the shock of his betrayal. He was in control, and his mind was working rationally again. There was still fury in his heart, but he could contemplate it, hold it up to scrutiny without it exploding, choking him. He tried to keep it from the forefront of his thoughts, to give his brain a rest.

The first half-hour after he had been bundled from the dock

the day before had been the worst. In the holding rooms below the court, he had faced Sir Cyril France wild-eyed, like something out of a painting from the Civil War. The barrister, divested of his wig and gown, looked small, and weaselly, and nervous.

'Michael,' he had said. 'What can I say? My dear chap, this is such a terrible, terrible shock to me.'

Masters was still beyond coherence. A shock to him! He, the barrister, Sir Cyril France, QC, had been one of the authors of the deal. He had persuaded Masters just how clever it would be to play it this way, just how easy it would be in Ford.

'The bastard,' breathed Masters. He was not trying to keep his voice low, despite the officer who was sitting nearby in the windowless room. 'The bastard was coming to my house. The bastard was—'

A look of panic rose in the barrister's eyes. He put his hand across the table to touch his client's arm. Masters' face was wild and pale.

'No,' he said, quietly but with desperate authority. 'Michael, I implore you. Don't say anything. No!'

Masters was breathing shallowly and rapidly, halfway between rage and disbelief. He remembered the judge's look of distaste over his half-moon spectacles. But Masters knew things about Mr Justice Harper that would have brought the public gallery baying to its feet. He crushed his fists into tight, shaking knots. To hell with it. To hell with all of them.

'Michael,' said Sir Cyril, carefully. 'Something has gone badly wrong. I don't know why, and I don't know how. My first job is to find that out. My second—'

Masters shot a hand across the table and gripped the thin, weak wrist. As he squeezed, a dew of sweat broke out upon the brow of Sir Cyril France. Over a fifteen-second period he paled until his skin was sickly yellow. But he suffered in silence. When his wrist was freed, he could no longer move his fingers.

'Your first job,' Masters told him, 'is to get me out of here. You know who I'm protecting, Cyril, and you know what I know. You can give them all the news, can't you? I want out.'

The barrister's sick, frightened eyes slid towards the guard. His face implored his client to say no more.

'We might appeal,' he muttered. 'Perhaps if—'

Masters' voice was harsh.

'You can't appeal against what we've already admitted, can you? And you can't appeal against the sentence until you've found out whose idea the sentence was. Geoffrey Harper's a puppet, and you know it. Now get out of here and ask the questions.'

'Michael, please. Be careful what you say. You're still in court. The precincts.'

He stood up, with an ingratiating glance at the officer, a big man in his middle-fifties. Masters spoke to him.

'Would you be surprised,' he said, conversationally, 'if I told you Mr Justice Harper wore women's underwear and spent his cash on kiddie-porn from Holland?'

The barrister emitted a small sound of genuine distress. His face went grey.

'You,' said the usher to Michael Masters, 'have got a nasty mind. I take it you've finished with your visitor?'

Masters felt better. His emotions were coming back under control. He knew he'd put the fear of God up France.

'Get the shitbag out of here,' he said. 'I think I've made myself clear.'

Sir Cyril France tried to pick his briefcase up in his right hand, but winced. He took it with his left. The officer opened the door and he left with small and rapid steps.

'You,' the officer said. 'This way.'

As Masters passed him, he said: 'Is it true about Harper? Kiddie-porn?'

'Nah,' said Masters. 'He's a boring little fart. I doubt if he's even got one.'

'Oh,' replied the guard. 'A lot of them are bent, though. We've got a lady judge sleeps with her alsatian. Straight up.'

'Straight up? Well, that's something I suppose!'

They both laughed.

To Rosanna Nixon's annoyance, the rain in Glasgow made her late for work. She had dearly wanted to be in the news-room when Maurice Campbell arrived, and she had wanted to present the ultimate picture of the cool, collected newshound putting one over on her curmudgeonly cynic of a boss. Instead, she had arrived twenty minutes late, by taxi, with laddered tights. She also had wet hair, soggy shoulders, and dirty hands.

The news-room was long, airy and modern. Each desk had a computer and VDU instead of a typewriter and spike, and the floors were carpeted. Rosanna left a damp trail in the pale rose as she walked, pulling her coat off on the way. Campbell, in isolated splendour at his desk at the end, watched with amusement. He had a secret.

'Sorry I'm late,' said Rosanna. 'Car wouldn't start. And the kitchen flooded, and I couldn't get a taxi.'

'S'all right by me, hen,' he said. 'Nothing's happening yet awhile, you're first in except for wee Barry. Whyn't you go to the ladies and dry off?'

'No!' said Rosanna. She shied her coat six feet across the room at a chair. The seat rotated lazily under the impact and the coat fell to the floor. Rosanna grinned at him, her damp face shining.

'Well,' said Campbell, carefully. 'The day in Buckie seems to have done you good. Or did you stay in bed?'

'I did not. You were right, though. I didn't find a thing. You were absolutely right.'

Campbell dipped his head.

'No sign of the diving boy? Well, I thought there wouldn't be. You seem damn cheerful about it, though. Come on, what's up your sleeve?'

What's up yours, Rosanna thought. She knew him well enough to realise there was something. Surely her mystery caller had not . . . ? No, stupid. She stopped beating about the bush.

'Look,' she said, 'I know we nearly fell out about the diving boy, but I wasn't dreaming it. Buckie was a waste of time, but when I got home last night, this morning – I had a phone call.'

She was a nice wee thing, thought Maurice Campbell. Not exactly good-looking, not exactly the world's best journalist, but she had an open face, and she told the truth, and she was keen. He thought she was going to come a cropper yet again, and it pained him. He dropped the idea of making something of his secret. It would hurt her more.

'Before you go on, lassie,' he said. 'This phone call wasnae confirmation, was it? That someone died? Because I'm sorry, but I know. It's been announced. It's public.'

It was like stealing a toy from a child. Rosanna flushed brick red.

'Oh,' she said. 'But . . .'

Campbell picked up a piece of PA copy which had been face down in front of him. He handed it across.

'An overnight. It was in the tray this morning. It's very brief. I doubt it'll make a paragraph outside Buckie.'

The slip said simply: 'The Scottish Office announced today

that a prisoner involved in the recent rooftop protest at HM Prison, Buckie, collapsed and died yesterday, apparently from natural causes. His name will not be released until his next of kin have been informed.'

Rosanna stared at the yellow sheet in puzzlement. It was so bald. So meaningless. Campbell's ruddy face was sympathetic.

'But I know his name,' she said. 'That was what the man on the phone told me. It's James McGregor. James Malcolm McGregor.'

'So? So it could be John Two-three. He died of natural causes, didn't he? And we can't use his name. Next of kin.'

Rosanna's face was burning.

'But Maurice, for Christ's sake! It stinks! It bloody stinks! I see someone falling off a roof, the Scottish Office deny everything, and then there's a corpse! A heart attack, whatever! Nothing to do with anything! Natural causes!'

Maurice Campbell looked up and past her. Barry Robins and another reporter had come through the door. They were watching the scene, attracted by Rosanna's voice.

'Look, hen,' said Campbell, soothingly. 'Get a grip, eh? I'm sick to death of all this nonsense. I'm a reasonable man, but I can't spend my mornings wiping babies' bottoms. You've been in Buckie yourself, you learned nothing. Someone's died behind the walls and you think you know his name and he fell off. So what? If they picked the poor sod up by his testicles and kicked him over like a football do you think I'd put it in the paper on your say so? Get a grip.'

His voice had become lower and harsher as the other two had approached. Now he waved his hand at her, impatiently.

'Go away,' he said. 'I don't want to be giving you public bollockings all the time, Rosanna. Go away and dry your hair or something. Dry behind your ears while you're at it. You can have this morning to yourself, all right? You can try to crack the Scottish Office on the phone. You can speak to the new man down in London. Mr Ever-Open-Door Whatsisface? But by dinnertime I want you back on my staff as a fully functioning reporter without a bee in the bonnet. Do I make myself very bloody clear?'

Rosanna walked away with her lower lip bitten firmly between her teeth. When Barry Robins, sympathetically, handed her her coat, she turned away. She might as well have stayed in bed. Period.

* * *

Even with his brain in neutral, Michael Masters could not entirely ignore the processes he went through on arrival at the jail in Staffordshire. It was at once so similar to scenes he'd watched on film and television, and so completely different. The rooms were the same – drab, cream and green, impersonal – but they had a third dimension. As in the cells he'd stayed in overnight, it was mainly to do with smell, and heat. The air was almost palpable, redolent of boiled food and drains, so thick that he could taste it. Masters was not a particularly fastidious man, there was nothing fey or precious in his tastes, but he found himself reluctant to even breathe it deeply. It felt polluted, dangerous.

Then there were the processes. In the armoured prison van, the men who had travelled with him from London had seemed quite normal, unremarkable. Opposite had been a thin, handsome man with two-toned sculptured hair, who was possibly a homosexual. He had a cut lip and a swollen eye, but appeared quite self-contained. Next to Masters was a youth, a black boy of barely twenty. He said nothing throughout the long journey, merely wringing his hands together and staring at the floor. Two men – white and in their forties – had worn suits, another wore a tracksuit bottom and an anorak, and an older man, Irish, had slept noisily for most of the time. When he had awoken, he had demanded to be allowed to piss, then dozed off again. He smelled of drink.

But when they had disgorged, and been lined up to enter the reception suite, these ordinary, common or garden detainees – himself included – had apparently been transformed, turned into Martians, aliens, creatures from the Black Lagoon. It was a transformation invisible to the naked eye, and certainly unbeknown to them. But the prison officers could see it, and they had become fierce and animated. They had shouted, and cajoled, and pushed.

The apparent homosexual got it worst. Two officers ranged round him, at a distance of four feet, their eyes bulging like music hall comedians'. They pointed at him, pantomiming shock, while the man stared back at them, disconcerted, clearly beginning to be afraid. Masters, left alone for the moment with the others in the queue, watched fascinated. His mind was back in gear, but he could hardly believe the spectacle. It was like a comedy routine, like something from a play about conscription. The RSM's gavotte.

'Are you a bleeding poof, duckie?' said the leader of the double-act. 'Are you one of the stick-it-up-the-bum brigade? We'll have to get the bleeding tongs to you won't we, my girl? We'll have to bung you in the leper colony. I suppose you're HIV, you dirty little brown-hat bastard?'

Some of the men in line with Masters laughed. The target of the prison officers had gone white.

'You can't say that to me,' he started. His voice was well-educated, but not mannered. The double-act laughed, mockingly.

'Oh no, you're right,' said one. 'You're only on remand, aren't you? What is it? Drugs, assaulting a policeman, bleeding on the pavement outside the House of Commons? We've got your measure, Raymond Orchard. Come on, Cherry! Get in there!'

One of the officers moved fast, and pushed the prisoner from behind, slamming him into the door jamb of the reception suite. He gave a cry, and dropped to one knee. Both officers stood back.

'You've got to get them from behind,' one said to the queue. 'It's what they're used to.'

There was more laughter, but not full-throated. One or two of the men had lost colour from their faces, and the black boy was beginning to moan beneath his breath. Yeah, thought Masters, you're next, Sunshine. Pound to a penny.

But he was wrong. All the men were treated equally for a while. They were shoved through the wooden doorway into a changing room and told to strip. Only Raymond Orchard was segregated, and taken to a curtained area. As in changing rooms everywhere, some of the men tried to hide their nakedness, others brazened it out. To Masters' eyes, it was an unsavoury collection of manhood. Sagging breasts and bellies, hollow chests, fields of scarlet spots on pallid, narrow backs. The criminal classes, he reflected, were an unhealthy-looking lot.

The smell was much worse when the men were naked. God knows when some of them had last washed, let alone had a bath. The smell of feet, as socks were peeled off and dropped, became quite choking. As an overlay to the food and drains it was horrendous. Masters himself had only been able to splash his face and clean his teeth that morning, but he had showered yesterday, and his clothes, naturally, were clean. From time to time he felt himself about to gag.

A third prison officer – tall, broad-shouldered, smiling – noticed his discomfort.

'Nice, isn't it, your lordship,' he said. 'It's what we put up with all the time. The scum, the filth, the lousy stinking dregs. Nice, isn't it?'

Masters, naked, faced the prison officer. The smile appeared to be a genuine one, there was no sign of a sneer in it. The epithet 'your lordship' had been delivered straight, as if he thought that Masters was a lord. Masters sensed trouble.

The officer's uniform shirt was crisp, his boots were brilliant, his trousers quite immaculate. Hair clearly styled, with a firm wave in the luxuriant dark growth on top, and distinguished grey patches above each ear. He exuded self-regard.

Masters said: 'Why did you call me that? I'm not a lord.'

'Sir,' he said. 'Why did I call you that, *sir*.'

'Sir,' said Masters. That did not worry him. The edges of the officer's smile began to develop the expected sneer. Here we go, said Masters, to himself.

'You think you're a lord, don't you, though? The man with the millions. The man with the judges in his pocket. I'm going to take your clothes away now. You're going to get a pair of holey underpants some dirty coon's shit into. You're going to get a pair of socks so stiff with sweat they'll cut your toenails for you. You're going to have a shower that's got to last you for a week and I'll control the water. I'm telling you, *Mister* Masters, you'd better wash dead quick. I don't feel very generous to parasites.'

Masters bent to pick his clothes up, and the polished boot came down onto his fingers. Not hard. When he tried to remove them, the pressure increased.

'You look a bit of a nerd, bent down like that, a bit of a prat. Shall I get that raving poof to slip you one, shall I? An instant Aids injection?'

Masters said: 'If I told you what I thought of you, you'd crush my fingers, wouldn't you? Sir.' The officer began to increase the pressure. Masters said: 'I wouldn't do that, friend. I won't forget it.'

The officer, thus challenged, swung forward onto the ball of his foot. Masters gasped, feeling the knuckles crush and roll. Nothing broke, though. When the officer removed his boot, Masters straightened up.

'Well it hasn't given you a hard-on,' sneered the officer. 'At least you're not a pervert. How would you like to share a cell with one? We've got some nice ones here. Eh? Who do you fancy as a cell-mate?'

Anger was seated low in Masters' stomach. Without realising

it, he hit on the classic way to anger prison officers, the old lags' way. He did not answer. The man's face became suffused.

'I'm talking to you, cunt,' he said. 'What sort of cell-mate do you want?'

Most of the other men, their clothes collected, had moved into the showers. One or two were looking curiously at the battle. The prisoner seemed calm, the calmer of the two. He did not speak.

'You!' shouted the officer. His voice was rising, there was an edge of rage. 'You fucking answer me, you fucking cunt!'

Suddenly he swung his hand from up beside him, across his body, and smacked Masters hard across the face. As Masters leapt at him two other officers shot across the room. Masters, his hands reaching for the man's throat, was dragged backwards and thrown onto the tiles. He was kicked quickly and efficiently in the balls and stomach until he rolled up like a hedgehog, retching. Then he was dragged into a cubicle and showered as he lay. It was longer than he had been promised, but it was cold – to bring him round, presumably.

Twenty minutes later, Prisoner 137059 Masters, M., had been issued with dungarees and shirt, underpants and socks, and a pair of soft-soled shoes that did not fit. He had seen the medical officer and coughed, he had dressed himself, and he had signed for his own clothes and the contents of his pockets. The prison officer who had crushed his hand had unlocked a cell door on M-floor, flanked by two other men. Before he pushed it open, the officer had smiled his friendly smile.

'D'you like niggers, your lordship?' he said. 'Do you like violent men? This man should suit you right down to the ground, then. He killed a copper, didn't he? Matthew Jerrold's his name. He's an insane bastard, honestly. You'll like him.'

Without more ceremony, Michael Masters was pushed into the cell.

At 5.30 that evening, as far as she was able to remember, Rosanna Nixon had got herself the sack. Certainly, she pictured very clearly a cataclysmic row with Maurice Campbell, and she remembered storming from the office shouting insults. That in itself was not sufficient reason for thinking she was unemployed, because Maurice Campbell liked a slanging match. A stand-up dingdong between him and a reporter usually ended in a drink or two and reconciliations. But Rosanna had not stuck around.

She was at home now, sitting in her kitchen waiting for the electric kettle to boil. She had a mug in front of her, instant coffee standing in it, more spilled on the table. She had dropped and smashed a bottle of milk that she had bought around the corner on Hyndland Road. She was drunk.

Rosanna had started her telephone enquiries that morning from the office, but had abandoned the news-room after twenty minutes out of sheer embarrassment. She had gone to a small interviewing room and used the telephone there. Her questions could only be direct ones, because she could think of no way round that. She had tried the Scottish Office first, the jail, then the Buckie Sheriff's office. She had been put on hold, she had been transferred, she had been forgotten or fobbed off. Finally she had got through to the Prison Department of the Home Office.

'This is the East Kilbride News Service,' she had lied, for the sixth or seventh time. 'I'm enquiring about the PA report released last night. About the prisoner who died at Buckie Jail. I wonder is there anyone who could give me further details?'

If you asked the same question long enough, Rosanna was beginning to understand, it would eventually filter through to somebody who might know something about it. This time she was transferred to three junior functionaries in a row. They knew nothing personally, but the crisis was still vividly in everybody's minds. It came as a surprise to two of them to hear that there had been a death. One questioned her as to whether she was certain the announcement had been made by them.

Thus it came that a senior clerical officer, passing through an open-plan office, heard a junior call across the room to a fellow on the other side, 'Got a woman here who says someone died at Buckie. Is that right?' Thirty seconds later, although she did not know it, Rosanna Nixon had Christian Fortyne himself at the other end of the telephone. The accent, to her, was merely upper class and English. She did not recognise his voice.

'Can I help?' he said. 'I'm sorry if you've had trouble getting through. What is the problem?'

'This is the East Kilbride News Service,' said Rosanna. 'It's about the man who died at Buckie Jail. I wonder if there's any more information yet?'

Alarm bells were ringing gently in Fortyne's head. He remembered the small woman at the press conference. Could this be her?

'I'm afraid the press release said all we have to say at present. What else would you like to know?'

'Well. The PA piece said natural causes. Has that been confirmed?

'Not entirely, although there's little reason for doubt. The medical experts have yet to report in full. A post mortem might be called for. Possibly an inquest in due course. A fatal accident inquiry as you call them in Scotland, I believe.'

'Why? Were there . . . are the circumstances suspicious?'

There was something much too eager in her voice. Something Fortyne did not like. He pressed the mute button on his handset, and motioned a secretary to him. He pointed to the phone.

'Get a special trace on this for me. Top priority.' He released the button. 'No, not at all. But it is sometimes deemed appropriate in a case like this. The circumstances at the jail were hardly normal in themselves, were they?'

'When will it be? When will the post mortem be?'

Fortyne glanced at the secretary. She was talking rapidly into the phone. At Queen Anne's Gate, naturally, there was a system.

'I did not say there definitely would be one,' he explained, patiently. He could afford to be patient, he wanted time. 'It might be that the death certificate will be entirely straightforward. But in any event I know nothing fresh as yet. The press will be informed, obviously. At present we have not even been able to contact the next of kin. Many prisoners, you know, lose contact with their families, sometimes for many years. In case' – he laughed urbanely – 'in case your next question was when and if we could release a name.'

Rosanna licked her lips. Now or never.

'I know his name,' she said. 'Can you confirm it for me? It's James Malcolm McGregor.'

Christian Fortyne's eyebrows lifted imperceptibly. But his voice betrayed nothing. He did not miss a beat.

'I'm afraid the name means nothing to me,' he said. 'That's not my department. But I do know we could neither confirm nor deny it anyway. Until the next of kin have been traced and informed we would not wish it to appear, naturally. The distress would be enormous.'

The secretary approached with a piece of paper in her hand. On it was written the name of Rosanna's paper and the company that owned it, with an address. Fortyne nodded his thanks.

'By the way,' he said. 'What agency do you represent? Did you say—'

Rosanna Nixon put the phone down. Fortyne smiled.

'Too late, you bitch,' he said.

After that, Rosanna left the office. Although it was not much past eleven, she began to tour the bars. She was not drinking, she was looking for somebody. A former crime reporter called Adrian Rafferty, who was now a full-time drunk. She ran him to earth in the Arlington at five to one. He was already half seas over, but he was on his feet. He was at the bar, shouting at the top of his voice as every drinker does in Glasgow, and sliding down fifths of Grouse chased with halves of Belhaven. He did not recognise her despite the fact he'd torn her blouse off in a club one night and had his glasses smashed into his face.

'Adrian!' she shouted. 'It's me! I've come to buy you that drink!'

Rafferty blinked at her through smeared lenses. He was a tall man, who had once been smart as well as legendary. He wore a crumpled double-breasted suit, a stained white shirt, and a bow-tie.

'And who might you be, lassie?' His voice, once sonorous, was cracked. 'Never mind. I'll take a Grouse with you. And a half-pint of the heavy.'

Rosanna had to drink with him, or she would have got no information. Maybe he had nothing to give. She sipped a half of lager and listened to his ramblings for a while. Then she dropped the name. It was a very long shot. Jimmy McGregor was probably of no significance at all, as convicts went. But Rafferty paused. He drained his spirits glass and pushed the pair of them across at her.

'Wee Jimmy,' he said. 'That's Angus's kid brother. You know Angus, hen. The Animal. Wee Jimmy's not just any old McGregor, know what I mean? And is he dead? Hell's teeth.'

By 2.15 Rosanna had dragged Adrian Rafferty out of the Arlington and taken him on a taxi tour of bars as diverse as the Copper Kettle and the Saracen's Head. She knew all there was to know about wee Jimmy's brother except what jail he was in. They had spoken to well-heeled drugs men who wore their criminality as insultingly as their dark glasses and white jackets, they had stirred the bleary memories of men whose faces still bore razor scars from the great days of the fifties. By five o'clock she was woozy, and Rafferty was still much as she'd found him four hours before, neither incapable nor sober. He was refusing staunchly to join her for a bite to eat.

'I'll go down to the Three Tuns if you insist on spoiling a pleasant afternoon,' he said. 'There's a man might be in there will have our answer for us in a jiffy. I can guarantee it. Give me twenty pounds.'

She had already spent about thirty, and had no hope at all of claiming anything on expenses. But she paid up, and stopped the taxi at the first cashpoint she saw on the way back to the office. The drink had made her quite euphoric. Whatever Maurice Campbell thought, whatever he said to her, she was beginning to feel she might bring off a coup. She might present him, yet, with what they would have called a scoop in the good old days.

That was when she walked into the firestorm. Campbell was red with fury, shouting and waving his arms. He practically dragged her into his inner office when she began to bellow back, and he quickly quietened her with the intensity of his anger. He told her that the Scottish Office had been on, accusing her of professional misconduct, underhand behaviour, and bringing her newspaper into disrepute. They had accused him of being prepared to intrude on private grief, to spread malicious falsehoods, and to ignore directives expressly issued for humanitarian reasons. For a few moments Rosanna had been almost penitent, until she began to wonder how they had traced her call. The row flared up again, they spilled into the news-room, and she'd been sacked. She had stormed out to the Three Tuns, without the meal, to speak to Adrian Rafferty. Who, inevitably, had not been there.

When she had tracked him down, two hours later, his mood had changed. There was a mystery about the Animal, he said, but he would not elucidate. He muttered something about England, he demanded eighty pounds, and he turned ugly when she refused. He mocked her as a professional virgin and a whore, and tried to grab her breasts. She got home at last, drunk and furious.

The telephone awoke Rosanna. She was slumped on the kitchen table, her coffee still unmade. The kettle, if she had ever turned it on, had turned itself off again at least an hour ago. It was Maurice Campbell.

'Rosanna? Listen, hen, how you feeling?'

She felt terrible. Her head was poisonous and her throat was worse.

'Terrible. You sacked me, didn't you?'

'I did. However, we could come to some arrangement. I'm a sucker for a pretty face.'

Rosanna made a noise. A sort of croak.

'What a pity I haven't got one,' she said. 'What are you offering?'

'Oh, everything as normal. No change, nothing. So long as you keep your heid shut about the diving boy. All right?'

She did not even need to think.

'Maurice,' she said. 'You're probably right. I'm probably mad. But I saw what I saw and I heard what I heard. They traced a telephone call today. They warned me off.'

'Ach to hell! The Scottish Office probably rang round till they found you out. They probably—'

She interrupted him.

'Maurice, I didn't phone the Scottish Office. I phoned the men in London. The big boys. I phoned the Home Office.'

Maurice sighed.

'Ah well, hen. I didnae really expect you to say yes. So what's the next step?'

'London,' said Rosanna. 'I'm going down there. I'm damned if I'll give up yet awhile. Degree or no degree!'

She did not tell him about the Animal. Coming from Rafferty it was probably garbage anyway. She felt ill. She wanted bed.

Maurice sighed once more.

'Tell you what I'll do, Rosanna. I'll put you down for holiday, right? Take a fortnight. Three weeks. See how it goes.' He laughed. 'Don't burst into tears or anything, eh hen? I know I'm wonderful.'

'Yeah,' she said. She did not know what to say. 'Yeah, thanks. I'm sorry about the shouting at you.'

'See,' he said. 'Correct me if I'm wrong, but you'll not know anyone in London, I suppose?'

'Of course I do, God's sake! I'm not planning to doss down in the gutter, if that's what you were thinking!'

'I meant in the trade. Someone who could put you right. You know, contacts.'

She shook her head, as if he could see her.

'I'll be all right,' she said. 'Honestly. I'll make out.'

'Well listen. There's a guy down there you ought to talk to.

Serious. A guy called Forbes. He's not Scottish, but he's the next best thing. He married a lass from Govan. More important, he's an expert on the spook trade. You know what I mean?'

'Not exactly.'

'He's into corruption, and the secret boys, and bent police and so on. He's not a very popular turn in some high places. Go and see him.'

'But why should he want to speak to me? He doesn't know me.'

'I'm telling you, that's all. He's written books on the subject. He's the king of the conspiracy theorists. He'll try to screw you, by the way. He's a bit mad, some people reckon.'

'Oh thank you.'

'Nah, nah, I didn't mean it that way, hen. Listen, he can be bitter, all right? He may tell you to piss off. But he's shit-hot at his job, it's worth a try. Just go and see him.'

Half-bemused, Rosanna wrote down the details. Later, in her bed, she tried the London number.

There was no reply.

The rain in Sheerness was extraordinary. Throughout the first part of the day it had been moderate, then, as darkness had fallen, it had increased. By 6 p.m. there had been traffic jams, and by eight some roads were blocked. It had eased off, from cloudburst to steady downpour, and the traffic was moving once more. Andrew Forbes, sheltering under a harbour crane on the inner fortifications, was damp but satisfied. He was about to watch the arrest of Charlie Lister.

The Olau ferry from Flushing had nosed into the dock some minutes previously, and Forbes' companion, Peter Jackson, had left him on his own. Although Forbes had provided the information for the arrest, he would take no active part, of course. His reward, he hoped, would come on Friday. Alice Grogan would be free from fear.

As the foot-passengers began streaming from the terminal building in a dense crowd, Forbes realised he would be lucky to see anything, let alone anything spectacular. The Customs men would make the arrest quietly, and only when they were sure that Lister had brought no unknown friends from Holland. They still did not know exactly what the set-up was, but they knew – via Andrew Forbes and Alice – that they had to act. Charles Lister was about to disappear.

Forbes noted with interest that a police prowl car was nosing towards the terminal, across the stream of traffic disembarking from the hidden *Olau Britannia*. Behind a container truck in the lorry park, another car was visible, white and fluorescent red. Its lights were off, but there were men inside it. Maybe there was another arrest in the offing, he thought – or maybe it was routine. No policemen knew of this particular operation.

Suddenly, through the driving rain, he saw the beginning of activity. A group of plainclothes Customs officers appeared from behind the van he had been told to watch, while another group strode purposefully along beside the wire fence from the lorry pound. Simultaneously, the prowl car turned on its twin-tone blarer. Its blue light flashed, and there was a squeal of tyres as it accelerated.

What was going on? Andrew Forbes ran along the fortification wall, trying to get a better view. As he did so, the headlights of the parked police car blazed on, and it shot from behind the container truck, slicing through the stream of traffic to join the first one at the glass door of the terminal. The group of men along the fence were running hard, heads up, shouting, as policemen tumbled onto the pavement and joined the ruck. Passengers, some loaded down with luggage, scattered in alarm.

In seconds, it was over. The first car, siren blaring once more, cut through the line of traffic and accelerated towards the outer gate. The second followed almost instantly, its back doors flying open. By the time the blue lights had dwindled, Forbes had joined his friend. The Customs men were devastated, wild with anger, sick with hate.

It was four in the morning before he and Peter Jackson headed back to London. It had still not been established which police department – which force, even – had lifted Charlie Lister. The faint hope was that it was a genuine mistake, a breakdown in communications, some crossed lines somewhere. Neither of them believed it for a second.

'They've got you bugged,' said Jackson. 'They've got you taped and tapped.'

Andrew Forbes studied Jackson's face. It was thin, and lined with tiredness.

'We were ultra careful, weren't we?' he replied. 'We never used the telephone, clean or not. It's a bit special, isn't it?'

Jackson grunted.

'Alice Grogan won't be best pleased, will she? When she hears he's flown. Any way we can get in touch?'

'No.'

'It's a bastard, isn't it?'

Forbes gazed miserably at the rain-drenched road ahead.

'I hope she's safe,' he said. 'I hope to Christ she's safe.'

FIVE

The dinner party that Donald Sinclair felt obliged to give to mark his confirmation in Cyril Richardson's job was not exactly a sparkling affair. The gravel drive outside the modestly proportioned but rather beautiful Surrey house had space for seven cars, and another two could join the family vehicles in the garage. There was, in fact, just one outside the front door steps, a white Mercedes belonging to the Secretary of State. It was not his official car – that was a Rover. But Gerald Turner, patriotic though he undoubtedly was, had had a long affair with the products of the Stuttgart factory, which Lady Elizabeth viewed comfortably as no bad thing. He had driven it to the Sinclairs' house himself, taking simple pleasure in trying to shake off his bodyguard. They were in a Cavalier, parked discreetly out of sight of the front door. Everything was under very close surveillance.

Donald Sinclair's wife, a beautiful and thoughtful woman in her late thirties, had vetoed his original guest list on the grounds of good sense and of tact. For although congratulations on his appointment had flooded in, Mary was very well aware of what it must have meant to Cyril Richardson. He was an ineffective man, true, even a feeble one, and he had certainly not been entirely up to the job. But one of the reasons for his difficulties had been the liberal quality of his views – a quality which had found increasing disfavour at the very top. The trouble was, her husband was a liberal in his way, although a much more robust and hard-headed one. To invite the sycophants, as she saw them, would be to invite at least two undesirable things: unbearable derision at the fate of a sick man, and a malicious testing of her husband's mettle. Either of them, had he responded badly, could have done incalculable harm.

Sir Gerald, she had pointed out, was a far better choice alone. Despite being a member of both the aristocracy and the Establishment he too had a liberal turn of mind, and would undoubtedly welcome the opportunity to test his new junior's thoughts and aspirations in a relaxed and private atmosphere. What was more, his own brains could be picked as to the climate at the top.

Sinclair, who hated formal parties anyway, agreed at once, while hardly seeing that Turner would accept. Mary however – whose family lineage was impeccable – had had no doubts. The Turners had visited before, although never alone. The relationship should now move on.

Turner, for a senior politician, took his high office apparently very lightly. During the first three courses – avocado mousse, Dover sole, rack of lamb – they talked amiably and easily about a range of topics, with the conversation more or less equally divided between the four of them. Mary, who had been educated at Benenden and in Switzerland, had a horror of the sort of dinner-table talk that split by gender. If they could not involve men and women, husband and wife, in a discussion, she maintained, they should not bother to discuss. Only when the matter turned to politics, and Donald's appointment in particular, did the pattern waver. Lady Elizabeth, who liked to talk of many things, was not so keen on that.

'About this job,' said Turner, over a second cup of coffee. 'Have you waded through the bumph yet? The PM had a word with me today. Very excited over the press we're getting. It never seems to end. Very excited indeed. You've made a hit.'

'Gerald,' said his wife, not quite imploringly. 'Must we, darling? Mary's telling us about the new greenhouse project.'

Mary returned, carrying a decanter. One of her little foibles was to keep the servants hidden from their guests.

'Won't be long, my dear,' said Turner, to his wife. 'Must congratulate young Donald properly, mustn't we? Perhaps you and Mary might care to . . . '

He caught sight of Mary's expression, and made a face of mock shame. She laughed. One had to like him.

'I'd really rather like to hear your thoughts myself,' she said. 'If you don't mind, Lady Elizabeth? Poor Donald's been worrying himself silly. It's a gigantic responsibility, isn't it?'

'Worrying!' said Turner. 'Nonsense and poppycock! What could Donald possibly have to worry about?'

'Well,' rejoined Mary. 'There is a crisis, isn't there? What a nightmare if the whole thing blows up now, in Donald's face. Would you like some port?'

'I would, I would! Eat, drink and be merry, for tomorrow we die! What a pessimist your wife is, Donald!'

Donald smiled supportively at Mary.

'Now come on, Sir Gerald. I won't have that. There's nothing pessimistic in recognising there's a crisis, and there's nothing poppycockish in my worrying. I would have thought they were both necessary responses.'

'Poppycockish!' said Lady Elizabeth. 'What a lovely word! Does it exist?'

Donald smiled at her. But kept his eyes on Turner.

'In fact,' he said, pouring himself a port, 'it wouldn't be too pessimistic to say the thing was out of hand. More than fifty thousand in a system built for less than forty-three, God knows how many being held in police cells, and a positive cascade of new convictions. Tell the judiciary not to jail so many people, and they tell us not to interfere. It's enough to give you ulcers.'

Lady Elizabeth said, wide-eyed: 'But Donald, we can't just let them go, can we? They're criminals.' To Mary she added: 'Gerald once had ulcers, did you know? It's the stress. Does Donald have them?'

'Why not ask him?' said Mary, a trifle edgily. 'I somehow doubt it. But he has been mumbling statistics at me solidly, since he got the call from on high. Sir Gerald, be frank. If Donald is half-expecting trouble, is that so foolish?'

Gerald Turner reached for the decanter. He poured and sipped more port, reflectively.

'Well,' he said. 'I'm not going to sit here and deny it's possible, Mary. That's not my job. But I do feel bound to point out that that's the main reason why I recommended Donald. More or less forced it through, in fact. I don't do these things lightly, you know.'

Mary put her head on one side, half-understanding.

'What do you mean? Exactly.'

'Well,' said Turner. 'Look on Buckie as an exemplar. The Scottish prisons are a problem. They make the English ones look good. Richardson muffs it up, as usual – but Donald sorts it out. Brilliantly, in less than eighteen hours. So the PM is delighted, naturally. The man for the job, at last. The crisis has thrown up its own solution. And if there's any bleating about something should be done, and magic wands, and suchlike nonsense – well there he is, spouting new initiatives at every breath. A new initiative on legs. Wonderful.'

He laughed, to break the moment.

'Come to think of it, laddie, I'm going to watch my back from now on. In case you decide that you'd like my position next, never mind poor Cyril's.'

No one else laughed. Mary was deep in thought, and his own wife was beginning to look bored, but controlling it.

'But if it's accepted that things are bad in Scotland,' Mary Sinclair said, 'surely an inquiry might produce a real solution? Isn't that what they're always asking for? If they do have reasonable grounds for complaint, shouldn't they be investigated?'

'We know the problem and we know the answer,' replied Turner, soberly. 'The system doesn't work. It's brutal and repressive and expensive. And it can't be changed.'

'Why not?'

Sir Gerald made a small noise in his throat. He would rather not have answered that.

'I shall sound cynical,' he said. 'Oh what the hell, it is cynical. The system can't be changed because it's too difficult. Too expensive, too politically damaging. The trouble is, at base, the people want prisoners to be degraded. They want them kept like dogs, in fact. Starvation and whipping wouldn't be too much, you check the Sunday papers. And some of them, as you know, go further. However hard prison is, it's far too soft. Hanging is a better way. Hanged men don't take up beds, and they don't eat food. They also win votes.'

Mary would have liked to have taken the subject further. But Turner's wife was dabbing her lips determinedly.

'Gerald,' she said. 'This really is the most unsuitable topic. Don't you think we ought to think of going home? It's rather late.'

Donald, the perfect host, began to rise immediately. But Sir Gerald indicated that he did not wish to move. Donald hovered.

'Mary,' Turner said, 'is there any chance of just another cup of coffee, please? Is it any trouble? Driving, you know.'

The cafetière was empty. Mary, with a smile, left for the kitchen to make some more. Lady Elizabeth, gladly, asked if she could help. Perhaps collect the cuttings that had been mentioned earlier. Alone, the two men poured more port.

'Funny, isn't it?' Donald Sinclair said. 'How you have to pussyfoot around with women. How can I tell Mary it's not just Joe Public who's out for blood? Hasn't she noticed the backwoodsmen? Hasn't she noticed the baying lunatics at the party conference? Hasn't she noticed that even at the very . . .'

He stopped, and raised his glass. He was not about to mention names, however tempted he might be. He knew about survival even if his wife did not. He sighed.

'The more I look at the whole sorry situation,' he told Turner, 'the more I feel despair. It's a powder keg. A bloody powder keg.'

Sir Gerald Turner said: 'I heard about the death today. McGregor. Why didn't you tell me earlier?'

Sinclair's palms began to dampen. But he looked at Turner calmly.

'It was a tragedy,' he said. 'An awful tragedy. Quite honestly, until I'd seen my way through it, I thought it better left unsaid. I'm afraid I took Fortyne's advice on that. I'm not blaming him, I agreed with every word. I didn't want to burden you with the details.' He paused. 'Did I do wrong?'

After a moment, the Home Secretary shook his head.

'I will say this,' he said. 'It's not the way I would have handled it. But once the accident had happened, there was little choice, I suppose. You couldn't risk the whole shebang. You should have told me, though.'

Donald accepted the rebuke.

'I've had the idiot responsible carpeted,' he said. 'A small thing, but mine own. And I'm learning all the time, I promise you. I really mean it, though, we're sitting on a pile of high explosive. I've taken more pre-emptive measures today, and I've got another package for tomorrow.' He smiled, tentatively. 'I know how busy you are. Do you want the proposals all in writing? Down to the last detail?'

'Give me an outline.'

Sinclair ran quickly through the list. He had held secret talks with the Prison Officers Association, who had been operating one of their periodic bans on accepting certain new prisoners into jails. This would bear immediate propaganda fruit, as well as clearing about fourteen hundred people from out of overcrowded police and magistrates' court cells into proper prisons. It would cost some money, but not too much. His bargaining counter had been extra manpower and his quid pro quo a certain secrecy – no announcement of the number of new jobs would be made. He had also set up working parties to re-examine the military cover at all the top-security jails. Meetings would be taking place as a matter of extreme urgency with senior personnel from the Army and the Royal Air Force, and mobile task forces, with agreed response plans, would soon be in position. Coupled with the high-profile action to give known big-time criminals tougher sentences, which had proved so popular in the case of Michael Masters, there was to be a serious and sustained effort to actually cut sentences for petty and non-violent crimes. He hoped, finally, to persuade the judiciary to use other options, to keep more prisoners out of jail.

Sinclair held his hands out, palms downwards.

'That will be the toughest nut to crack,' he said. 'And in the end, Sir Gerald, I'm afraid it will come down to you. You were brilliant over Masters' sentence, utterly fantastic. I'm going to draw up the detailed proposals, and I'm studying new ideas. But I've got no influence at all with the wig and gown brigade. No one has. Unless . . .'

Sir Gerald Turner smiled at the thought left hanging in the air. He had been a politician for a very long time, and was not susceptible, any more, to the flattery of the young and ambitious. But he did agree with Sinclair's assessment. Unlike many of his fellow rulers of the realm, he believed that the prisons needed emptying. Fast. The pressure had to come off.

'I'll back you, Donald. I'm not so pessimistic as you are, in any case. The prison cauldron's been simmering for years. With luck it won't go off, with luck and a cool summer. You seem to have sorted Scotland out for the moment, and I'll back the follow-up to the hilt. I think you're the right man for the job.'

The two women were approaching from the kitchen. Mary, picking up the last words as Sir Gerald had intended, laughed with pleasure.

'He's going on a world tour next,' she said. 'When he's screwed the lid down temporarily. And he's not taking me. Isn't that beastly?'

'If he's looking at prisons,' said Lady Elizabeth, 'you can thank your lucky stars. But can't we change the subject, please? Let's just have one last cup of coffee without a bitter taste.'

Half an hour later, the Sinclairs stood in the driveway as Sir Gerald prepared to move off. They heard the motor of the Cavalier cough into life further down the drive. Sir Gerald nodded for Donald to put his head close.

'When you do talk to the military,' he said quietly, 'don't expect them to do exactly what they agree to, will you?'

'I beg your pardon?'

Sir Gerald put the Mercedes into bottom gear. He began to move forward, very slowly.

'It was the SAS,' he said. 'On the roof. You wanted Major Edwards' bollocks on a plate, I understand. You're not likely to get them, laddie.'

'Goodbye!' said Lady Elizabeth, gaily. 'And thank you for the cuttings, Mary. They're beautiful!'

'Goodbye!' said Mary. 'It was a lovely evening! Goodbye!'

Donald Sinclair said nothing. His arm, lifted in a wave, stayed where it was for several seconds.

'What lovely people,' said his wife. 'What a lovely man.'

He dropped his arm and watched the dwindling tail lights. So when did you know that, Sir Gerald, he asked himself. Whose game is this, anyway?

Richard Pendlebury, governor of HM Prison Bowscar, sat at his broad mahogany desk staring at the papers spread across his blotter. He touched one with a pen, then pushed it aside to reveal another. But he was not seeing them. He was waiting for the knock, for the union representative to arrive. For the next round in the gruelling fight to start.

Pendlebury had been governor at Bowscar for four years, four years in which it seemed to him the struggle to maintain anything remotely resembling decent standards, human dignity, basic hopes, or rights, or aspirations, was being lost inevitably and at an accelerating rate. The last twelve months had been the worst, no question, and the last few days the heaviest of all.

He could remember, if he forced himself, the courage and determination he had been able to summon the day he had first stood outside the iron-studded gates. He had served in more modern jails before, and he knew that in some obscure way the Prison Department of the Home Office were punishing him with this appointment. Richard Pendlebury had proved himself a liberal in their eyes, and had latterly become quite vocal. He had written to *The Times*, and then – much more unacceptably – allowed himself to be interviewed on television. His thesis had been simple, and in his view neither original nor left wing: the prisons were overcrowded, a disgrace, an affront to civilised society. He had been summoned before the Board immediately and reprimanded, despite the fact, as he had mildly pointed out, that he was paraphrasing what two Home Secretaries had said before, in print. Apparently, in their eyes, his outburst carried more weight. In fact, he guessed, he had broken an unwritten rule: he had spoken as a servant, not a master. It was not his place.

But Pendlebury had had hope. He knew he was no firebrand, he knew he hated violence, deceit and criminality as much as anybody else. He hoped that despite the air of gloomy misery that hung over the building, despite the lack of proper sanitation, the damp, the cockroaches, he could do some good. He firmly believed the official line, that prison existed to provide humane containment, that loss of liberty was the punishment itself. His job was to contain people, not to brutalise or torture them. Given goodwill and circumstances, some of them might even leave jail 'better men' than they had arrived – not just better criminals.

Richard Pendlebury was not naive. Although like many governors he had done some service as a prison officer, he did not fool himself that he was one of them in education, background or in attitude. He had a degree, and although poor, his parents had been 'genteel' – he had spent his childhood first in a country rectory, then in a very different one in Salford. Not only had his father's parishioners been poverty-stricken, but in his early teens he had rubbed shoulders with criminals, sometimes voluntarily and sometimes as a victim. It had had a strange effect on him, instilled a certain latent sympathy. Most of his prison officers utterly despised it.

So the four years, from the very first week, had been a catalogue of conflict. He had sympathy for the officers themselves, which they also latched onto, perverted, and despised. He recognised them as victims of a system – mainly ignorant, under-educated men, many of them veterans of the services. As a body, they had the minds of NCOs – they sensed themselves to be the salt of the earth, the power that kept the system going smoothly, but to be somehow undervalued, objects of contempt. They were right, of course. The power of disruption they had, the industrial muscle, extended only as far as the power basically to make life more miserable for the prisoners. Once, in 1986, they had worked to rule throughout the country, and the system had almost exploded. The prison officers, frightened, had backtracked immediately, had made it clear they were responsible men and women who knew their duty and would stand by it. The Home Office had acknowledged and rewarded this restraint with a systematic attack on their wages and their staffing levels, hypocritically presented as a restructuring of their careers to give them self-esteem. They still needed a minimum of education, they still had only twelve weeks' training, they still faced daily danger to life, limb and health, but they were forced to work shorter hours for less pay. Because Pendlebury sympathised, they hated him. They thought he equated them with the inmates, who were dregs, animals, scum. It was unbearable.

As the years dragged by, other factors were thrown into the cement mixer that was concreting the grave of Pendlebury's hopes. Bowscar Prison, built in 1872 for seven hundred men, held eight hundred and eleven when he came to it. As the law and order clarions sounded ever louder, as the measures of repression grew, the numbers climbed inexorably. Measures to keep people out of prison – like electronic tagging, punishment in the community – were counterbalanced by stricter rules of evidence, the loss of a suspect's right to silence, which dragged more in. Suspended sentences and parole, designed to shorten terms in prison, were craftily manipulated by a judiciary blind to any evidence, however good, however respectable, that prison did not work. Except, of course, thought Pendlebury, as revenge. At that, it seemed to satisfy quite well.

Sitting in his office, waiting for the battle which was due at any moment, Richard Pendlebury was frightened. The memo on his blotter, placed there that morning by one of his assistants, swam into focus. The POA, it said, had suddenly agreed to withdraw their ban on admitting certain prisoners. The nine men he had received yesterday had brought his total up to one thousand and fourteen. Now thirteen more had been allocated to Bowscar, thirteen men who had been locked in police cells, some innocent, some guilty, some violent, some aggrieved. He already had sixty-three men three to a one-man cell. God save us all, he thought, just how long can this go on? Unbidden, his thoughts turned to his wife, who had died two years ago, from heart disease. A brisk knock at the door jerked him, mercifully, back to the present.

The two officers, tight-faced and formal, had come on union business. One of their members had reported, and another two corroborated, that he had undermined their dignity and integrity as prison officers in a Board of Visitors complaints procedure held that morning in the matter of Prisoner 651304 Hughes, A. Hughes had brought a complaint against Senior Officer Bernard Burnett, not here present, alleging assault on the aforesaid Hughes in the D-floor sluice. The case had been a straightforward one, which the Board of Visitors had dismissed out of hand. Prisoner 651304 Hughes had been awarded three months loss of remission, plus the removal of televisual privileges for six weeks.

Pendlebury listened to the staccato institution-speak with distaste but little interest. The officer delivering it, Christopher

Abbey, was a man he particularly disliked. He had a very high opinion of himself, and a very low one of almost everybody else. He was the mouthpiece for every grievance held by the officers.

'I take it,' said Pendlebury, when Abbey had concluded, 'that Mr Burnett objects to the opinion I expressed to the Board of Visitors when the evidence had been heard. Is that right?'

The rigid, humourless mouth opened woodenly.

'Prisoner 651304 Hughes is a well-known troublemaker. The case was a straightforward clash of evidential statements. Either the prisoner was lying, or our member was. Our members, as the other two corroborated the evidence in chief. Your comment, in our respectful opinion, tended to cast doubt on their veracity.'

The governor put the tips of his fingers together as if deep in thought. His statement had indeed cast doubt on the officers' veracity, as it had been intended to. The officers, after all, were lying.

'Alan Hughes,' he said, 'claimed that Senior Officer Burnett had been racially abusing a coloured prisoner.'

'Not true!'

'Hughes further said that the officer was wearing a tie-pin representing a black man hanging from a tree. I told the Board of Visitors that I had seen the pin myself, six months ago.'

Abbey's handsome face flushed with anger.

'It was not a black man,' he said. 'It was a monkey. Senior Officer Burnett comes from Hartlepool. Apparently it's a local symbol. Hughes is a troublemaker, and you backed him up. My members are furious.'

If it had not been so serious, it might have been funny, Pendlebury thought. These grown men expected him to listen to this tripe. They were angry because their juvenile sham had been seen through. He had expressly condemned the wearing of the badge on the first occasion it had emerged. A year before it had been golliwogs the officers had affected, enamel brooches worn on the inside of lapels. Outside the building many of them were quite open in their racism. But that, he was not expected to have noticed.

'Senior Officer Burnett,' said Christopher Abbey, 'agrees with us that he has been professionally slighted. We have therefore been mandated to seek an apology. On this occasion, sir, a verbal will be acceptable. Unless you would prefer to write it down.'

Pendlebury stood. He was a tall man, but thin now, painfully thin. He overcame his stoop to stare contemptuously at the officer and his silent, uncomfortable companion.

'Alan Hughes is a strange man,' he said. 'But when he appears before me with a black eye and a broken tooth, accused of assaulting an officer, I tend to feel a small suspicion in my breast. I will never know the truth of it, that much I guess is guaranteed. However so, the Board of Visitors backed your Mr Burnett, despite my desperately insulting and wholly indefensible remark. They chose to decide that the prisoner was lying, and for all I know or care, they were right. If that is not enough for you, Mr Abbey, I despair. But you can tell your colleague this: if I ever see him or any other officer wearing badges which are deliberately designed to insult again, I will move heaven and earth to have that officer sacked, or failing that removed. Do I make myself clear?'

Pendlebury was trembling, inside and out. He was not afraid of men like Christopher Abbey, he was sick of them. He looked the officer in the face for a few seconds more, then sat.

'I am a busy man,' he said. 'With me, this will go no further. I suggest you tell Mr Burnett and his friends to forget the whole thing. If there is nothing else, you may go. I am very busy.'

Somewhat to his surprise, the two men left. No doubt, he thought, to report that the governor – soft as ever – had apologetically admitted that his words had been 'insulting and wholly indefensible'. So what did it matter? Pendlebury shuffled through the papers, his eyes hardly focused, his mind not quite engaged. By tonight, perhaps tomorrow, he would have a thousand and twenty-seven men inside. Inside this dustbin that the authorities were pleased to call a prison. He had murderers, addicts, sex offenders, blacks. He had a tiny, sullen coterie of Irish terrorists, the feckless, the half-insane, the drunks, the homosexuals. He had Angus John McGregor, too, the man they called the Animal. Pendlebury suspected his officers did not wish him to enquire too closely after this one, so that must become a priority. Also, he must speak to someone in the Department, urgently. Why was McGregor to be held in isolation? How long was the order expected to hold?

It was not yet lunchtime, and the day stretched out before him like a long, unfriendly road. There was a knot of tension in his stomach, and a sour taste beneath his tongue. Richard Pendlebury feared that the mood in Bowscar Prison was becoming critical. He had told the Prison Department of the Home Office, had warned them many times. The sum effect, he imagined, had been to confirm his image as a troublemaker and a bore. Perhaps the new man – Donald Sinclair, was it? – perhaps he meant the platitudes reported from his press conference, the promises to listen and to learn. Perhaps Pendlebury would try again, just one more time.

His daughter Eileen wanted desperately for him to stop. To retire early, or just give it up.

If he did not do it soon, he thought, it would be too late.

Now that they were absolutely certain that the house in Stoke Newington was unsafe, Andrew Forbes and Peter Jackson worked from the Customs officer's flat. Where Forbes' bachelor style was seedy-nudging-sordid, his friend – who had been divorced for nearly five years – had gone the other way. The place was tiny, a tiny bedroom, kitchenette and bathroom, but it was almost antiseptically clean. Unlike Andrew Forbes, Jackson had little interest in hunting women. His eight years of marriage had been savagely unpleasant and had driven him (as he saw it) deeper and deeper into work. When his wife had gone, he had watched her take the house, the car, the money, everything – with a feeling only that he wished she'd be quick about it so that he could return to the job in hand. Luckily, they'd had no children.

As an undercover investigator of total dedication, Jackson sometimes wondered how he'd ever teamed up with Forbes, let alone become a kind of friend. He spent his life in tortuous research, detailed detective work, hundreds of hours of surveillance, with occasional bursts of energetic pursuit and awful terror. In his head he carried details of shipping patterns, lines of international criminal communication, airline schedules. He had an encyclopaedic knowledge of drugs in every state, from seedlings in the High Andes to the latest refinements designer-made for the West Coast millionaire. He spoke three languages fluently, and had intimate contacts in the police forces and Customs departments of Holland, France, America and Hong Kong. Andrew Forbes, on the other hand, was a slob.

He knew his job, however, and – peculiar though it struck Peter Jackson as a way to earn a living – clove to it with a half-amused mild passion. He was in a kind of limbo, neither a journalist nor an academic seeker after arcane truths. He did write articles, true, he did write books and provide background information, usually uncredited, to television documentary teams. But his driving force was neither money nor fame. He was interested, merely, in criminals and criminal corruption, with the British secret state his speciality. He was an amateur and a slob, and Peter Jackson liked him. They had met in a dockside pub in Portsmouth three years ago, and apart from drinking, the only thing they had in common was that neither wore a gun. Jackson's job did not allow it. Forbes just thought they stank.

In the hours after Charles Lister had been lifted from Sheerness Docks, both men had worked frantically to find out who and why. The fact that police cars had been used did not necessarily mean the police had been responsible, but as they worked through their contacts to extract the vital pieces of the jigsaw it appeared most likely that they had. The cars were London-based, and both assigned to special uses or departments. Given the labyrinthine organisation of the giant force, it was impossible to be more accurate than that.

By the early hours both men were pale with exhaustion, coffee and alcohol. Jackson's shiny little formica kitchen table was shiny no more, smeared with the spilled ash of many cigarettes, milk and beer. They had not eaten, but neither were they hungry. The kettle had just boiled for the umpteenth time, and Forbes was making instant coffee with a hand that trembled slightly. Jackson sat at the table licking his teeth, which tasted rank.

'So what we got?' he said, as the coffee mug appeared before him. 'What have we got, and where can we go from here, and is it time for bed, mother?'

Forbes pulled his hand vertically down his face, rasping the stubble on his chin. He had stomach ache and a headache. He filled his mouth with coffee, wincing at its heat.

Jackson continued, answering his own questions.

'What we've got is this. He's been lifted by the Mets, and they're hardly likely to have done it to save us trouble, are they? What's more nobody – if they know where he is – is letting on. Now, he'll be in police cells somewhere which means in effect that no one can keep tabs on him. The system's so overloaded prisoners get shunted all over the place wherever there's a vacancy. My guess is they'll put him on a holding charge, and move him around, then he'll mysteriously escape. He might even appear before some half-wit magistrate in Cumbria or Poole or somewhere and get let out on bail – same result. That's the scam, Andrew. Bet on it.'

'Yeah,' said Forbes. 'Brilliant as ever, maestro. But why?'

'You're knackered aren't you, chum? Brain's gone. Your lovely black bit told us, didn't she? There's a ship out on the pond that Lister's got to meet, OK? Alice put us onto him, but somebody told Lister you'd been talking to the lady, I'll find out who for you later. So Lister talks to someone else – let's say our friends at Sheerness – and they whip him, by appointment, from underneath our noses. So he can still meet the ship. Next thing we'll know is when he's back in Florida, which de Sallis tells us.'

'De Sallis?'

'My oppo over there. US Customs. We've been working on this together for three months. John de Sallis will not be polite. We've been screwed, my friend. Comprehensively.'

Forbes, who had lighted a cigarette and drawn on it, made a face and stubbed it out on the edge of the ashtray. It tasted ghastly.

'Talking of which,' he said, 'which side of the bed do you want? There's nothing we can do now, is there? Until we find out where he is? Let's sleep.'

Jackson raised a smile. He yawned.

'If you dream I'm Alice Grogan,' he said, getting up, 'remember I'm a virgin. If I wake up with your dick in my pyjamas, Andy-boy, I'll cut it off. OK?'

Later that day, as Forbes and Jackson still searched fruitlessly, Charles Lister, much to his surprise, ended up in Bowscar Jail. The order to pack his plastic bag and shift out of cells in Hertfordshire neither interested nor disturbed him, as he had been told what to expect. Talk in the armoured van of a sudden ending to a POA dispute meant nothing, as he had heard of neither it nor them. The gates of Bowscar were shut and locked behind him before the truth began to dawn.

'Say, what the Jesus shit,' began Charles Lister. Two prison officers, burly men with kindly English faces, had just requested him to remove his clothes.

'Now now,' said one of them, the smile broadening at the unexpected accent. 'None of that here, Yankee Doodle Dandy. You'll get your clothes back after you've had a shower. You're only on remand.'

'You're innocent,' said the other, his eyes lost in a fat, satiric smile. 'Until proved guilty. Get your clothes off, mate. Let's see what an American one looks like.'

Charles Lister stripped in silence. Somebody was going to pay for this.

* * *

Rosanna was in the bath when the telephone rang. Normally, she would not have bothered to answer, but her taxi was due fairly shortly, to take her to the station. She counted twelve rings before she stood and stomped wetly into the kitchen, wrapping a towel round her, skimpily. If one of her high-minded Hyndland neighbours happened to look through the window, she'd be in trouble with the residents' association yet again, but what the hell? She was off to London, and for all she cared she need never return.

Even the sound of Adrian Rafferty's voice was not enough to upset her mood. So what she'd soaked the kitchen floor? So what the old drunk was probably going to proposition her, or ask for money, or something equally ridiculous. She did not give a toss.

'Is that you, hen? Rosanna? Listen, I phoned to say I'm sorry, so I am.'

'Don't give it another thought, Adrian,' she said. 'If I'd thought you were a gentleman, I'd never have talked to you, would I? Anyway – you gave me the goods.'

'Well, better than that,' said Rafferty. 'In actual fact. You see the Animal, McGregor. I told you he went to England, right? Well he went via Durham, then Hull, got that? Durham and Hull. Then the trail's gone cold.'

'Hey, that's terrific! Ach, thanks Adrian, thanks for calling.'

'Listen, hen,' he said. 'If I can help in any other way, all right? You've got my number. Ring me. From England. Reverse the charges. Maurice told me you were off.'

She laughed aloud.

'You're raving, man! I'll do no such thing! You only insulted me, you know, it was nothing serious. If I need to ring you, I'll let some other bugger pay, like a good wee journalist!'

'Aye, right,' he agreed, sounding more cheerful. 'But seriously – I'm sorry for last night. It was the Irish in me.'

This time Rosanna hooted.

'Funny that,' she said. 'I thought it was the Scotch!'

Two minutes later, towelling her hair, she heard the phone again. Still naked, she strode into the kitchen. She guessed it was Adrian with a good reply.

'Go on,' she said. 'But for God's sake hurry up!'

There was silence. Then an English voice said quietly: 'Did you ask about Jimmy McGregor yet? Did they tell you anything? Except a pack of lies?'

Rosanna swallowed. She gripped her towel, hard. Her heart was pounding.

'They said . . . they—'

'Shut up and listen. Ask them what knocked him out. Ask them about the drug. Ask them how it got there. Ask them about the gun.'

Rosanna's mouth was open. She tried to force her mind to work. She heard the phone go down. The line went dead.

When she went to catch her train to London, there was a British Telecom van parked opposite her Renault, beside the residents' private park.

She did not notice it.

SIX

Michael Masters was in his bed when Alan Hughes was returned by the prison officers from his Board of Visitors 'trial'. He had covered himself with a blanket, and he was thinking of Sarah Williams. His memories of her were so specific that his desire had become almost a pain. Feeling his penis through the denim of his trousers, he could feel the texture of her cunt, feel the slippery, moulded flesh, feel even the damp hair fringing his stroking fingers. He saw, with brilliant perfection, her body, naked, on the canal boat's double bunk, and he groaned.

Immediately, a grunting laugh came from the bunk above him, snapping Masters' consciousness to the present. He realised that he must have made a noise, and irrational shame flooded him. There was a heavy creak as Matthew Jerrold rolled onto his side.

'Go on, do it, man,' he said. 'You'll have to do it sometime, won't you? Nobody mind in here. Somebody do it for you, if you want.'

Masters did not reply, but he was surprised. This was the first time that Matthew Jerrold had actually spoken to him. Before, he had glowered, had muttered threateningly, had made rapid, violent movements designed, quite clearly, to intimidate. He was not a very large man, but he had an air of power in his body and an aura of barely suppressed rage. He was very black, almost ebony, with a bony, skull-like face that could have been especially designed to make him feared and hated by a white man. Masters knew that he had killed a policeman with a fireman's axe and that he was violent, dangerous, and prone to fits of screaming rage. The prison officers had told him all this, with glee. That was why he was in with him.

The voice from above him, though, had sounded less than threatening, almost friendly. It was a softish voice, with the normal accent of a London-born West Indian. But for Christ's sake, Masters thought. Am I to have a conversation about sex! About Sarah's body? About this massive hard-on? He noticed that the hard-on had gone, had slipped away unbidden. That was no surprise.

Jerrold said: 'I been here for thirteen months. Thirteen months down, twenty-four years to go. Before I come in here, man, I was a pussy freak, know what I mean? I used to eat it, and drink it, and work it, and sleep it, and fuck it. You go ahead and have your wank, guy.'

Masters was lying on his back, the wire bed-springs and the dusty white ticking less than two feet from his face. Jerrold was on his back too, presumably, staring at the yellow-painted ceiling. An absurd picture, Masters thought. An absurd set-up. The millionaire and the monster, staring upwards, talking sex. Except that he had not yet spoken.

Michael Masters had never really understood racism, perhaps because he'd never had to. Where he'd been brought up there had been few blacks or Asians, and those he had seen had never troubled him. His father hated them as some kind of alien blot on the landscape, but to Masters and his generation the British landscape, and the television, were a multi-cultural experience and always had been. He remembered his Uncle Geoff, seriously damaged in the war, screaming passionately at one family Christmas 'Five years of my life I gave to keep the fucking Germans out of England, and now it's overrun with fucking nignogs!' Michael, assuming it was part of the Christmas fun, had laughed. His father had hit him across the face and knocked him down. In his meteoric rise through the world of money, he had treated blacks as he had treated everybody else – if they could do it they were fine, and if they couldn't he despised them. He'd fucked a black girl once, at a party. It had been very pleasant, but hardly very different.

'Look,' he said. 'It's nice of you to worry about it, mate, but when it comes to wanking, I can handle it myself.'

The man above him gave a cough of amusement. There was another creak as he rolled sideways. A pair of naked black legs appeared over the edge of the bed, then two hands, beside the thighs. Jerrold leaned forward, bending at the waist, and jumped to the floor. He was wearing only a pair of baggy underpants. He grinned at Masters, and sat facing him on the bed on the other side of the cell. They were only two feet apart.

'How come you talk like that? How come you ain't got no accent? You a millionaire, ain't you? You a rich twat.'

Masters smiled. He pulled the blanket aside, and waved his

hand across his body to indicate the clothes. See – no sex. He sat up. They had to offset themselves, there was not room enough to sit face-to-face.

'I got rich, I wasn't born rich,' he said. 'I went to a comprehensive, just like you I expect. And I'm not a millionaire. That was just for starters.'

Jerrold laughed again, a solid, fruity laugh. He thrust his hand across the narrow gap, to shake. Masters, half-surprised at the formality, took it.

'Matthew Jerrold,' said Matthew Jerrold. 'The Beast of Buckingham Estate. If you haven't heard of me, I can show you my cuttings. The *Sun* one's best. They wanted to castrate me, then send me back to where I come from. Up my mother's birth canal, I guess. In Wandsworth High Street!'

It had been one of the summer riots, Masters remembered. Two days of mayhem, three people killed. Firebombs, baton charges, the policeman cut off from his unit and set upon. He'd read about it from his house in Tuscany.

He said politely: 'Wasn't there some doubt about the evidence? Weren't the police accused of some dubious practices?'

Jerrold's ebony face split in amusement.

'You *can* talk posh! Dubious practices, I like that! They was lying through their fucking teeth, man. I wasn't even in the same street!'

'You would say that though, wouldn't you?'

For a moment, the smiling face opposite clouded, and Michael Masters felt a touch of apprehension. Because Jerrold acted as if normal did not mean he was. To take the piss out of a psychopath was a pretty stupid thing to do in any circumstances. A prickle of sweat started in his armpits. If Jerrold jumped him, what would happen? Size meant nothing. Madmen killed.

But Jerrold only sighed. He made a dismissive gesture.

'Suit yourself. Every other bastard did. But I tell you this, guy – if I was really mad, I'd've gone insane in here, know what I mean? You'll find out soon enough.'

I won't though, Masters thought. If Sir Cyril France doesn't shift me soon, there'll be hell to pay. But before either of them spoke again, the spyhole jerked open with its characteristic bang to reveal Chris Abbey's face, the narrowed eyes searching for signs of ambush. The key turned in the lock and the door swung open. Alan Hughes stood between two officers, with Abbey to one side. The prisoner was smiling.

Abbey, looking from Masters to Jerrold in some surprise, stepped halfway in.

'Well well,' he said. 'What a touching little scene. Who was underneath? Jerrold, what is it about you that turns nice white men into nigger-lovers? Have you got two dicks?'

As he said it, he stepped backwards. The other two officers propelled Hughes into the cell with a shove in his back. Jerrold, rising, was forced to catch him.

'*Mister* Masters,' said Abbey. 'As you're so fond of shit, you can do a little job for me in the morning. Goon Squad. I'll call you early with a nice cup of tea, shall I?'

The door slammed shut, and the spyhole cracked across. The three men sorted their limbs out. The plastic bucket had gone flying, and the lid was in the corner. Fortunately, nobody had had to use it. Hughes motioned Masters to shift along the bed a little, and pushed Jerrold down with a hand on his shoulder. He sat beside him. Jerrold's face had become tight and hard and dangerous. He was breathing swiftly through his nose. Hughes smiled across the cell at Masters.

'Charming lads, when you get to know them,' he said. 'Chris Abbey's got a wife and two lovely kids, you know. Caravan in Scarborough, nice old dog. Even Hitler loved his dog, until he poisoned it. Are you a nigger-lover?'

Masters glanced at Jerrold. The black man's face was loosening, becoming more relaxed. Hughes' smile grew broader.

'Sorry, friend. Bit unfair to put you through it, isn't it? I expect you've had enough. It's the amateur psychologist in me. I can't switch off. I'm like most psychologists, I suppose. Mental.'

'What's the Goon Squad?'

'Change the subject, eh? Very wise. Or are you perhaps an egotist? You must be, you've made a fortune, haven't you? You pick up shit.'

Since he'd been in the cell, Masters had hardly communicated with Hughes, who had been away a lot – having treatment for his broken tooth, conducting his defence. He wondered if he always spoke in this elliptical, mocking style. And if so, whether he would ever understand it.

'Is that the answer, or a question?' he asked. 'What d'you mean, I pick up shit?'

'Will you tell him or shall I?' Hughes said to Jerrold. Jerrold shook his head.

'You,' he said. 'You got a better turn of phrase. Alan,' he said to Michael Masters, 'he's got education, guy. Not like you'n me. He went to grammar school. University.'

'I taught there, too,' said Alan Hughes. It was not a lie, or a boast. He found it quite amusing, apparently. 'Now, the Goon Squad lecture. Or would you prefer it brief? Unvarnished? The simple, unattractive facts?'

'Yes. Please.'

Hughes pointed at the yellow plastic bucket. He had replaced it on its spot and put the lid back on.

'That object there, as you perfectly well know, is our lavatory. As you will also have discovered, prison food makes you fart. I don't know exactly why this is, I've only been eating it six years, but although the data are neither complete nor conclusive, I suspect the effect's deliberately designed. The ingredients – while being the cheapest available, naturally – are carefully selected for their propensity to generate wind. Fat mince and soya extract mixed, sprouts boiled to a mush, desiccated onions fried in oil, that sort of idea. Ten minutes after any meal, the inmates of this glorious institution start to fart. A thousand men and more. With windows that don't open, or open enough to let an anorexic mouse crawl through. It saves on heating, I suppose.'

He paused, to assess the audience reaction.

'Go on,' said Michael Masters. 'This is the *brief* version?'

'Oh very brief,' smiled Hughes. 'It can be very boring inside here, can brevity. Everything gets relative.' He indicated Matthew Jerrold, who appeared to have gone to sleep. 'And there are ways round it. Nobody has to listen. Where was I? Farting. Eructation. That's bad enough, I suppose, but it leads to worse. You probably won't have had the pleasure yet, because the first few days are usually blessed with constipation. But there comes a time, friend, when the farting has to stop. You have to shit. How does that grab at you?'

Alan Hughes had a thin, intelligent face. His hair was greying at the sides, bald on top. Masters guessed his age at fiftyish, maybe considerably younger. He never doubted for a moment that this man had taught at university. There was a bizarre element of the tutorial even in this disgusting conversation. He responded almost as a student might have done.

'It doesn't sound too good,' he said. 'But does it happen very often? In the cell, I mean? Aren't we allowed to ring the bell?'

Jerrold, his eyes still closed, grunted.

'Oh, of course,' said Alan Hughes. 'Indubitably. And the screws are allowed to answer, there's no rule against it. But they don't like disturbing people on the landings, you can understand that, can't you? Those heavy boots. The rattling of the locks. I told you, they're thoughtful people, some of them, too nice for their own good. Ring that bell at night, friend, and an officer might come. How long can you hold it, by the way? When it's touching cloth? You learn all sorts in the Scar, for sure. Sphincter control is one of them. But you can't keep it closed for ever.'

The smell in the cell was revolting. Masters looked about him. Two double bunks – one top bed unmade – a chair and two small stools, a tiny table. The bucket stood alone, but he could hardly see how one could use it. To stand and hold it up, to piss, fair enough. He had not done it yet, but he thought he would be able to, when the need arose. But to squat over it? Feet from people's faces? With the smell already thick with sweat, and warmed up, breathed out, non-circulated air? And after meals, as Hughes had so lovingly elucidated, the farts. Which he, alone of the three men, so far tried to save for bed, to filter through the blankets, to hide the point of origin.

'Look,' he said. 'Thanks for the briefness of the version, but I've had enough. What if I throw up? Would they come for that, if I rang the bell?'

'He think he in the Ritz,' Jerrold murmured. 'Alan, finish now. He goin' be sick, the man say.'

'The Goon Squad,' said Alan Hughes, incisively, 'is the detail that picks up the bags of shit. Some people, sensitive souls like you, can't bear to do it in a bucket. OK? Fair enough. They do it in their underpants, or failing that a copy of the *Sun*. Even your common or garden con can see the symmetry in that. They chuck the parcel through the window, through that little slot up there, so God help their armpits if it's runny. It splatters on the ground below. The Goon Squad picks it up. Some jails it's called the Barmy Army, the Shit Shovellers, you name it. Chris Abbey doesn't like you, does he? Tomorrow you pick up shit. Incidentally, if you do decide to do it in your pants, remember you only get one pair a week in Bowscar, and you don't get talcum powder after your shower, however well brought up your balls are! You don't get a shower if you don't apply in writing, by the way – did they tell you that? Get a docket from the office.'

There was silence for a considerable while. Then Jerrold pulled himself upright on the bed, and shook his head to clear the drowsiness away.

'The best way, Michael,' he said, 'is if you has to, go ahead and shit. First few times is terrible, I ain't denying that. But you get used to it, you got to. Your own shit you don't mind the smell of, right? No one does. You got to look on us as if we was you, your sort of brothers, right? That man's stink – I can take it like my own, although I ain't up to enjoying it, yet! Look Michael, do I call you Michael, Mike? Look, man, we your friends, OK? We your fucking friends.'

Jesus Christ, thought Michael Masters. This can't be happening. He thought of the original agreement, signed, sealed and agreed. Four months in an open prison, with a telephone, a room, a bed. He thought of his friends, the men he was protecting, one man in particular. He thought of Sarah Williams. Jesus Christ, I've died and gone to hell. I've gone insane.

'You see,' said Hughes, 'out there there's people who want to humiliate you. Grind you down, destroy you. You've either got to take all this, you've got to stomach it, join in, or you'll go under. Shape up or ship out, as the Yanks said over Vietnam. Except you can't ship out. You're stuck.'

Michael Masters' eyes were bright in his powerful, determined face.

'I can stand anything,' he said. His voice was low and intense. 'I can take the lot. But I'm damned if I'm prepared to. I'm *damned*.'

Hughes turned to Matthew Jerrold. He raised his eyebrows lightly, and his voice was dry.

'Bravo,' he said.

Donald Sinclair, as he admitted later to his wife, got quite a bruising when he met the military. He went into the briefing feeling one hundred per cent on top of the subject, sure of his facts, certain of his back-up. They did not exactly eat him, but they did their level best.

The meeting came at the end of an almost incredibly busy morning. Since taking up his post, and kicking off at such high profile, Sinclair had been made to realise for the first time in his political career just how many people would make demands if they were given half a chance. Judith Parker, his adviser, treated a minor complaint about it with her usual scathing logic. He had announced the ever-open door, she pointed out. He had boasted of his ever-listening ear. Now would he cut the whingeing and let her get on organising the tour? Or was the trip to examine foreign systems going the way of his intensive visits to British jails – into the ever-pending file?

For twenty-four hours – and Donald Sinclair felt as if he were working on the problems even in his sleep – he had had to dodge, and weave and delegate. If he left the Home Office he was set upon by pressmen, when he lifted his head from one telephone call another three were waiting, and representatives from prisoners' rights groups, prisoners' wives support committees, re-offenders' sheltered homes organisations and umpteen other sane and loony fringes were clinging to the coat-tails of the prison officers, governors and reformists who wanted, quite legitimately, to state their own views and to listen carefully to his. He had had to cancel some meetings and reschedule others, he had given Christian Fortyne – now confirmed as his principal private secretary – carte blanche to handle certain people, and he had developed, in pure self-defence, the ministerial trick he had long despised in others: pretending to listen seriously to serious statements, then dismissing them with some half-cooked platitude he'd thought up halfway through the exposition. The military briefing was his show, however. He entered the airy, modernistic conference room with relief. He could spare an hour, and they would be pleased to listen, not to talk. It would be almost relaxation.

The first slight shock came as Fortyne steered him through the door. General Forsythe, he reported, the most senior Army officer due, had had to cancel. His expert on the subject, Brigadier Robert Sherwood, was standing in. He would, of course, report back on all deliberations, and the net result would be the same. It was unfortunate, but not a tragedy.

'Look, Christian,' said Sinclair, testily, 'the composition of this meeting was chosen with the greatest care, and well in advance. What reasons has Forsythe given?'

'Operational. Some NATO blow-up. I expect the Americans wanted him for something. They are in charge, you know.'

The two men smiled. Sinclair still had no real idea how deep Fortyne's cynicism really ran. It could not all be humorous.

'What about the others? Will they be here?'

They were. The meeting consisted of an expert personally appointed by the Royal Air Force Chief of Staff, two lower-ranking men who co-ordinated peacetime air manoeuvres on the British mainland, and three Army officers including Brigadier Sherwood. The Prisons Board, which controlled the day-to-day running of the service, was represented by its assistant director general, and David Cheek, junior minister at the Ministry of Defence, was present with his PPS. The formal introductions over, they took their places, prearranged by Fortyne's staff, at the long and polished table. Before each man was a thick pile of briefings in colour-coded files, copies of which had been circulated in advance. Two shorthand writers were the only females present.

While Fortyne went over the ground to be covered, Sinclair marshalled his own requirements. Unlike most of his colleagues in the higher ranks of government, he had gone to a minor public school rather than to Marlborough, Eton, Charterhouse or the like – and despite a mother obsessively determined that he should be educated above their class, he still spoke English, he did not quack it. Some quackers, Fortyne among them, he had learned to admire and respect. But military men still worried him. At school the worst sort, the aristocratic dunderheads, had gravitated towards the cadet forces, as they had at university. And here they were again, fifteen or twenty years on, superbly turned-out men, their hair short and sleek, their heads held high like hunting dogs, their accents quite extraordinary. Maybe it was tiredness, maybe Sir Gerald Turner's warning, maybe only prejudice. But he distrusted them entirely. Especially their ability.

The purpose of the meeting was simple. Every one of Britain's top-security jails was covered by a contingency plan, which was theoretically constantly under review. In the event of any trouble, whether serious internal disturbance or outside attack, both the Army and the Air Force were continuously held ready to respond. Each governor and his senior staff had codewords and a series of emergency numbers to get them through to the designated controls. In the past few days Sinclair had required the military to review the procedures, extend them to selected extra prisons in blueprint, and suggest upgrades in the level of security and response.

For half an hour the meeting was routine. There were grumblings from David Cheek about the cost of extending the cover to five new jails, and resistance from the junior Army men to the idea that several fast response vehicles would have to be held on twenty-four-hour standby, always, to provide cover for the remoter prisons being brought into the scheme. Sinclair explained, patiently, that because of increased and increasing over-crowding in the system, distinctions had been blurred. Training prisons, that would not in normal times have held the most dangerous types of inmate, had been forced to accept a smattering of Category A men, while Category B prisoners had universally increased as a corollary of the government's determination to combat violent crime by ever-more savage sentences. The accompanying increase in such crimes – a logical hiccup that he skated over so smoothly that they did not notice it – had done the rest.

'I can assure you, gentlemen,' he said, 'that we are making every effort to ensure that the new measures will not cost you anything. I entirely take your point about the extra vehicles needed, and I will raise it with the Home Secretary at the earliest opportunity. As you know, I am taking a long, hard global look at the whole knotty problem of the prisons, and I hope to come up with some more positive approaches soon. In the meantime, I can assure you that the Prime Minister is taking a keen personal interest and has expressed concern. Between these four walls, I think we can take it that that will mean more money.'

They laughed urbanely, but Sinclair could still detect an edge, he thought. Paranoia? The disconcertingly young faces of these high-ranking officers were closed against him, he was sure of it. But nobody had contradicted, or even argued hard. He glanced at the clock, stark on the white-painted wall. It was almost time to draw the strings together.

The brigadier led the attack. It came so subtly, in such honeyed tones, that Donald Sinclair failed at first to recognise it. The man was only his age or a little older, with a friendly, handsome face and slightly curly hair. He, of all of them, looked least like the military stereotype. The accent was there, though. No doubt his family had been soldiers for generations, had probably fought Napoleon.

'Minister, we do all understand your difficulties, and the financial hints are heartening, of course. But where I and my colleagues are to a degree unclear, is why some of the measures have been thought necessary. The new cover, obviously, yes, and it will be provided. But in all the briefings your department circulated, one could not entirely perceive a rationale.'

A moment of panic shot through Sinclair's brain. What was he talking about? But the other military faces were smiling and nodding in unison. Suspicious unison. Christian Fortyne slipped easily to his rescue.

'Are you suggesting, Brigadier Sherwood, that the review of the procedures for the original nine jails was unnecessary? That the contingency plans already covering them are adequate?'

The brigadier became more wary. He knew that here he was on equal terms, that in upbringing and accent Fortyne matched him exactly.

'Well,' he replied, 'there was an element of that. General Forsythe in particular felt . . . well . . . time-wasting might perhaps be too strong an expression, but—'

Sinclair cut in: 'Are you telling me that General Forsythe missed this meeting because he thought it was a waste of time?'

One of the stenographers, who appeared to be able to write shorthand in her sleep, came out of her coma. She pulled her skirt down with an interested wriggle. She picked up a fresh pencil.

'Good lord, minister, no,' replied the brigadier. 'General Forsythe was most regretful that he could not be present. Surely his apologies were conveyed to you?'

'Of course, of course.' Sinclair was furious. 'But if you want it straight, Brigadier Sherwood, yes I *do* consider that the present arrangements are inadequate. Not in theory, maybe, but definitely in practice. When one considers . . .'

Sinclair forced himself to stop. This was going wrong. If he brought Buckie up, and Major Edwards, and the death of James McGregor . . . Opposite him, Fortyne's glasses glinted. Stop, he was saying silently. Do not go on.

Donald Sinclair drew a deep breath. He would not go on. But he was damned if he would let them get away scot-free.

'Gentlemen,' he said. 'I do not wish to deal with specifics, and I do not wish to criticise the here and now. Sir Gerald Turner, were he here, might have some words to offer on the subject of the Buckie roof but I will not. Suffice it to say that criminals are more daring and better organised today than they have ever been, and you must try to understand that. There are political prisoners, IRA men, terrorists. In Paris there have been recent airborne breakouts, in Ireland we saw Portlaoise. You would agree, I trust, that Gartree was an appalling gaffe?'

They all exude efficiency, he thought, and fail to deliver. Then they pass the buck. Well if the prisons blew up, the buck was his. He was marking their cards, that was all. Letting them know he had their measure. Gartree would clinch it. That would give them food for thought. He did not need to spell it out for them, the insult was elegant enough this way.

Unfortunately, David Cheek was in the room. Whether by foolishness or deep design, he dropped the question Sinclair did not want.

'Gartree? I don't think I understand the reference. What happened at Gartree?'

Fortyne, trying to close the subject, said dismissively: 'A breakout. Nineteen eighty-seven. Only two escaped, by helicopter. Nothing too significant.'

'But you said an appalling gaffe, Sinclair. How was that?'

Sinclair looked at the soft, unlined face of his fellow junior minister with loathing. He looked a fool, but he was rising quickly in the Ministry of Defence. Was he deliberately sliding in the knife? The irritation and the tiredness got the better of him.

'A helicopter landed in the playing fields,' he said acidly. 'The governor rang the nearest RAF station to scramble intercepting aircraft. It was the sort of plan we're talking about today, precisely. The sort of plan that General Forsythe does not consider needs improving. Operation Rogue Elephant, it was called, and the governor, naturally, used the codeword. Operation Rogue What, said the RAF? Never heard of it, old bean. Where's Gartree, anyway? Try dialling 999.'

There was a cold silence in the room. Cheek timed his last card brilliantly.

'I don't think that sort of thing is very helpful to these chaps,' he said primly. 'Some things, Donald, are better left unsaid. Let's pass on.'

Later, over pâté and cold Beck's in Christian Fortyne's office, Sinclair spat out his irritation at the way the meeting had gone. Judith had joined them and was sitting on the edge of the desk, cool and severe as ever in a tailored suit. When she had heard the story she laughed.

'Do you know,' she said. 'I think you've got an inferiority complex, Donald. Why should they rattle you just because they went to Eton? Christian went to Eton and he's all right, isn't he? They're cannon fodder.'

'The reason they rattle me is because that's just what they're not. They're fireproof, untouchable, unshakeable. You give them orders, and they smile. They make a cock-up, and they smile.

You point them at the enemy, and God knows what they do. Stab you in the back, maybe? If it suits them. Christian?'

Fortyne took the top off a second bottle. He poured, sipped, savoured.

'There is a certain superiority,' he said. 'It comes, I think, from knowing that when the war breaks out you'll always be in a hole in the ground directing it. I don't think it's anything to do with Eton, though. That just makes them happier in the company of men.' He took another sip. 'Or grown-up boys, at least.'

Sinclair checked his watch.

'Back to the grind in five minutes,' he said. 'I'm sorry about the outburst, Christian. I must be a trial to you sometimes.'

Fortyne shook his head.

'You can never tell with the military,' he said. 'Who knows, you might have impressed them. But as a general rule, Donald, a bit more sang-froid. If you don't mind my saying so?'

Judith slid lightly from the desk.

'He's exhausted, poor thing. I've put three more appointments off this afternoon. Why don't you catch up on some report-reading?'

'If you mean have a doze in the armchair,' said Sinclair, 'there's no chance. Any calls I ought to deal with?'

'Ah,' she said. 'Pendlebury rang. In fact, he's rung three times. I think it's one for Christian, though.'

Fortyne groaned.

'Pendlebury?' said Sinclair.

'Governor of Bowscar,' said Fortyne. 'Where we put the Animal. He's a bit of a liberal, I'm afraid. A bit of a pain.'

'Now now,' said Judith, lightly. 'Donald's a liberal as well. We're a liberal department now.' She laughed aloud at Sinclair's face. 'Oh you do look tired! I'm honestly not mocking *very* much. But Pendlebury's something else.' To Fortyne she added: 'He wants to know why, and for how long, McGregor has to be kept in cellular confinement. Which he called solitary. He's worried by the implications.'

Fortyne nodded.

'I'll sort him out,' he said. 'Maybe another move. The Scar's ideal for McGregor, though. Nice and isolated. I'll think about it.'

Sinclair did go home early that evening. He left much work undone, and he cut a cocktail party at the House which the PM was scheduled to attend. He dined alone with Mary, after a long hot bath, and he split a bottle of wonderful claret with her, then drank vintage port. By the time they went upstairs Mary's eyes had darkened visibly, and she returned from her dressing room languorously naked. Their love-making was relaxed, and comfortable, and afterwards they mulled over the day again. The memory of the meeting restirred Sinclair, though, and the excitement began to trickle back. He talked of the new contingency measures in terms of rings of steel, of flexible responses, of going in hard and strong. He sounded like a military man himself.

'You sound as if you're enjoying it,' said Mary. There was something in her voice.

'Yes,' he said. 'I am. Is there anything wrong with that?'

The lamps were off, but the curtains were open. He could see her face, shadowed and highlighted, in the moonlight.

'I suppose it's part of a larger strategy,' she said. 'But it doesn't sound exactly . . . reformist yet, does it? Rings of steel . . .'

'What are you suggesting? That I'm going to join the hang'em and flog'em brigade! Come on, darling! But if there were another riot. If there's another Buckie . . .'

'That man died, didn't he?' said Mary. 'That young man on the roof. Elizabeth Turner told me. He was only twenty-three. That's awful, Donald. That's terrible.'

He lay beside her in the softly lighted room, staring at the ceiling. Somehow, it had not occurred to him to think of James McGregor in those terms. Twenty-three. A young man. Dead. He'd paid lip service to the horror, to Sir Gerald in particular, but it did not actually *feel* important. What did, increasingly, was what had sprung from it. The sense of excitement. The sense of possibility. The sense of power. He leaned across the pillow and kissed Mary lightly on the cheek.

'You're right,' he said. 'But I have to try not to brood too much. That would be fatal. I've got to build.'

Mary did not reply. She had closed her eyes.

'Goodnight,' he said. 'I love you.'

It was the funny looks that he was getting that finally shifted Andrew Forbes from the foyer area of the Shaw Theatre and Camden Library onto the Euston Road. He'd been there, on and off, for nearly two hours, and he felt a bloody fool. The trouble was that he did not fit the proper category. He did not look like the sort of person to be seen staring at the modern paintings and the works of sculpture, not even for ten minutes. Least of all did he look like the sort of man who would study them, come back to them, ponder them. He was a misfit.

He had gone to the foyer after a long and fruitless morning with Peter Jackson, continuing the search for Lister. With daytime, and with a reasonable five hours' sleep beneath their belts, they had been able to tap more sources. Both men had contacts in the Met, and both had followed leads. After two hours on the telephone, they had gone their separate ways. Jackson used a car in London, despite the hassles, and he dropped Forbes off near Wormwood Scrubs, where he had arranged to chat with a prison officer whose finger was generally on the pulse. They'd arranged to meet in the Princess Louise near Centre Point between five and seven in the evening. Andrew Forbes did not mention it, but he hoped to introduce the Customs man to Alice Grogan. That would shake him!

He cursed himself, as he walked down past the British Museum, for the sublime nebulousness of the arrangement. He'd let her leave his flat, had let her go, with a half-arsed farewell and a quarter-arsed belief that they had some kind of a date. He hunched his shoulders into his coat, smiling in self-mockery. He was getting old, and daft, and stupid. Why should lovely Alice bother with the likes of him? She shouldn't. And she hadn't.

The pub was crowded, but Jackson was watching out for him. He shouldered his way to the door, with a full pint he had been guarding on a table. His own half-empty one was in the other hand.

'Health,' he said, passing the beer to Forbes. 'What do you want first, the good news or the bad news?'

His thin, tired face was enlivened. Well, thought Andrew, at least someone's had a happy afternoon. He took two large mouthfuls quickly, savouring the bitter flavour.

'Good,' he said. 'The good news. I need something to cheer me up.'

'He's in Bowscar Jail,' said Jackson. His grin grew bigger. 'They took him there this morning. From St Albans nick. He never even realised it, apparently. He thought he was going to another lock-up. All part of the plan.'

'Fuck,' said Forbes. 'Miraculous. But was it a scam? What went wrong?'

'I don't know all the details yet. Who gives a shit? We've got him, Andy-boy. Bowscar's a bastard. Bowscar is tight. We've got the bastard nailed.'

Forbes emptied half the glass in three more mouthfuls. He reached for Jackson's empty.

'Again?' They always drank Ruddles in the Princess Louise. He did not need to ask. 'Oh – and what's the bad news, by the way?'

'Lister's lady,' said Peter Jackson. 'The black girl. They found her body in a flat this morning. Nosy neighbour job. Single stab wound to the heart. Dead as mutton.'

Andrew Forbes took the glasses to the bar. He ordered the bitter, and put his mind carefully into neutral. He saw a face in the mirror behind the Australian giantess pulling the pints. It was his own. He looked old, and tired, and fed up.

He was.

'The man's a pill, the lowest of the low. Riff-raff. What pains me, Robert, is that fellows like that are on our side these days. My God, you'd think he'd have the decency to cross the floor.'

Brigadier Robert Sherwood, deep in the leather armchair, chuckled.

'I think if you'd shown up at the meeting, sir,' he replied, 'you'd probably have frightened him into it. He might have resigned at least.'

'Rattled, was he? Good. My God, these little shits. Wet behind the ears. You didn't mention Edwards, I suppose? Not by name?'

'Oh no. But I made it clear we thought the whole shake-up thing was nonsense. That if anybody made mistakes it wasn't us. Rattled he quite definitely was.'

'D'you know, Robert,' said General Forsythe, 'I can't imagine what goes on inside the heads of some of these jumped-up politician johnnies. They dream up harebrained schemes, they put good men at risk, then they try to stick the blame on someone else. A pill. The man's an utter pill.'

Sherwood pulled himself from the armchair and picked up their empty glasses. He had not mentioned Sinclair's counterblast about the Gartree job. He did not want to spoil Forsythe's fun, and in any case, that had been an Air Force cock-up, nothing to do with them.

'I'll get two more,' he said. 'It'll save old Clarence's pins, won't it? D'you know, the oddest thing was, he seemed to be implying it was Turner wanted Edwards' guts for garters, not him. Would that be likely?'

The general shook his head.

'Doesn't sound like Gerald, does it?' He barked with laughter.

'On the other hand – he is a politician. Anything's possible!'
'Yes. I suppose so. I'll get the drinks.'
'Good man.'

SEVEN

Paddy Collins and the fat man were in the Lada when Rosanna Nixon arrived at last at Andrew Forbes' door. She had turned up the previous afternoon and waited for ten minutes, but other men had watched her then. She was not expected, because although she was theoretically under watch in Glasgow, their counterparts up there had not realised she had crossed the Border, going south. Rosanna Nixon had rung Andrew Forbes' number twice yesterday, from her London friends' house, and got no reply. This morning she had rung again, early, and somebody had picked the phone up. Before she could speak, however, they had let it drop. Rosanna had caught the Tube to Highbury and Islington, and walked.

From a distance, to the watching men, she looked interesting. She was female, which was almost good enough in itself, and she was very small and neat. It was cold, and she was snug in a long wool topcoat, with a white scarf and a dark, fluffy, peakless cap. Her eyes were bright, her face quite pretty, and there was something waiflike and defenceless about her. Paddy Collins, who had always had a yen for childlike women, got quite excited. When she turned up Forbes' steps and rang the bell, he groaned.

'Jesus Christ,' he said. 'Not another one. We're in the wrong job, mate, d'you know that?'

His companion pressed the button and the camera's computer bleeped. The aerial was already trained on the door. He waited for the woman to turn her face back to the road.

'You're bent, you are,' he said. 'She only looks fourteen. My daughter's that age, pervert.'

Collins said nothing. He knew his oppo's daughter, and, secretly, he'd have given his left arm to get across it. Rosanna, impatiently, looked at her watch. She rang the bell, then hammered with her fist.

'He's in,' said Paddy Collins, conversationally. 'Unless Jeff got it wrong. They logged him back at three o'clock this morning. Drunk as a fiddler's bitch.'

The camera beeped twice as Rosanna turned her head to survey the road.

'She's not that good-looking,' Collins said. 'And I bet she's thirty if she's a day.'

Above Rosanna's head, with a painful squeak, the bottom sash of a window was dragged open. Three pairs of eyes turned upwards. The two men in the Lada grinned at the sight. Rosanna stopped herself, but only just.

Andrew Forbes, what you could see of him, was naked. His chest was white, with tufts of sparse black hair about his nipples, and there was a clear line at the base of his neck where the darker skin began. Here was a man who rarely took his clothes off out of doors, even Doctor Watson could have worked that out. The colour of his facial skin was more problematical. It was pale and blotchy, almost grey in parts, and stubbly. The two men in the car could sympathise. They could almost feel his hangover.

'I'm asleep,' said Forbes. 'What do you want? Why don't you go away?'

'Get one for the files,' hissed Paddy Collins. 'Casanova in repose. The seamy side of subversion.'

The fat man grunted in agreement. The camera swivelled in the aerial tip. Beep.

'Excuse me,' said Rosanna Nixon. 'I'd like to talk to you. I'm sorry if I've come at an inconvenient time.'

The two men in the Lada were too far away to hear what was being said, but they knew full well that Forbes would let her in. She was a woman, wasn't she? After a couple more minutes of talking, the tousled head withdrew. To their amusement, Forbes banged the back of it against the bottom of the raised window. Two minutes later, apparently draped in a sheet, he opened the door and Rosanna disappeared inside. For a moment there was silence in the car, save for the sucking of the fat man's teeth.

'The black tart's dead, did you know that?' Paddy asked. 'I wonder if this is her replacement? Lucky bastard.'

'It's not been in the papers. How would he know it? I don't know. Maybe he does.'

In the hallway, Andrew Forbes was thinking of Alice Grogan. She was the last woman who had been inside his house, and he had hoped that she would come again. His head hurt badly, because of Alice Grogan. Upstairs in his bedroom, still in its box, was a new duvet, and a duvet cover, and a bottom sheet. What a twat, he thought. What a hopeless prat I am. He was aware of the stink of stale beer on his breath and body, and he was half-aware of this new woman, standing in front of him. The silence was becoming embarrassing.

'Look,' he said. 'Did you say Rosanna? Look, Rosanna, I shouldn't have let you in. I'm shattered. Wrecked. I was on the bash last night till God knows how long. Then some swine rang me up this morning, early. I want to go to bed.'

Forbes was not a tall man, but Rosanna barely reached his chin. She bit her lower lip, not knowing what to do. If only Maurice Campbell could see me now, she thought! The off-white sheet the man was holding round himself was coming open down his front. Already she could see a thigh, white and hairy. She made a rather desperate gesture.

'I've come from Glasgow,' she said. 'Look, you're coming apart. Look – where's the kitchen? You go back to bed and I'll bring up a cup of coffee. I've got to speak to you. I mean it. I mean – I really do need to speak to you.'

She had already told him where she'd come from, on the doorstep, and mentioned Maurice Campbell. Through the pain, Forbes was quite amused by her tenacity.

'Oh balls,' he said. 'I can't argue any more. I'm on the first floor. Follow the groans. The kitchen's in the basement, down those stairs, and you won't find any milk. I think you're mad.'

He turned away, and the sheet fell to the ground. He cursed, and picked it up, groaning at the effort. Unseen by him, Rosanna blushed. He went up the creaking stairway like an old man.

Rosanna Nixon was a well-brought up girl, in the Scottish tradition. She had been born and raised in Milngavie, a quiet, wealthy Glasgow suburb, and she had done everything well, and according to plan. At eleven she had gone to private school, where she had sung in the choir, been good at games and excellent at practically everything else. She had passed her highers well, and had been accepted to read English at Glasgow University without a struggle. Like most Scottish students she had continued to live at home while an undergraduate, travelling daily to her classes on the bus, then in the car her father bought her for her twenty-first. She had had one boyfriend for many years, and being religious, and not exactly wild about him in her private heart, had remained a virgin. Heavy petting, fine – or friskiness, as she liked to call it. It could be made to last all day if the mood was right, it could be reasonably squared with her belief in God's morality, and it enabled her to keep a distance. When the boyfriend, at the age of twenty-three, had got fed up with it and gone away to England, she'd been relieved. Six months later he was married, and they still sent each other cards at Christmas and on birthdays.

In her parents' eyes, things had started going wrong when she had got the journalism bug. After university she had trained as a teacher, and when she had the paper qualification, had travelled for a year. In Dublin, she had fallen in love with a reporter on the *Irish Times* – a married man, a Catholic – and, more strangely, with his job as well. After eighteen months she had lost plenty. Her virginity, naturally, the man, of course, a tooth and a fair amount of blood when the wife, hysterical with grief, had attacked her in a singing pub in Merrion Row, her happiness. Her parents did not know any of this, or if they did would not admit it. What really angered them was that she clung onto her stupid love for journalism. She took another course, began to drink a lot, moved into the flat in Kingsborough Gardens, and mixed with really quite unsavoury people. They were not entirely mollified when she got a job at last, and all their friends kept pointing out her by-line in the paper. They suspected, rightly, that she was not religious any more. Nor their little girl . . .

Rosanna, at twenty-eight, was wary now, about men and sex. In the course of becoming a reporter and getting herself accepted, she had developed a technique for fending off her colleagues without offending them too much, or herself by her apparent complicity in the rather grubby game. It would have been a lot easier to keep her self-respect intact if she had told them to piss off and go back to their mammies – where she suspected most Scottish men actually belonged – but she did not hate them for it, merely felt it was a pity, a bit pathetic. She had come to terms, also, with the fact that it usually happened when drink had been taken. One love affair, while it may have torn her guts to ribbons, did not, she supposed, mean she was attractive.

Learning to be a reporter, too, had taught her about men's homes. About run-down, dirty, unswept rooms in damp, unpleasant houses, in which she had lost the occasional battle on a greasy sofa. But so far, she had encountered nothing like Andrew Forbes' kitchen. Standing amid the grime, and remembering the drink-shattered white blob almost crawling up the uncarpeted stair above, she wondered if she had gone crazy. Then, gritting her teeth, she filled the one clean pan with water, lit the gas, found the instant coffee, which was lying on its side, lidless, with half the contents spread across a fish and chippy plate. Five minutes later she stood in the doorway of Andrew Forbes' bedroom. He was asleep.

The officers of Bowscar did not know what to make of Charlie Lister. He had been committed on remand on a charge of assaulting a policeman and he had spoken fewer than twenty sentences to anyone since he had arrived. He had stripped and showered in silence, submitted to his medical examination and an anal search, and been taken to his cell. There was one other man in it, an old recidivist from Manchester with a drinks problem. Outside jail he lived on VP wine and babbled incoherently. Inside he just babbled. But where Lister had merely ignored the prison officers' talk, except to answer formal questions in polite, toneless monosyllables, he had warned his cell-mate off. He had told him twice in twenty minutes that he did not want to talk, and on the third time he had taken him in a throat-hold and slowly throttled him until he was black and barely conscious.

'Listen,' said Charles Lister. 'If you speak to me once more, without I give you my express permission, I'll do this to you properly, OK? I'll starve your brain of oxygen until it dies. You'll be a vegetable. Deaf and fucking dumb. If you understand me, collapse.'

He let go, smiling sardonically as the man crumpled to the floor. You had to keep a sense of humour, didn't you? The prison officers knew that he had done something, and it intrigued them. Old Mickie White made no complaint, and there was not a mark visible on him. But the next time they had opened up the cell, he had been staring at Lister in transparent terror, pressed against the wall beside his bed. The officers had asked him what was wrong, and he had violently shaken his head. Maybe, they thought, he'd bought a drink somehow. More likely, this strange American had got to him.

Most of the officers in Bowscar were reasonable men, who disliked and despised only the vile and violent specimens among the inmates. Some of them had a sneaking regard for a number of the prisoners, although any fraternisation was considered dangerous and unprofessional. People like Mick White they were in general sorry for, and regretted the mockery and beatings they received, even when the perpetrators were their fellow officers. But in this case, none of them could see a way to signal to the American that White should be left alone, or that there would be trouble. It was inexpressible, naturally, but they all knew it: they were intimidated.

On the second day, three officers were detailed to take him to a contact cell for interrogation. Two plainclothes policemen, rumoured to be Special Branch, had arrived by prior arrangement to question him on matter or matters unspecified. They were large men, broad-shouldered and fit, and they made little effort to conceal their higher status in the world of fighting crime. They informed the duty officer who allocated the contact room that their requirement was for absolute isolation, with no chance of being overheard. No hovering, they implied. No little boys trying to muscle in on big boys' games.

Lister, when his cell was opened, was sitting at the small table with a pack of cards in front of him. He had not cut them, but was holding them face downwards in a deck. If the spyhole on the cell was opened at almost any time during the eighteen hours or so that he and Mickie White were normally locked up in it, he would be found like that, not moving, not playing with the cards. Poor gregarious Mickie, these times, was usually on his bed, stone silent.

The two detectives were seated at one side of a plain formica table. The prison officers guided Lister in, then stood awkwardly, unsure what to do. Normally they'd have exchanged a word or two, had some banter. The detectives remained hard-faced.

'Charles Lister,' said Officer Ted Taylor, finally. 'We won't be far away. I expect you know how . . .'

What had he been going to say? 'Dangerous?' Whatever, the detectives did not leave the silence hanging long.

'Sit down, Charles,' one said. The screws were ignored entirely. 'We've got some questions for you.'

When the officers had gone, one of the detectives drew a packet of Marlborough from his pocket and offered it. Lister took a cigarette, and the lighter. He inhaled deeply. He gestured round the small, bare room.

'Is this clean?'

'It's a prison, Charlie. Not the Lubianka.'

The American's eyes were pale blue through the smoke. He took another draw before he spoke. He was breathing deeply.

'Then why the fuck,' he said clearly, 'am I in it? What the fuck went wrong? And when the fuck do I get out?'

The bigger of the detectives had close-cropped, greying hair. He took his lighter off the table and fiddled with it.

'Something went wrong,' he said. 'It took us by surprise. Everybody by surprise. Some politician pulled a stunt, changed the whole scenario overnight. Everybody on remand, everybody in the cells, all over England. They got shifted. Dispersed. By the time we got the buzz, it was too late. We sent a car to St Albans so fast a policewoman's knickers melted. You'd gone. Short of ramming the prison truck we'd blown it.' He snapped the lighter on. 'It was a fuck-up. Grade A. Sorry.'

The smaller man was sweating. He brushed his temples, from back to front, with the thumb side of his hands. Charles Lister let smoke trickle from his mouth and rise beside his nostrils. Whatever they'd expected, he stayed calm.

'We had a deal. I've got to be out of England by a date. A lot of organisation's gone into this. A lot of love. I've got sixty million dollars riding on this date, and that's only an instalment. When do I get out?'

The spokesman tapped moodily at the formica table with the plastic lighter.

'We know who fingered you,' he said. 'If it hadn't been for him the Customs wouldn't have had to go for you just yet. We wouldn't have had to start this bloody farce.'

Before Lister could reply, the smaller man put in: 'His name is Forbes. Andrew Forbes. Some sort of journalist. A writer. He'd . . . he'd been knocking off that woman. Alice Grogan. They'd been having an affair.'

'She's dead,' said the other. 'The plods were called in by a neighbour, nothing to do with us. I suppose you knew that did you, Charlie? Alice Grogan's dead.'

Behind their still faces, both were suffering. Lister crushed the cigarette out between his thumb and index finger. He rolled the filter, then flicked it. It was noticeable that his fingers were very slightly shaking. His voice betrayed no strain.

'I don't exactly know what you're trying to say to me,' he said. 'But let me tell you something straight. I'm working for an outfit, right? It's an outfit that stretches right across the world. If I don't get out as per schedule to meet a certain boat, that outfit is going to be gunning for somebody. Not any somebody, right, but you somebody.' His finger stabbed. 'You, and you, and all the other little yous who got me in this mess, OK? We're talking business here, OK? The biggest business in the world. And we're talking an arrangement you fucked up.'

The bigger of the two detectives said quietly: 'We work for an outfit too, you know. We're not a one-man band.'

Lister gave a single shout of laughter. No more needed to be said. He stood up and gestured at the door.

'Why don't you fuck off before I lose my cool? Why don't you call the Mickey Mouse squad in? I'm fed up of your company.'

'Andrew Forbes,' started the smaller one.

'Shut up,' said Charlie Lister. He went and hammered on the armoured door. Booted feet approached. 'I'll expect a visit soon. Very soon.'

As the door opened, he added: 'Or it won't just be Andrew Forbes.'

Richard Pendlebury renewed his efforts to speak to somebody at the highest level after finally achieving an interview with Angus John McGregor. At Queen Anne's Gate his call was expected, and the people in Christian Fortyne's office had been briefed. Neither Mr Sinclair nor his highest aides were available, the governor was told, but he would be contacted as soon as possible. How soon? Well, difficult to say, as they were in a meeting. Within an hour, possibly. After two, Pendlebury rang again, and was again put off. He was promised a response, however. Probably within an hour.

The visit to the strip cell where McGregor was incarcerated was conducted in conditions of the highest security. Although he was the governor, Pendlebury was well aware of how little actual operational power he commanded in the face of a well-organised and obstructive staff. Many reasons had been given for the delaying of his interview, all of them presented in terms of his personal safety. Although McGregor was not conducting a 'dirty protest' as he had done in his Scottish jail, he was still refusing to wear clothes, and his attitude was one of barely repressed violence. It had been noted by the Chief Medical Officer that he had long nails, deeply stained and packed with hardened dirt and faeces. He had not been tested for HIV or hepatitis, but it was considered highly likely that he was infected with one or both. Drug injection was thought to be far more rife in Scottish prisons than in English, and the junkie population of Edinburgh was the biggest pool of HIV in Britain as a whole. If McGregor did not inject with the shared and filthy needles or sharpened ball-point pens he undoubtedly shed blood in fighting other prisoners, and probably had anal intercourse. All this had been explained, with proper gravity, by a delegation of officers and a junior MO. Pendlebury had kept his counsel, and insisted. He wished to interview McGregor, and he would.

The meeting, inside the antiseptic, glaring cell, was totally bizarre in Richard Pendlebury's view. The walls, of padded vinyl, reeked of disinfectant and reflected crazily the bright bulb, recessed in the ceiling in a bulge of armoured glass. Pendlebury, in a dark grey suit, stood between two officers who looked like Martians from a children's comic. They wore white overalls and rubber boots, red industrial gloves of heavy PVC, neck protectors and visored helmets. Outside, he knew, were three more men dressed the same, carrying weighted billyclubs. He sympathised with their position, but only half. Whatever else Aids meant, he recognised it as another opportunity to enhance the trappings, to indulge the myths of danger and of power. Angus John McGregor was a violent, dangerous man. But you would not, he thought, approach a pain-crazed tiger in this fashion. And tigers went armed.

McGregor was a small man. He sat in front of Pendlebury on the only piece of furniture in the cell, a narrow padded bench built along the angle of wall and floor as part of the structure of the room. It had no sharp edges, no brick or concrete exposed. Even if you put your chin on it, and banged your head down with your tongue between your teeth as frightened kamikaze pilots were reputed to have done rather than fly their missions, you were unlikely to bite it off. Pendlebury, who would perhaps have killed himself two years ago if he had not loved his daughter, had often pondered the morality of such places. To be unable to harm oneself, when so many people were doing one such harm, was peculiar. But like so many other moral questions he had had to face since joining the prison service, he had yet to find an answer for it. He wondered if McGregor might have an opinion to express.

McGregor was naked, and he sat with his thighs together and his hands held, as if in prayer, along the vee they formed. His face was pale, thin-cheeked, and stubbled. He was allowed an electric razor twice a week, but it was a lightweight battery-driven toy, encased in soft rubber to prevent use as a weapon. His body was thin, almost emaciated, his rib-cage hollow. Although he looked incapable of doing physical harm to any normal healthy man, Pendlebury did not doubt that he could be transformed in violence. It seemed to him, from observation, that many legendary 'hard men', like Glaswegian fighters, drew their power from other sources than the power of their bodies. The violence came from inside. The spirit, maybe. The frustration and the rage. The myth itself. Angus John McGregor had murdered several times, with weapons or with his bare hands. I wonder if he had his reasons, thought Pendlebury.

'Good morning,' he said. 'My name is Richard Pendlebury, and I am governor of this prison. You may find this peculiar, but this visit is in the nature of a courtesy call. You are being held in these conditions of maximum security for reasons of your own safety, because of the information we received when you were transferred. Personally, I would wish at the earliest opportunity to transfer you into the main body of the prison, possibly via the hospital wing if that might be beneficial. There are other factors to be taken into account, but your attitude and demeanour is the most important one. What do you think?'

Pendlebury, glancing to left and right, could almost feel the contempt emanating from the prison officers. Their assessments of the state of McGregor's mind had reiterated one point: he was unprepared to co-operate, or indeed to communicate. He had not offered violence, but had made it clear that he would take no part in any dialogue. His attitude, they had reported, was similar to the Irish terrorists in H-wing. He was withdrawn, calm, determined. Concomitantly, unprepared to recognise the system. Pendlebury actually saw both of them jump when McGregor raised his head and answered him.

'Excuse me, sir,' he said. 'But I think somebody's kidding you. I was not moved here for my own safety, and you should know that. Maybe you do. If so, you're a fucking evil—'

Beside Pendlebury, the prison officers tensed themselves to spring. McGregor saw the movement and stopped talking. He grinned, through his bruised lips. Neither they, nor his other facial wounds, looked fresh to Pendlebury. That was something.

'Look,' said the governor to the prison officers, gently. 'I have heard these words before, you know. If Mr McGregor wants to ask me if I'm a fucking evil liar, I think in the circumstances he's entitled to. Mr McGregor?'

Behind the visors, the faces had set. Pendlebury could hear breath hissing through one man's nose. One day, they'll jump on me, he thought. Maybe I deserve it.

McGregor raised his head higher than it had been so far. He thought for a moment, then decided.

'You're a queer one, aren't you, Mister?' he said. 'I'll level with you. I've no idea at all why they sent me into England. It happened in the middle of the night, and they moved me from pillar to post till I lost myself completely. That was intended, any fool can tell that much. But if they expected me to still think I was in Scotland, they're fucking mental. Even full of Largactil I can tell an English accent, can't I? I don't know where I am exactly, but by their accents it must be Birmingham or somewhere. Am I close?'

'Sir,' warned one of the officers.

Pendlebury ignored him.

'You're in Staffordshire,' he said. 'What you might call the Black Country. It's a deadly insult to say the accent's like Birmingham but we'll forgive you. This is HM Prison Bowscar.'

'Ach, the Scar. Well, thanks for that. But why? If you could tell me that. It'll be something to do with my wee brother?'

Pendlebury said: 'I honestly know nothing about anything like that. We've had no requests to visit you. Does your brother know where you are?'

'How would he, then? No fucker knows. Anyway, he's inside himself, he's in Buckie.' McGregor's voice had become low and flat. 'He was on the roof. Is it over yet? Are they down?'

His head had dropped forward. Now he snapped it back. His eyes began to shine, the pupils to dilate.

'I need to know! I need to fucking know! It's driving me insane!'

Momentarily, Pendlebury saw the mask of the beast slip into place. The atmosphere in the little padded room became charged. McGregor's eyes were widening, his lips pulling back to expose his teeth. His hands left his thighs and clenched into fists beside his cheeks. The bodies of the prison officers altered in stance. They braced themselves, leaned slightly forward. Then the moment passed. McGregor slumped, dropping his open palms onto his legs. Everybody's breath was clearly audible, quickened.

Pendlebury said: 'All this is new to me. I ask you to believe me. I'll do my best to find out the answers.'

McGregor's eyes were dull. He did not speak.

'In the meantime,' said Richard Pendlebury, 'would you consider wearing clothes? It's very difficult to relate, you know. A naked man, sometimes . . .'

Angus John McGregor's chin was back on his chest. His hands were in the prayerful attitude, between his thighs. Shortly, the three other men left the cell.

When Christian Fortyne at last rang Bowscar Prison, Richard Pendlebury had made a list of queries and worries concerning Angus McGregor. His original unease had been solely with the idea of solitary confinement – by whatever euphemism the Prisons Board cared to use for it in these enlightened days. Solitary confinement in a strip cell, with no communication or association whatever, for a period unspecified. Now he wanted to know other things from Fortyne. Why, for instance, had a Scottish prisoner been transferred to England? Why in the dead of night? Why had he been drugged, why held incommunicado? Was it to do with his brother, and if so why? Were there any other next of kin? Had they been informed?

Christian Fortyne had not sought to evade. He had spoken of the deep regret that was felt within the department at the measures forced upon them by the current ferment in the Scottish system, and their hopes that the latest moves, and moves that were being considered at this very moment, would bring a much-needed and lasting stability. There were certain elements, he said, that threatened to destabilise the whole Scottish experience, involving a network of irredeemably evil and highly motivated men. Government investigations into the events at Buckie, which he did not have the authority to disclose, had made it absolutely clear that McGregor should be moved.

When Pendlebury had tried to question further, Fortyne had allowed himself to sound a little irritated.

'Mr Pendlebury,' he said. 'At the Prison Department, your concern for the welfare of the men in your establishment is well understood and I promise you appreciated. But you must allow us the global view, the ability to make wider decisions based on a knowledge of all the facts, not just some of them. If you wish it, we will issue a CI 10/74 and have McGregor transferred by tomorrow morning. That may be the best thing. But I'm afraid I absolutely cannot discuss the details of his custody any further. Angus McGregor must be kept segregated until further notice, and he must be guarded constantly, as I'm sure your excellent officers understand. Now – shall I authorise the transfer?'

Richard Pendlebury did not want that. It would have been a defeat, a defeat for everybody. How easy to let him go, to see 'The Animal' shunted from prison to prison to be possibly brutalised and surely forgotten. He expressed careful regret if he had voiced his concern too robustly, and took note of Fortyne's strictures on the global view. He put the phone down and wondered, for some while, how much of Fortyne's rigmarole he had believed.

At the other end, Fortyne banged the phone down and made a face at Judith Parker.

'God save us from good men,' he said. 'They just don't understand . . .'

It was nearly two hours before Andrew Forbes woke up again, two hours in which Rosanna Nixon had made herself familiar with both his house and most of what she presumed to be his secrets. She had not done it deliberately, in the sense that she was seeking anything, but once she had started she had been quite systematic. From time to time in her perambulations, she had paused to look in at his door. He had remained flat on his back under a thin and lumpy duvet, snoring. The room, apart from the mattress on the floor, was remarkably bare, barer even than her own. A chest of drawers, a pile of clothes, a radio. Most noticeably, a cardboard box claiming to contain a duvet, with two soft brown paper packages resting on it. The curtains were open, but the view outside was restricted by a double layer of grey net nylon, hanging down at one side.

It was a big house, with a bathroom and a boxroom on this floor, and two attic rooms above. Everywhere was piled with cardboard boxes, and bulging plastic bags, and electrical devices – once shifted by removal men but never yet unpacked. Only in the room downstairs, the living room that stretched from front to back, had there been an effort at homemaking, civilisation. It held a polished table, sadly stained, some easy chairs and a sofa, thousands of books, on fitted shelves and lying in heaps across the floor, and a television set with video recorder. The time was fixed at 15:32, flashing greenly. It looked to Rosanna as if it had been flashing since time began.

She glanced at the newspapers. The *Guardian*, *The Times*, the *Independent*, the *Observer*. All old, most of them unread. The only area which was not entirely chaotic was a small corner, squeezed between the rear window and one of the knocked-through room's gas-fires. It contained another table, fifties, square, with pull-out leaves, on which there was a word processor. There were neat boxes of discs, some of them labelled, and a pile of tightly written notes beside the keyboard. Rosanna looked at the notes, but found them uninteresting, not to say incomprehensible, possibly in some sort of code. She was halfway up the basement stairway, deeply discouraged, with a third cup of milk-less instant coffee in her hand, when she heard Forbes coming down the upper flight. She held her breath, wondering what horror of mankind he would present to her this time. But after the bare feet came trousered ankles, and above the belt a shirt. Even his face looked better, less cadaverous. When he saw her, he stopped.

'Shit,' he said. 'I didn't dream it after all. Is that for me?'

Rosanna walked up to street level.

'You might as well. You probably need it. I was only doing it out of boredom, actually. I've searched the house.'

Forbes summoned up a laugh without wincing. He took the coffee and tried a mouthful or two. He walked into the living room and sat beside the word processor, assuming she would follow. She did, sitting on a wooden straight-backed chair.

'You could be anyone,' he said. 'Walking in on a hangover like that. Did you find anything worth photographing?'

'I'm sorry,' she said. 'I got bored. I guess I thought you'd be sort of – high-powered. You know, full of, you know. Maurice told me you were shit-hot.'

Forbes made a face.

'This tastes of fish and chips,' he said. 'Good old Maurice, eh? How is the twat?'

In a stupid way, Rosanna felt extremely happy. For the first time in quite a while, she felt that she was getting somewhere. But that is stupid, she told herself. I'm sitting here with a man who looks like liver failure, who I don't know from the Pope, and we're talking nonsense. It felt right. Bloody marvellous.

'What time is it?' asked Andrew Forbes. 'Time for a drink, surely? I don't suppose you dragged all the way from Bonnie Scotland just to say hello, did you? I'm old enough to be your brother, anyway. Are you on expenses? You could take me for a meal.'

'All right,' she said. 'I'm not on expenses, but Maurice didn't sack me in the end, so I've got a wage. Where shall we go?'

'Well, that depends,' said Andrew. 'What do we want to talk about? I mean, if it's really intimate, we could stay at home. Mull it over underneath the sheets.'

Rosanna recognised the ploy, the loaded joke, and recognised the sofa, even. But to her surprise it did not annoy her. It was said without any hard intent, she thought, without malice aforethought. It was friendly.

'Andrew,' she said, 'I've already seen you naked, and we've not been properly introduced. Let that be enough for one day, yes? You'll probably find when you know me that you lose interest. In Scottish journalism they call me the Wee Mouse. But I do need you to be sober. Soberish. If we go to a pub now, can I make an appointment for another day?'

'Bloody hell,' said Forbes. 'They've got you wrong, love, you're a shrew not a mouse. So what's the subject? Tell me.'

While Rosanna Nixon outlined the story, Forbes wandered round the room. He pulled books out of bookshelves, and pushed them back. He looked at himself in a mirror on the mantelpiece, and grimaced. He found some toast and marmalade underneath a newspaper, and ate it. When she had finished, he let the pause hang for quite some time. There was intermittent traffic noise from out front. A child shrieking nearby. He sat down.

'Well?' said Rosanna.

'The trouble with being English,' Andrew answered, 'is the imperialism. It's bred into the bone. I mean – sure, I've heard of Buckie, I heard about the siege. But what's his name again? Jimmy McGregor? I mean – is he really dead? It didn't make the papers this end, I can tell you. Or if it did I never saw it. Nobody died, surely? The Army moved in maybe, maybe not. The new junior minister, whatsisname? Donald Sinclair. He did a secret deal. They came down off the roof, everybody clapped their hands, and Bob's your uncle. Two days later Sinclair gets the screws back on the job and clears the cells of remand prisoners. For once, I've never heard *anyone* complaining. He even did a little job for me, indirectly. Put somebody inside. Too late, but never mind. We can't have everything, can we?'

Underneath his untidy, lightish hair, Forbes' grey eyes clouded. The smile around his lips faded, leaving them, to Rosanna's eyes, quite grim. Herself, she was hollow. He was being honest, she could not complain, but it left her in the pit. Scotland – where was it? Jimmy McGregor – who was he? A conspiracy to murder – so what?

'He didn't just fall off, you know,' she said. 'I don't expect you to believe this, so I didn't say it. But he was drugged. The soldiers went onto the roof and they shot him with a dart or something. Oh, I don't know. Maybe it was just to keep me interested. The man who rang me up. He mentioned drugs. He said to ask them about how they got into his body. He said to ask about the gun.

Then they moved the brother. They whipped him across the border and he's disappeared. A man called Adrian Rafferty told me. He's—'

'Christ! You don't know that old drunk do you? Is he still alive? And what does he reckon? If Rafferty thinks there's a story in it . . . Jesus, last time I spoke to him the quacks had given him two months. That was in 1984!'

Rosanna was glad they had not gone out to a pub. Forbes, as far as she could tell, was still riddled with booze from the night before. She was reiterating constantly, going carefully over the same ground time and time again. Was he grasping it? Was he doing it deliberately, to tease out everything? Or was his mind following Rafferty's, on the downward, drunken path?

'Adrian says the Animal's untraceable,' she said. 'After Glasgow—'

'Hang on, hang on! Where does he come in? The Animal? Isn't he the guy who minces prison officers? And prisoners, and friends, and— Oh. Angus McGregor. And the guy who died – Jimmy. Why didn't you say so? It's his brother?'

'I did. I . . .'

Andrew Forbes laughed at her.

'It's hard, isn't it?' he teased. 'To be so young and earnest. Do you think this is important, Rosanna Nixon?' He did a stupid, hippy voice. 'I mean, really, really important?'

You shit, she thought. Has all this been just to take the piss? You boring, useless shit.

'As a matter of fact I do,' she said. 'But as I can see you don't, I might as well sod off, I guess. I guess you've got bigger fish to fry. I'm sorry I wasted your time.'

As she stood, red-faced, Andrew Forbes stood with her.

'We'll have to walk,' he said. 'I'm afraid my Porsche's a bit fucked just at present. Can you see my jacket anywhere? It's not far to the pub.'

'I'm hungry,' said Rosanna, belligerently. 'If you want to spend my money, you'll have to eat.'

'For a wee sleekit cow'rin' beastie,' said Forbes, 'you're quite hard, d'you know that? I suppose if I said they did sandwiches at the pub—'

'You'd be on your own. I'm fed to death of drunken journalists.'

'I'm not a journalist, you cheeky bitch,' he said. 'I've written *books*.'

In the photograph, standing outside the old and flaking front door, they were laughing. To Paddy Collins' lustful eye, they already looked like lovers.

EIGHT

It had not occurred to Barbara Masters that Saturday was the worst day possible to visit her husband in prison, and nobody had told her. Sir Cyril France, QC, barrister and family friend, had hinted that it might be possible to squeeze some extra time out of the system – after all, he smiled, twelve half-hours a year could hardly be considered generous – but for the moment, he had said, best play it by the rules. Like Barbara, he was not constrained by time as ordinary mortals are, and like her he assumed unthinkingly that there would be something extra pleasant about a weekend visit, something almost festive at the end of a long dull week. Although he had been in prisons, naturally, he had hardly noticed them in detail, and categorised them, when he bothered to at all, as rather inferior hotels. Barbara had seen photographs, and expected to find the architecture interesting, but beyond that she had an open mind. Bowscar would be nasty, she guessed. But it was a prison, wasn't it?

The drive had been quite pleasant, and the weather fine. The BMW had eaten up the miles, with the CD system enabling her to fill her mind with music. In some odd way, both she and the boys – who luckily were away at school, so had no decisions to make concerning visiting – had come to terms with the whole affair. She found it devastatingly sad, still, but she had lived with the elements of shame for so long that they were no longer sharp. What was more everybody – her friends, Michael's business associates, the financial press – had behaved wonderfully towards them both. It was their universal opinion that he had done nothing wrong beyond what everybody did, that he was a victim of hypocrisy, a scapegoat for the envious millions. Only her parents had not embraced this view, but that, she thought, was the shallowest of opportunism on their part. They did not like him, and they never had done. Not because of any perceived failings in his moral code, not because his business practices could be said to be so very sharp, but because he was not one of them. He was of a lower class and it amused him – in their company – to revel in it.

Truth to tell, thought Barbara, as she drove the last few miles through the Staffordshire countryside to Bowscar, I don't like him much myself. The idea amused her, for a moment – or more particularly, the fact that it had slipped into her mind so easily. Here she was, the wife of a millionaire, humming through the sunlit countryside in a wonderful limousine towards his prison, and she could be so disloyal! That in itself warmed her to him, and she revised the mental statement. 'No,' she said aloud. 'I don't dislike you, Michael. But I can stand the thought of prison, you bastard! Oh yes, I can stand the thought of prison!' She had not, as he had half-suspected, been behind the betrayal of the deal, she had not known that one existed. But when all was said and done, he had had something coming to him, hadn't he?

Barbara Masters, after fourteen years of marriage, could contemplate her feelings quite dispassionately. For the first six, Masters' joint passions – making money and making women – had set up an odd conflict in her emotions. The money side amused her, because she was rich herself, and found his naked lust for it somehow endearing. But the woman side, when she had discovered it, had been an appalling, searing shock. Because she had thought their love and sex life perfect, it made her suspect, horribly, that her wealth had been the first, perhaps the only, thing about her that had actually attracted him. She had been wrong, but it had taken her six years and three minor affairs of her own – affairs of desperation, not of love – to make her realise it. Since then, slowly, she had come to accept Michael as a man who needed certain fixes to stay alive. She no longer hated him for the women, nor even cared that much, and she was totally faithful sexually herself, although her love was deeply modified. She did not know of Sarah Williams.

It was the sight of Bowscar Prison that brought the sadness back. Like many of the great Victorian piles, it had such a presence that it stood out from the landscape as a shock. The houses of the village came quite close to it, but it was oddly out of scale with them. It was much too large, as if somehow over the years of its existence it had grown by sucking the life from its surroundings. It had an enormous tower, with a gallery around its higher part exactly positioned on its length as the glans of an erect penis would have been. The walls were vastly high, the windows tragically small, in minuscule, inhuman scale. The integrity of the architectural vision, Barbara found amazing. It was not so much a building as a nightmare, genuinely made real. The day it was finished, it would have been as awesome and as awful. While men believed in retribution, it could never be knocked down.

And her husband had been sent here for four years? Barbara Masters knew, clearly and simply, that it could not be. He would not stay, he could not. She was close to tears.

An hour later, humiliatingly, the tears were falling down her cheeks. She was sitting opposite her husband, at a bare deal table with uneven legs, and she could not speak. Masters, sardonically, observed that her distress was selfish, or at least, not to do with the state she found him in. He gathered that she had had a hard time of it. Had found nowhere to park the BMW, had had to queue for ages, surrounded by the lower orders and their squalling brats. In an odd way, it gave him satisfaction to see the slim, elegant woman so unhappy in such squalor. Barbara had pretensions to liberality which occasionally irked him. Now, like Natella Abashvili, she was apparently discovering that the lower orders were giving her a migraine.

'What did you expect?' he asked, impatiently and coldly. 'A major-domo to take your coat? For God's sake dress the part next time. If there is a next time.'

The words went in like knives. Barbara had genuinely been looking forward to seeing him, and had genuinely been overwhelmed by the horror of the physical reality. It was Saturday, the day when the women who were lucky enough to have jobs could take time off. When those with children who wanted, or were prepared, to see their fathers were not at school. When those whose new lovers, maybe, would drive them, and hang around outside wondering what the hell they'd done it for. There were more than three hundred women at Bowscar this day, and about a hundred children. The visiting hall held thirty prisoners at a time, with the waiting wives and children left in the street until they were counted in like sheep to slaughter. Bored children, after waiting for an hour, became uncontrollable. The toddlers wet themselves, dramatically, on their fathers' knees. The women, trying to kiss the men, and say they loved them, or that everything was all right, were knocked into by flying kids, looked at slyly by other women who knew their deepest secrets, vomited over by their babies. Over all, on a small raised dais, sat five officers, bored but vigilant, hating every minute of it. Every half an hour, they cleared the room, trying not to share the utter misery of the scene. Even the hardest officers, men like Ted Taylor and Chris

Abbey, could not take the looks of shocked disbelief on the women's faces when they realised their time was up, that the visit was over for another month. But they hadn't said . . . But he hadn't smiled . . . Was he *trying* to be a bastard, or was he just upset . . . ?

With this all round her, Barbara Masters discovered the other great agony of being a visiting wife. For all but a very few couples, words were too difficult to say. All over the crowded room, men and women were facing each other across bare tables, saying nothing. To every question, the man would fence an answer. 'What's it like?' All right. 'Are they . . . do they, you know, treat you all right?' Yeah, not too bad. 'What's the food like?' Shit. Like your Mum's. 'I *love* you.' Yeah, shut up, willya, keep it down. Small children wound themselves around their fathers' necks and wondered why they looked so wild and sad. Others, inevitably, mentioned unmentionable names. Uncle John came last night. He was still there in the morning. And do you know, Dad – he ate *three* shredded wheats.

Barbara sat opposite her husband, wishing she were dead, and Michael Masters sat staring at her, almost sightlessly, wishing she were someone else. His need for Sarah Williams – no longer doubted, no longer wishable away – was triggered by his wife, his heart ached and his stomach muscles contracted, progressively, into a knot of terrifying hunger. As Barbara spoke to him, he answered Sarah, in a silent shout. Oh Sarah, Sarah, Sarah. That was all.

He had not asked her how the boys were, he thought dully. Or had she told him? He had not asked about the house, the cars, the staff, the dogs, the horse, her parents. He had not asked her how she was making out, if Sir Cyril France had been in touch yet with a plan, or whether she would come again or if she'd be surprised to find that someone had let her tyres down outside or scratched the paintwork with a knife. He had not asked her why she'd worn such ridiculously opulent clothes or whether she was mad. He had not asked her if she would divorce him or give a message to Sarah, or kill herself and set him free. As the half-hour ground on, or flew by, he thought he was going to shout at her, to scream, or strike her. He had grown pale, he knew it. For the first time in his adult life he thought he might lose control.

But I can take anything, he told himself. I can, anything. Sarah. Until I met you. You bitch.

When the handbell rang, Masters stood abruptly. There was a

sheen of moisture on his brow, and the muscles in his jaw were locked. Barbara's eyes were frightened. She reached a hand out and he flinched.

'Darling,' she said. 'I'll speak to Cyril. This is . . .' She stopped herself. This was wrong. You had to be brave, didn't you? She couldn't leave like this. It was disastrous, insupportable. She tried to smile, but it was a ghastly mask.

'I love you,' she said. The tears began again, flooding down her cheeks. She turned, stumblingly, and banged into a couple at the table behind her. They were locked, astonishingly, in a passionate embrace. As she hit them the woman, who was slewed halfway across the table, seemed to grip the shoulders of her man to stop herself from falling. They moved sideways, still locked mouth to mouth, the table legs scraping noisily across the floor. Only after Barbara passed, trying to mumble an apology through her sobs, did they separate. The woman, who was thin and small and furiously angry, shouted at her: 'You clumsy fucking bitch! Why don't you look out what you're fucking doing!'

At another table, as she bore down on it, Barbara came across two young men, both weeping as they gazed at each other. One, the inmate, was tall and beautiful, with hair that looked as if chunks had been hacked off with a knife. Patches of skull showed through, and the remains were straggly, and different colours. The visitor was short and stubby, with a black motorcycle jacket and tight blue jeans. As Barbara passed, a tiny woman, spiderlike and venomous, spat at him. The two men's hands, which were almost touching, drew back. Neither of them said a word.

Outside, the air was still clear, still clean, still beautiful. But most of Barbara's elegance was gone. She had the clothes, but she had lost the ability to walk properly. She did not exactly stagger, but there was a lumpishness in her gait, a lack of balance. She felt as if she had turned into a crab, a hermit crab with long, useless legs and a hugely heavy shell. When she reached the BMW – untouched, unscratched – she found it hard to get the key into the lock. She leaned her arm on the roof and touched the metal with her forehead, and concentrated. Her arm, she thought, smelled of the awful room. Of dirt, and sick, and poverty. Inside the car, she sat for minutes, smelling the same smell. It was stronger than the smell of leather from the seats. She pressed the button to take the window down but the ignition was not on. She sat.

Two hundred yards away, the thin woman who had shouted at

her approached an old blue Transit van. As she neared him, Peter Smith leaned forward and started up the engine. Thank Christ that's over, he thought. He did not normally go on jobs. He stayed strictly far away. But this was urgent. There'd been no choice.

The woman jerked the door back and climbed in. She glanced at him, with little interest, then away. She lit a cigarette.

'Go all right?'

He banged the gear-stick into bottom and eased the clutch out. Despite his care, the van juddered before it moved away. The woman did not answer.

'I said,' said Peter Smith, 'did it go all right? No problems?'

'Some stupid cow,' she said. 'I nearly bloody swallowed it. We was just passing it, she knocks into me. Stupid cow. Rich cow.'

'Shit. What, you were actually passing it? In the johnnie bag?'

'I got it stuck on my tooth. Tony were trying to get it clear with his tongue. He nearly bloody choked me. Then this rich tart.'

Peter Smith juddered the Transit cautiously through a junction, heading for the trunk road. Jesus Christ, he thought. Only the trigger mechanism!

'You done it, though? Tony got the gear?'

She dragged deeply on the cigarette.

'Don't shit yourself. It's twenty quid. I need it, don't I?'

Smith had his foot hard on the floor. The van's speed climbed towards twenty-eight. When it got there, he changed up to top.

'Make it thirty if you like,' he said. 'You've done good.'

The woman was surprised.

'What? Thirty? Just because of that? For doing good?'

Peter Smith showed his teeth. They were yellow.

'Don't be stupid, love. My name ain't Father Christmas. I want to fuck you, too.'

'Oh,' she said.

She wound the window down and threw the fag butt into the road.

'Thirty-five,' she said.

'Get stuffed.'

Much to Rosanna's surprise, Andrew Forbes did not drink anything with his lunch. She offered to buy a bottle of wine – even offered to share it – but he shook his head.

'If we're going to do business,' he said, 'you're going to have to revise your opinion of me. Having once been married to a Scot, I know all about your hang-ups. I'm not an alcoholic, and I never have been. But there's only one way to convince a Scots woman of that, and that is not to drink. I'll have a Perrier water. Please.'

While he studied the menu, Rosanna studied the top of his head. He had a lot of hair, growing out of his scalp at every angle. It was light brown, and – at the moment – not very clean. She guessed his age at forty, perhaps a little older, but his general unkemptness made it difficult to judge. He was wearing a suit, and that too had seen better days. It was brown, too pale to ever have looked good, and like the rest of him, it was rumpled. His hands, holding the menu, were pale and soft, not working hands, but the nails were split and dirty. Washing-up would sort that out, she thought tartly, then mocked the thought. The wee Scot of his dreams!

Forbes caught her studying.

'Careful,' he said. 'Thinking a man needs mothering is the easiest route to finding yourself in bed with him. Curb yourself, Rosanna, curb yourself.'

She blushed.

'I'm only reading the menu to impress you, that's another thing,' he said. 'I always come here when I'm hungover. Their lasagne's like aromatic concrete. You could plug a fashion-conscious dyke with it.' He paused, the fraction of a beat. 'What do you fancy?'

Rosanna fancied regaining the advantage, if she'd ever had it. She'd expected their conversation to be oblique and bantering, with a sexual sub-text, because that was the way such conversations went, in her experience. But Forbes' technique – if technique it was – left her streets behind. Mocking her he undoubtedly was. But was it a seduction line?

'She came from Govan, didn't she?' she said. 'Your wife. Why did she leave you?'

'Oh nasty,' replied Forbes. 'Which big-mouthed ex-mate do I have to thank for that?'

'Oh come on! You can't have all the attacking lines! It was Maurice, actually. Campbell. He sees you as a sort of honorary Scot.'

'God spare the mark,' said Andrew, soberly. Again the well-timed pause. 'She died of cancer. I'm a widower.'

Not since she had been in love had Rosanna Nixon felt such complete mortification. Forbes' eyes were on her, and he knew precisely the effect his words had had. His eyes were clear. You asked for that, they said.

'I'm sorry,' Rosanna muttered. 'That was stupid. That was really bloody stupid.'

He reached across the table and tapped the back of her hand with two of his fingers.

'Maurice would have been too polite to say. People are, I've noticed. Even saying cancer scares them, in case it brings it on or something. Rosanna. I did that deliberately, you know. I don't need mothering. It's a warning. I do all right.'

They sat in silence for a while, occupying themselves with the food when it arrived. It was a business-like restaurant, with no suggestive wagglings of pepper-mills over Rosanna's plate, and the food was good. Gradually, she relaxed. Andrew Forbes had mentioned doing business. After ten minutes of quite friendly silence, she began to realise he could possibly have meant it, literally, just like that. When she analysed it, he wasn't putting pressure on at all.

'Andrew,' she said. 'Are you going to help me? Do you think it's worth it, there's a story there?'

'Yeah,' he said. 'There might be. It's worth a try. I'm doing bugger all else that's interesting at the minute, that's for sure. How are you for cash?'

'Well you won't have to keep me,' said Rosanna. 'But I'm not precisely loaded. You're not – you weren't thinking of charging for your services, were you?'

He hooted.

'What a brilliant idea! I sometimes think I'll have to do something to raise some ready cash! But no, I wasn't. I've got enough to get me by for a month or so, and if we get somewhere we'll find a market, won't we? Luckily, the overheads on my life are pretty low. That's the advantage of widowhood over divorce. But it could take time, and travel. A bit of bribery and corruption. If we run out of cash, it's finished, that's the truth of it. When I need to pay the mortgage, I have to work. Real work. I do subbing shifts on the *Sun* and *Daily Mail*. It confuses the Special Branch no end.'

After they had eaten, they strolled slowly down towards the centre. Rosanna, who did not know London well, found Stoke Newington and upper Islington alarmingly cosmopolitan and rather cramped, with lower, meaner buildings than Glasgow and a scandalous amount of traffic. But her interests lay elsewhere.

As they walked, she tried to extract a schedule, or a pattern, or a plan. She wanted to know, simply, what they were going to do.

'Right now,' he said, as they walked across High Holborn, past the *Mirror* offices, 'we're going for a drink.' He caught her look. 'That's right, it's not yet four o'clock. And if you complain, Miss Mouse . . .'

She bit her lip, mock ruefully.

'Sorry,' she said. 'I could actually do with one myself. It's just that—'

'You want to see some action? Well this meeting's by appointment, see? With a man who I want you to meet, a man I think can help us. Ah, you say – I didn't see you ring him up. No, I say – I didn't. One of the little mysteries of the game.'

The man was Peter Jackson, and the 'appointment' had been one of habit. Not having families, and having practically no interests outside their work, they shared a well-worn circuit with a fluctuating number of other people on the fringes. They were mostly men, and mostly connected with the law or breaking it in some way. The Princess Louise was more a private spot for Forbes and Jackson, though. Jackson, not even sure that his friend would turn up, had bought *Private Eye* and was reading it in a corner. The first he knew of the company was when Forbes slid a full pint in behind the magazine for him. Jackson touched it with a finger-tip.

'Cheers,' he said. He saw Rosanna, hovering slyly at Forbes' elbow. 'Christ,' he added. 'That period of mourning was a short one, mate. Going for the record?'

Andrew indicated the plush upholstered bench and Rosanna sat. She was holding half a pint of lager.

'Rosanna Nixon,' said Forbes to Jackson. 'Sorry about the lager, she's a Scot. This is Peter Jackson,' he told Rosanna. 'He's an investigating officer with the Customs. Which information, naturally, is classified. It's all right, Peter. You can trust her. She's in the game. It looks as if the end of that jail siege up in Scotland was not so brilliant after all. The death or glory boys went in after dark and cocked it up, as usual. They killed somebody. Sixty-foot dive job, onto granite.'

The thin-faced Customs man did not bat an eyelid.

'It didn't say that in my paper,' he said. 'Didn't Donald Sinclair do it single-handed? Or did he deny he did it single-handed, I can't remember? Anyway, so what?'

The thing that fascinated Rosanna was the desultory nature of the conversation. When she spoke of James McGregor, she got quite animated, and Jackson listened carefully – until he broke her off halfway and went to get some drinks. When he returned he moved into another topic, with Andrew joining in. This was not small-talk, either. She heard of Lister, and a multi-million pound drugs operation, and a false arrest. In a Glasgow bar with journalists on a Saturday afternoon, she thought, we'd be onto mortgages and cars. Indeed, Forbes and Jackson treated their subject just as lightly. She was delighted.

'What's the score on Charlie?' Andrew asked. 'Have you pinpointed the opposition yet?'

'We're pretty sure. Not centum per centum. I think we've spiked their guns, though. It's gone to Foreign Office level. De Sallis might come over from Miami to add a bit of muscle if we need it. Any chance the Mets might have snatched to move him out of the Scar for further questioning – ho ho – has been well and truly bolloxed. Side from anything else, they'd give themselves away. We'd know for sure.'

'Sorry to be so ignorant,' said Rosanna, 'but am I understanding this? Are you saying the police tried to prevent the Customs arresting somebody? To help him to escape?'

'Put it down to friendly rivalry,' said Jackson. 'It happens all the time. And what's your next move on the McGregor thing? Infiltrate the SAS? Persuade the Prison Department to tell the truth for once? You're too late to get Sinclair to admit he pushed the boy himself. He flew out this morning on his tour. That's the life, eh? Jetting round the world to look at other people's cock-ups so that you can say that by comparison we're doing not so bad. Prats.'

'Right now,' said Forbes, 'we're going to jump a cab and bugger off home. I'm beginning to feel the urge for a civilised evening's drinking coming on. A bath first. A change of clothes. What about you?'

Jackson nodded.

'Sounds OK. I've got to see an oppo first. Should be through by nine o'clock. Dog and Partridge?'

Rosanna was not mentioned, so she made no comment or assumptions. In the taxi she tried to ask Forbes what *was* their next move, but he told her it was now officially Saturday evening, and work was therefore banned. In the long, chilly living room of his house she tried to make some sense of the past few days. Particularly the past few hours.

'Listen,' she said. 'I don't know if you're expecting me, but I can't come out this evening. Sorry.'

'Oh aye?' replied Forbes. He was sorting through a clothes horse near the front gas-fire, looking for a shirt. 'Why's that then? Got a date?'

'No, not exactly. I mean, the people I'm staying with, they're expecting me. We'll have a meal I should think.'

'What! Two meals in a day! You'll lose your girlish figure if you don't watch out. Where is it? Far away?'

'Mm. Clapham.'

'Drag. When we start working properly, you're welcome to stay here, you know.'

He raised his head from the clothes maiden. Rosanna flushed.

'I'm not sleeping with you. Sorry. If that's what you mean.'

He kept a straight face.

'No, I wasn't meaning that. We can easily make another bed up. You'll have noticed I have several. I've even got a new duvet for you. How about that?'

Rosanna, feeling very foolish, turned away. Outside, the light was fading rapidly.

'I don't know how you manage it, Andrew, but you make me sound ridiculous. Everything I say sounds ridiculous. Even the reason I came here sounds ridiculous. Prisoners, and poison darts, and cover-ups. It sounds ridiculous. And now I refuse to sleep with you and you haven't even thought of asking. Ridiculous.'

She became aware of him standing just behind her in the gloom. Her body tensed, involuntarily. But he pointed through the window, over her shoulder. His tone was conversational.

'See that car over there? The old green Lada? How ridiculous would it sound if I told you it was watching us? How ridiculous would it sound if I told you it had probably caused a woman to be stabbed to death this week? Probably by the American we've just been on about in the Princess Louise? How ridiculous would it sound if I said your photograph was probably on file, already, since you came hammering on my door this morning?'

Rosanna stared across and down the road at the Lada. It was squat and lumpy, with a vinyl top and a roof-rack. Inside, she thought she could just make out two human shapes in the growing darkness. Why would men be sitting there, in the dark?

'Where?' she asked. 'On file where?'

'Who knows? Special Branch, MI5? The one thing you can be sure about in Britain is that you can never be sure. Jackson found out about the car for me after something happened. I'd never even noticed it. But even he's not certain what it all adds up to. I wouldn't be too surprised myself if Charlie Lister wasn't working for the Brits. Maybe they want to get him out legitimately. Even if he did kill Alice Grogan. If he did.'

Rosanna moved back into the room. It was dark now, but she did not want a light on.

'Alice Grogan,' she said. 'Is that the woman? The one you didn't mourn for very long?'

'There wasn't much to mourn,' said Forbes. He gave a short laugh. 'Let it be a warning, though. Women have a habit of dying on me, don't they? Get out while you can.' He sighed, and followed her into the middle of the room. He switched the light on.

'Of course your bloody tale's ridiculous,' he said. 'We live in a ridiculous age. But anyway, what does it matter if they used a drug or not? I wouldn't be surprised if they imported a tribe of pygmies with poison blowpipes. They love their toys, these lads, they're wedded to them. But it's irrelevant. You're telling me that somebody got killed, whether by accident or design, and the big lie's under way as usual. A prisoner gets dead, his brother disappears, and nobody knows damn all. Rosanna, isn't that enough? Do you want jam on it?'

For once, he had become animated. There was even colour in his cheeks. Seeing her look, Forbes turned away, grabbing up her coat from the back of a chair. He threw it at her, and she caught it.

'Come on,' he said. 'Fuck off and let me bathe my body in ointments and exotic unguents. Someone might get lucky tonight, who knows? You go and share a bottle of Wincarnis with your respectable friends. You can take me for another lunch tomorrow, if you're free.'

Outside, although it was not in her direction, Rosanna walked past the Lada, looking at it from the corner of her eyes. Inside were two men in boiler suits. They stared at her quite openly, and she was afraid.

In the aftermath of his wife's visit, Michael Masters was provoked almost beyond the edge of reason. He managed to control himself, just, and was delivered to his cell at last by his tormentors. Chris Abbey, Ted Taylor and Simon Petter, as a final gesture, pushed him through the door with enough force to knock over Alan

Hughes, who was sitting at the table reading. Jerrold, who was lying on his bed, swung his legs out, glaring balefully. Not, as the officers hoped, to start or join an attack, but to hinder Masters if he lost his temper and sprang for them. But Masters had won the battle with his rage five minutes before. He lay in a heap with Hughes, saying nothing, moving not at all. After a few insults about homosexuality, inevitably, the officers left. Hughes pulled himself slowly to his feet.

'My my,' he said. 'Your relationship with Mr Abbey seems to be coming on a treat. What have you been up to this time?'

Masters stood. He was pale, and at the sight of his face Jerrold swung his legs back onto his bunk.

'You leave the man alone,' he told Alan Hughes. 'I want to sleep. I don't want no talking.'

Hughes picked the table up and retrieved his book. He sat down and found his page. He began to read. The silence of the prison, a noisy silence composed of distant clangs and yells, the booming of ancient heating pipes, the sighing of the wind, settled on the cell. Masters lay down on his back, regulating his breathing carefully. He had to keep his mouth open, to relieve the tension in his muscles. He felt on the verge of explosion, or hysteria, or going mad. He almost wished he had jumped on Abbey.

Ordinarily, the incident would not have bothered him. He had the measure of Abbey and his clique, and he treated them with polite contempt. It was a technique he would have developed for himself, but Jerrold and Hughes were both past masters, and good tutors. The politeness was essential, the most important element, because it left the officers in the position of low-grade thugs if they used violence. Also, if it was done elegantly enough, it confused them, with the stupider ones sometimes believing it was real. Abbey was no fool, though, and he chose his moments carefully. After the visit from his wife, he had judged, Masters would be vulnerable.

The incident had happened in the corridor outside the visiting room. When their half-hour was up, Masters and his thirty-odd companions had been herded out, and lined up along one wall. Along the opposite one were the next contingent, a mixture of hope and apprehension in their faces, as well as acute discomfort at having to face the men who had finished the ordeal. It was one of the more refined pieces of torture in the Scar, to mix them. And had probably first been done, like so many other savage things, with no intended malice.

Abbey, surveying his little flock, had homed in on two prisoners, Michael Masters and Raymond Orchard, the tuft-haired homosexual. His psychology was excellent, because several others were suffering more visibly. A young deaf and dumb man was crying horribly, a snuffling, snoring sound, and a black of about fifty-five was punching rhythmically at the wall, ignoring or unaware of the blood flowing from his knuckles. Abbey took the homosexual first.

'You,' he said. 'You disgust me, do you know that? I watched you, in there, with your little bum-boy. Touching fingers, trying to get your slimy little tongues in each other's mouths. Are you in love?'

Raymond Orchard did not reply. He was a quiet man, and his eyes were dull with misery. The visit had been especial agony for him.

'You must be, mustn't you?' said Abbey. 'Too much in love to talk. I've heard of that. But you're wasting yourself in here. You could make a fortune with an arse like yours, hasn't that occurred to you? What you need's a pimp.'

He laughed, and flicked Orchard's cheek with his fingers. Few prisoners joined in, although there was little sympathy for Orchard in the jail. His lips were trembling, his face on the point of collapse.

'I've had some interest expressed, I'm serious,' said Abbey. 'Perhaps we could do a deal. You provide the orifice and I'll provide the plugs. Twenty-five per cent.'

Well satisfied with the effect he'd had, Abbey turned away. He spoke to Masters.

'Talking of prostitutes, what a tasty little wife! What a lovely little knob-sucker, eh? Did you see her crying? Did you see the tears of shame? Mixing with the common bastards, was it? The sluts and snotty kids? The old lags and their slags? My God, Mister Masters, she must be proud of you!'

The knotted fist in Masters' abdomen rose to his gorge and choked him. He put his hands behind his back, pressed them into the cold, painted brickwork. Sweat broke out again, as it had inside the room. A horrible nausea rose within him. Chris Abbey, clearly, was impressed and pleased. He called to Petter and Ted Taylor.

'Mr Petter. Mr Taylor. Come and look at this. Should we call the MO do you think? Do the regs cover a millionaire having a heart attack? Or is he having kittens?'

The prisoners on the other side were shuffling in for their visits. At the end of the corridor, a door banged open. A principal officer called loudly: 'Let's be having you! Shift yourselves! Mr Abbey? What's the hold-up?'

Masters managed to speak. His lips were drawn back from his teeth and his pulse was throbbing. He said to Abbey: 'I'm going to kill you. I'm going to have you killed.'

Abbey's smile of satisfaction grew less. Masters' face was white, his pupils dilated to enormous size. His breath was shallow and uneven.

'Was that a threat?' asked Abbey. 'Would you care to repeat that?'

Masters, with an extraordinary effort, prepared to do so. He had controlled his desire to physically attack, and it had drained him. But he had faculties enough left to know he had got through.

'Yes, I'll repeat it.'

But Abbey, suddenly, pushed him along the corridor, by his shoulder. Other officers pushed or led the rest. Three times they tripped him on the journey to his cell, four or five times he was cuffed or hit. But thinking about it on his bed, Masters was confident. He had frightened Abbey.

'I'm going to have him killed,' he breathed.

He slept.

The junior minister had told his assistant to keep it simple, and Judith Parker had. Although their visit to the States was on official business, many of the trappings had been dispensed with. Donald Sinclair's relatively lowly status had been their best card, coupled with the small size of the delegation. The minister himself, Miss Parker, and two clerical civil servants to collate, to note, to photocopy. It was a fact-finding mission only, they had emphasised, and should rate low on pomp.

They had been met at O'Hare and driven straight to a small reception at the State Department in Chicago, where local politicians had assessed what benefit, if any, they could extract from associating with this tall, suave Briton. They loved his accent and his style, but Sinclair made it very plain that he was moving on. It was a whistle-stop tour, in which at least twenty prisons would be visited, and he hoped there would be no TV or press. The politicians ate their pretzels and drank their drinks and faded. Not much more than an hour later, the Britons were in the Federal Bureau of Prisons offices, and down to work.

Sinclair's guide to the complex subject, it turned out, was a woman named Myra Fischer, who was some years younger than himself, and black. She had only a hazy idea of Britain's prison problems and little interest, but she was fiercely brusque about outlining those of America. As of this moment, she declared, some eight and a half hundred thousand Americans were behind bars, which was a higher figure than the populations of no fewer than eight states of the union. About one thousand new inmates were admitted every week, and the Big M – the millionth prisoner – was clear on the horizon. Each cell cost around a million dollars for the thirty years it was designed to last, and an unknown percentage was destroyed each year by riots. Prison, she added, did not seem to work, on any terms. But in the public mind, prison was what criminals deserved, unless they could be gassed or shot or electrocuted. Most prisoners, she added drily, were black.

The statistics went on and on, with little concession made to her audience's capacity to absorb. Myra Fischer knew her subject, and spoke to it with an oddly detached passion. After an hour and three-quarters, Sinclair's brain had turned to mush. Whether she had noticed this or not the woman, shortly, stopped.

'That's just the tip of it,' she said. 'Tomorrow I've worked out an itinerary that will show the nuts and bolts. Your cars will be outside the hotel at 6 a.m. Do you have any queries, please? I'm afraid I must get back to my work.'

In their hotel, cool and air-conditioned, the four of them sat in a small private lounge studying the itinerary Ms Fischer had provided. The only facts that meant anything at this stage were the distances to be covered, and the times of start and finish. The two assistants, a man of fifty called Preston and a slightly younger woman called Royds, were pale with tiredness. Donald Sinclair finished his coffee with decision.

'You two look all in,' he said. 'It's been a long day and a hard one, and I thank you both very much indeed. I suggest we all dine in our rooms tonight, at our own pace. That way nobody will feel any pressure to be sociable, will they? Miss Parker, though, I must ask for one last effort. There are two or three things I have to check and understand before the morning. Look – perhaps we'd better have a shower first, and freshen up? Could you come to my room in forty minutes, say? It won't take very long.'

Miss Parker, tiredly, agreed, and the party, with wan goodnights and more marvelling at the terrifying energy of the Americans, split up. Donald Sinclair was sitting at his desk when Judith Parker tapped on his door. He called that it was open, and she came in.

Sinclair was in a swivel chair, and as she approached him, still in her severe grey suit, he turned himself away from the kneehole desk and stretched his legs in front of him. Without a word, Miss Parker knelt between his thighs and unzipped his fly. She must just have cleaned her teeth because her mouth, as it closed gently over his erection, was cool. The contrast was delicious. Sinclair rolled his head back, his eyes closed.

'Ah, Christ,' he sighed. 'That's lovely.'

NINE

Unlike her lover, Sarah Williams had never had a moment's doubt about whether she was in love or not. As she picked her way down the muddy bank onto the towpath of the Oxford Canal, her only uncertainty was that she could bear it for much longer. Since she had seen him last, she had lost three pounds and slept appallingly. Just now, driving down the narrow country roads, she had passed a tractor on a near-blind bend and narrowly been missed by a milk-tanker. She did not care. She would not have cared, she thought, if she and her little car had been crushed to scrap.

Since the cold snap had ended, the spring had become progressively more lovely. But Sarah, who lived alone in a small country house left her by her parents, had hardly noticed the change. It was only sixteen miles to Michael Masters' house from hers, and it had been like a magnet to her. She had stopped going into London to her work, she had stopped talking to her friends, she had stopped everything. Four or five times, since he had gone away, she had driven to the outskirts of his land, and had switched the engine off, and sat and watched the house, half-hidden in the trees. She had been aware of the stupidity of it all, but she had not been able to stop.

Sarah worked for a publisher in London, one of the few small independents as yet not gobbled up by the conglomerates. She was not short of money, and did not need to work, but that apart, nobody minded much if she was absent. She had phoned to say she was unwell, but nobody believed her. It was well known that Sarah was in love with a married man, and most of the women there were sympathetic. The one man who mattered, the managing director, was half in love with her himself, and hoped that one day she would respond to him emotionally, as once he had thought she was going to. He was married, naturally, but that seemed unimportant. To be fair to him, Sarah too had gone quite blithely and with open eyes into her love affair with Masters. It was the done thing, it was normal, it did no harm to anybody. She knew much better now.

She had met him – appalling cliché of London literary life – at a launch party for some book or other. It had been in that time, post Big Bang, when everyone was talking money with a capital M, the sexiest thing around. Sarah, whose family had always had it, found it boring and a trifle vulgar, with the rash of plays and books on how to be an instant millionaire, how to disguise pathological greed as business acumen, how to judge the emptiness of someone's soul by the fullness of their wallet, basically uninteresting. In the giant crush in Michelin House she had stood alone after a while, munching quails' eggs and sipping champagne, bored stupid. She had probably been looking at Michael Masters' face for five full minutes before it registered. He was gazing at her from beside a display cabinet, and he was smiling. As Sarah jerked her brain back to the present, he began to move towards her.

'Oh God,' she thought. 'He thinks this is a come-on. He thinks I was staring at him. Transfixed with his beauty.'

Michael Masters was beautiful, of that there was no doubt. He was tall and tousled and self-confident. She had a moment of panic. Was he the fêted author? But no, he looked too bright for that. Too human. When he reached her, she put on a smile. That, she supposed, was what she was being paid to do.

'Hallo,' she said. 'Sorry about the manic stare. I was miles away.'

'Snap,' said Michael Masters. 'What were you thinking of?'

'Oh. Well – well, actually I was thinking of my canal boat. I'm going away on her this weekend, and I'm having trouble with my injector. At least, I think I am. There seems to be a leak in the seating. I don't think it's serious.'

To the man in front of her, it might have been the most natural subject in the world at a literary launch. He bent his head down towards her, because the room was very noisy and she was rather short.

'Only one injector?' he said. 'What engine is it? Volvo Penta?'

'Sabb. Eight horse. It's very good. Very economical.'

He lifted his head back into the clouds and drained his glass. Sarah liked the way the muscles in his neck stretched. He leaned past her to put the glass down on a shelf.

'I know them,' he replied. 'Good engine. Where's the nearest bottle, any idea?'

Sarah was a little disappointed. After that unusual opener, he was trying to get away. She was not that disappointed though. After all, he didn't look much like a diesel fitter.

'I could get you one,' she said. 'I'm meant to be here officially, although it's not my office. We've got an interest in this book. Rights of some sort. You could have mine, in fact. I don't really want it.'

'Thanks,' he said. And took it. He swallowed half of it in one mouthful. He rolled it round his tongue.

'I like champagne,' he said. 'It's one of the great things about being rich.'

Oy oy, thought Sarah. Here we go. But she kept her features in control. They stood in silence for a moment. Then Masters said: 'Do you know what I was thinking? Watching you?'

'No.'

'I was thinking how much I'd like to eat your pussy. Sorry, it must be the surroundings. It's a literary reference.'

'Yes,' said Sarah, levelly. 'You must be older than you look, you patronising git. *Portnoy's Complaint*.'

They erupted simultaneously into laughter.

'It's the only line I remember,' he said. 'That and fucking the family dinner. Talking of which, how about it? The dinner I mean, of course.' He dipped his head abruptly, and read the badge pinned above her left breast. 'Ms Sarah Williams.'

He did not ask if she were married or engaged or attached, he probably didn't give a toss what she replied. Sarah, quite definitely, thought it would be very nice, Portnoy or no Portnoy. They became lovers the following Tuesday night. By the weekend, she was lost.

Standing in the sunshine beside her boat, *Cynthia's Beam*, Sarah Williams knew that she was truly lost now, more alone than she had ever known was possible. During the years of the affair there had been bad times, inevitably, times of anger, hatred and despair. Michael had insisted on ground rules, and some of them had been emotionally disastrous for her. Complete secrecy for one, which was based, he said, on the simple facts of his life and how he made his living. For him, as for Iago, reputation had been everything, worth all his other skills and cleverness. The bitterest thing, for Sarah, was that when he had been arrested, then charged, then convicted, his loss of reputation did not apparently matter in the slightest. In her bleakest moments, she suspected that the secrecy was a convenience. If nobody knew about her – except as a casual fuck, which naturally would have been entirely unexceptionable – he would never have to undergo the embarrassment of complete acknowledgement. The concomitant of that was the awful question: did he love her? London was full of mistresses, and she knew many of them. For all of them the equation was the same, for all of them unstated: he stays with his wife whatever he might say – he must prefer her. She did not believe it, but she did. Beside the canal, alone, she could believe anything.

In the end, Sarah had to force herself to get the keys out and open up the boat. There were other boats nearby, owned by people who knew her, and for all she knew she had been standing motionless for hours. She felt in the pocket of her short blue jacket and opened the side door. She dropped through the hatchway, into the doghouse that contained the engine casing and her tools and junk, then unlocked the communicating door. The main cabin was warm, and shaded by the drawn-to curtains. The double bed was unmade, rumpled from the day before he had gone away. She could see him lying there, grinning as she passed him gin and tonic. Tears slowly filled her eyes.

Sarah had received a letter from Masters that morning. The joy when she had seen his handwriting had nearly choked her. The letter, when she had steadied her hands sufficiently to spread it out, had been like a bucket of icy water. She had read it quickly, then slowly, then line by line. It was empty. It was a letter from a stranger. The only note of intimacy was a reference to the boat. Which was why, against her better judgement, she had come.

Sarah, her eyes wiped, sat on the bed and took the letter from the inside pocket of her jacket. It was written on lined paper, yellowish and cheap, of a type she had imagined had disappeared with the sixpenny exercise books of her childhood. It had a prison number written in the corner, and it was sixteen lines long.

'Dear Sarah,' it said. *'I'm sorry not to have been in touch before, but as you can imagine, things have been pretty hectic and confusing. I've never been so disoriented in my life, although I have to say everybody has been very fair to me, and things "inside" are not as bad as I expected. I'm sharing a cell with two other men, but I don't think I'm allowed to tell you what they are in for. They're both OK, however. They seem to accept me for the criminal that I am! (Joke). It would be very nice to see you sometime, although not easy, naturally. Twelve visits a year (thirty minutes plus) don't leave much hope with such a*

family as I suffer with! However – give my love to Cynthia (in person) please. I'd love to see her too. We have such memories, we three. Yours, Michael.'

The word *'yours'* was underlined, and reading it for perhaps the twentieth time, it finally occurred to Sarah that it was written with a censor in mind. She was filled with horror, then with rage. But surely not? Surely Michael had told her . . . ?

Yes, he had told her he would write, as soon as he got to prison and knew the form. And yes she could write back, long and passionate letters, he had said, that would give him something to get hold of . . . But that was the open prison, wasn't it? That was Ford. And he had gone to Bowscar, where presumably some goon . . . She was sickened. Could she write back? Would the same goon read her letters? How could she find out . . . ?

'Yours, Michael.' The words came into focus. Good God, couldn't he even admit her existence inside a jail? Couldn't he even say he loved her? Or would the censor think it rude? Or pruriently enjoy it? Or – oh Christ, she thought she'd guessed it. Or could it somehow be used against him?

Other words came into focus. *'Cynthia . . . I'd love to see her, too. We have such memories.'*

Slowly, a plan began to form in Sarah's mind. A mad plan, instantly dismissed. Then resurrected, looked at, turned over, tossed about.

She went to a shelf beside the iron stove and pulled out Nicholson's Guides to the Waterways. Bowscar was in Staffordshire, wasn't it? And Staffordshire had canals. She found the relevant volume and began leafing through. Excitement was mounting inside her. She'd take the boat to Bowscar. Well, near enough, she thought she could get within a mile or two.

Then somehow, *somehow* – he could see his Cynthia again. And his Sarah. And they'd see him.

For the first time in ages, Sarah Williams was hungry.

If Christopher Abbey had backed off a little, Masters might have dropped his plan to get his own back. When the emotional turmoil of the visit had died down, he recognised it would be easier, and probably more sensible, to revert to his old technique of acceptance and contempt. But Abbey, locked in his own confusion of greed, and envy and morality, kept the pressure on. The following day, on goon squad, Masters got particularly soiled from a bursting parcel of faeces he picked up. He was not allowed a shower, and as he washed, Abbey harassed him, verbally and physically, while his friends looked on.

It was after lunch that Masters raised the subject of revenge with Hughes and Jerrold. That amused him, because it was a conscious parody of the way he might have entered into business before the world of Bowscar. They had dined substantially, off thin tomato soup, spaghetti and chips, and a steamed pudding that had been injected with watered blackberry essence. Singularly – a city gent might have considered – it had all been consumed from one plate, a stainless steel compartment tray that one held out at the kitchen hot-plate for the regulation portions to be flopped upon it. Once upon a time, he had been told, the men would then have eaten it in some companionship in the dining halls. Nowadays, the pressure of numbers was far too great, and the number of staff (the POA insisted) far too small. The privilege of eating in a community had gone the way of other privileges in the Scar, like proper exercise, and education classes, and work. At mealtimes now, each man took his tray – heavy or light depending on whether the server liked, or loved, or owed, or hated him – back to his cell, along with a plastic mug of tea. The only thing missing was a glass of crusted port.

'Well,' he said. 'That was excellent. I think I'll just wander back to the office and have Miss Fairfax on the filing cabinet before I curl up for a kip. Before I do, though, I want to have somebody killed. Hughes – when you've finished your Stilton, of course – how does one go about that sort of thing?'

Hughes was rolling a cigarette. His packet of Golden Virginia was almost empty, and he was laying the tobacco strands along the inside of the paper.

'Hang about old chap,' he said, joining in the game. 'I'm just nipping the end of the old Corona. Are we serious, or is this some sort of joke?'

Jerrold was already back on his bed. He was less jovial.

'You forgetting the lesson, man. Ignore that twat. Abbey just fancies you, it'll pass. Ignore, guy.'

'Fancies! Jesus, Matt!'

'It's possible,' said Hughes. 'Doubtful, but possible. But the first part's right, though. You don't want to get Abbey knocked about. Do as we tell you. Listen to the experts. Let it ride.'

'You start going for revenge,' said Jerrold, 'and you'll end up crazy. Look at me. One wholly innocent man banged up for life. Do I complain?'

He laughed, richly and deeply. Of what he was charged, Masters now knew and believed, he was probably innocent. On the night of the riots he had been on the Buckingham Estate but he had killed no policeman. He had been convicted on confession evidence that would certainly not have withstood the scrutiny of the European courts, if Jerrold was the sort of man with the sort of lawyers who could get the case that far. His philosophy was that he was stuck with it, and if he ever got the chance he'd kill one next time, because of what they'd done to him, so that was fair enough. And was he crazy? The prison officers thought he was, and outside the cell he was a surly, dangerous presence whom very few dared speak to or approach. Masters was not sure.

He said to Alan Hughes: 'You don't let things ride. You're always causing trouble. You've got no remission left, you can't watch television, you can't associate. Jesus, Alan, you've seen the Board of Visitors so often it's a wonder they haven't co-opted you.'

Hughes was lighting his thin cigarette. The end flared, but he got two puffs from it before he nipped it out for later. He nodded.

'I do that for amusement,' he said. 'I've been in prison for six years and I don't suppose I'll ever get out, do you? I don't know that I want to. But us ex-*Guardian* readers need a bit of fun. A substitute for Araucaria. Being in prison's like being in a mental home for the sane. It's the system that's cracked, the system and the doctors. I like to play with it.'

'He's a liar,' Matthew Jerrold said. 'He cause trouble because he likes to show the fascists up. He always get in trouble protecting people, standing up for them. Screws call him the nigger-lover, but he'll stand up for anyone. No taste. He's indiscriminate. Last one was a black boy lose his cool when he discover all the best ganja come from the prison officers, when he just got six months for possession! They rough him up for being cheeky and Batman here step in. One bust tooth, one black eye, one good kicking. What he do? He complain the boy's been racially abused! Insane.'

Hughes said to Masters: 'That's exactly what I mean. The complaints procedure's the best game of the lot. You can end up petitioning the Home Secretary himself – I used to know him, incidentally – but only when you've been through all the channels. First channel – complain to a prison officer, tell him you need the form. Because one of his oppos has been tearing up the rules, I ask you!'

'Ah, but that's another thing,' put in Jerrold. 'We don't know the rules, neither. We know they exist, and we see some of them on notices, but we got no right to see them written down – that's a rule. Screw once say to me: Best way to find out if something 'gainst the rules, man, is to do it. I soon tell you if it is or not!'

Jerrold let out a rumble of a laugh. At the same time, he farted. Dead on time, thought Michael Masters. Pass the After Eights . . .

'If you do get past the screws to the Governor or the Board,' Hughes went on, 'the farce gets funnier. Because Rule 47, Section 12 says if you can't *prove* that this officer did what you say he did – and you can imagine how easy it is to get a witness in this place, can't you? – you've made "a false and malicious complaint". Which means instead of him getting punished *you* do, although it's not a punishment it's an *award*, which if you've got the sense you'll thank them for. If you want to carry on the case, and they don't stop you in your tracks with Section 16, you can write to a solicitor, or your MP, or the Home Secretary himself, except that they read your letters in case you're telling lies about them which is not allowed. It's some catch, that Catch 22. It's the best there is.'

After a few moments, Masters said: 'Alan. I don't know you well enough to be certain if you're joking. If getting kicked in the mouth to relieve the boredom works for you, fair enough. But just hypothetically, if I wanted to get Chris Abbey killed, or smashed about a bit, could I do it? Without taking the blame, naturally.'

'Oh naturally,' said Jerrold. 'You're a millionaire, ain't you?'

Hughes inserted his tiny cigarette into his mouth and struck a match. He hunched himself forward.

'Look Mike,' he said. 'You can do anything in here when you know the ropes. You can shoot heroin, smoke dope, sniff cocaine. You can buy a gobble from a con any time you like and a prison officer if you pick your man and moment. You can fuck, you can drink, you can watch porno movies, you can even use the telephone. There are networks, there are undercurrents, there are little businesses. Everything works in fractions. A fraction of the screws are corrupt, a fraction are fascist morons; most of them are ciphers with a chip on their shoulder about how *they* get treated, never mind the lags. A fraction of the cons are gangsters, a fraction do the gangsters' business for them, a fraction are the victims. Most of them are nothing. Pathetic little no ones, soft as shit or hard as nails, the matrix. You could get power in here quite easily, you're the type. You're even too intelligent to try and fight for it. You'd do deals, spend money, make alignments. I can see you now, you and Brian Rogers, kings of the Scar. You could get Chris Abbey's best friends to beat him up within a fortnight, no problem. But what's the use? That sort of power's got nothing that you'd ever want. Your power's outside this nightmare. Your power's in the real world. The only thing you can't get in this place, my friend, is out. And that's where you want to be.'

There was a creak, as Jerrold rolled heavily onto his side. His face was serious.

'Tell him about the escape plan, man,' he said. 'Let's enrol him on the old committee.'

A look of irritation crossed Hughes' face. He shook his head, and spoke to Masters.

'*Boy's Own Paper*,' he said. 'Matthew's being childish. There's no escape committee. It's a game we play. An intellectual exercise.'

Jerrold grinned. He rolled back out of sight.

'I the intellectual,' he said. 'You got to believe it, Mike.'

But Masters was not interested. For two convicted murderers, he could not imagine a pair less likely to be the brains behind a break-out. He had more concrete leads to follow up.

'Who's Brian Rogers?' he asked. 'Should I have heard of him?'

Hughes picked wet paper from his lower lip. He seemed to be considering.

'You don't smoke, you don't shoot up, you're not an alcoholic, you keep your nose clean. No, I suppose it's possible. He's one of the big boys. He runs the place. The unofficial governor.' He chuckled. 'Poor old Pendlebury,' he said. 'If he had half the control over his staff that Rogers does! He might be able to get you to a phone.'

'Mm,' said Masters. He aimed for casualness, but Hughes' eyes had narrowed with amusement.

'Mm,' he mimicked. 'I thought that would interest you. Mm.'

'Did you really know the Home Secretary?' Masters said. Hughes was full of tricks. Or mysteries. 'Or is that another . . . drollery?'

'Oh no, I knew him. He wasn't Home Secretary then, of course. He wasn't even "Sir". Gerald Turner. I used to live just down the road. Me and my wife. My second wife.'

Hughes had killed his wife, so Masters understood. The subject, so far, had not been broached. Hughes' gaze was steady.

'I often think it would be interesting to have a little talk to him,' he said. 'About the prisons, life inside, morality, crime and retribution. You know, stuff like that. I imagine you wouldn't mind a little tête à tête, yourself.'

'How do you mean?'

'Well, we have the radio,' said Hughes. 'Two wavebands only, according to the Act! I occasionally see the newspapers. I got the impression that Sir Gerald got you into here. Had a word beneath their lordships' wigs or somesuch. Probably just a nasty rumour . . .'

'Yeah,' said Michael Masters. 'Yes. Maybe I will have a chat about it some day. My wife can ask him to dinner. How do I get in touch with Rogers?'

Alan Hughes sighed.

'Revenge or telephone?'

Masters considered.

'I want the telephone,' he said. 'The rest depends. It's Abbey's smile that interests me. I'd quite like somebody to take it off his face. And tread on it.'

'I think I ought to warn you,' said Alan Hughes. 'About currency. The basic units in this place are sex, drugs, tobacco, money, information, promises. You're a millionaire. If we showed you the ropes you'd have no trouble getting currency. But smiles interest Brian Rogers a lot as well. And bodies. He's not precisely short of cash.'

Indeed, as they were talking, Brian Rogers had just taken delivery of a present. His door had been opened, and it had been pushed inside. The door had been locked, the spyhole closed.

It was Cherry Orchard.

The problems of secrecy, of running a clandestine affair, had never given Judith Parker pause for thought. As the Bureau of Prisons limousine swept her along the busy freeway to the airport, she watched the back of Donald Sinclair's head, turned in conversation with Myra Fischer. He was very sexy, certainly. But he was a politician, and he was a star ascending. That was the important thing.

Judith, at twenty-six, was very pleased at the way her career was shaping up. She had taken the not abnormal route to mainstream, rightish orthodoxy by a basic grounding in left-wing student activism. Three years as a national officer of the union had given her both a taste for power and an awareness of the debilitating effects of believing in things too much. She graduated brilliantly – to the amazement of all her friends, who thought she had been much too busy with the important things to work – then shocked them even more by walking into a House of Commons job, at the heart of the system she despised. When it suited her, Judith argued that she was acting as a sleeper, or a mole, but she did not keep up the pretence for long. Within six months the early chapters of her life were firmly closed. She neither saw nor spoke to any of her old acquaintances.

Many people, both inside and outside, had warned her vociferously about the Palace of Westminster. It was, some said, a gigantic rest-home for several hundred men and some token women with massive egos and tiny intellects. Others likened it to a kind of whorehouse, where drunken oafs debauched young women like herself while their wives and children suffered in silence back at home. But Judith believed in politics – despite the high percentage of the feckless and the witless in the place – and she loved the sexual undercurrents. It seemed wholly fitting to her that she should be able to locate and target some suitable male – and hitch her star to him. She did it only once, because she knew the fate of beautiful and brilliant young hopefuls who thought that they could play the field at leisure, and she chose extremely carefully. It was a bonus that Donald Sinclair's lust for power gave her a lust for him.

Seducing politicians, she knew, was very easy. There was a vast number of good-looking, smart young women in the Palace, and most of them, whether they realised it or not, were there to get a man. Almost all MPs were married, because perceived morality deemed it necessary, and many of them – especially the homosexuals – were desperately unhappy in the state. Further, the aphrodisiac of power worked both ways. Even the ugly, hopeless, stupid ones felt attractive because of their positions, and dared to tilt at false bastions of virtue which – miraculously! – fell. Judith was more rigorous. This atmosphere of the knocking-shop, the knowledge of all these rather mediocre men and women finding solace and fulfilment of a kind, she found distasteful. When she and Donald finally went to bed together, it was unmessy, mentally and physically. They both intended to keep it that way.

In a way, they had. It was a matter of some satisfaction to her that in the office, in the bars and eating places of the House and its environs, nobody, however closely involved in work they were, had ever suspected anything. Even on this trip, with Julian Preston and Yvonne Royds staying in the same hotels, there had been neither the slightest hint nor the smallest suspicion. Some of the guards in the prisons they had so far visited, and many of the inmates, had clearly found her severe, stitched up English elegance provoking. But side by side with her boss, the laid-back Englishman, she had not been taken for his sexual partner.

An hour later, then, when they had taken a formal farewell from the formidable Ms Fischer and were relaxing over dry martinis as their Boeing 747 flew them west, they were able to sit side by side in the deep loungers and discuss their experiences so far with an easy intimacy they knew would not be correctly interpreted by their harassed aides. So far, they had visited seven jails, and the picture they were building up was fascinating. As in most things, America's scale of operations was bizarre, unreal, absurdist.

'It's the money I can't get over,' said Sinclair. 'The cash they're pouring in. Imagine a system where the prisoners can sue you if you put them in an overcrowded jail! We'd be bankrupt in two months! And the cells. You've got to admit it, some of the cells we've seen weren't as bad as some hotels I've stayed in!'

'Not much good for a dirty weekend though. I thought the individual stainless steel lavatories were rather chic, but having one wall made of iron bars did spoil the effect, rather!'

He laughed.

'It's a good example of the lunacy of it all though, isn't it? They've poured cash in, they've built hundreds of new jails, and the crime rate's rocketing. What's more, they admit it! Myra works for the government, and she says quite freely it's a disaster. Rum.'

'What's so rum about that?' teased Judith. 'Isn't that what you're always telling everyone?'

He raised his eyebrows.

'Some damn hopes,' he said. 'After Buckie I was allowed to be critical as a counterpoint, the voice of reason and humanity. Normally, anything that might make life easier in prisons has got to be presented as a crackdown. The law of propaganda as expounded by Velma Goodman. She's right as well.'

'Thank God for that! I was beginning to think you were going soft on me!'

He grinned.

'I'll pay you back for that,' he said. 'I'll be as soft as I need to be, just like I was at Buckie. In any case, it's not exactly what you do that counts, it's how it gets perceived. Look at Gerald Turner. He knocks off civil liberties like other men kill lice, and people call him liberal. He's in a great tradition, granted. The Cabinet of Cowards, jumping when the PM blinks. Secrets Act, tagging, the right to silence, immigration, jury vetting, you wouldn't have believed it ten years back. And good old Gerald sails his boat and drives his Merc and everybody says he's such a nice chap, so damned civilised. Even Mary, who ought to know better. She thinks he's wonderful.'

He caught a glint in Judith's eye, and knew he had transgressed. There was a rule when they were alone or intimate. Mary was not mentioned. He tried to cover.

'Mark you,' he said, 'I don't think Gerald plays the game because he's brilliant or anything. I think he's weak, he's like a weather vane, so he's bound to seem amiable. If liberality ever became an albatross round his neck he'd probably be stuck with it. I wouldn't though. If I could reform the system it would be the most fantastic coup. But I'm not going to improve the lot of fifty thousand criminals if I end up on the scrapheap doing it, believe me! That's not the plan at all.'

That night, although he came into her room, Sinclair did not pay her back as he had threatened to – she paid him. She lay passively beneath him as he made love to her, and she thought about his wife. She felt his body coldly, and tried hard to despise him. He would never leave his home, she knew. Mary Sinclair – Mary Bacon as had been – was the power behind his throne, the wealth, the breeding, the connections, and Donald was a man who knew with utter clarity which side his bread was buttered on. But she would never want him to move out, she told herself, for she was using him in her turn, he was her vehicle. In many ways, she had the upper hand.

For Judith did have hopes, inevitably. Above all she was politically ambitious. One day, in her scheme of things, she would be recognised – probably through her work with Donald – and would be given a seat to contest and win. Whatever other reasons she might have for not rocking his boat, that one was paramount. Everybody knew what happened to political mistresses who made waves. Even if they were abandoned, pregnant and publicly betrayed, they could expect no quarter. The forces of darkness, in their familiar disguise as the forces of light, would be mobilised, and the woman would be destroyed, humiliated.

When Donald Sinclair had come and she, conspicuously, had not, Judith pushed him off her and carried on the punishment. It was petty but not unsatisfying, she was in total, cold, control.

'Do you still do it?' she said, lying rigid on her back. 'With Mary? I suppose you do.'

'Not very often,' said Sinclair, truthfully. 'One has to, doesn't one? But it's not very good. I don't enjoy it very much.'

The sudden stab of pain shook Judith. It was not in the game.

'Not even as good as *that*?' she said, sarcastically.

'Nothing like as good as that,' he said. 'I don't think she actually likes me very much.'

'What?' She opened her eyes. 'What are you talking about?'

'I think she thinks I'm a bit corrupt,' said Donald Sinclair. 'Funny, isn't it?'

Judith closed her eyes again.

'Well, aren't you?' she said quietly.

On his journey to Brian Rogers' cell, Raymond Orchard had been left in little doubt about what lay in store for him. The prison officers, whose rampant homophobia did not stop them grabbing parts of him and squeezing them, and fondling his bottom and his thighs, had been quite ecstatic. Apparently, they said, Rogers had spotted him on association and been excited by his appearance. This, to Orchard, would have been amazing, except that his capacity to be surprised was by now diminishing hourly. His face was cut and battered, his hair had almost gone – partly pulled out in handfuls by other prisoners, the rest shorn off in self-defence – and his clothes were torn and soiled. When he had entered Bowscar Prison, Raymond Orchard had been an actively politicised gay – homosexual and proud of it. Now, still untried for any crime let alone convicted, he was an emotional wreck, with cuts, bruises and abrasions thrown in. He did not know the ins and outs of Rule 43 yet, which might have saved him pain and trouble, he did not know the rules at all, although he was often said to be in breach of them. He had written seven letters out, which had been refused on grounds of censorship which the prison officers would not explain. He had received none, on the same grounds. They had told him, with satisfaction, that they had returned eleven.

Orchard – Cherry, universally, to officers and inmates alike – had been exotic. He was tall and thin, and had worn his clothes proudly, like a model or a star. Even on the gay rights march he had stood out, and he had taken no filth or sarcasm from the police. Consequently, he had been arrested and charged with assault and other things. It was nothing new, and he was glad in some ways that it was him. He was clever and articulate, politically aware, and capable of impressing even magistrates who hated queers like poison. He knew he would probably be acquitted, and he knew he could show the police to have been lying, he had done it all before. Because of this, perhaps, they did it properly. They planted a cut-throat razor on him – how wonderfully archaic, he laughed at first – and a package of cocaine. He was remanded in custody before he had time to blink – and ended up in Bowscar.

Raymond Orchard did not have Aids. More precisely, he was not HIV positive, and neither was his lover Kevin Clarke. Where Orchard was exotic, Kevin tended to the prosaic. He liked motorcycles and swimming, and holidays abroad. They had been together for six years, and since the Aids scare, had sworn an oath of sexually exclusive loyalty, on a hill in Lancashire. They were in love.

Now, Raymond Orchard faced his fate. His back was to the door that had been locked behind him, and his upper arms were being gripped by two strong inmates. In front of him stood Brian Rogers. He was taking off his clothes.

Orchard did not know what to say. The sickness in his stomach was so enormous that he dared not open his mouth. But had he done so, he would still have been speechless. He did not know what to say.

Rogers was a big man, with a face that seemed intelligent despite a domed, bald skull protruding from a mass of lank, long hair that reached his shoulders. His chin was heavy, stubbled black, and his stomach, as he exposed it, was fat but powerful, with black hair rising from his pubis to his navel. His penis was large, half-erect, and throbbing rhythmically, gaining size and height. When he stood naked, the men holding Orchard began to take his trousers off. He hunched forward, white and nauseous, as if to protect himself. But he did not try to resist. They pulled his shirt up his back, also wordless, and bent him across the bare pine table. One of them clamped a hand across his mouth as Rogers thrust his penis into him, to stop him crying out.

After Rogers, one of the other men raped Orchard. Because he was weeping, the third man, who apparently did not care for sex like that, was allowed to beat him up a bit. Then Rogers, pulling out his shaking hand, put a packet of dope into it, and a box of matches and some Rizla. Outside, the officers could be heard, preparing to unlock the door.

'Dry your eyes, you silly fucking poof,' said Rogers. 'It was only a bit of fun.'

They were the only words that had been spoken in the cell.

TEN

The first breakthrough for Forbes and Rosanna came three days after they had gone back to Scotland – although at first Forbes failed to spot its full significance. A seventeen-year-old chambermaid – English – identified a photograph of Donald Sinclair that he showed her. She had recognised him on the TV news the day after the prison siege had ended, she said, and had wondered why, as a hotel guest, he had been called Mr Philip Swift. When she had mentioned this to the under manager, though, she had been sworn to secrecy and given a ten-pound bonus. A woman reporter had come round snooping later, she had been told, but she had not seen her.

The conversation took place in a small café on the other side of Buckie, and Forbes had already paid the girl fifteen pounds. They both laughed about the legendary meanness of the Scots, and Andrew had given her another fiver to go on talking.

'Really,' she said, 'it's not the money. I mean, I was a bit insulted that they thought I needed bribing to shut up, I'm a loyal employee, aren't I? He was only up here for the night. He never came out of his room in daylight.'

'How do you like it up here?' asked Andrew, sympathetically. 'Are you London? It's a bit quiet, isn't it, Christine?'

'Like the grave,' replied Chris Richards. 'Croydon. That's where I'm from. I mean, that's another thing. They're not only dead mean, they're dead boring, aren't they? I don't like it here, it was a big mistake. I won't be staying long. I don't feel I'm doing wrong, telling you. They've not been nice to me.'

God save me from whingeing children, thought Andrew Forbes. What did she expect in the wilds of north-east Scotland? Never mind. The girl had done him proud.

'So you don't know much else?' he said. 'You only saw him two or three times, and he'd left before you started in the morning? There haven't been any rumours, have there? Since the siege?'

'What sort of rumours? About Mr Sinclair?'

'About anything. No tales of prisoners falling off roofs or anything? No bodies smuggled out of prison in the dead of night?'

She was regretful.

'No. Nothing like that. It's not likely, is it? The trouble was, they finished it at night. They could've sent the Scotch Guards in, kilts and bagpipes the lot, and no one would've noticed, they go to bed at ten o'clock. I mean it! I go out with fellers sometimes. Nothing steady. And they take me back at ten o'clock! Sometimes it isn't even dark. Oh God, it's so boring. You just wouldn't believe how boring they are up here.'

Driving back to Glasgow in Rosanna's Renault, Forbes thought on balance he agreed with Christine over that. He had been in the town for two days, and he had learned nothing of value at all until he had picked the girl up as she left the Fox Hotel on her afternoon off. The locals, now the siege was over, were uninterested, almost embarrassed by the memory. Most of them appeared to handle the presence of the jail by pretending it was somewhere else, that it had nothing to do with them. He had spoken to tradesmen, launderers, the wives of prison officers, people in bars – to no avail. Some knew things and could or would not say. But the attitude of most was that there had been some trouble, it was over, and please God there'd be no more. The place should never have been built there in the first place.

Rosanna had already gone to bed when Forbes got back, but she got up and put a robe on when she heard his key in the lock. She entered the kitchen to the sharp hiss and click of a ring-pull.

'You didn't ring,' she said. 'Was that bone idleness, or did you find out something for my ears only?'

He told her, and Rosanna's eyes lit up. She got a can of Stella from the fridge. She raised it in a toast.

'Congratulations,' she said, half-seriously. 'The hand of the master where the feeble apprentice failed. That's fantastic. Look, come through to the bedroom. My feet are cold.'

Forbes followed her through to the big, bare room at the front. He watched her jump into the empty bed with regret. She did not invite him in. He pushed her clothes off the chair and sat. He took a pull of beer.

'Well,' he said, 'it's not fantastic but it's something. Another little coffin nail.' He was feeling drained. 'How have you got on?'

'Hold on! Hold on! Surely it's more than that? I know it's a hell of a drive from Buckie, Andrew, but surely . . . Well, I mean, that's enormous, isn't it? The man was lying. A minister of the Crown! You've found him out!'

He nodded.

'According to Christine Richards, fine. But what does it add up to? I've told you before, none of this means anything until it's solid enough for somebody to print it. We need proof.'

'Proof!' said Rosanna, heatedly. 'I think you're being really downbeat. We've got the chambermaid, a name. And the false one Sinclair used as well. For God's sake, let's at least hit the swine with that.'

A small smile crossed his face.

'He's abroad. Who'll pay our fares?' He sighed. 'In any case, has he broken any law? If he didn't just deny it, he'd call it a precaution, he travelled incognito. What's wrong with that?'

'Nonsense! It's a serious embarrassment, he's been lying through his teeth! And if he's abroad he can't deny it, can he – even better! What about the register? Did you look?'

He shook his head.

'What for? To read the name Philip Swift? Where does that get us?' He upended the can into his mouth and swallowed several times. 'You know,' he said, 'it's the Army angle that still intrigues me most. I wonder what their game was with the drug tale and the rest of it. If there was just a way of cracking that.'

Rosanna was getting angry. She was quite red.

'We spent two days in Hereford and two hundred quid in information money, didn't we?' she snapped. 'For what? Your SAS contact couldn't even tell us it was them, or wouldn't. A real no-no.'

Andrew crushed his empty can.

'That's the way it goes,' he said. 'That trail's a dead'un, realistically. Unless we get another call. Look, I'm not saying the Buckie lead's not a good one. We might be able to frighten something out of them with it. We'll think tomorrow. But we need the Animal. He's the only next of kin. We can ask about Wee Jimmy until we're blue in the face. You have. And they don't even have to answer.'

Rosanna put her half-empty tin of Stella on the floor.

'Andrew,' she said. 'You're a constant wonder to me, so you are. You get the goods in one fell swoop, and you think you've got damn all. They refuse to answer all my questions, but the man in charge is Donald Sinclair. Nothing happened at Buckie, they assure us, but the man who wasn't there was Donald Sinclair. Don't you see it? Somehow or other he's involved, he's got the answers. And if he *was* there, when Jimmy McGregor got knocked off – Jesus Christ! No wonder he denies it! I say tomorrow we go and talk to Maurice Campbell, try and get it in the paper. This chambermaid. Is she pretty? Would she make a picture?'

Andrew actually laughed.

'Sordid cow!' he said. 'The language of the gutter press!' He made a rueful face. 'No, is she buggery, she's 'orrible.'

'But is it worth a try? With Maurice?'

Forbes thought. He scratched his forehead with the empty can.

'Realistically,' he said, 'there's nothing that he'll use. You don't risk everything on the ramblings of a spotty adolescent. We'll go and see him, though, have a drink, remind him we exist, he's a bloody useful contact. You're right to bollock me, I'm getting stupid, potentially it's terrific. Another thing we'll do is hunt down Rafferty. We've *got* to find the Animal.'

Rosanna looked gloomy.

'I spoke to him today. Completely drunk. Is there no way we can follow up that trail ourselves?'

'Now who's being defeatist? Adrian Rafferty is brilliant, when he's sober. And short of going up to every jail in England and shouting through the keyhole, we've got no chance, without him. We'll hunt him down, and sober him up, and bribe him. How about a feel of arse till payday?'

'For Adrian or you? Either way, it's no. Oh Andrew! We will get somewhere, won't we? It's not just all a lousy waste of time?'

Andrew Forbes stood. Rosanna was very tiny in the big, square bed. Small, and tousled, and troubled. Very carefully, he did not step towards her.

'Of course we will,' he said. 'We'll bowl out in the morning, and we'll sock 'em dead. In the meantime, I'm exhausted, you're fed up, so this is absolutely and completely the wrong time to ask you: can I sleep with you tonight?'

Her small face lit into a smile.

'Fuck off,' she said. 'I've told you, Andrew. I'm a wee Scot with a hang-up about sex.'

'I don't believe you. Anyway, I'm very good at therapy.'

'Aye, I'm very sure you are. Now go to bed. You can take this tin of beer if you like. I've touched it with my lips!'

Next morning, on a whim, Rosanna went to the public call box nearby in Hyndland Road and rang the Fox Hotel in Buckie. Christine Richards, she was told, did not work there any more. She had gone away to London, they believed.

* * *

The latent violence in Bowscar Prison exploded, surprisingly, around Raymond Orchard. It started as the extension of the normal taunts and insults that he suffered, and, for the taunters it came from nowhere. They knew he had been raped, but they did not think he would react so violently. It was, they after all assumed, what he really wanted, wasn't it?

The incident happened on the B-floor sluice, when Orchard was slopping out. He was seen to be walking oddly as he approached, which in itself was cause enough for hoots and catcalls. When it was his turn to empty the contents of his bucket, the chorus became louder.

'Let's see the turds, Cherry!' shouted one prisoner. 'They reckon Brian Rogers has got a triangular dick, is that right? Have you been shitting pyramids?'

Orchard gritted his teeth and took the lid off the bucket. Since the incident, two days before, he had been in considerable pain. He had also lost a fair amount of blood.

'Did you hear about the poof that went to the doctor with Aids?' said a prison officer. He was standing in the sluice-room doorway, as far away as he could be from the reeking drains and lavatory bowls. 'The doctor told him to go away and eat as much hot curry as he could, vindaloo, then drink a dozen pints of beer and take a laxative.'

Orchard, who had heard all the foul jokes a thousand times, looked at the contents of his bucket. It was a quarter full of urine, and of faeces streaked with blood. He had visited the prison medical officer the day before, and received as little sympathy.

'Why's that Doc? says the poof,' the prison officer continued. 'Will it cure my Aids?' He started laughing. 'No, he says, will it fuck as like. But it'll show you what your arsehole's really for!'

Quite unexpectedly, to him as well as everybody else, Raymond Orchard swung the bucket sideways, grabbing at its bottom as he did so. Wild-eyed, he turned towards the doorway, to the crowds of laughing men. The prison officer, realising instantly what was going to happen, jumped sideways. He trod hard on the foot of a man who had just entered, who had not joined the laughter, who did not appear to understand what was going on. It was Charles Lister.

As Lister lashed out at the officer, the contents of the bucket hit them in their chests and faces, spraying half a dozen other men. Outside, the bouncing bucket hit another in the mouth and drove two teeth into his lip, before it clattered over the iron railing of the balcony and landed in the suicide nets. Prisoners two floors below watched the liquid dripping down, saw the furious tussle, and cheered.

The reactions of the men inside the sluice were quite irrational. Because Orchard was gay, because there was blood, they knew there must be Aids. But even those who had not been flecked attacked him, and then each other. They were out to kill, and in the mêlée they were smeared, and punched, and cut.

The prison staff were quick off the mark. Within seconds, three officers who had been close to start with, as back-up for the officer at the door, were pounding along the gallery to protect their colleague and assess the situation. Other prisoners who had already slopped out stood about uncertainly, their reactions slower. If it was a bit of fun, fair enough, they would join in. But it was a dangerous game. If you got caught up in trouble, it could cost you very dear. The thundering of boots up iron stairs, the clanging of the alarm bell when it started, mesmerised some of them. Before they had recovered, officers were bundling them through their cell doors, quickly, urgently, and locking them with relief. Once inside, though, many had an immediate reaction. They became wild with fury, started crashing about. Men who had been standing at their doors, wondering what was going on, found themselves attacked, or pressed themselves into corners while their cell-mates wrecked the place.

On paper, the officer to inmate ratio in the Scar was quite good. But because of overtime restrictions, court escort duties, sickness and so on, the position in reality was never so favourable as it looked. In any case, the call on manpower when things got out of hand was horrendous. The first priority, the vital, overwhelming necessity, was to get the prisoners in their cells. But where in normal circumstances it was usually a formality, when trouble started each prisoner might need one officer, or two, or a small army. It depended on the level of excitement, and the level of preplanning.

The alarms themselves caused problems. Although the flare-up was on B-floor of D-hall, the bells were audible all over the prison. Officers peacefully going about their duties on other galleries found themselves confronted with suddenly animated, inquisitive, nervous men – whom they had to guide back to their doorways and bang up, abruptly and with no adequate explanation. Instead of the number of colleagues noticeably increasing in case of need, they noticeably decreased, as principal officers detailed extra men to D-hall by internal telephone. And the bells were not the worst. They triggered in the men a weird, harsh roar, an amalgam at first of cheers and shouting, that gained its own momentum. Even when the alarms were switched off, the throbbing cry continued.

For men already locked into their cells, like Masters, Hughes and Jerrold, the sounds induced mixed reactions. For Masters, strangely, the overriding one was fear. As the bells began, as the shouts and screams increased, his mouth grew dry, his stomach tense. Jerrold, on his bunk as usual, played Joe Cool, but his eyes betrayed him. Alan Hughes, seated at the table, leaned forward, his breath coming much faster.

In the next few minutes Masters, for the first time in his life, experienced claustrophobia. It was extraordinary, he thought, that they could be so intimately involved in something, and have no sight of it at all, no perception other than through their ears. The cell became smaller in his mind, the walls moved in, the ceiling and the floor began to crush him, suffocate him. He had to get out. It was impossible to be locked in so small a space. He had to *know*.

'What's going on?' he said. His voice had thickened, and he cleared his throat. 'What's happening?'

Alan Hughes walked over to the door. He took the knob and shook at it.

'Christ knows,' he said. 'It's a riot of some sort. Christ knows.'

There could be anything out there. What if the prison went on fire? What if it was on fire, this was not a riot? Would they all be burned to death? Locked up like rats? Masters sank his face into his hands, seated on his bed. He had to know.

For the governor, the disturbance meant extreme and unexpected danger. Ten minutes before, he had been conducted into Angus McGregor's isolation cell by his spaceman escort, to continue the dialogue he had been trying to establish. As the days had passed and his hopes of getting any information, let alone a genuine response, from the Prison Department had dwindled, he had been well aware that the dialogue was at best lop-sided. As his creativity in expressing hopeful signs had diminished, so had McGregor's willingness to talk at all. Today, after a half a dozen grunts, he had come out with only this: 'I don't want to talk about it. I don't want to talk about anything. Except my brother.' Momentarily, his eyes had gleamed. Then they had dulled, almost glazed. The deadness, which was becoming rapidly a characteristic of his expression, Pendlebury found horrifying.

When the noise of the alarm bells erupted through the jail, McGregor responded like a wild animal. His head jerked backwards and his eyes widened. The shoulders, which had taken on a slumped, acquiescent form, braced back, while his hands, open and slack upon his thighs, clenched involuntarily into fists. As he half-rose, Pendlebury could see his eyes dilating. Beside him, the watchful officers matched his movements. It was like a gridiron football confrontation – with one man naked.

'No!' shouted Pendlebury. It was too late. All three protagonists jumped simultaneously, and the governor was thrust to one side. He tripped and fell heavily, banging his head against the padded wall. As he clambered to one knee, the double door flew open, and two more monstrous spacemen burst in. The noise from outside increased, the bells, the baying, the wild cheers. A third spaceman slammed the inner door, then came to Pendlebury, lifting him upright by one arm.

On the padded floor, McGregor was struggling with terrifying abandon. Pendlebury saw feet and claws, caught a glimpse of wild eyes, foam-flecked screaming mouth, as the officers tried to contain his violent motion. Their cumbersome white bodies covered his, their thick arms sought to get behind his neck, to pinion his flailing limbs. Within a short time he was trapped, on his back, rigid. But his mouth was open, bellowing, his diaphragm pumping air up through his throat, rocking the huge men who lay across his chest. His eyes had rolled, white, into his skull.

The battle at the sluice room was bloodier, but far more diffuse. Lister, who had hit the prison officer backhand across the face before the contents of the bucket soaked him, had not followed up on the attack. The officer was an easy target, gasping, white-faced, dripping mucoid liquid, defenceless. But Lister had no quarrel with him, nor with anyone. He wanted to escape the danger zone. Before the going got rough.

At first, he did not achieve it. There were three or four men at the doorway with him, and two of them attacked the officer, as if by reflex action. Lister, who needed to get past and away, grabbed one of them to drag him off, just as the first of the back-up officers arrived. He piled into Lister – very bravely, considering his fear of him – with a flurry of punches to the face. Lister rode this, dropping back and keeping calm. As the officer followed him, it opened him to attack from the side, and Lister could withdraw still further. When the other two arrived, Lister was well clear, not posing any threat.

'Inside!' he shouted. 'They're murdering the faggot.'

Three of the officers, pushing aside the struggling inmates, drove themselves, wedge-like, through the door. Despite the sound and fury, several of the men inside were in fact already beaten, the exhilarating burst of energy and anger gone. They were staring at their hands and arms, dazed, dragging flesh across cloth to try and clean it. Others still punched and kicked each other, bouncing from the cubicle walls and wash basins, and some turned towards the screws with indiscriminate fury, only to be jumped on by other prisoners from behind. But although the fight was barely minutes old, the men were tiring. They also wanted, most of them, to submit. Enough damage had been done. Enough bridges had been broken. If they were lucky, they would avoid a kicking. That would be sufficient.

Raymond Orchard was in a lavatory cubicle, and it had saved his life. As the first wave of furious men had attacked, he had been knocked fortuitously backwards, cracking his head against a vertical doorpost. There were no doors on the lavatories on B-floor, so he had collapsed into it, driven before a flurry of fists and feet. For a moment he had balanced on the toilet pedestal which – seatless – had half-cradled him. Then he had been knocked sideways and backwards as the first three men jammed themselves into the cubicle to continue the kicking. Orchard, coming round as his face touched the cold wet quarry tiles, saw the U-bend, the four-inch soil pipe, the small, cramped space behind the pan. He pushed his head far into it, wrapping his arms around the base of the pedestal. Kick and scramble as they might, the men could not get their boots to bear on his face or head. The rest of him they hammered.

By now, the galleries of B-floor were thick with officers. Charles Lister, his back still to the wall, held his hands out, palms upwards, warily. Although below him he could still see fighting men and officers on A-floor balcony, the officers approaching him had cleared their territory. Many of them held sticks and short-shields, and one or two had combat helmets on. As the men spilled from the sluice they were jabbed and herded with the sticks along the walls. Lister, silent, was silently surrounded. It was a golden opportunity to bring him down, and he assumed that they would take it. OK, he thought. Every dog has his day. Today it's yours, tomorrow . . .

At that moment, though, two things happened. The last of the inmates in the sluice were driven out, followed by three prison officers carrying Raymond Orchard. Below, on the main hall floor, Richard Pendlebury, with a praetorian guard of Martians, appeared in his grey suit. He raised his arms, peculiarly, in some kind of supplication. Lister could see his mouth was open. Presumably he was shouting.

As if he had not been hearing it, Lister became aware of the noise around him. It was thunderous, a swelling, pulsing din. Hundreds of prisoners throughout the jail were clattering on their doors with fists, pots, anything. It was arhythmic, but a rhythm was emerging. Gradually, as the shouts and screams died down, the battering took over. Close to him, the screaming of Orchard, whose left arm was broken and dangling as the officers hurried him along, was thin and insignificant.

'OK you guys!' yelled Lister to the men surrounding him. 'I didn't start this, see? I'm an innocent bystander. Get me back home in one piece, and I'll buy you all a drink!'

Pendlebury, on the main floor, watched the riot fizzle out. Above him, the last prisoners were being pushed through doors, some of them under raining blows from fist or club. The flags beneath his feet were strewn with broken cups, slop-pot lids and other missiles, slippery and dangerous. He was alone, an old, grey-haired man, stooping in a wilderness. He began to move towards his office, stepping carefully, to make his phone calls. It occurred to him that the men behind all this, the men in ultimate charge, would not even be at their work in Queen Anne's Gate yet. Ah well, all the better. It would give him time to think.

For the next hour or more, however, coherent thought was virtually impossible. In the offices, there was a constant stream of reports and messages coming in, filtered for the governor by his duty-deputy, Ian Serple. The senior officers from every hall concentrated first on injured staff, then on injured inmates. Then there were preliminary assessments of the numbers in each cell, and the totals for each floor and finally each wing. Nobody had been seen to escape, or try to, but the numbers in the jail had obviously to be verified with the utmost urgency. Given the number of injuries and the speed with which the landings had been cleared, this would not be easy. Many men had gone into the wrong cells, some onto different floors. Many of the prisoners were refusing to be counted, covering their spyholes and hiding under beds when a visual check was made. Eighty cells had been barricaded, and about forty were known to have been wrecked. After ninety minutes, worst of all, the rhythmic banging of the doors had hardly diminished. Even in the admin block – far away and thickly carpeted – it could be heard. It was unnerving, demoralising. And nothing could be done about it.

Pendlebury, when he judged that Christian Fortyne's secretarial staff would be at work, put in a call. As expected, he had not arrived, so Pendlebury left his name. He would like to be rung by Mr Fortyne immediately he reached his office, he told the girl – it was extremely urgent. When he put the phone down, he smiled at Serple.

'That'll give us a nice long breathing space,' he said. 'Remind me to ring again in an hour or so. If I kept it up all day and never mentioned a riot I could make him look a complete and utter fool.' The half-smile left his face. 'And I'd get the sack.'

Ian Serple, observing the thoughtful look that settled on the boss's tired features, made no comment . . .

When Christian Fortyne did ring back at last – several hours later – and found out what had happened, he did not waste his time on anger. He knew full well he had been outflanked, and he appreciated the neatness of it. He listened carefully to the governor's dry outline of the disturbance, and he asked him about the current situation and his assessment for the immediate future. As soon as he had put the phone down he contacted Sir Gerald Turner's private secretary and made an appointment. His own urgency received a much more positive response.

'The question I most ask myself,' said Fortyne, after he had briefed the Home Secretary thoroughly, 'is whether to contact Donald Sinclair. The prisons are very much his baby now, although he's in America. I suppose he ought to know?'

Sir Gerald made a steeple with his fingers. He had been talking about Sinclair in his club the night before. There were questions in his mind.

'Well,' he said. 'Donald certainly would be interested. But I am Home Secretary, you know. I trust you're not suggesting I can't handle the prisons on my own if need be?'

There was a twinkle in his eye, which Fortyne acknowledged, warily, as indicative of a minor joke. But he knew he had to demonstrate where his loyalties lay, that at least he had not become Donald Sinclair's exclusive creature.

'Good lord no,' he said. 'And if you think so, there's no pressing reason why I should let him know. It's just that the ball was in his court, rather, with all his statements after Buckie and so on.'

Turner nodded, the twinkle growing.

'He did perhaps give the impression that everything was solved,' he said. 'However, this is by no means a major outbreak, and in general things have been very quiet, on both sides of the border. I suppose you're not suggesting Donald's made a muff of it?'

Fortyne was suggesting no such thing, and Turner knew it. He was merely providing both of them with an escape route, and himself perhaps a weapon, in case of need. Christian Fortyne was a very useful man. With an excellent nose for the winning side.

Turner continued: 'In any case, this won't get into the press, I trust? After all, for once there was nothing visible. No madmen on the roof, no fires, no people hopping over walls. There was the noise, I suppose, there's always noise, but it's not a lot to go on. Visiting cancelled, of course. If anybody does ask questions, it won't be for days. Then it's old hat. The one thing is, it's proved Pendlebury right. About the state of Bowscar. How much should that be worrying us?'

'Well that's not exactly for me to assess,' said Fortyne. 'I think that when Mr Sinclair returns he will want to address himself to that. But more trouble there seems rather unlikely in my opinion, however pessimistic Pendlebury may be. There have been problems and now the boil's burst. It should take a damn long time to grow again. More importantly, I think, it won't infect the other jails. It won't become a *cause célèbre* if no one knows about it. That was what was so damnable about the Scottish problems. The copy-cat syndrome.'

'Yes,' said Turner. He remained silent for almost half a minute, by the digital display. Then he raised his eyes to Fortyne's.

'About the press,' he said. 'I'm getting reports. I needn't say who from. Always the same two names. Andrew Forbes, Susanna Nixon. Tell me what you know about them.'

Christian Fortyne cursed inwardly. But his face and manner were unchanged. Suave, bland, his eyes untroubled behind his spectacles. You're getting in the mire my boy, he thought of Donald Sinclair. He cleared his throat.

'Rosanna, I believe. Not Susanna. She's a Scottish journalist, apparently a freelance now. Andrew Forbes is a well-known bloody nuisance. Wrote a book about the secret services, inevitably. One we *were* able to stop, even before the Act. He makes a living on the fringes of journalism, bit of TV specialist research. Obsessive dislike of the status quo.'

'Subversive?'

Fortyne allowed himself a minimal raising of the eyebrows. He had not expected such a crudity from so sophisticated a minister. Sir Gerald saw the movement and smiled.

'You know what I mean,' he said. 'I'm using PM-speak for convenience. I know full well that people who question our God-given right to government aren't all Soviet agents. Even Soviet agents aren't entirely, these days! But he's seriously digging, is he? And the woman. Do we know exactly why?'

Briefly, as it was not his place to lie, Fortyne outlined what they knew. That Nixon had seen McGregor fall, had been pressing for a post mortem result, the inquest date. Forbes had joined her, for reasons as yet unknown. Most lately, they had discovered evidence that Sinclair had been in Buckie on the night. What they hoped to do, eventually, was unclear. But Sinclair's advice, from experts, had been that all the time nothing could be proved, they were unlikely to make waves, or even ripples. They had no muscle.

Sir Gerald Turner mused. So that was it at last. He had known the basic cover-up, of course. But the significant lie – to the extent that Sinclair had withheld the truth from him – was the fact that the fall had been observed. It was a huge omission. It was the sort of omission that, if held up to the light of day, could bring somebody down. A Secretary of State. Something else slipped into place. In all his public utterances after Buckie, Sinclair had bent over backwards to share the credit, to keep Sir Gerald Turner's name in public view. At his club the night before, a military companion had berated him for things he'd never said and thoughts he'd never had about the ending of the Scottish siege.

Aware that time was passing, Sir Gerald thanked Fortyne and dismissed him. He did not actually know that Sinclair was being less than one hundred per cent with him, and he did not necessarily believe the signs. But perhaps he was reaching too high, too soon? A touch of hubris creeping in? Maybe the Bowscar thing should be given to the press after all? A small, judicious leak to bring him down a peg or two?

But no, thought Sir Gerald. Time enough for him to dig his

own grave if need be. Rope enough for him to hang himself. Truth was, that he thought very highly of Donald Sinclair, still.

Although not highly enough to let him steal his job.

ELEVEN

Peter Smith was very happy when he at last got home that night. To put it another way, he was legless. Since getting off the bus from Chorlton Street, he had been in four of his local pubs, and he had bought drinks in every one. Not just for himself, for all his mates as well. Not mates, acquaintances, he scorned to call them mates. They thought he worked for a metal fabricator in Trafford Park, they thought he was a labourer. He told them, as he bought them drinks, that he'd come up on the horses. He was not even tempted to tell them the truth. Secrecy was the name of the game. He was good at it. They drank his ale, they played him at darts, they patted him on the back when he went to his next pub on the crawl.

The house, when he got back to it, was cold and rather lonely. Peter Smith turned all the lights on, and two of the gas fires. He switched the television on, quite loud and sod the neighbours, and rummaged in the cupboard for a bottle of Scotch whisky. He poured himself a tumblerful, and sipped. He thrust the bottle back into the cupboard, out of temptation's way.

What a triumph it had been – world class! The memory of the fat girl's face as she had struggled off the Bowscar bus with her buggy and her brats had been enough. She had seen him waiting, and she had forced a smile. Yes, it said. No problems. Peter Smith had actually gone to help her. In the café, he had offered her a cake. He had bought plastic cups of insipid orange for the kids.

'They had a riot there,' she told him. 'On Wednesday I think it was. Wayne said. He said I was first batch to be allowed back in. First visitors. Lucky.'

Bleeding hell, thought Peter Smith. You don't know how right you are, you great fat tart. In his elation, he wondered if he ought to proposition her. Give her some extra for a romp around the bed. He wondered what she'd look like, naked. Like a mountain of blancmange, wobbly. He wondered how he'd ever find the hole. Stick a little flag in maybe, like on a golf course! Get her to fart, to give him a clue! But he dismissed the thought. Her face was just too much. Tonight he'd do a little drinking.

He did not tell the woman that the job was finished, that she would never see him again. Unless there was another one to be smuggled into Bowscar, before her Wayne was out, and that did not seem likely. When he had finished his tea, he slipped her the envelope with the twenty pounds in it, he left and caught his bus, and he metaphorically hugged himself in glee. Four grand this trick had earned him so far, with another grand to come. And the satisfaction, he told himself piously, of a job well done.

With his nightcap whisky only half-finished, Peter Smith decided to have a little gloat in his emporium. He switched on the light at the top of the cellar steps and clattered down. Another switch, and his workshop was bathed in harsh, clean working light. Light enough for engineering to the smallest tolerances. Light enough for making guns. Peter Smith ran his eyes, then his hands, lovingly over his two small lathes, vertical and horizontal milling and drilling machines, his neatly stacked supplies of steel, from mild to carbon of the highest quality. On the workbench, in a vice, was part of a finely detailed model of a triple expansion steam engine, that was his cover. If a team of detectives searched the workshop for ten days, they would find no trace of anything that spoke of guns. There was nothing written down, nothing drawn. He held it in his head. Everything.

The last job had been one of glorious satisfaction, the specification a challenge of the truest sort. It was a single-shot pistol, of only .22 calibre, that was capable of discharging a sporting cartridge of enormous power. It had to be small, it had to be accurate, it had to be reliable. But most of all, it had to be dismantleable. It had to come to pieces, easily and quickly, into a minimum possible number of simple, foolproof parts. And a man, possibly under pressure and without instruction beyond a basic expertise with firearms, had to be able to assemble it. He could imagine it, fondly, lying loaded in the palm of someone's hand in Bowscar. The fat woman had bangled in the fifth and last bullet today.

Peter Smith jumped when the doorbell rang, then looked at his watch. Ten minutes to midnight. He closed his eyes to concentrate, being fuddled, but no explanation came. The boys were due tomorrow with his last payment, weren't they? Sure. Tomorrow. But maybe it was them. No other bugger ever called. He put his whisky down, turned off the lights, and clambered heavily upstairs. Boy, but he was pissed.

Not too drunk, he told himself. Not too drunk to put the chain on. He did, then called softly: 'Who's that? I'm in bed.'

There was a short pause, then a muffled laugh. A voice said gruffly. 'Open up. It's the police. We know you're in there.'

For a moment his stomach lurched, then Peter Smith laughed in his turn.

'Daft bastards,' he muttered. He unhitched the chain, and turned the Yale knob. 'Daft bastards,' he said, opening the door. 'You're early.'

The two men were both small and stocky. One, with blond hair, was in his twenties. The other, older man was bald. They both wore short open overcoats, over suits.

'Never mind that,' said the older man. 'We've got the money. What more d'you want?'

They walked before him, into the living room, and warmed themselves in front of the gas fire. The blond man went to the back window, which overlooked a garden, then over the backs of other houses. He pulled the curtains closed.

'Want a drink?' asked Peter Smith. 'I've got one somewhere myself. It's whisky. Want some?'

The blond man was looking round the room. The television was still on, quite loud. He went and stood beside it.

The other man said: 'So what went wrong?'

Peter Smith, by the bottle cupboard, turned, startled.

'Nothing!' he said. 'It all went perfect. She done the job.'

'Aye,' said the man. 'We watched.'

'So what's up then? Here – you're not trying to get out of that last grand are you? Fucking hell.'

The man reached into his jacket contemptuously. He withdrew a brown envelope and tossed it onto the sofa.

'She opened up her fucking mouth, didn't she?' he said. 'She was in a pub in Gorton, wasn't she? Clacking on. She got pissed and fucking maudlin, didn't she? Said you made her smuggle stuff, and then you fucked her. Said you were a bastard, said her old man'd kill you when he comes out of the Scar, you're a bastard.'

'But I didn't fuck her! What, that fat tart! I didn't fuck her!'

'Not the fat one, cunt. The thin one. Tony Geraghty's tart. She's put it all over Gorton, hasn't she?'

Peter Smith found himself a tumbler and poured whisky into it. He had gone white.

'Oh Jesus Christ,' he said. 'Not about the gun? She didn't know it was a gun. I never told her nothing.'

The young man spoke from beside the television. His voice was very light.

'Fair play,' he said. 'We don't know if she said it was a gun. Fair play.'

Smith had an overwhelming surge of relief. He took a mouthful of neat whisky, gratefully, and coughed.

'It's not my fault,' he gasped. 'I made the fucking gun. I arranged to get it in. I did everything. It's not my fault if some moronic tart . . . I'm not responsible for that.'

They waited patiently until he got his breath back. He was still very pale. The older man said quietly: 'You're responsible for everything, Peter. That's the deal. This woman could have caused a lot of trouble. People are upset.'

'Yeah,' said Peter Smith. His eyes moved to the fat envelope. 'I can accept that. I'm sorry, honestly. What are you going to do to her? Do I have to buy her off?'

'No need for that,' said the bald man. 'She's dead. We've got her body in the car. We want you to look after her.'

Peter Smith looked from one to the other. All the drink he had taken began to rise against him. He felt sick.

'Is this a joke?'

The young man said: 'No joke, Peter. You've got your little cellar, haven't you? You've told us lots of times. Your security is excellent. Brilliant. Nobody ever calls. Not even the milkman or a paperboy.'

The older said: 'That's why we chose you, Peter. For the job. That and the fact that you're the best. It won't be for long, old son. Just temporary. Come and help us in with her.'

'I've got to go upstairs! I'm going to throw up!'

He had gone greenish. The bald man sighed.

'We'll do it then, you idle bastard. Off you go. Peter? Don't close the door on us, will you? We're very serious men.'

He shook his head, willing his stomach not to lose control. He ran up to the bathroom. When he returned, shakily, the men were in the living room, as before. But he had heard what they had done, while his head had rested on the cool porcelain of the cistern.

'Sorry about that,' he said. 'The booze. Where is she?'

'Downstairs, as agreed. No one saw. The only problem is, Peter, that you're going to have to join her, mate. Sorry.'

He stared like a mesmerised rabbit as the older man withdrew a pistol from his belt. It had a silencer he recognised. He had made it.

'I won't tell anyone,' he said. His voice was just a croak. 'You might need me again, you know. I'm the best.'

The bald man smiled, regretfully.

'You are,' he said. 'A genius. You just shouldn't have blown the cover, should you? And for a bit of skinny little cunt.'

Peter Smith's head was rising. His neck was stretching. His eyes were opening wide. He was about to start to scream. The younger man, bending swiftly, turned the TV volume up, loud, to cover the two shots. Then down again and off. It sounded as if someone had accidentally turned the knob the wrong way. Drunk, no doubt. Peter Smith, once drunk this night, now dead, had jacknifed to the floor. The blond man checked his pulse.

'Only twenty-nine,' he said. 'Tragic, isn't it? And what an armourer. A magician.'

'Good time to go, though,' said the older man. He opened the cellar door, so that they could push him down the stairs. 'I mean, he would have had an awful bloody hangover!'

Five minutes later, both bodies were sealed in vacuum bags in the coolest part of the cellar. The men sat in their car in the deserted street, outside the darkened house, satisfied that nobody had noticed anything unusual.

'They'll do there,' said the older man. 'Who were they anyway? Nobody'll miss them.'

They drove away.

'What are you missing, guy?'

Michael Masters, lying on his back in the bunk underneath Matthew Jerrold's, considered the question. He did not know whether he had made a noise, a sigh or a groan, or if the black man was just making conversation. But he was missing. He was missing everything.

'It's a long list, Matt,' he said. 'But nothing interesting. No pussy in it. Not directly.'

The bed-springs creaked.

'Cunt not everything,' said Jerrold. 'Know what I miss most? Not always, some of the time. Tube trains. The smell of the Tubes. Know what I mean?'

Masters, at that moment, had been missing jazz. Not just the music, for the group he had in mind were not the nation's finest, but the place, the company, the smell, the taste of beer. It was a small country pub he and Sarah went to, many Monday nights. A barn, admission free, room for thirty or forty people at the most, jostled round the walls and by the bar. The musicians were all fortyish and fiftyish, and did other jobs. The leader was a milkman, the drummer an accountant.

Alan Hughes said: 'I miss my garden. I had a lovely garden.' He made a peculiar noise, halfway between a sigh and a snort. 'It got a really good digging over, one way and another. When they tried to find my wife.'

Normally, if Hughes had expressed a willingness to talk about his wife, his crime, Masters would have been eager to glean everything. He was building up a piecemeal knowledge of the story, but it was far from complete. Alan Hughes liked to be elliptical about some things, and he liked to amuse himself by dropping clues. He knew that Masters was fascinated, and had once told him it was because of Sarah Williams. All married men with mistresses, he said, had fantasies of murdering their wives. Later, if things took their normal course, the mistress became the object of the homicidal dreaming. By now, the men had pooled some of their emotional secrets, to make their stunted sex lives bearable. Some, but not all.

Today, though, Masters did not follow up the lead. Today, he was too involved in his own sense of loss. Since the riot all of them had been depressed. Not just them, either. Everyone in the Scar. It was an emotional wound that would not quickly heal.

'I had a thought,' said Matthew Jerrold. 'Talking about wives. I had a philosophical thought.'

Masters said nothing. He was thinking of the closing number, the sign-off that the small band always played. 'Springtime in the Rockies.' Ridiculous. Oh Sarah.

'Go on,' said Hughes. He put down his book. It was a paperback, from the library's stock of about eight hundred trashy titles. He had had it out three times before.

'Women,' said Jerrold, slowly, 'only tend to masturbate, yeah? – good word! – when they can't get it off their husbands, right? But men – we have to wank when we can *only* get it off our wives! Yoh!'

'Bloody Mary,' said Alan Hughes. 'You'll be regius professor at Oxford if they ever let us out. Along with all the other wankers.'

Masters swung his feet out from his bed and put them on the tiled floor. It was hot in the cell, with the radiator clanking moodily from time to time. Some of the other cells, they knew, were cold, and running with the damp that only constant heating kept at bay. The smashed-up cells – still inhabited, many of them – would be repaired very slowly. It had led to further overcrowding in the rest. Masters said to Hughes: 'Look, Alan, I've had enough of this. I've got the horrors coming on. Something's got to happen. I'm serious. I'm going mad. I'll have to see the doctor.'

It had come so suddenly, and his voice was so unharsh, unstrained, that for a moment Hughes only stared. Jerrold put his face over, concerned.

'You serious, Mike? What goes off?'

Masters stood up, cracking his shoulder against the upper bunk. His face was white, beaded with sweat. His upper lip was trembling. Hughes stood too.

'Steady, steady feller,' he said. 'Steady on.'

He moved uncertainly towards the bigger man, and Masters came towards him. For a moment it looked as if they might embrace. Then Hughes guided Masters past him, to the chair beside the table. Masters sat. He had covered his mouth with one hand, to try and still his shaking lips.

There was nothing to be done. No glass of water could be fetched, no tot of spirits, or cup of tea. No garden that he could be led to, to get a breath of air. There was hardly room for him to throw his arms back, fill his lungs and shout. Which might have had the side effect of summoning an unwanted visit from a screw. Masters sat, one hand to his mouth, his left fist clenched on the table top. Jerrold, quietly, left his bed and came to stand nearby.

'Talking of philosophy,' Alan Hughes said, after a long silence. 'What you're suffering from, my friend, is a blocked catharsis. There was a blow-up, a releasing of emotions, an orgasm if you like. Only for you – for us – it didn't happen.'

'Come again?' said Jerrold. It was a joke.

'Fuck off,' said Hughes. 'I'm trying to be serious. Michael's got a problem. Michael needs to get out. So let's talk about it.'

Masters smiled wanly. His colour was returning, his lips were still.

'This is the mystic escape committee, I suppose,' he said. 'Listen, Alan, don't mock the afflicted. Escape fantasies I can do without. I had one of my own.'

'Michael,' said Hughes. 'I'm not saying I can get you out of here. Not on your own, just like that. But there are things going on in prison. Things I've thought about for years. I'm an academic, remember? I've got this highly organised brain that I can't switch off, I've got this theory. You've got to believe me, mate – reading the complete works of Barbara Taylor Bradford seven times just ain't enough!'

Masters wiped the moisture off his face. The worst part of the crisis was gone. Listening to one of Hughes' mega-fantasies would be soothing.

'Go on. I'll buy it. Do you want your chair back?'

Hughes did not. He was settled on his bunk. Jerrold, the excitement over, climbed back onto his.

'You know how the place has been since the riot,' said Hughes. 'The screws bad-tempered, two sluices closed down, the cons all suicidal. It only needs another trigger, some other incident that gets under anybody's skin, and it could go again tomorrow. Or today.'

Masters considered it. To him, that was quite feasible. If he was banged up next time, he would go stark insane. Hughes carried on.

'The point is, Michael, that if it does go again, if it did go again, it might be just a waste of time – again. Alternatively – well, that's my theory. I'll tell it to you, although you'll probably think I've lost my marbles. Just shut up till I've finished. Think about it. Me and Matthew have. A long, long time. Then we'll talk.'

Baldly stated, Hughes' theory did sound pretty strange to Masters. But not entirely daft. What it added up to was that prisoners, without being aware of it, actually consented to their state, acquiesced in it. They were sentenced to a loss of liberty, sometimes arbitrarily, often unfairly, and they accepted the idea – and the deprivation – as their part in some kind of ritualistic bargain. In a country which saw itself as civilised, super-civilised compared with foreign lands, they allowed themselves to be locked into prisons which by anybody's standards – even their own government's – were unfit and inhumane. To be fed bad food, breathe bad air, use sanitary arrangements that were incredible, and risk a variety of illnesses, lately as terrible as hepatitis and Aids. If they decided, Hughes' thinking ran, to one day withdraw that consent, to just say 'No, we've had enough, we will not stay in prison' – they would be unstoppable. Except, he added, by the use of the most brutal, and quite unacceptable, level of force. He expounded the thesis calmly, like a lecturer talking something through with a valued tutorial group.

'Well?' he said. 'Any questions?'

'You said I ought to think first,' Masters said. 'But as a snap reaction, there seem to be some holes. Like most of the prats in this place can't be persuaded to fart in unison, let alone do anything constructive. And even if we did orchestrate a protest, how would we get out? They're hardly going to unlock the doors for us, are they? Just because we say we're going home?'

Hughes was slightly hurt.

'That's where rioting comes in,' he said. 'Haven't you been listening? We need a riot as the basis, but we've had one, haven't we? We've got the atmosphere, the seedbed. We're in a riot-situation. It could go off again. It could be made to go off.'

'I notice,' said Matthew Jerrold, 'that Mick referred to "we". If "we" orchestrated a protest. That's good, eh? Mickie – why not, guy? Our riot come along, we got two chances, like the man say. We get our rocks off, treat it like a gang-bang – or we do it proper. We make it work for us. What say?'

It was a long-term joke, Masters could read that, a routine they'd developed over time to pass the time. But there was serious intent, he could read that too. Before he had a chance to ask them any more, the spyhole clattered back. They were investigated, and the door was unlocked. Outside stood four prison officers. They were carrying a mattress, blankets and a pillow. Hughes got up.

'What's this?' he said. 'No room at the inn. Haven't you read the European Convention on prison overcrowding, sir?'

'Don't blame us,' said one of them. 'We didn't start the riots. You've got a spare bed, we've got a spare bod.'

'That's not spare,' said Hughes. 'There's just no one on it. This is a one-man cell, remember? Circa 1870.'

The officers were unrolling the mattress onto the top bunk above where Hughes slept.

'You'll have to sort that out with your new bum-chum,' the screw said. 'He fell out with his last two cell-mates, though. He wouldn't stay with them. They seemed . . . how shall I put it? Shit-scared of him. Poor old Mickie White, you know?'

With a swift movement, Matthew Jerrold sat upright. His dark look, the look that made men nervous, clamped down on his ebony features. The officers regrouped imperceptibly.

'Not that Yank?' he demanded. 'You ain't putting that Yank in here?'

'Yes we are,' said the spokesman. 'And you call us sir remember, black boy. Two gorillas in one cage. All the shit in a single bucket.'

They were waiting for him to jump. They were looking forward to it. Jerrold did not move.

Alan Hughes said: 'Officer, I'm not trying to be funny. Sir.' He indicated Masters. 'This man here is suffering from claustrophobia. Badly.'

'Tough,' said the spokesman. 'He should have gone private, shouldn't he?'

The other three guffawed. One said: 'Maybe Mr Pendlebury'll let him use his suite. He's fucking soft enough.'

'I think if the MO,' began Hughes. He was not allowed to finish. The spokesman took him by the shoulder and pushed him down onto his chair.

'Listen, you barrack-room lawyer twat,' he said, 'I said tough shit. Now why don't you just sit quietly and think how you can make your visitor welcome? The Bowscar Gentleman!'

Another officer jerked the blankets and pillow up onto the bed.

'For starters, why don't you make his bed up for him? As a gesture. And I wouldn't advise you to apple-pie it!'

Laughing, the prison officers left. For the first time, Masters shared the nervousness of waiting for a new cell-companion. But Charlie Lister, they knew about already. Everybody did . . .

Judith Parker was quite surprised by Sinclair's response when he was finally told about the Bowscar problem. The information was dropped into a telephone conversation by Christian Fortyne, and Sinclair, as far as she could see, took it at face value. He did demand to know, quite sharply, why he had not been informed earlier, but Fortyne soothed him easily. It was, as Sinclair told Judith afterwards over a drink, a very minor affair, that need not affect his strategy in any way. One broken arm, fifty or sixty thousand pounds' worth of damage, no escapes. What was the problem?

Judith was not so sure.

'It's the timing, that's all. I mean, you're out of the country, and in the public mind that's because you've solved the immediate problem. Now this happens and you're away. You can't defend yourself, explain it.'

'But the public doesn't know,' he said. 'I told you.'

'But they might find out. So might prisoners in other jails. You know the grapevine. Are you sure we hadn't better go back, just in case?'

Donald was sure, or at least insistent. But after he had talked it through with Judith, he went alone into his hotel room to ring his wife. It was an action that surprised her, certainly – content as she had been to receive the usual postcards – but Donald denied any ulterior motive.

'No, there isn't any reason,' he laughed. 'You're suspicious, aren't you? Think I'm checking up on you?'

Mary, who had been preparing gazpacho in her sunlit kitchen, rubbed her nose with a garlicky finger.

'You're the one with all the opportunity, darling,' she replied. 'I'm just a little housewife. Although I must admit dishy Geoff Dunning's coming to dinner tonight. But so's his wife, unfortunately, and two other couples! How's it going, anyway?'

'Oh fine. We're off to Marion this afternoon. That should give me food for thought.'

'Should I know her?'

The banter, for no reason, grated. An hour before, Donald had showered with Judith Parker after their morning work session, and they had made love. Now he kept glancing at the hotel door, oddly fearful that she might walk through it.

'It's a jail,' he said. 'Quite a novel one, I believe. The men are kept in chains and never touch another human being.'

'Chains? You can't be serious?'

'Of course I'm serious. Leg-irons, waist-bands, manacles, it's the coming thing. Look, Mary, never mind all that, now. How's home? Quiet?'

He could hear the strain in his own voice. He hoped that Mary, three thousand miles away, could not. Faint chance, indeed.

'What's wrong?' she asked. 'What is it exactly that you want to know?'

Something like fury flashed over Sinclair's brain. His grip on the receiver hurt his fingers.

'Nothing! It's a simple question for Christ's sake! England. My country. How's it getting on?'

Go on, you fool, he thought. Why not just come out with it? Any riots, by the way? Any problems at the Scar! The transatlantic line was so good that each could hear the other's breathing, plainly. A sharp, unhappy sound.

Mary said: 'It's getting on all right as far as I know. The government hasn't fallen without your presence, if that's what you mean. The main news today was about the Channel Tunnel, as far as I remember. Don—?'

He interrupted her.

'Look, darling, I'm sorry, I didn't mean to snap, forgive me. It's a killing schedule over here, and I'm due off to the Far East in a day or two. Only the Iron Maiden and two cabbages for company, I'm going up the wall! Forgive me.'

The lightness was distorted by his voice. Mary strove to ignore that.

'Yes,' she said. 'Of course. It was nice of you to ring anyway; thoughtful. Listen – don't get seduced.'

There was silence. Then:

'What can you possibly mean by that?'

'That prison. Marion? In the land of the free! Don't let them take *us* back to the Middle Ages, will you?'

Donald Sinclair laughed, with sudden, real, relief.

'But it works,' he said. 'That's the interesting thing. It works!'

Later that evening, surrounded by her friends, Mary listened to the latest marriage scandals, the divorces and adulteries, with amusement. No, she said, she never worried about her husband, what was the point? He was away a lot, of course he could be gallivanting. But all she asked of infidelity was that she did not know, when all was said and done! In any case, she suspected he was far too busy.

But afterwards, drifting into sleep, a cloud was in her mind, the shadow of a cloud. It was not to do with sexual faithfulness, but with ideals, perhaps, political integrity. Tiredly, Mary Sinclair tried to pin it down, but it was so nebulous. In the morning, she told herself, it would have gone . . .

Raymond Orchard lasted only five and a half hours in the hospital wing before he was moved to an isolation cell. In that time he had been mysteriously attacked three times, during the last of which a determined effort had been made to break the plaster cast on his left arm. His nose was bloodied, a tooth had gone, and he had been tipped onto the floor and kicked.

Orchard, according to the medical staff who moved him, seemed resigned to the attitude of his fellow prisoners. The cell he was put into was not a padded one, because he was not considered to be a danger, either to himself or others. It had a standard door and standard window fittings, but a hospital bed instead of the regulation bunk. He spoke little during the transfer operation, although he was in some discomfort. Strangely, as the cell was a secure one, he was noted over the next few days to have sustained several new injuries and abrasions of a minor sort, which were assumed to have been self-inflicted. When asked, Orchard made no comment.

He had been in the isolation room for nearly a week when an orderly, alerted by a noise as he passed at 2.40 in the morning, flipped back the spyhole cover and looked in. On seeing Orchard hanging from the ceiling light fitting, he immediately raised the alarm. He then waited until three prison officers arrived to unlock the cell, when Orchard was cut down and given artificial respiration and cardiac massage. By coincidence, one of the first officers to arrive was a man called Arthur Probert, who had been involved in the fracas at the sluice room which had caused the prisoner's injuries. After giving mouth-to-mouth resuscitation he became visibly upset, and was then sick in a corner of the cell. Later, the MO put him under mild sedation.

At 3.17 a.m., Raymond Orchard was pronounced dead, and the cell was cleared. The local coroner's officer was informed of the tragedy at twenty-five minutes to ten that morning, and an hour later the body was removed from Bowscar Prison for a post mortem examination in the town thirteen miles away. The cause of death was quite straightforward: asphyxiation. Raymond Orchard had hanged himself with a bandage.

TWELVE

'Dulce domum,' said Andrew Forbes flatly. 'You've read *The Wind in the Willows*, I suppose? Dulce fucking domum.'

Rosanna, standing in the desolate room, looked at him to see how upset he really was. They had been celebrating for most of the evening, and they were both quite drunk. They had been with Peter Jackson in the Princess Louise.

'I don't quite see you as Mole,' she replied, lightly. 'And I don't think we'll be visited by any carol-singing fieldmice, do you?' She paused. Forbes was looking round the room, his expression bleak. 'They've made an awful mess,' she added, soberly. 'I suppose it wasn't burglars, was it?'

He grinned tightly as he passed her on his way to the front window. He pulled the curtain back, a bold, open gesture.

'Fat Ivan's gone,' he said. 'The old green Lada. They'll be somewhere out there, in one of the old wrecks. I ought to flog them the Porsche, didn't I? They could sit right outside the door. They probably think they deserve a Porsche. More their image. Bastards.'

'Could it, though? Be burglars? I mean – well, it is a pretty rough area, isn't it? And they've made an awful mess.'

Forbes, returning from the window, nodded to the TV set. It had been kicked over, probably wrecked, but it was still there. As was the VCR, upside-down, with its wires jerked out from its back.

'Burglars take videos,' he said. 'They sell them in the pub, or swap them. Burglars don't take floppy discs.'

He went to the table where his word processor had been. It was on the floor, the keyboard stamped in. The plastic racks of discs were empty.

'Not a disc to be seen,' he said. 'How much crack would you get for them? Do me a favour, little Mouse. The mess is a statement of intent. To tell us something.'

'I need a wee,' said Rosanna. 'Will you . . . would you come with me, please?'

'What!'

'Oh get that stupid grin wiped off! I'm scared. There might be someone here. That's all.'

They walked up the carpet-less stairs together. As they did so, Forbes tore a long strip of hanging wallpaper off.

'It must have been quite frustrating for the lads, trying to make a mess in this place. It would have been more unsettling if they'd redecorated it for me! I suppose you don't want me to come inside and hold your hand?'

Rosanna turned the bathroom light on, apprehensively. Everything was normal. Towels everywhere, the hand basin tap dripping onto a mushy bar of soap, a toilet roll on the floor.

'You could check the bedrooms,' she said, closing the door. 'It might seem normal to you, my pet, but it's not to me. I mean being burgled by the secret services, not watching someone have a pee. I'm nervous.'

To satisfy his own mind as well as hers, Andrew did a quick tour of the house. He was not upset, nor even angry, at what they'd done. He found it vaguely depressing, merely. Everything, every box, every pile of books, every unhung picture had been kicked over, or trodden on, or messed about. It was so crude, so pointless. Rosanna's mattress had been dragged onto the floor, and her dressing-table drawers had been tipped everywhere. He was standing in his room when she rejoined him.

'Jings,' she breathed. 'Steamer in a Snowstorm. How nasty can you get?'

There was little in the room to touch. Practically nothing. So the spooks had slashed the duvet, and shaken it. The bare wood floor was ankle deep in places with white feathers. The red plastic of the telephone, peeping through the down, looked startlingly like a gutted duck at first glance. Forbes bent to pick it up. He checked the dialling tone.

'They're not completely daft,' he said. 'They've left their little bugged device intact. Maybe they've put some more in. So that they can listen to us talk. Or have a pee! D'you want a coffee? I doubt if they'll have rolled the kitchen. Scared of getting botulism.'

Later that evening, Forbes and Rosanna went to bed together for the first time. It came as a complete surprise to Forbes, and not much less of one to Rosanna Nixon. She had not known for certain that it was going to happen until they were in his bedroom again, surveying the soft white chaos. He looked so lost.

'Andrew,' she said. 'I'll get my duvet from my room. Can you clear the feathers off the mattress?'

'What?'

'You heard. You did warn me once, I seem to remember. Beware of the mothering instinct, or helpless men, or something. Well it's happened.'

'Good God. Are you sure?'

She bridled.

'Are you serious! Are you trying to turn me down!'

'No! Christ, no, not at all! But . . . fuck!'

'Not necessarily,' said Rosanna, rather primly. 'I want to talk, that's all. Well . . . And anyway, you said they might have bugged the place. They won't have bugged my pillow, I suppose.'

Forbes' face lit with pleasure. He looked into a corner of the room and gave the thumbs up sign.

'Thanks boys,' he said. 'You can raid me any time!' He started brushing at the feathers with his hands. 'Don't mind me,' he said. 'It's only because I'm pleased, Rosanna. Please don't change your mind.'

When she returned, towing the duvet behind her, Rosanna had already put on a long red cotton nightdress. Her small face, framed by its short, dark hair, was serious. As she threw the covering across the bed, a cloud of feathers scuttled across the floorboards, rose, then softly fell. Andrew Forbes, who was not the world's shyest man in normal times, was suddenly very shy.

'You get in,' he said. 'I'm going to the bathroom. I hope the bastards aren't listening, Rosanna. But they might be.'

When he returned, wearing only his shirt, he turned the light off at the doorway and slipped under the duvet with her. For a moment they lay quite rigid, then turned to face each other, lying on their sides. Andrew put his right hand on her shoulder, and Rosanna touched his hip.

'We can be very quiet,' she said. 'Anyway, it's their problem more than ours, I guess. Perverts shouldn't worry us.'

'No,' said Andrew Forbes.

Rosanna moved her head forward in the darkness and kissed him, dry and gently, on the mouth.

'It's good about McGregor, isn't it? Fancy old Adrian Rafferty finding out at last. You're a clever little devil, Mr Forbes.'

'Fancy it being Bowscar. Peter was amused. The Animal could be sharing with his Yankee chum! Anyway, you started it, Wee Miss Nixon.'

'We've got to confirm it though,' said Rosanna. 'You know what a lush old Rafferty is. And he said it was two weeks ago. His last information. How can we confirm it?'

They were quiet for a while. Andrew moved his hand down from her shoulder and put it on her rib-cage. He could feel her ribs.

He said: 'Rosanna. How old are you?'

'I told you. Twenty-eight. I'll soon be twenty-nine.'

'I'll soon be forty. Why are you in bed with me? I didn't ask you this time.'

'No. You didn't ask me. This time.'

She lifted her hand from his hip and laid it on the side of his face. In the dark, he saw her smile.

'I want some peace,' she said.

For the first hour after Charles Lister was moved into their cell, Masters, Hughes and Jerrold hardly spoke. Considering the conditions they were living in, Masters in particular was surprised by the sense of invasion that he felt. Not the physical one, of crushing, claustrophobic proximity, but a corroding of his mental state, the indescribable resentment that his territory was under attack, that an alien being had been forced into an enclosed, self-sufficient unit. The violence in the air was not from him alone. Jerrold's face was a mask of repression, while the very fact that Hughes had taken to his bunk spoke loud. Alan Hughes hated his bunk, except as a place to sleep in. Now, without a confrontation, he had no choice.

The American was a stocky man, of enormous latent power. His face bore neither smile nor scowl when the prison officers delivered him, and they did not enter into the normal banter, friendly or aggressive, that they shared with every other prisoner. He held a washbag and a towel and a few small items, and he wore jeans, a dark shirt, and a denim jacket. When he entered the cell, Jerrold was already lying on his bunk, and Masters was seated on his. When Hughes stood, there was no room to move. Too many legs, too many bodies, in too small a space. Masters swung his legs onto his bed and Hughes, allowing the newcomer to squeeze past him, lowered himself onto his. Lister stood for perhaps half a minute, watching them, feeling the resentment grow. Then he sat, and stretched his legs in front of him. He produced a pack of Golden Virginia and began to roll a cigarette. A fat one.

'I guess you guys don't mind if I smoke?' he drawled. Not waiting for an answer, he struck a match.

Horribly, for Masters, the feeling of resentment, of dislocation, was gradually replaced by a growing need inside him for the lavatory. It was almost certainly a claustrophobic reaction, which somehow made it worse. Since the riot, his confidence in the strength of his own will had been devastatingly undermined. He had dreamed several times of being securely locked up, with screams and smoke and bangings assailing him through the heavy door, and he had awoken streaming sweat. The presence of another body in the cell was turning his resolve – and his stomach – to water. He could feel his face paling with the effort of control. His breath got shorter. He laid his forearm across his mouth to mask the noise. It must not happen. It must not.

But it did. After a bitter struggle, Masters crushed a cry, and stumbled to his feet. He began punching at the night bell, his stomach cramped, his body bending forward. Hughes stood beside him, touching him lightly on the back. Jerrold's face twisted with anger at the screws, the new man, his friend's predicament.

'The bastards,' he spat. 'The bastards never come. The bastards.'

Throughout the next few minutes, which were to Michael Masters completely horrible, Charles Lister did not say a word. He moved back into a corner to give Masters room to use the bucket, and he rolled and lit another cigarette, quickly. He angled the chair away from the agonised man, looking up at the high ceiling, smoking impassively. Jerrold and Hughes both glanced at him, at first accusingly, as if it were all his fault. Lister, unmoved, smoked on.

When it was over, when the lid was on the plastic bucket, Masters moved towards his bed once more. He felt in some strange sense violated, as if he had performed an unnatural act. The irony of that was not beyond him, despite his sense of shame. He forced himself to acknowledge Lister.

'Sorry about that,' he said, aiming for an even tone. 'It won't be what you're used to.'

Lister flicked ash.

'How come? Americans do have assholes, believe it. And even your Queen must stink like us when she takes a shit, I guess. Anyway, I chose you guys for the conversation, not the airs and graces.' His thin, dangerous lips slowly took a curve. 'After that performance, Mr Masters, can anyone be in doubt? This is a water closet, not a cell. A rathole. I want out. Like you.'

His words, slowly spoken, deliberately chosen, caused a sensation in all three men which they all tried to keep well hidden. He was telling them, apparently, that he had engineered his transfer to their cell, that it was not a whim of some sadistic prison officer. He was telling them, apparently, that he knew something, however little, about their . . . well, one could hardly call it a plan. It was left to Hughes to speak.

'What have you heard?' he asked. 'And how do we know whose side you're on? You get visits from policemen, don't you? Detectives with London accents. Then you get "transferred" to our cell. Four men in a room thirteen by eight. We're not mad, Mr Lister. What are you? Some kind of *agent provocateur*?'

Lister was rolling cigarettes, fat cigarettes. He offered them around, and Hughes, the only other smoker, took one. He touched it with his lips.

'He must be, guv,' said Jerrold. 'Ordinary con don't have cigarette like that. A corona corona. Tell us your story. Give us a laugh. Only don't expect us to believe you, right?'

They did believe him, though, remarkably quickly. He told them his tale with vigour, pinning each of them, one after the other, with penetrating eyes. He told them that he was in the middle of an operation, and that the clear-out of police cells had caught him on the hop. His contacts, the men with London accents, were indeed detectives, what he called undercover men, and they had failed to get him out. He had scratched the surface of the corruption in the jail, among the officers, but it was at an amazingly petty level. He held the cigarette up, ironically. Fags or faggots, no trouble. Drugs and booze, any time, if you had the necessary. But if you mentioned getting out, everybody went completely blank. No one did that sort of thing. They'd get found out. It would look badly on their record sheets, ruin their promotion. Lister, with a grimace, crushed his cigarette. His contempt was palpable.

'Little England,' he muttered. 'Ratshit city. Well – I believe it, guys. I do believe it now.'

'And us?' said Hughes. 'How did you get on to us, then? I've spent a lot of time in this place, and I've done a lot of talking. But I don't imagine I've made enough impression for anyone to care about my theories. Let me guess. You're here for Michael Masters?'

The American studied them in turn, from under lowered brows.

'Sure,' he said. 'Masters. That's the reason. I've heard about you, sure. Alan Hughes, the guy that knows the systems, that knows his way around. Also, the guy that people like, except the screws. They say you're a nigger-lover, right? Also a faggot-lover, the man who sticks his head out for the underdog. Pity Cherry Orchard never made the connection, huh? What's your problem, friend?'

He spoke to Matthew Jerrold, whose head was hanging heavy over his bunk.

'You say nigger,' Jerrold said. 'What you hear about me, honky?'

'Nothing bad,' the American said, easily. 'It's a word, OK? Some of my best men are niggers. Some business colleagues. My lady was a nigger. All I hear about you, is you are mean. And dangerous. I like the sound of that. That makes me feel at home. You look after Hughes, he looks after you. A team. If we're going to pull anything in this pen, we need a team.'

Jerrold rolled back onto his bunk. Masters spoke.

'So what about me? Why am I the reason? I'm like you, I got conned. I know nothing about this place, except I don't like being here. So far, I can't see any way of getting out. So what's this reason?'

'Think about it,' said Lister, dismissively. 'You don't even need to ask. Everybody knows your story, you were set up. You played Patsy so that some big boys would live. You're a rich man, everybody says. If you had even half the money you're credited with in here, you'd be Croesus. You're also one hard guy, check? When you get out, blood is going to flow. You stay here, you're dead, you'll eat yourself alive. And me – I got sixty million bucks riding on a date. We're in the same boat, understand? We're going out.'

There was a low whistle from Jerrold's bunk. Sixty million. Jesus. Nobody else made a sound.

Then Lister said: 'I told you a little lie, just now. About Mr Hughes and Mr Jerrold. Nobody says much, but I figured that there must be a direction going on, you know? Hughes the fixer, Jerrold the muscle. And Michael Masters just happens to end up in their cell. Call it a smell, I don't know. I needed to be in.'

Masters laughed.

'It was an accident,' he said. 'No plan, no plot. Coincidence.'

'Bullshit,' said Charles Lister. 'So you don't trust me, fair enough. But look at it this way. Where's the percentage if I lie to you? If there's a break-out, someone will get hurt. Lots of people. If you thought I was double-crossing you, you'd have me killed,

I guess. Even if you had to wait. And I tell you all this stuff, my business details, stuff like that, on the same strict understanding. Anything goes wrong, any betrayal, and you're dead men, the same. Masters, tell me, now: you're going out of here, ain't you? You're fucking leaving?'

Michael Masters stood. He seemed lost in thought. Then his face cleared.

'Yes,' he said. 'I am.'

He thrust his hand out, and shook Lister's. Alan Hughes moved across the tiny room and took a cigarette from the small pile on the table. He struck a match.

'Matthew,' he said, 'get up and celebrate, you idle sod. I think the bus is moving.'

'Yoh!' said Matthew Jerrold.

Richard Pendlebury took his daughter Eileen with him when he visited Arthur Probert. But as they drove down the quiet cul-de-sac towards the council house on the edge of Bowscar village, he reiterated his warning that the prison officer would probably prefer her to wait outside. They had met before, at social functions involving Bowscar staff, and Eileen remembered Probert. He was an old-school prison officer, a little stiff and formal, and he had shown compassion and concern when her mother had been dying. Eileen, when she had heard of his collapse after the Orchard affair, had wanted to be of comfort, if she could. In any case, she'd said, she'd do the driving.

Suicide, Pendlebury explained to her, often had a traumatic effect on prison officers, even those who maintained an ultra-tough exterior. It was usually the inadequates who killed themselves, the men whom everybody – including the government that ran the system – knew should never have been sent to prison in the first place. And it always fell to prison officers to cut down the corpse, to try resuscitation, to be drenched in body fluids, to be attacked by hysterical prisoners who had woken to find their cell-mate hanging, dying. The Orchard case had been particularly hard for Probert, as he had been involved in the sluice-room debacle, and because Orchard had been gay.

'But Arthur Probert isn't gay, is he?' asked Eileen. 'I mean, he's a bachelor, but . . .'

'He lives alone,' he said. 'I think he's what we used to call a confirmed bachelor. No, I shouldn't imagine for a moment that he's gay. But there's Aids to think of, isn't there? And apart from anything else, his duty – and his desire, knowing Arthur Probert – was to save Orchard's life. He gave him mouth-to-mouth.'

Eileen drew the car up outside the small, grey-wash council house. She switched the engine off.

'Was Orchard HIV?'

'I shouldn't think so. I received a letter from his, ah, partner. They were practising homosexuals, and they had both had tests. Negative. They'd been monogamous for years, and intended to be in future. A sort of married couple.'

'So Arthur's in the clear. He can't get Aids.' She glanced at him, sharply. 'What do you mean, you shouldn't *think* so?'

Richard Pendlebury put his hand on the door latch and pushed it downwards.

'I think he was raped,' he said. 'Some days before the violence in the sluice. I'd be the last person to know for certain, but I'm fairly sure. There's no general testing of prisoners for HIV, so even if I'd known who raped him I wouldn't know the level of the risk. He was raped by more than one, though. That's normal. Poor old Arthur would know their names. I'll wave you in if he wants to talk to you.'

There was no wave, and Arthur Probert kept himself well hidden, behind the door frame. Eileen switched the radio on.

Inside the house, Pendlebury was quite shocked by the condition of the prison officer. He had known the governor was coming, and he was up, in pyjamas and a dressing gown. The table had been laid, formally, for drinking tea, with two plates of biscuits, one plain one chocolate. But Probert, normally a ruddy, open man, was pale and waxen, quiet and withdrawn. They made the preliminaries, then lapsed into silence while he made and served the tea. Then, without noticing that Pendlebury was sitting uncomfortably at the table, he slumped into a deep armchair beside the gas fire. Although it was warm and pleasant outside, the fire was burning. It was some while before either of them spoke. Pendlebury began.

'Arthur,' he said, 'I know this will sound like dreadful platitudes, but I had to come along and talk to you in person. I appreciate you've had a terrible time, and I want you to know how bad I feel about it. Don't feel any pressure to hurry back to work, although we all hope you feel better soon, naturally. We know how you must feel.'

'No,' said Probert. His voice was weak, but he repeated it, more loudly. 'No,' he said, 'you don't. The funny thing is, that I feel guilty. Not about that fellow killing himself, but about the state I'm in. Look at me, I'm collapsed, I'm a total wreck, I'm on tranquillisers. When we cut him down, there was stuff coming out of his mouth, Mr Pendlebury. Yellow, bitter stuff. It tasted disgusting. It blew into my mouth, he sort of chucked it up, expelled it, despite him being dead. And I was scared. I have been scared, I am scared, ever since. I know it's irrational, I know it's stupid, but I've got this total fear. I'm ashamed.'

He stopped talking, and he sipped his tea, his eyes large and anguished. Before Pendlebury could think of a response that would sound even half adequate, he began again.

'It's the shame that disgusts me,' he said, quietly. 'If I catch Aids, if I died from it – they'd think I was a queer. All my mates, all the people in the service, all the people who knew me in the Navy. I'm sorry, Mr Pendlebury, but I'm not a queer. I'm sorry, but I think that sort of thing's unnatural, it's disgusting, it's *unchristian*. I mean, I feel sorry for them, especially in prison. Not just the homosexuals but the rest of them. I know many of them just lack self-control. I mean, if they didn't, they wouldn't be in prison, would they? They're not like real people, not like normal people, they can't stop themselves. But if I got Aids, people would say I was a queer. I'm a bachelor, I live alone, I work in prison. It would be obvious, wouldn't it?'

'But you were attacked! You were cut, scratched. Then you gave artificial respiration. And in any case – why should you catch it? We don't know that Raymond Orchard had it. You must have tests. Arthur, I am certain—'

Platitudes again. He cut it off, before he could compound it. Arthur Probert had fixed his gaze on the rag rug in front of the gas fire. A strangely archaic piece of furnishing.

'Nobody would care about the evidence,' said Probert. 'Would they? Bloody hell, Mr Pendlebury, be your age. But what's the odds? For a start-off, the government wouldn't admit it, would they? They wouldn't allow it for a second. What d'you think they'd do, if an officer got Aids, or died? Give us a pension? Give us a big lump sum? Look after our families? You must be joking. They'd deny everything, and threaten us with the Official Secrets if we tried to tell. They're hypocrites. One day the thing will go sky-high. There'll be an epidemic. When everyone in prison has got Aids, what will happen then? Close down the jails? Bring in gas chambers? Deportation?'

Pendlebury said: 'Maybe the whole thing's a lie. It's what my daughter thinks, in fact. The government latched onto Aids as a sort of moral crusade, a plague to scourge us with, to make us better people. I.e., according to Eileen, to make us stop enjoying sex. But after the first outswelling, there's not much there. No monster epidemic. Embarrassing.'

Rather to his surprise, Probert was prepared to give Eileen's theory – a joke, as Pendlebury thought – consideration. There was more animation in his eyes. Anything, presumably, was better than brooding.

'I'm a religious man,' he said. 'But I do think there's an element of truth in that. It's to do with sex, for sure. Look at the condom-thing, for instance, what a farce! They won't issue prisoners with French letters because a homosexual act's illegal in a public place – and that includes prison! I ask you! Tell the public that. Tell a convict he's in a public place when he's banged up. But we all know the real reason, don't we? It's because a homosexual act's revolting to most people, they don't want to even think about it. The bum-fucking, and the sucking, and the wanking, and the raping, and the dirty magazines and videos some bastard screws bring in to make a profit and besmirch the service, they just don't want to know. And the government, the hypocrites, who know there's votes at stake, they say: male sex isn't nice and in prison it's illegal, aren't we good? What's more, if we issued condoms we might encourage it. I ask you, Mr Pendlebury, as if the poor bastards *liked* sticking it up a nasty shitty jacksie instead of a nice warm . . . Well, all except the perverts, anyway.'

Arthur Probert had turned his head to Pendlebury, and he looked half surprised, as if he had been less than aware of what he'd been saying. Then he sighed.

'Is a condom meant to make it pleasanter, or something? Is that what would "encourage" them? Not in my experience. Not with normal sex. No, what they mean is this: sex is dirty. The voters don't like sex, so we don't either, it's worse than all the other natural functions rolled into one. They don't mind, incidentally, men shitting into a bucket in front of each other, do they? Stinking themselves to death? Shaming themselves to death? But they can't ban shitting, see, and they can ban sex, or pretend they can. And anyone who defies the ban, anyone who does have sex, is lower than an animal and deserves everything he gets – including spreading it to innocent wives and babies. Innocent? Did I say innocent? If wives don't want disease, they shouldn't go with animals, should they? It's corrupting, Mr

Pendlebury, we're all corrupted. Most officers aren't cruel men, even the Chris Abbeys of this world. But we're stuck in at the sharp end, and no one will respect us for it, or pay us for it, or even listen to us. We're forced to control something that's out of control, and Raymond Orchard's dead. It's *corrupting*.'

Pendlebury's cup of tea had been finished long ago, so had Probert's. The governor picked his up, merely for something to occupy his hands, then put it down again. Probert, taking it as a cue, slowly stood. He walked to Pendlebury, very sombre.

'You know what's thought of you, don't you?' he asked. 'You won't be offended, Mr Pendlebury, if I tell the truth. You're thought a soft sod. Coons, queers, mental cases, nonces. You prefer their company, that's what people like Abbey think, do you know that? You prefer the company of criminals, dangerous, dirty criminals, to the company of your own, and that reflects on us. It makes life dangerous. I'm giving you a warning, Mr Pendlebury. Do you want more tea?'

He picked the cup up, rattling on the saucer. He walked into the kitchen. Pendlebury heard the tap run, then the click as the electric kettle was switched on. Probert appeared in the doorway.

'Don't trust them, sir,' he said. 'There's officers in there, who I have to say it, hate you. They'll try to bring you down, to denigrate you. It's funny, really, because if we worked to rule, tried to make a mark with the department, you'd probably back us, where no other governor would. You actually believe we've got a grievance, you know we're being used. But that doesn't count for anything, I'm afraid. They wouldn't back you, sir. If push came to shove. They wouldn't be behind you.'

The kettle boiled, and Probert made more tea. But, although Richard Pendlebury tried for more enlightenment, the officer retreated into platitude himself. He thanked him too profusely for the visit, and said he felt a great deal better – which, surprisingly Pendlebury thought, he did look to be. He said he would be back at work next week, which the governor said must be left completely to the doctor, and deprecated himself for a somewhat foolish over-reaction to a bad event. By the time the governor stood up, both men were relieved that the visit was at an end.

As he opened the door though – still keeping well out of the line of vision of the woman in the car – Arthur Probert said to Pendlebury: 'What if I did get Aids? No, not me, anybody? What do you think will happen when the first prison officer does get Aids? Do you really think things will go on as before?'

Pendlebury, on the doorstep, had no answer. He shrugged.

'It's a thought though, isn't it?' said Probert. 'But Aids or no Aids, Mr Pendlebury – something's going wrong at Bowscar. Don't trust them.'

He began to close the door.

'I appreciate the visit, sir,' he said. 'I do. And thank your daughter for the kindness of the thought.'

Pendlebury's daughter, he could see as he approached the car, had gone to sleep. She looked very young and pretty sitting there, her head on one side, her mouth slightly open. His face softened, and he tried, foolishly, to open the car door without awakening her. She blinked, then smiled at him.

'Hallo,' she said. 'You've been ages. Was he all right?'

'All right,' said Pendlebury. 'Yes I think so. He's all right.'

She waited for more as he climbed into the car, folding his tall frame like a clasp-knife. But he did not speak.

'Are you going to talk about it?' she asked him, starting the engine. 'There's a pub in the next village that stays open. I'll buy you one.'

Richard Pendlebury nodded wearily.

'We'll talk,' he said.

Although it was only shortly after eleven o'clock at night when the telephone rang, Sir Cyril France was asleep. The voice at the other end sounded fuzzy, but familiar. Vaguely familiar.

'I beg your pardon?' he said. 'Bad line, sorry. Who?'

'Masters. Michael Masters. Shut up and listen, I haven't got much time.'

Sir Cyril France's stomach dropped with shock. He opened his mouth, but his lips only made a small wet noise.

'Listen,' said Masters. 'I don't know if this line's safe but I'm giving you an ultimatum. Things are happening. Tell the man who got me in here it's been too long. Time's running out. Understand?'

But Masters is in prison, thought Sir Cyril France. He's locked away in jail. This can't be happening.

'France? Are you listening?'

France whispered: 'But we've tried. There's nothing we can do. The climate's just not right.'

There was a harsh noise. A croak. Masters said: 'Tell the man, my friend, that it's a damn sight worse in here. It's fucking terrible. Tell him – tell all of them – it's raining cats and dogs.'

Brian Rogers, attracted by the cell-phone's final beep, pushed open the cell door. There was a sneer on his lips.

'What are you looking so scared of?' he said. 'You don't have to be so quick, you know, it's safe. Unless I tell anyone what you've said. It's completely safe.'

I'm afraid of this place, thought Masters. I'm afraid of what we've started happening. I'm afraid to ride the juggernaut.

'It can't be safe. No cell-phone's safe. It's done by radio signal. It can be intercepted. They don't mention it, that's all, in the rental contract. They leak like hell.'

'No wonder you're the millionaire,' mocked Rogers. 'Mister Know-all. That's still two hundred and fifty you owe me, though. No need to write it down. I think you're stupid. Why waste two-fifty when you could get it for free? I suck your cock, we get mutual pleasure, and it's money in the bank.'

'No thanks,' said Masters. He thought, appallingly, of Sarah. 'No.'

An odd expression passed across Rogers' broad, cruel face, an expression Masters could not read. He raised thick eyebrows.

'You know best,' he said. 'You're the millionaire. I'll call the serf.'

As Masters was escorted to his cell, it occurred to him that since he had been dealing with Brian Rogers, he had been taken off the goonie squad. Chris Abbey and his sidekicks quite noticeably left him alone.

He thought of the cell-phone, and of the currency Rogers wanted him to use. He thought again of Sarah . . .

THIRTEEN

Rosanna Nixon, once she had committed herself to Andrew Forbes, did it with whole heart. She had not made love properly for several years, and she had told herself she did not miss it. After three days with Forbes, she revised that slightly: she did not know what she had been missing.

On the morning after they first slept together, Forbes had brought her a mug of – milkless – coffee in bed, and made a tent of the duvet for them to drink it under. It was, he said, so that they could talk without the boys listening in, and that may well have been true. It also gave them the opportunity, in the light-spill as they moved, to study each other. Rosanna, at first, was shy. Forbes, for the amusement it afforded him, pretended still to be.

'You look to me,' he said, lifting the covers slightly and angling his head, 'to be a skinny sort of piece. Under eight stone did you say? Your mammy would reckon you weren't getting enough haggis and neaps. If your mammy could see you now!'

Rosanna blushed.

'You're quite fat,' she said. 'I'm not surprised, all the beer you drink. But you're rather revolting, if this is honesty time. You ought to keep your mouth shut, in case I change my mind. Come to my senses.'

Resting on one elbow, his coffee mug on the mattress in his hand, Andrew reached across and took her nipple between his finger and his thumb. He stroked the thumbnail gently downwards.

'You've got quite hairy nipples,' he said. 'Is that a sign of something? Your tits aren't very big.'

'They're not hairy! There's two hairs out of that one, and three out of that. It's not my nipples, anyway. It's the areolae.'

'Christ,' said Andrew. 'Sorry I spoke. I like them, anyway. Lie down.'

'I'm finishing my coffee. Lie down yourself and have a fantasy. Andrew. Stop it.'

Shifting her mug from one hand to the other, Rosanna rolled onto her face, propping on her elbows, slopping coffee.

'Shit.'

'Why?'

'I've spilt my coffee.'

'No, I meant why stop it? I'm not doing anything.'

Andrew sat up, and threw the rest of his mug down his throat. His action had uncovered Rosanna, face downwards, naked. He put his mug down and put his right hand on her bottom.

'Oh, I don't know,' said Rosanna. 'It's my upbringing, maybe. The religion. I'm not much good at this sort of thing, I never was. I was terrible last night. Sorry.'

'You were great,' said Andrew. 'We were exhausted. There's nothing nicer, sometimes, than just to be received. A nice, warm, welcoming cunt, expecting nothing in return. It's relaxing. It's generous. I slept like a baby.'

'I know. I did get something in return, though. I wanted it. You. It was nice. It was what I wanted.'

Andrew turned to her, and put her mug down on the floor. He turned her over onto her back, half-covering her with the duvet. Rosanna put her palms under the back of her head, eyes closed. Outside there was birdsong, and early traffic. He studied her. Her armpits were unshaven.

'You're very tiny,' he said. 'But you don't look like a girl, at all. Your nipples are dark brown, aren't they? And I love your breasts. Even lying on your back they've got that shape. And what do they call these hip-bones? Is it salt-cellars, or is that up near your shoulders? They're lovely. You could eat your dinner off your stomach. How are you on coming? Orgasms? Being religious and all that.'

The flat white stomach convulsed twice, smoothly, as she laughed. She kept her eyes closed, and Andrew noticed that she coloured slightly.

'Being religious,' she replied. 'I've never had one. That's my story, anyway. I've only had one lover, as you know. An Irish Catholic. I'm lucky I'm not still a virgin. Actually, I think it's something in myself. There seems to be a sort of mechanism. It stops me, when I think I'm going to start. That's *my* religion, I suspect. To be fair to Irish Catholics. Adulterers.'

Forbes had dropped his hand onto her lower stomach. His third finger was moving through her pubic hair, into the cleft above her clitoris, very gently.

'To be fair to Seamus,' he said, quietly.

'His name was Des,' she said, calmly. 'As you know. Mark

you,' she added, 'I've got nothing against the idea. In principle.'

Slowly, almost imperceptibly, she drew her heels towards her, and moved her knees apart. Her thighs were very slim. Equally imperceptibly, Andrew moved his finger into the wider cleft.

'You've got the longest hair I've ever seen,' he said. 'It's very lovely. It's straight, and it's glossy. Most unusual. Most cunt hair's curly. And short.' He gave a little laugh. 'Hence the name. You've got a grey hair here.'

Rosanna sat up, eyes open, anxiously.

'I haven't! You don't get grey hairs there, surely?'

Forbes dropped his head onto her stomach. He spread the dark mass of her hair with his left hand, and tried to catch the elusive silver hair with the fingers of his right. Rosanna, resting her weight on her arms, leaned back, but craned her head forward to see. She noted Forbes' tousled hair, and the stubble on the curve of his cheek. His penis, moving gently to a rhythm of its own, lay partly on his slightly chubby stomach, amid its own, regulation short and curly hair, and partly on the duvet. There was a silver dribble coming from its head, which Rosanna, slightly to her surprise, wanted to taste.

'There,' he said. 'One grey hair. Christ, it's about three inches! Shall I pull it out?'

He tugged it, very softly, and Rosanna had a thrill of shocking, lovely, pain. Her thighs were wide apart now, and Andrew's lips were touching the topmost hair. She could feel his breath on her right thigh, and she heard him breathing deeply. He was smelling her, revelling in it, the smells of last night's love-making and today's. Laughing, he left the silver hair to hide itself, and separated the rest. Her labia, opened with his fingers, glistened. Slowly, Rosanna lay down on her back once more. One hand she laid across his head, and ear.

'Your clitoris is very sweet,' he said. 'It's very small and pink. What's wrong with your thigh? Why are you moving it?'

She was, although hardly consciously. She was moving her left knee inwards rhythmically, then letting it drop out. Each time the long tendon twanged tight it was exquisite. Having Andrew nestling between her legs, his head being banged by the thigh, was wonderful. His head was moving underneath her hand, turning. She wound her fingers in his hair, taking desperate care not to pull too hard. She was coming.

'I'm moving it because I like it,' she said. 'Is there any rule?'

She did not know what Andrew was doing with her now, or with what. She knew nothing, except that her thighs were strained outwards, and her stomach and back were arched, pushing, pushing. There was a feeling of heat, of electricity, a sudden, spreading shock. Sudden but slow. Then a wonderful, extraordinary, release of energy, that she could not stop. She twisted, joyfully, like an animal, throwing one leg over the other and rolling right across the bed and Andrew, almost pulling off his ears. She ended up on her back again, lying on the bare board floor, legs stretched across the mattress, open. Her eyes were open, too, and she was laughing.

'Christ,' she said, 'I've done it. You've done it! Andrew! Come into me! Oh Jesus.'

Andrew covered her body, and her mouth, and everything, with his, and came into her. They were lovers.

After Richard Pendlebury and Christian Fortyne had left his office, Sir Gerald Turner sat silently for many minutes. Normally, he would not have agreed to speak to an individual governor, any governor. But Pendlebury, who thought he had come to talk to Fortyne alone, had Bowscar. And Bowscar had Michael Masters.

In terms of publicity, Turner mused, Masters had been a thorn in his side since his arrest so many months ago. His image as a big fish in the murky pool of high finance, the widespread belief that he had the establishment, the judiciary, and possibly most members of the government in his pocket, had made a seemly handling of his case most difficult. Even when the balance had been tipped, though, and the big fish had gone to join the various small fry who *had* been made example of, the problem was not solved. The press, as usual, had changed sides and had done many features on the devastated children and the lonely, lovely wife. And Sir Gerald, in his club, at dinner parties formal and informal, and in hurried conversations with the noble and the mighty, had heard the rumblings. It was not only publicity, it appeared. Something had gone wrong somehow, somewhere down the line. What Sir Gerald could not understand, was what it had to do with him.

The latest bleat about the 'problem' had been the most bizarre and worrying – not least because it had come at ten past seven in the morning. Sir Cyril France had been extremely agitated, and not the slightest bit apologetic. In fact, he said, he had held off as long as this only because he had not thought the matter through. Michael Masters was issuing warnings in the middle of the night – and issuing them by telephone.

'By telephone?' said Turner. 'But that's impossible.'

'Impossible or not, that's what he's doing,' said Sir Cyril. 'And he said to tell the man who put him there that time is running out. It was a threat, Gerald. A threat of violence.'

'But what's it got to do with me, for God's sake? What does he think I can do about it? I can't get him out.'

There was a dismissive exhalation from the other end of the line.

'Quiet words in ears in clubs,' said France, bleakly. 'Mr Justice Harper surprised us all, remember? I'm not asking if you spoke to him, but Masters clearly thinks it. I'm telling you.'

When Sir Gerald had called Pendlebury and Fortyne into his office and told them of the alleged telephone, he had expected Pendlebury to deny it, even laugh it out of court. Quite frankly, he preferred not to believe it, and hoped for confirmation. But Pendlebury, after shock, then thought, had said that it was possible.

Sir Gerald said angrily: 'But good God, man, that's appalling! A telephone in a prison! A secret telephone! You must have the place searched. You must find it. Surely your prison officers can find an object like a telphone?'

Pendlebury, who had spent half an hour trying to convince Fortyne of the appalling danger they were facing, made a wry face. If there was a telephone, he explained, it would be owned and operated by the staff. It would be a way, in their eyes, of eking out their salaries.

'But don't you *know*?' demanded Turner. 'You're the governor, for Christ's sake. Don't you know?'

'I know what I am told,' said Pendlebury, crisply. 'As I keep trying to explain. Including officers and other staff there are nearly two thousand people in that building. Many of the prisoners know more about the real life of the place than I do. It's a secret world.'

Sir Gerald Turner was far too wise a man to rant. He felt helpless. He began to appreciate the helplessness that Pendlebury's frequent memos and appeals had doubtless struggled to convey.

'An effort must be made,' he said. 'Perhaps Fortyne could advise? Perhaps more staff . . . Jesus Christ Almighty. If the newspapers got to hear such things . . .'

Pendlebury, before he had left, had raised the subject of McGregor yet again. But it was too much for Turner. There was too much on his mind.

'Fortyne,' he said. 'What is the position now? What is our line? Tell Mr Pendlebury.'

'I have told him,' said Fortyne. 'McGregor must remain confined, on the basis of the medical reports we have received. I apologised for not informing him they were being sought, which was an oversight, but the MO's adamant. McGregor is totally unstable, and would probably suffer a schizoid breakdown if he was told too much. I attempted to explain, yet again, that we must take an overall view of what should be revealed and what withheld about the brother. I rather hoped that Mr Pendlebury, this time, had taken the point.'

'I did,' said Pendlebury. 'But—'

Sir Gerald interrupted.

'Mr Pendlebury,' he said. 'Please. I trust Mr Fortyne in this matter, so must you. Quite frankly, there seem to be more pressing things at Bowscar than the welfare of one prisoner. Leave it all with us. We must obviously think hard. The telephone in particular. I want something done about that. That is intolerable. Now please. We are so very busy here.'

Alone at last, Sir Gerald Turner pondered. There was too much going on, he thought, too much going on. After a while, he reached for his internal telephone and punched buttons.

'Fortyne,' he said. 'Where's Sinclair now? No matter – I want him back. Yes, today. Tomorrow. As soon as he can break engagements and get a flight. Don't tread on any important foreign toes, of course. But back here, fast.'

After a minute more, he dialled an outside number. He wanted to have a quiet, confidential lunch. With the managing editor of the *Daily Telegraph*. Then Gerald Turner phoned 10 Downing Street. He asked for an appointment with the Prime Minister. As soon as ever possible.

'It's time young Sinclair faced the music,' he told himself when all was done. 'It's more than time.'

The realisation that Sarah Williams was moving slowly up-country with *Cynthia's Beam* had amazed and warmed Michael Masters when he had worked it out. At first, until she had learned how to handle censored letters, she had been circumspect to the point of practical obscurity. She had talked of her and 'Cynthia' taking time off work to make a trip, but she had been totally vague about when it was to be, and where they might be going. Her regulation four sides of five-by-eight-inch paper (there was no official rule about it, but that was all the officers would deign to read) were usually filled up with painfully formal talk of jazz and mutual friends, so well-designed to hide the scent of their relationship that she might have been a maiden aunt of Masters, not a lover. At last, though, she had suggested that his wife be asked to bring Nicholson with her when visiting her husband, because he was 'good on the area and might be interesting'. The censoring officer had assumed Nicholson was a friend, another officer had formally granted leave for the canal guide to be one of the dozen books he was allowed to keep, and Barbara, unwittingly, had done the rest. Subsequent letters referred only to pubs and restaurants that Sarah and Cynthia had visited, and he was able to check them in the book and plot their progress week by week.

Because she had a scheme, however crazy, to hold on to, Sarah had picked up her normal life again, and returned to work. She was moving the canal boat at weekends, comforted by the knowledge that she was drawing always nearer to the prison, and the fantasy that she and Michael would sit on their bed again, and hold each other, and make love. Two nights before, he had devastated her by ringing her at home at midnight. He had been very brisk and brief, and told her to get a mobile phone for him, and give it to Cynthia for her birthday. He'd need the serial number of the agreement, naturally. Sarah, racked with joy at the sound of his voice, had been incoherent, but had worked out that that would be the way to convey the cell-phone number. She was trying to work out how to say she loved him with equally harmless words when he said the real ones for her, tersely, softly, but definitely. Afterwards she had cried, and he had masturbated. He had come luxuriously in the private aromatic refuge of his bed, to rich imaginings of their first night together on *Cynthia's Beam*. It would be not only marvellous, but safe. Canal boats were anonymous, untrackable, unnoticed. The slowest and most secure getaway vehicle ever dreamed of. And nobody, nobody in the world, would link the boat with him. She would be just another early summer mover, with two quiet people holidaying on board. Soon he would have a date, and Sarah would have a telephone. Soon, it would be safe to hint at more, of a good pub lunch perhaps, through their Nicholson code. They would disappear.

Now, thirty-six hours later, Masters lay on his bed, not in it. For once, there were only three people in the cell – himself and Hughes and Jerrold – and to all of them, the place felt unnaturally empty. For although Alan Hughes had provided the spark, Lister had rapidly assumed command of operations. Jerrold and Masters, at first, had been inclined to feel aggrieved by the very dynamism of the American, the ruthless speed at which he worked. But Hughes, to their surprise, had sided with him. What did you expect, he asked on one occasion? A vicarage tea party?

In fact, Hughes had pointed out in the earliest talks with Lister that his 'philosophical proposition' could never be as neat and clean as it sounded. Talking about 'withdrawal of consent' was one thing, but getting the mass of prisoners to do it was quite another. The project, once it was up and running, would be fraught with danger. It would involve violence, intimidation, bloodshed probably, and close association with men who might at any time turn against them to the point of maiming or even death. It would involve bribing both the barons and the corrupt officers who oversaw the sub-society of rape, drugs and prostitution in the jail. To Masters – who still saw prison life as transient, a fleeting nightmare that was divorced from actual life – it came as a shock to realise that to many it *was* life: that trying to make them leave Bowscar would be to ask them to destroy a society and a livelihood. Hughes and Lister also agreed very early on that someone would be needed 'on the ground', someone who could move men around, control the disruptive elements, make contacts, arrange meetings. There was no question about who it had to be: Brian Rogers.

For Masters, who feared and hated Rogers, this was a sticking point. He knew the man wanted to make love to him, and that it was only his great wealth and the power that conferred that saved him from rape. The fact that it was not a homosexual lust he found more chilling. Rogers wanted to rape him because of who he was, as he would have wanted to exercise primeval dominance over any strong woman. It was not only a question of the lust and violence in the big man's eyes, either. Masters thought he was a liar and a fantasist. He claimed to have been in the SAS, and to control a crooked network outside prison that amounted to a private Mafia. In fact, Alan Hughes had told him, Rogers had been leader of a gang of extortionists and bankroll raiders who had been relatively successful by dint of obscene violence and utter lack of pity. His power in the Scar, allied to large wealth amassed inside through drugs and deployed in bribery, was similarly based.

When Masters had objected, though, it was Lister who had argued.

'Michael,' he had said. 'That man is what we need. You just can't have it both ways, feller. He's dangerous, he's hard, he's got the business. He also has mobility. You and me, we can't walk this jail at will, OK? What's more, we don't know who we need to speak to, do we? We have to talk to the Irishmen, right? We have to talk to the gays, the blacks, the fruitcakes, the Forty-Threes. I don't even know what blocks they're on, for fucksake. Nor do you. Alan does, and every time he sticks his nose out of the cell some screw punches it. Matthew they watch like Dolly Parton's tits in spades, no pun intended. We *need* that monster.'

'Jesus,' put in Jerrold. 'Are we letting the Irish in on this? Jesus Christ.'

'We're letting everybody in,' replied Lister. 'Are you serious or what? If this job's going to happen, it happens one hundred per cent or it fails. Of course we tell the fucking Irish.' He turned to Hughes, in appeal. 'Alan? What is this shit?'

Hughes nodded. He gazed at Matthew Jerrold, then at Masters.

'We tell everyone. Everyone who can be trusted to join in or gum the works up. They don't have to know what's behind it, most of them. For God's sake, some of the poor bastards can't even get their cocks out for a piss. But the place has got to fall to pieces. We've got to swamp the system, clog it up completely. We're getting out, remember? It's not a jamboree.'

Lister crushed a cigarette.

'Those Irishmen are serious, right? They're terrorists, for fucksake. Give them the news in time, give them the date, and they'll have an armoured car outside. A tank. Bazookas. Whether you like it or not, Mike, that's where it's at. We're talking war. You'll have guys outside, yeah? I sure as hell ain't waiting for a bus. This place has got to explode like a hornets' nest that someone kicked. We tell everyone.'

'Who can be trusted,' Hughes reiterated. 'Which is where Rogers and his thugs come in. He'll know who to tell, and who to frighten. Even the bentest screws probably wouldn't keep a full-scale riot underneath their caps, so we need secrecy. Everybody knows that if they cross Rogers they end up dead. He's our man.'

From the first formal meeting, Alan Hughes was proved to be right. Thug he might have been, but Rogers was not stupid. He digested the outline of the plan, then the details, then came back with angles of his own. He organised meeting times and places, and he began to put out feelers to his fellow barons in the other wings and halls. In his opinion – in his humble opinion he said, gazing ironically at Masters with his bright, lubricious eyes – they needed a military structure of control. They needed a cadre who would activate the blow-up on the day, in every area, with precision.

'I was in the SAS,' he said. 'I was a sergeant. We had a rule. Never move until you're set. Until everything is set. Another thing. We need guns.'

This time, it was Hughes who made objections. Guns, he said, would shift it up a gear. If men had guns, men would shoot. His theory, at its purest, would involve only minimal violence. The system would break under the strain of numbers, not of blood.

'Bollocks,' Rogers said, brutally. His red-haired henchman, Billy Ford, nodded at his side. 'Some of the screws are fucking barmy. They'll try to keep us in. They won't see reason.'

Ford did not have the irony, but he shared the view.

'Aye,' he said. 'Some of them need shooting, any road. And some of the other cunts in here. I'm going to kill a nonce or two, no danger.'

'But if we had guns,' Hughes argued, 'they'd crack down harder. There'd be people killed, they'd send the Army in. It really would be war.'

'They'll send the Army in anyway, you twat,' said Rogers. 'They've got a plan, haven't they? After Buckie. Don't you listen to the radio? That Home Secretary.'

'Sir Gerald Turner,' murmured Hughes. He did not like the talk of guns. He could imagine some of the consequences. 'I know him. Knew him, once.'

'No,' said Rogers. 'His sidekick. Donald Something. Donald fucking Duck.'

'Sinclair,' said Masters. 'Yes, that sounds like Sinclair.'

'Bloody Ada,' said Billy Ford. 'And you know *him*, I suppose? How about the Queen? Prince Philip? Couldn't you tap them up for some guns? They're always popping pheasants, ain't they? Here, that's a thought, Brian! That farmhouse that we done that time, with Terry. Down in Hampshire, somewhere. What was it, World's End?'

'World's End,' said Brian Rogers. 'Pratt's Farm. They go in for funny names in Hampshire, don't they? So what? We're in Staffs.'

'He had guns though, didn't he? That old prat what lives there. All alone with all them shotguns. We could get someone outside to do him over, couldn't we? It's lonely enough. An easy roll.'

'You're fucking barmy,' said Rogers. 'What use are shotguns? How we going to get them in, up your Lynn's jacksie? And it's in bleeding Hampshire, ain't it? It's fucking miles away. Two hundred.'

'If it comes to that,' said Masters, sarcastically, 'I've got an uncle with a full-scale armoury. My wife has, anyway. He's even got an elephant gun. He could pull a helicopter down. He lives alone as well, on a Scottish bloody island. Jesus, *I've* got guns at home. Finding them's not the problem, is it?'

'What guns?' said Lister, sharply. 'Handguns?'

'Yes, three or four. But so what, Charlie? They're in a locked steel cupboard. They're not accessible. D'you think my fucking wife's going to bring them in? If I even suggested it, she'd go straight to the law. I promise you.'

Billy Ford had got excited. He pushed his hair back from his eyes.

'We could get it done! Give us the details, Mike! We could get them lifted! We wouldn't do no damage!'

Even Brian Rogers laughed.

'I can just see it, can't you?' he said. He fixed his eyes on Michael Masters, and his smile was hungry. 'Mikey gives us the details, and we send some boys in. You be careful, we tell them. Make sure you don't fuck up the carpets. Or the children. Or the little wife. Don't get out of hand, lads. Don't do anything I wouldn't do. Be your age, Billy, for Christ's sake.' He paused, for a fraction of a beat. 'We'll bear it in mind for some other time, though. I expect you're in the phone book aren't you, Mike?'

There was an uncomfortable silence, which Brian Rogers broke. He reached into the pocket of his dungarees and produced a flick-knife. Snapped open, it had a polished, pointed, six-inch blade.

'Without no guns,' he said, 'we've got much less control, that's all I'm worried about. I mean, knives, razors, knuckles – they're all right, but there's too many of them for comfort, isn't there? I mean, we'll get tooled up from now on, we'll start to organise some blades, try and arm the important ones, like us. But you never know who else is going tooled. There's some dirty bastards in this place, and I don't just mean the screws. But they'd be capable too. A little bit of sweet revenge. And what a tragedy, eh? All the other cunts escape, and we end up fucking slaughtered. Charlie, you know guns. You'd rather have one, wouldn't you?'

Charles Lister reached downwards and tucked two fingers underneath his trouser leg. When he straightened, a thin and wicked piece of steel glittered in his hand. One end was buried in a cork.

'My mama told me never walk naked in the big bad world,' he said. 'Sure I'd like a gun. But I can kill you with this if I need to. Or my fingers. I only tell you this, friends, in case there comes a time . . . But we're all buddies, OK? Alan, Michael, Matthew?'

'I got nothing,' said Matthew Jerrold. 'My mummy told me the opposite to yours, Charlie. She said ask a policeman. And look where that got me!'

'You lying nignog twat,' said Brian Rogers. 'We all know about you and coppers, Sunshine. You chop the fuckers up.'

'There's a moral dilemma and a half,' said Alan Hughes, sardonically. 'Who should you hate most, blacks or policemen?'

'I fucking hate them both,' said Billy Ford. 'No contest. I bet you're ironed up to fuck, you lying bastard.'

Jerrold's sculpted face was glistening and still. For a moment he said nothing. Then: 'You better had believe that, Billy. You better had believe that.'

In meeting after meeting Rogers worried at the gun idea, even while he organised the constant stream of kitchen knives, bodkins, razor blades and other weaponry for distribution to his chosen NCOs throughout the Scar. As an idea, it never ceased to unnerve Alan Hughes, a feeling which he tried to hide from Lister, but not from Jerrold or Masters. 'Webster,' he once quoted to them both, 'could see the skull beneath the skin.' It was a line of T. S. Eliot's, he added, about a Jacobean playwright. They laughed at him for being an over-educated prat. But they knew exactly what he meant.

Two days after Masters' call to Sarah, Charles Lister returned after an absence of more than an hour, and led him, alone, to a mysteriously empty cell. He had spoken to his friends, he said. It had been a difficult but important conversation. The upshot was, that they would bring the guns in. The handguns. They had absolutely insisted that they could not provide the weapons, that was impossible. But they could bring them in. All that was needed was for Masters to provide them. Masters was aghast.

'But it's impossible! I told you! They're locked away. It's a combination lock. My wife would tell the police.'

'You've got the girlfriend, haven't you?' said Lister. 'You can find out when the house is empty. Give her the number to the alarm, give her the combination to the secure cabinet. We need those pistols, Michael, we need them to survive. I'm talking you and me, friend, not anybody else. Not to shoot our way out, but to survive. They'll cut us down, Michael. They'll fucking cut us down.'

It was news to Masters that Lister knew about Sarah Williams, but not a shock. Nothing shocked him any more about the Scar. Presumably Rogers knew as well, the man who ruled the phone. The man, quite probably, who indeed would cut him down.

'I'll call her,' he said, quietly.

'You better had.'

Thirty-four miles from Bowscar Prison, two men drove sombrely back to London. They had spoken little since they left, but they were both obscurely afraid. They knew now that Lister had somehow been in touch with his American associates, and they knew that something big and terrible was going to happen. Like Michael Masters they were a part of it, and like him, they could see no way out. They were riding a tiger.

It was Rosanna Nixon's idea to speak to Richard Pendlebury directly, and it was she who had tracked down the village where he lived. Her main reason for the suggestion had been that they would escape the spooks by going to a small country hotel a couple of miles away, and among Forbes' reasons for agreeing was that that idea appealed to him mightily. He and Rosanna had spent most of the intervening days making love in one way or another, and neither of them could get enough of it. But they had tried hard to keep the seriousness of their purpose in mind, and had spent two days – between romps in the large and ancient bed they had acquired with their sixteenth-century room in the Fradshawe Arms Hotel – on reconnaissance. This evening, after a bite to eat, they were confident they would beard the governor in the lonely country pub he favoured. When they arrived, on foot, they identified his car, and exchanged a smile.

'Here goes,' said Rosanna. 'Christ, Andrew, I'm on pins. Give us a kiss.'

Despite their gleanings that Pendlebury was considered to be a liberal in the service, they both assumed the expression would be relative. In their terms, he could only be right-wing, and would inevitably meet their combination of revelation and demand with lies, evasions, and possibly threats. All they really hoped for was to get him to reveal – probably by default – that McGregor was indeed in Bowscar, so that they could present it to the Home Office as concrete fact, and force an answer from them. Pendlebury disarmed them completely.

He was sitting alone at a table when they entered, with a pint of bitter at his hand. Forbes bought bitter for himself, lager for Rosanna, and presented the pair of them in front of Pendlebury. He came straight to the point, using their real names and stating their business. Pendlebury did not look the sort who would respond to tricky questions, or even answer them. He considered them for a long moment, then invited them to sit. Rosanna, who had never really done anything quite like this before, was bubbling.

'You must understand,' said Pendlebury, 'that I could lose my job by talking to you. Especially if McGregor *were* in Bowscar. I'm afraid you'll have to explain in detail why you want to know.'

Between them, Rosanna and Andrew Forbes outlined what they understood. Pendlebury listened impassively until the death of James McGregor was mentioned. They both saw his eyes widen as if in shock.

'Didn't you know that?' asked Forbes. 'We thought . . .'

'It was announced,' said Rosanna. 'Well, it made the Scottish papers. Although they didn't make the connection. The fact that he was Angus's brother. Oh.'

'Oh indeed,' said Pendlebury. 'Oh indeed.'

After that, he listened with his forehead resting on one hand, his face half-hidden. When they had finished, he stayed deep in thought although oddly, in Rosanna's view, he continued to drink his bitter. Before he spoke, he went to the bar and bought another round, for all of them. More thinking time. Returned, he sat and raised his beer in a joyless toast.

'Angus McGregor is in Bowscar,' he said. 'And like you two, I think that it is scandalous. More than that, now I have heard your side of the story, I think it is obscene. Quite simply, McGregor is the victim of a conspiracy.'

'But why?' asked Rosanna. 'What's it for? What do they hope to gain by it?'

'Peace,' said Pendlebury. 'They're terrified by the state of the prisons. They're terrified about what would happen if the Scottish violence spread. They're terrified.'

'Well that,' said Andrew Forbes with satisfaction, 'is not our problem, is it? Perhaps when this comes out it'll force the smug bastards to do something about it. It'll go against the grain, but they might even have to let some people out. Cut the prison population, improve conditions. Mr Pendlebury – this might just be a turning point!'

Pendlebury's pale, exhausted face was like a mask. He moved his head from side to side, slowly.

'You can't publish it,' he said. 'It's far too late. My prison's like a powder keg, an unexploded bomb. Mr Forbes, Miss Nixon – that is not the way.'

'It is the way!' said Andrew, angrily. 'That's always their excuse, isn't it? It's the great British parrot cry: suppress it! It's just too easy, Mr Pendlebury. Think of Angus McGregor for once. Think of James. We've got to tell the truth!'

Pendlebury, for a moment, responded to the anger.

'The truth is this,' he snapped. 'If you want blood on your hands, go ahead and publish. Publish and be damned is the expression, isn't it? But don't fool yourselves that you will be the ones who suffer, will you? You won't be damned. I will. My daughter will. Angus McGregor will, and all the other men involved. Good God, man, I've had enough of bashing my head against a wall of cynicism and incomprehension at the Home Office. Won't *you* see sense? Do you *want* a bloodbath?'

They were in an alcove, and the inn was old. Nobody had noticed the raised voices, or the passion. Forbes and Pendlebury stared at each other. Forbes shook his head.

'No,' he said. 'We don't. If it's a matter of that, we don't. But what will happen? About McGregor? It can't just go on, for God's sake. Can it?'

Pendlebury clasped both hands around his beer pot.

'No,' he said.

Before they left, the governor took their number at the Fradshawe, and at both their homes. He did not smile when they told him the latter two were bugged, but he said he thought his own home number – ex-directory – was safe. He would tell his daughter Eileen all about them, he said, so that she could help if he was not there. He asked them to make nothing known, and not to try the Home Office, until they had spoken further.

That night, underneath the eiderdowns of their monumental bed, they talked for hours before the idea of sex occurred to them. The sweet taste of success had turned slightly bitter.

FOURTEEN

The aspect of his recall that upset Donald Sinclair most was the crudeness of the way it had been done. As he sipped a heavily watered whisky only seven hours after stepping off his flight from Sydney, it became increasingly obvious, and increasingly a matter of private outrage, that he had been set up. The fact that he had been summoned to this party after thirty hours non-stop travel, the fact that Mary's presence had been more or less required, was confirmation enough. Somebody, for some reason, was intent on humiliating him.

As he ranged the plush reception rooms of the Home Office, bent mainly on avoiding contact with people who wanted to ask about the tour, Sinclair knew he would look in vain for Judith Parker. The news that his wife was coming up from Surrey had visibly upset her, and after helping with a punishing press conference pre-organised by Christian Fortyne, she had announced her intention of going home. Fortyne, half-jokingly perhaps, had warned her that her absence would be frowned upon – the Prime Minister, after all, did not recognise the existence of mythical ailments like jet-lag or exhaustion – but Judith had responded angrily. The PM had not, in the event, turned up.

Sinclair was jet-lagged, there was no doubt of it. He felt irritated and strangely fragile, as if he were recovering from a severe bout of flu. To his surprise he missed Judith instantly and quite considerably, and could remember only too plainly the jolt he had felt on seeing Mary again. Not a jolt of pleasure, by any means. He looked at her now as she walked into the room in conversation with a civil servant. She was cool, and beautiful, and elegant, and contained. He did not love her.

The time abroad with Judith had been an odd one for their relationship. They had never had the luxury of hours, days, unbrokenly together before, and once they had relaxed into a routine their pleasure in each other had blossomed. 'Alarmingly', had been Judith's word for it, as they had talked after making quite glorious love one day in a sheltered hollow deep in the Tasmanian bush, and alarming it had been. Both of them knew that their 'love' had been in some ways a convenience, a kind of mild excitement with career overtones, and both of them knew it had altered. There was a danger in it, and intensity. Although Judith Parker avoided jet-lag when they returned to Britain, her temper was uncertain and her underlying mood was fiercely black. Donald Sinclair, who had trodden this path before, experienced the fear and desolation as potential, rather than reality. He would have to wait and see.

Their tour of foreign prisons – the good, the bad, the extraordinary – had forced them to hammer out political points, as well. One in particular, the penitentiary at Marion, Illinois, that he had clashed with Mary briefly over, had led to arguments. It was a lonely fortress of a jail, with gun-towers and high fences reminiscent of a concentration camp, where America's most violent men, the men who killed fellow prisoners and prison officers, were taken and contained hermetically until the poison of their psychopathy was drawn. Once released back into the 'mainstream' of the system, they had been told, few of them returned.

To Judith, these tales of 'cure', however well documented by US penologists and shrinks, rang false, they reeked of wish-fulfilment. Apart from anything else, she said, the Marion regime was not far removed from the sort of vile and violent treatment that had once made Scottish prisons the most infamous – and least successful – in Britain. Repression not only smacked of the medieval – it did not work.

But Sinclair's view was complex, and ironic.

'What we need in Britain,' he said, 'what I'm working for, is a radical solution. I don't want to squander billions on ten new jails in seven years to fill with drunks and misfits and fine defaulters and mental cases, I want to close some down. I want a smaller, leaner, more efficient system that doesn't gobble money and probably cuts the crime rate, too. I'm talking cash, Judith, a system that not only works, but pays. It's a political dream.'

They were standing alone, amidst the ruins of another great experiment in penology, in Port Arthur in Tasmania. It was a sunny day, with a cool breeze blowing off the creek where the convict ships had once discharged their loads. Sinclair's hair was tousled, his face enlivened by debate. Judith touched his hand.

'Fine,' she said, 'that's fine. I agree with every word, Donald, it's got to happen. But how is Marion going to change it? Look at this place. They brought these poor devils twelve thousand miles and locked them in a place like Marion. It's madness. It's insanity.'

'No! It's the key! We spend millions and millions a year unnecessarily. We've got top security until it's coming out of our ears, and security costs money. With Marion as with Port Arthur – all the worst scum in one sink. The other jails get down-rated. Low security, *no* security in some of them! Then we clear out remandees, bring in other measures, cut the prison population to the bone. Jackpot!'

'But men in chains. It's almost torture. It's inhuman.'

'Exactly!' His eyes were laughing, now. 'How else could I get the money? We English are a mean-spirited lot, my love, mean-minded. I'd never get the funding in a million years to reform the system on a humane ticket, however much it needs it. Think of the PM. Think of the backwoodsmen. But they'll run amok with joy at this, they'll see votes galore in it. And when it's working it'll be too late, the bastards will have voted for it. They'll be hog-tied.'

'It would be quicker and cheaper,' said Judith Parker, drily, 'to bring back hanging. More popular with the PM, too.'

'If we could hang them all,' said Sinclair, cheerfully, 'I'd agree with you – but we can't! Anyway, you're being cynical and I, for once, am not. Look, there are some animals in the jails, Judith, you can't get round that simple fact. There are some men who need a Marion, possibly even death. In any case, to change things, you need power. A regime like Marion would give it to me, and the real reforms could follow. Believe me. First you need the power.'

Judith did believe him. As they made love that night, they talked about it more. Their fucking was fantastic these days, and they often found themselves, until the crucial stages, talking about their work. Political animals, Donald had dubbed them, as they licked, and nibbled and discussed. They loved it. Later, as she lay beneath him, building slowly to orgasm, the thoughts became opaque, they flitted through her mind. She wondered what he'd sacrifice for the power itself, never mind ideals and all the rest. She wondered if he ever thought of James McGregor, or remembered him. As she came she thought: you are corrupt, my darling, I know you are. Delicious.

The journey back had been a strange one, largely because Sinclair had been unable to find out why he'd been recalled. The news had been brought to him before breakfast, and it was simple: they were booked on a flight from Hobart, via Sydney, and they would be on it. In London, feeling dreadful, and betrayed, and put-upon, Sinclair had had the shortest of meetings with Christian Fortyne, then been ushered into a VIP reception room to face the press. Sensing a blood sacrifice, they had jumped on him like lions. All Sinclair knew for certain was that the rioting at Bowscar, and Raymond Orchard's suicide, had been leaked. Would he now, at last, announce firm measures, stop the rot?

He was infuriated. Had he not been so badly jet-lagged, had Fortyne offered a more efficient cover, he would have fielded it all with ease. But he could smell assassin, and it rattled him. He talked about the need for firmness, certainly, and foolishly he mentioned Marion, then bogged down in its relevance or otherwise to Britain's situation. He waffled. The cameras, their flashbulbs flickering like summer lightning, captured it all perfectly for next day's front pages. Even down to the dark smudges underneath his eyes and his slightly misplaced tie.

At the cocktail party, Sinclair was noted – with a certain jocularity – to be in a foul temper. And at nine o'clock, having been told by Mary for the second time that he was being paranoid, he decided to take her snapped advice and have it out with Turner. He hung on the fringes of a group until the others took the hint and left them alone, then, slightly pale but apparently collected, he confronted him.

'Sir Gerald,' he said. 'I feel undermined. I've been dragged back from Australia for no sufficient reason, I've been set up for the press, and I've been required to turn up here like a performing dog. What upsets me is it's all been so bloody obvious. What have I done wrong? Been too successful? Trodden on your toes? What's going on?'

He was aware as he was speaking of sounding clumsy, arrogant. Indeed, Sir Gerald Turner responded with a mixture of amusement and irritation. His eyebrows rose slightly in his bland, unthreatening face.

'Too successful?' he said, with a small edge of contempt. 'My my, Donald. Did you not hear the questions that were put to you? Has Fortyne not briefed you fully yet? I'd hardly say successful.'

'I'm sorry,' said Sinclair. 'That came out wrong. What I mean is—'

'What I mean is,' Sir Gerald interrupted, 'that the peace you promised me is a damned long time a-coming. You swan off round the world, and leave me to hold the baby. Well the baby's shit itself, and I won't change the nappy, understand? You've got above yourself, laddie. To mix yet more metaphors, you were trying to run before you could walk – and I've clipped your wings.'

He turned away, attaching himself seamlessly to another waiting group. Sinclair, with an effort, composed himself and sauntered to another room.

Right, you bastard, he thought. So you're going to make a fight of it, are you? A dirty fight. Well, that's all right by me . . .

Before Richard Pendlebury spoke to Angus McGregor entirely alone, he almost had to physically fight with his own prison officers. The three men in their protective clothing who accompanied him to the door were deeply worried at his decision – genuinely, he knew and acknowledged – while Christopher Abbey, as union representative present at their behest, displayed a far more ambivalent attitude. He appeared quite happy at the prospect of the governor walking into a lion's den alone – but not if it should rebound upon his members.

'It is not my opinion,' he intoned, 'that this is a reasonable thing to do. It is all very well for you to undertake this act, but I must ask you to reconsider it. The consequences for yourself I cannot comment on. But my members, if anything goes wrong, will have to pick up the pieces. That will be unpleasant, sir. It could be dangerous.'

Pendlebury, having reached his own difficult and dangerous decision after many hours of mental anguish, was not inclined to argue. He moved a step nearer the strip cell.

'Mr Simons,' he said to one of the officers, 'I appreciate your concern. I have taken everything into consideration, and I have consulted with my deputies. Now will you kindly let me in?'

As he took another step forward, Abbey moved to block him. Pendlebury's face flushed with unaccustomed anger.

'Abbey,' he snapped. 'I am telling you. Get out of my way, and stop interfering in my work.'

Christopher Abbey had put himself into a difficult position. He was facing the governor, chin to chin, and he could only give way. Suddenly, with a turn so swift it was almost a flounce, he did. His shoulder brushed Pendlebury, pushing him aside. Whether it was deliberate or not, the governor chose to ignore it. Abbey, without looking back, walked off.

Simons said quietly: 'I still wish you wouldn't, Mr Pendlebury.

It's suicidal, sir.' But he opened the outer, then the inner, door. 'We'll be ready,' he added. 'We'll be close.'

As Pendlebury entered the strip cell, he saw that McGregor was waiting for him. He was standing at the farthest point of the cell, with his blanket wrapped and tucked so that he did not have to hold it. His eyes were unreadable, but his face was open. In fact, he was curious.

'What was that all about?' he asked. 'Are you having trouble with the staff again?'

It was a joke, which surprised and reassured Pendlebury. He was also surprised that McGregor did not appear to question that he should have visited alone.

'I didn't realise you could hear,' he said. 'I thought these pads were meant to be soundproof.'

'I hear enough. I heard that bastard Abbey, didn't I? Any enemy of his is a friend of mine. I'd offer you a seat . . .'

He indicated the padded bench. It was smeared with excrement. The cell smelt bad.

'It's not that I've gone dirty,' explained McGregor. 'It's just that some of the gorillas have started fun and games. No names no packdrill, eh? I wouldn't want to get them into trouble!'

The two of them had spoken since the Orchard flare-up. They had patched things up. But Pendlebury was aware that some of his officers had not forgiven McGregor. He understood their fear, their attitude, but still it filled him with disgust.

'You seem to take it very well,' he said. 'I'd apologise on their behalf if that wouldn't sound like arrant nonsense. Some of them are good men. Most of them. Which doesn't help you much.'

McGregor, unusually relaxed, went and sat on his bench. He stretched his thin, pale legs.

'Nothing helps me very much,' he said. 'If I'd had Barlinnie and a man like you – Barlinnie in the old days, the Dobson days, before the bastards ruined it – if I'd had that I might have been all right. It might have saved me. It's too late now.'

'No. Not too late. You're a sane and intelligent man, Angus. You must never say too late.'

McGregor lowered his head and smiled a private smile.

'A sane and intelligent man,' he repeated. 'I've killed more people than you've had hot dinners. Although I'm sorry for it, so I guess I'm not quite lunatic. No, I'm not sane. Not entirely. By the way, don't call me Angus, eh? It makes me feel bad, because I can't call you by your name. I know you say I can, but I can't.

So call me McGregor. Anything. The Animal. Not Angus. What's the purpose, by the way? Why are you here? Why the visit?'

'What do you mean?' said Pendlebury, playing for time. 'It's been some days. I just thought—'

'Awa' to fuck,' jeered McGregor. 'Come off it, sir. Why the ruckus with the spacemen? Why all alone? Talking of sanity, what the fuck are you doing in here, with me? Come on!'

Pendlebury's mouth was drying. It was not exactly fear. He licked his lips.

'Look,' he said. 'I want you out of here. You've been in solitary far too long, and I don't like it. Within reason, I'd be prepared to let you choose your cell mates. That is, if you did not fit the first time, or two, I'd let you change. Monitor the situation. I will not have you in a strip cell any longer.'

'Aye,' said McGregor. 'Acknowledged. But why?'

Now Pendlebury was afraid. It had to be said, though. He would no longer be a party to deception.

'Mr McGregor,' he said. 'The fact of the matter is that you were brought to Bowscar because of an appalling situation in Scotland. Since then, as you know, I have tried to get some decency, some humanity, some answers. I have failed. It is, of course, a matter of your brother. And now I am acting entirely on my own.'

McGregor did not respond for a very long time. Pendlebury, standing, was aware of enormous tension in himself. His fists were clenched, the back of his neck was sharply painful. He had absolutely no way of knowing what would happen next. He would have loved to have left. He remembered Rosanna and Forbes in the pub, his warning of the consequences of the story getting out, of McGregor hearing of it. He tried to wet his lips once more, without being noticed, without making the smallest noise.

'He's dead,' said McGregor. 'He's got to be. That's it, isn't it? He's dead.'

'Yes. I'm very sorry.'

'How?'

Now it was Pendlebury's turn to be silent for an unnatural length of time. He had been through it all a hundred times, but he had reached no firm decision on what would be best to reveal or suppress. He had left it till the moment, told himself that the right answer would reveal itself. But it hadn't.

'He was on the roof at Buckie,' said McGregor, flatly. 'Did they murder him?'

What if Forbes and the Scottish girl were wrong? What if

they were liars, gutter journalists looking for good copy? But Pendlebury did not believe that. He trusted them.

'According to the Home Office,' he said, 'your brother died of natural causes.'

There must have been something in his voice, an element he could not control. Angus McGregor raised his head.

'You don't believe it?'

'No,' said Pendlebury. His voice was strangled. 'I do not.'

In his mind's eye, as he had gone over the possible scenario time after time, the governor had seen this moment as the point of maximum danger. But as the prisoner stood and walked towards him, he felt nothing but relief. The man's face was calm. He was digesting. A process was working through. He came close, and the governor did not flinch.

'The Home Office,' said McGregor. His eyes were blank. 'That's Whatsisface. Sir Gerald Turner.'

'Not him personally, necessarily. It was a press announcement. Released in Scotland.'

'He'll do, right enough. He's the man in charge. I'll maybe kill him, one day. That would be the best. And Jimmy's gone.'

McGregor was talking absent-mindedly, half-musing. Pendlebury wondered if he would do what he said. He doubted it. It was like a dream, like therapy. The blankness in McGregor's eyes was clearing.

'Thanks for telling me,' he said. 'I guess I knew, but thanks. I'd like to leave this cell. Thank you.'

Pendlebury, unhappily, took the proffered hand.

'I'll sort it out,' he said.

Sarah Williams stood in the shadow of Michael Masters' boathouse and listened to the soft wind sighing through the trees. It was not a cold night, and she was well dressed up, but she felt chill and sick. She could still hardly believe that she was doing this. She could hardly believe that Michael had asked her to, or that he had meant it. She was still unsure why she had finally said yes.

The call had come while she had been picnicking beside the canal one sunny afternoon. She had moored *Cynthia's Beam* on her spikes, shut off the engine, and pulled a bottle of Vinho Verde from the fridge. She had prepared a salad, taking her time, and laid out a selection of meats, sausage and cheese. If Michael had been with her, they would have sat and watched the sunlight on the water and talked. As it was, she read a book. *Cynthia's Beam* was only two days' running from Bowscar. Whatever that meant in reality, it felt hopeful. She was quite happy.

The warbling of the telephone inside the boat increased her happiness with a bound, because it could only be Masters. She glanced at her watch and jumped up, her light skirt whirling. It took her half a minute to clamber down into the doghouse then through to the main cabin. 'Hallo,' she said, still wary of the magic of it all. 'It's me.'

Michael's voice had been anxious, and his message grim. He had little time, he said, and she could not argue. It was vital that she did what she was asked, and did not worry about the implications. He promised her that it was safe, if she was careful. If it failed, if she failed, he would be stuck in Bowscar. He would not get out.

Until now, she had not known that the plan was to escape, but she had understood it in her heart and hopes. Otherwise, why the telephone? She knew that she had been waiting for a call, and for a rendezvous. She had left her job, on some bold pretext of going abroad for a long while, and she was living on the boat. She had been enjoying herself, fantasising, thinking it would be easy. Now this. Michael Masters was giving her a time, and a day, to break into his house and take his pistols.

The breaking in was not the difficult part. It was a big house, with three separate burglar alarm systems. Masters used one part of it almost exclusively as his own, especially when his sons were away at school. It contained a games room, a squash court, a billiards room, his study. In the study were two steel cabinets, one for his shotguns, one for the pistols. There was also a bed. Some nights, when he was busy at the battery of computers and tape machines he used to juggle fortunes with, he stayed in the room all night. He slept there. Some nights, Sarah Williams opened a small side door with her key, tapped in the digits that silenced the alarm, and went to join him.

'It'll be a piece of cake,' he said. 'An adventure. Barbara never goes into my wing, and anyway, she'll be in bed by midnight. I'm sorry to ask you, Thing, but there's no alternative. Sarah?'

But you can't, she thought. You can't ask me to go into your house. Where your wife is. You can't ask me to break the law, to risk being caught by her! It's horrible.

'Sarah? Listen, for Christ's sake, darling. Listen, they're only target guns. There's not going to be a shoot-out or anything. Sarah!'

Sarah had been gazing through the window of the boat. Two swans had swum by, majestic on the sparkling green-brown water. She could hear the thud of a diesel slowly coming nearer. She did not speak.

'Sarah!' Masters' voice was raised, insistent. 'For Christ's sake, do you think this is *normal*, using a fucking phone in prison? Answer me!'

'Yes,' she said. 'I'm sorry. But Michael.'

He cut in, harshly.

'Will you do it or won't you? That's all I need to know. If you don't – I'm finished.'

'Yes,' said Sarah Williams. 'Of course I'll do it, Michael. Of course.'

He did not waste time with thanks. He was speaking fast now, blurting.

'It must be Tuesday night,' he said. 'I won't give you the combination, but it's the burglar alarm backwards, right? You must be clear by 2 a.m., then wait in Abel's Lane, near the split tree, with me? A white Polo will arrive, with two men in it. They'll say "Cynthia's Beam is bright tonight". You give them the pistols. And ammunition, of course. That's in the cabinet as well. It's all in one box, mixed up.'

'But Michael,' she croaked. '*Cynthia's Be—*'

He cut in urgently: 'They won't know what it means. They're policemen, for God's sake! Coppers!'

There was an angry voice at a distance from the telephone. An argument. The line went muffled, then dead. Sarah too, or so she felt. Slowly, she replaced the receiver and sat heavily on the bed. She watched the long dark shape of the other narrowboat slide by, its diesel thumping loudly. The man on the tiller saw her through the window and waved.

'*Cynthia's Beam*,' she heard a woman shout. 'What a lovely name!'

Sarah, as she slowly turned her key in the side-door lock, could not keep down the thoughts of criminality that had assailed, assaulted, her since Masters had given her this mission. It was a subject that in the past she had been able to keep at bay, although she had known almost from the first that his fortune was the result of some kind of tightrope act, he had revelled in it. His attitude had been that the whole thrust of government was based on buccaneering, an invitation for the clever and the daring to play ducks and drakes with lumpen regulations – and in any case nobody, but nobody, had ever been hurt by his activities. Even when he had been imprisoned it had still been easy, because of the injustice somebody had done him, because he'd been betrayed. But she had, inevitably, wondered how other women managed – as they so often and so publicly did – to stand behind more truly awful men. Now he was after guns, which could only mean one thing. He was going to become a criminal, even if he was not one now. And he was making her one in the process.

Worse. Sarah experienced a wrench of awful, physical pain literally in a flash. The beam of her small torch fell upon a large framed photograph on Michael Masters' desk. It showed his wife, Barbara, happy with their two sons. Sarah, unable to stop herself, ridiculously, turned it face downwards on the desk, furiously miserable. Where had it been before, when she had visited him? Nowhere. In a drawer. Hidden. She was on the point of screaming, rage and pain.

But she didn't. So you're a criminal now, she thought, not coldly. You're going to break out from prison using guns, and somebody will get shot. And you keep a picture of your darling fucking wife and brats on the desk you've fucked me on, do you? And she went to the pistol cabinet, and unlocked it, and put four pistols and the box of ammunition into a plastic bag. They were not target pistols, either, as she knew. There was a .25 automatic, nickel-plated, very old, a Smith and Wesson .38 revolver, a long, inelegant Ruger automatic and a stubby American .32 with its maker's name obscured. Michael was not interested in 'boys' toys' as he called them, but he let the children use them – under supervision – in the woods, the complete indulgent father. Now they'd kill someone at last. They'd come into their own.

She was almost tearful as she waited under the split tree in Abel's Lane for the white Polo to nose up to her, and a little frightened. There were two men in it, and in the darkness she could see that they were big and powerfully built. Her own car was a hundred yards away, and the nearest house was Michael's, nearly a quarter of a mile. The country lane was deserted, silent except for the soughing of the leaves, and absurdly dangerous for a lone woman to be standing in. If the men got out, she would run. She would try to. But to what use? She felt a flash of rage at Masters. You shit, she thought, you utter, utter *shit*.

As the car stopped she stepped firmly to the passenger window, holding up the heavy plastic bag. The pistols cracked against the glass before the man could wind it down.

'Go easy, darling,' he began. But Sarah, forgetting she was meant to hear a password, shoved the bag in and dropped it, heavy, onto his lap, and began to run. She ran away from her car, away from the direction they were facing, because they would have had to turn round if they wanted to give chase. She ran a hundred yards, to the edge of a small copse, and hid behind a tree. She could still see the car. One door was open, with a man standing beside it, looking down the lane towards where she was hidden. The interior light, switched on automatically, revealed the second man inside.

'You're all right, love,' the first man shouted. 'We're not going to hurt you. You're OK.'

Sarah waited, frightened by the harshness of her breathing. After half a minute the man got back into the car and slammed the door. He moved off smoothly, going quickly through the gears. The car was out of sight around a bend in moments, but the engine did not falter or slow down. Sarah, still afraid, went quickly to her car and got inside and locked the doors. She started up the engine.

So now she knew. She'd done it, she'd 'stood by her man'. You fucking shit, she thought, I fucking, fucking *hate* you. Her hands were shaking so badly that she started off in third, then could not get a better gear. She stalled the engine, and restarted it. She crunched it into bottom, and began to cry. She had never been so devastatingly alone.

After a mile or two she had to stop the car and give way properly to her tears. She switched the lights and engine off and held onto the wheel and sobbed and shuddered until she was exhausted. Then, calm, she blew her nose, and dried her puffed up eyes, and her cheeks, and her hands, and the steering wheel. She went round the inside of the car with a wad of Kleenex, to clear the condensation from the windows. She put her seat belt back on, and she prepared to drive back to her boat.

So now she knew. Like all the other stupid, tragic women, she would do anything for him. As she drove along, she began to cry again. But gently . . .

FIFTEEN

'But I don't know why you're telling me all this. It's a minor issue, a matter of regret. Something went wrong, the climate changed, the ball-game changed. I'm working on it.'

There was silence at the other end of the telephone. The call had lasted many minutes, and had got nowhere. One problem was that neither man knew for sure the line was safe. They were very circumspect.

'When you say you're working on it, what do you mean? I must have something to tell him. Something concrete.'

'You can tell him to stop whining, for a start. It may not have been intended, but most people think he got what he deserved. Tell him the best laid schemes of mice and men gang aft a-fucking gley. Tell him he's got my deepest sympathy. Tell him to wait.'

'I don't think you entirely understand. Sir Gerald's response was similar. But Mi— my client, is talking seriously of a major incident. He's being treated like an animal. He's talking of drastic action, some sort of explosion. He's talking of making certain items public.'

'He's in prison, for Christ's sake. He'll make nothing public. And if we're talking bloody revolution, tell him this, from me: when they start stringing people up from lamp-posts, he'll be the first to bloody dangle, won't he? Look, I'll say it just once more. I'm doing everything I can, and I'll continue to. Until then, tell him to keep his head down and his mouth shut. He hasn't been forgotten.'

Sir Cyril France, wearily, began another tack. But there was no one listening.

'And how's your man?' Peter Jackson asked Andrew Forbes. 'How's the Black McGregor?'

'Ah, the bloody story's turned to mush.' He shook the last drops comfortably away and zipped up. They were standing at the urinals in the Princess Louise. 'That's the trouble with the Scots. You just can't trust them.'

Jackson stepped back to the basin and rinsed his fingers.

'You married one,' he said. 'You're not about to repeat the prescription, I suppose?'

'Case in point,' said Forbes. 'The first one died on me. This one's pretty fragile, looking at her. I'm nae sae sure, Jummy, I'm nae sae sure!'

They collected the two pints of bitter and the half of lager they had ordered and rejoined Rosanna in a corner seat behind a table. They were on their third drink, and were feeling quite euphoric. Jackson, at least, had had good news to tell. John de Sallis, his American oppo, had picked up intelligence, good intelligence. Rosanna, not waiting for a sip, got back to the subject.

'And do they know why they're coming over?' she asked. 'Is it definitely connected?'

Jackson shook his head.

'Nothing's definite,' he said. 'But it must be our op, realistically. My guess is they're sweating nitric acid in the US because Lister's been inside so long. They're coming for a look, maybe. They've got to have that man.'

'Maybe they've got some spectacular escape lined up,' said Rosanna. 'Maybe they'll go in with a helicopter!'

'No chance at the Scar. The only put-down space is cabled. They'd lose their rotor. No, maybe it's panic, maybe they've got an ace. We'll have to wait and see.'

Rosanna's eyes were bright.

'Perhaps you ought to let him out,' she said. 'Couldn't you do that? Persuade the government, or something? Then he could, sort of . . . lead you to them?'

'It wouldn't work. He'd disappear. He's disappeared before. No, Charlie being stuck inside is the good thing, from our point of view. We don't know precisely why they're coming, but we know where they must end up. Without our Charles it's zilch, they're knackered.'

'I suppose de Sallis and his lot know where they're leaving from? Will they be tailed?'

Peter Jackson nodded.

'He's pretty confident. They've got a contact in Dutch Customs, a bent one, and we're tapped into him. It's looking good. Hey, by the way! What's this about your story going flat? Andrew said, in the gents.'

Rosanna tutted.

'Ah, that's him over-dramatising,' she said. 'The story's not exactly dead, it's just a wee bit dormant. I think when Pendlebury realised what he'd done he got cold feet. He's asked us to hang fire for a few more days. Until he's told the Home Office, at least!'

'Strange bedfellows,' said Jackson, with a smile. 'Sucking up to the Establishment now are we, Andy-boy? Do you think it means he'll give you a better cell, when you're inside? Hot and cold running chambermaids, governor's orders?'

'He's OK,' said Forbes. 'He's still nervous, that's all. McGregor hasn't pulled anybody's ears off yet, but it's early days. One swallow, and all that. And who knows, when the Home Office gets to hear, they could bung him back in solitary. Or whip him to another jail. Or the loonie bin. Pendlebury knows we're sweating on it, though, he won't let us down. It'll only be another day or two.'

'And the next step,' said Rosanna, with a grin from ear to ear, 'is a visit! When McGregor's ready for it, the governor's going to try and fix him to invite us in to talk. Now that would be a tale worth telling, eh?'

'They killed my brother and locked me in a padded cell – the Animal speaks, exclusive!' said Andrew Forbes. 'Let them pick the bones from that, my friend!'

'Yeah,' said Jackson. He paused. 'I hope to Christ they let you tell it, though. That's all.'

He had gone quite quiet. Rosanna felt a small clutch of fear at her heart. She looked at Andrew, seeking reassurance.

'Just let them try and stop us, mate,' he said. 'Just let them try.'

Whatever Pendlebury's intention, the news that he had defied Donald Sinclair in almost every particular was not long in reaching Queen Anne's Gate. It came in a phone call at the end of a long and gritty morning in which Bowscar Prison had been high on the agenda, and it raised Sinclair's anger and anxiety into another gear. It was an official call, or claimed to be, made on behalf of the POA in the prison. The caller was Chris Abbey.

Sinclair, still not entirely himself despite many hours of useful sleep and some time with Judith in the safe house, had made it his first priority since returning to his office to hammer out his differences – real or supposed – with Christian Fortyne. He had spent twenty-four hours at home with Mary which, considering the length of time they'd been apart, had hardly been a howling success. He had started the unpleasantness, despite himself, but Mary had fought back. The coldness of his demeanour had shocked and hurt her, and she had still been angry about his conduct at the cocktail party. The Home Secretary, she said, had given him every opportunity, and the sum total had been what? A boorish display, following a garbled statement at the press conference which was hardly worthy of a drunk backbencher. Where, incidentally, she'd added cuttingly, was his fabled liberal approach these days? There'd been precious little of it at that conference if the newspapers were to be believed – was that skin deep like all his other convictions? Afterwards, she had tried to backtrack, had wondered – in tears – why they were behaving to each other in this way, had apologised. But he had kept the quarrel going, had fuelled it with bitterness. He had slept alone that night.

Fortyne, a man with no discernible passion, was, however, hardly any easier to approach. His pale, clear eyes seemed constantly to speculate on Sinclair's grip on his subject and position. Sinclair, in a moment that worried him for its weakness, invited Judith into the office for the confrontation – then used the spark of self-directed anger that it generated to launch into the subject.

'Explain yourself,' he said. 'I may be quite mistaken, but I feel that something's going on, and I think you're part of it. When I went away I was flavour of the month, and you and I were totally in tune, I thought. I was pulled back, and I was thrown to the wolves. Why?'

The speculative gleam behind the glasses grew. Fortyne pushed them higher up the bridge of his nose with a delicate and manicured finger. The ambiguous curve of his lips became slightly more pronounced.

'I really do think you're being too bull-headed there,' he said. 'It's not as clear-cut as that. All right, so there's been some undermining. But you'd expect that, wouldn't you? It's politics. And I did tell you about the major problem. I rang you about Bowscar. That's top of the agenda, believe me.'

'You rang me days after the event,' said Sinclair. 'And you told me not to worry. As far as I can see I'm now in the firing line. According to Sir Gerald – silently, of course, nothing's ever stated – it's all my fault.'

'Sir Gerald is worried,' said Fortyne, simply. 'There's trouble in the air, and someone's got to face it. It's rule one, isn't it? If the buck is on the move, it doesn't stop with me. While you were away, the ground plan has been changed.'

'Hooray,' said Judith Parker, drily. 'So you've managed to admit it. What Donald wants to know is why he wasn't warned.'

'Of what?' asked Fortyne, warmly. 'There was nothing concrete, I wasn't really sure. And what could you have done? Come back because I said that Turner was possibly having second thoughts? Might, maybe, be undermining you a little? Nonsense.'

Judith let the moment hang, looking straight into his eyes.

'Or perhaps,' she said, 'you wanted to wait until a winning side emerged. Before deciding whom to back.'

Inwardly, Fortyne smiled at the accuracy of her thrust. His face remained serene and serious.

'Perhaps,' he said. 'But I doubt it. Consider: even sending Donald "naked into the conference chamber", so to speak, the press conference chamber, had the effect of opening his eyes, didn't it? And yours. Judith, trust me. Donald. There's going to be a fight. Let's all be on the winning side.'

It was shortly afterwards that Christopher Abbey rang. The governor, he told Fortyne, had removed McGregor from cellular confinement to the body of the prison, thereby putting the lives of officers and inmates at risk. Consequently the association were actively considering withdrawing to a holding position, that would amount to a work to rule. Coupled with the severe overcrowding and the state of mind of many of the inmates, brought about by the laxness of the governor and his reputation as a weakling, he and his fellow members considered that the situation in the jail was critical. Further – as had been reported to the governor – metal objects, including knives, had been disappearing from the kitchens and the workshops. There was real fear abroad, he said, that an officer or officers might soon be attacked with weapons. There might even be fatalities.

Sinclair came off the extension shaking with rage. Fortyne, impassively, motioned him to pick up the receiver again, and flicked a switch: the governor had been contacted and was waiting on the line. This time, Sinclair did the talking. He started at a shout, but Pendlebury was not cowed. It was the minister who had to find control.

'But why?' asked Sinclair, when he had done so. 'Why, given all these appalling facts, did you defy me? Why did you free McGregor? Was this not an insane act? You must realise I shall fire you? I have to fire you?'

'Fire away,' said Pendlebury. 'Truly, minister, it is a matter of complete indifference to me. Your department has consistently lied to me about McGregor, and the lie was finally confirmed for me beyond a shadow of a doubt. He knows his brother is dead, and as far as he is concerned it was not from natural causes.'

Sinclair's throat went tight.

'Who told you that?' he demanded. 'Where did this "confirmation" come from?'

His voice had changed in tone, and he forced himself to stop. Judith and Fortyne were watching, fascinated. Richard Pendlebury's voice remained quite calm.

'The fact that James McGregor died at Buckie,' he said, 'is a matter of public record. It was briefly reported, I believe, in some Scottish newspapers. The lie comes from your department, in that they deliberately withheld the fact from me, however many times I raised the subject. I shall prepare my resignation letter immediately.'

Sinclair was thinking furiously. Too many chickens were looking for a roost.

'You will do nothing of the sort,' he snapped. 'You will do nothing more until I tell you to. First, you will relock up McGregor. Immediately. That is vitally important.'

'It's too late,' said the governor. 'You just don't understand. In prison terms he's a celebrated man. It would be far too dangerous to try. Apart from anything he might do himself, it would almost certainly spark a riot. He has charisma.'

'Charisma! You're talking about a common murderer!'

'Yes, and Hitler was a mass one. I don't suppose you'll deny that he was charismatic, whatever else he was? McGregor is a figurehead. I can't put him back in solitary. I won't.'

Sinclair lifted his eyes to Judith's, and read anxiety in her face. He realised that his own must look worse. He heard Richard Pendlebury sigh.

'Mr Sinclair. Please listen to me. The trouble that is coming in Bowscar will not be caused by Angus McGregor, I assure you. There are a thousand other men. I implore you to do something. Act. But for God's sake don't think repression is the answer. It is not.'

Sinclair, after that, brought the phone call swiftly to an end. He decided, instantly, that he would have to trust Fortyne, because he needed him. He faced them gravely.

'Good God alive,' he said. 'This is appalling. No wonder Turner wanted me back in the firing line.'

Fortyne glinted.

'I'm not sure that he knows just what's on the cards,' he said.

'I rather think he just wants the security of having you around. In case anything does go wrong.'

'To blame?' said Judith.

'To blame,' said Christian Fortyne. 'Any more trouble in the jails will be political death for someone, and if Bowscar goes there are others that are bound to follow. Turner's preparing Donald's grave.'

Sinclair slowly drank some beer.

'The first thing is,' he said, 'to polish up our thoughts. Marshal them. Kick them into shape. Then I'll go and hit the old devil between the eyes. I'm going to screw him.'

'It won't be an easy fight,' said Fortyne. 'I suspect he's warned the PM that there could be gales ahead already. And about your dangerous tendency to softness . . .'

Judith, with decision, pulled a telephone towards her.

'So when do you want your appointment?' she said. 'For Round One?'

Once Angus John McGregor had been released from solitary – or cellular confinement, as the Prisons Board insisted it be called – the news of his presence in the Scar, long a solid rumour, spread within an hour to every hall and every floor. It was exciting news, because as Pendlebury had told Sinclair, his was a charismatic name, close to mythical. Rumour had it, also, that the screws were shit-scared of him, and would only handle him in threes. On the governor's instructions, he was put into a 'neutral' cell until he should express a preference, which privileged treatment upset and outraged many of the officers. Consequently the cell they recommended – which looked all right on paper – was occupied by Mickie White, the garrulous old drunk, and a mentally-deficient London boy who had tried to burn down the half-way hostel he was living in the night after the warden had seduced him over bed-time cocoa. To the disappointment of the officers, McGregor found neither the ramblings of one nor the unhappy sniffings of the other annoying, and was in fact a model cell-mate.

It had taken very little time for Brian Rogers to make contact. He had broached the subject with Lister on the morning McGregor had been moved, and they had developed the theme with Hughes, Jerrold and Masters later the same day. To Jerrold, who still managed to stay somehow aloof in the refuge of his bunk, it did not matter either way: he called himself the sleeping partner. To

Hughes and Masters it was another vague worry, an addition to their feeling that they had been marginalised, but nothing more – the argument for recruiting McGregor was unanswerable. When they met him – small, pale and quiet – they were even more disturbed. Was this the Animal?

McGregor did not seem excited by the plan. As Rogers had before him, he listened carefully, asking in a quiet, pleasant voice for certain points to be gone over several times. He wanted to know how it was an escape plan, rather than the blueprint for a riot, and nodded over Rogers' explanations. The key was hostage-taking, with threats of execution if doors were not unlocked immediately, he was told; there would be knives and guns. That was fine, he said, but threats of execution meant nothing, unless the people making them were capable of carrying them out. And he would want a gun.

Lister and Rogers smiled. In a way that rather sickened Michael Masters, they presented their credentials. And Rogers listed his team: Billy Ford, Tom Amory, Pat Parkinson, Mike Shaw – need he go on? They'd not only kill anyone who stood between them and their liberty, they'd bloody love it. For what had they to lose? They were in for life, the lot of them. If they were caught, so what? Another five years on the thirty? So fucking what? It would be a pleasure. And naturally he would have a gun.

The only stipulation that McGregor made was about the governor. He was not to be a hostage, nor was he to be killed. He was to be left alone, in fact. He did not bother to go in for explanations, it was a statement. But he insisted that it must be understood, especially by the heavy squad: it was a personal requirement. It bothered nobody, although it interested Alan Hughes. As Rogers said, there was already a list of screws who should be left alone, for favours done or services rendered, or because nobody had ever had a quarrel with them. Equally, there were others whose lives wouldn't be worth a panda's fart if they got in the way. The governor could join the first lot.

Hughes, who was incorrigible in his interests, talked to McGregor for hours in the following days, although he learnt little about what made him tick. At some point, to his annoyance, he learned that somebody had told a garbled version of his 'relationship' with Sir Gerald Turner, and it revealed an obsessive streak in the Scot. He wanted details of the man, his life, his personality. Hughes reiterated that he had been a neighbour, many years before, and had hardly known him or his wife and daughter except to nod to in the street. But McGregor had begun to seek him out, first to talk about Sir Gerald, then, increasingly, about himself. That was much more Hughes' territory, and the meetings ceased to be a pain. Like Pendlebury before him he thought he could discern a deep and deeply troubled man below the surface.

'What are you in for, Alan?' McGregor asked at one point. 'They say you killed two women. Two wives. Is that a fact?'

The men were alone, leaning on the rail around their balcony. Below them, through the netting, they could see other men, leaning, talking, walking. It was rather like the inside of an anthill, Hughes often thought, except more aimless. Ants were busy, they were workers. In Bowscar there was not a lot to do.

'It's what I was convicted of,' he said. 'There was only one body, though. The second wife. She fell downstairs and broke her neck. The first one was never found. She disappeared.'

'So did you kill them? They're all fucking bitches, women. I'd've topped my wife if I'd ever married her. She fucked off.'

'The judge was a fan of Oscar Wilde,' said Hughes. 'Not Reading Jail, of course. The Importance. To lose one wife could be classed as misfortune or whatever the old borc said. To lose two sounded like carelessness. Certainly I didn't care much when they sent me down. I'd had enough. You're right you know, Angus. I prefer wet dreams myself. You get a better class of person.'

Two of Abbey's men, Burnett and Simon Petter, were approaching, with the clear intention of separating them. To forestall their pleasure McGregor pushed himself away from the railing and turned towards his cell.

'You could kill the judge,' he said. 'We could go together. First Mr Justice Whatsisface, then Turner. Think about it.'

He was back to his obsession.

Richard Pendlebury did not imagine for a moment that he would find personal satisfaction in confronting Christopher Abbey, but he did hope something concrete might spin off from it. He thought carefully through his tactics before he called the meeting, determining above all to stay calm. The line he took was loyalty, or the lack of it, and he was after a definite response. He got it.

'I have been speaking to the Prison Department,' he said, 'and I am ashamed at what I've heard. In my capacity as governor of this establishment I made certain decisions, and had them carried out. To my horror, I find that those decisions have been relayed behind my back to a higher authority. The good of the prison has been seriously compromised.'

Abbey, who had been preparing to deny direct involvement, was astonished.

'The good of the prison?' he said. 'Moving a dangerous psychopath into an open hall? It was for the good of Bowscar that the approach to the Department was made!'

'By you?'

'It was a democratic action. It was decided on a vote. We understood that you were under orders which you chose to break. We took advice at a national level, and from colleagues in Scotland, men whose lives have been at risk for many years from this piece of . . . this scum. Mr Pendlebury, I have to say that my members are constantly concerned that *you* don't seem to have the good of Bowscar at heart. You don't know or care what's good for Bowscar.'

The officer's face registered his awareness of just how far he had gone. In any normal situation, with any normal governor, he could have expected the sky to fall on him. Richard Pendlebury, having deliberately provoked the anger, stayed calm.

'That's a matter of opinion,' he said. 'You are entirely entitled to believe it. Forgive me if it rings a little hollow though, coming from you. I understand there were threats to work to rule? A threat of partial withdrawal of labour? How is that for the prison's good? How will that contain the latent violence that I'm sure you feel and fear as much as I do? How, further, do you explain the fact that a telephone is being used? By the prisoners.'

Briefly, a shade of doubt slid across Abbey's face. Then he looked straight into Pendlebury's eyes.

'I don't know what you're talking about,' he said. 'I don't believe that's true. I would say, in fact, that it's impossible. Ridiculous.'

'Yes,' said Pendlebury. 'Given a better staff, given a staff more inclined to loyalty, to pulling together, to pulling their weight, I'd agree with you whole-heartedly. Nevertheless, it's true. Before you lecture me on the good of Bowscar, Mr Abbey, I suggest you set your house in order.'

Abbey's face darkened.

'If you're suggesting—'

Pendlebury stood.

'I'm suggesting nothing. With you, I've found it a complete and utter waste of time. Just go away and talk to your members. Try a little thought.'

They faced each other across the polished desk-top. Of the two, the officer was breathing faster.

'By the way,' said Pendlebury, almost casually. 'I advised the junior minister that to put McGregor back into solitary would be a thoroughly retrograde step. As far as one can make out, he agrees with me. Good day.'

The American associates of Charles Lister arrived in England on three separate days and by four separate points of entry, having fed false information to the corrupt Dutch Customs officer. They were two white men, Pete Delano and Al Pruchak, one black man, Sidney Gibbin, and a white woman, Syvil Hollis. Hollis reached England via Belfast Harbour Airport and Blackpool, Gibbin 'returned' on a charter flight from Barbados, Delano came by Olau Line from Flushing to Sheerness, and Pruchak caught a weekend flight from Jersey to Manchester. They stayed in separate small hotels among the visiting hordes of Kensington, and met in pubs, at night. Although by this time Lister had given them a contact name and number in London, they decided not to use it.

'Look what they did for Chuck,' said Syvil Hollis. 'And that was only one guy. With four of us, they could screw us up four times. What the hell we need them for, anyway? Once we get him out of the pen, we'll have him in Miami in fifteen hours. Screw the Brits. They're hopeless.'

Delano, who had done the hard work on the ground in Holland, agreed. He had brought five guns across, and innumerable documents. They had airline tickets, false ID, passports in various names and nations. The next task was to get some cars, go to Staffordshire, suss the prison out. The operation, with luck, would be relatively simple, efficient, clean. With their map books out, for God's sake, they even looked like tourists. People said to them, in that mocking British way, when they left pubs: 'Have a nice day!' Well, they intended to . . .

The 'inefficient Brits' had managed something, as the Americans later learned in a coded phone call made by Lister to a Rotterdam safe contact and passed on. Three days after Sarah Williams had thrust the bag of pistols through the car window in Abel's Lane, another interview had taken place in Bowscar Prison.

The men who brought the guns in had thought that Lister was insane, and begged him to take one or two this visit, the others at another time. Lister, with contempt, had secreted all four down the front of his trousers, the cold barrel of the long Ruger hard against his pubic bone. The belly of his shirt camouflaged the butts, and he carried a jumper, which hid the ammunition.

The hardware had arrived.

SIXTEEN

Despite the way his meeting with Sir Gerald Turner was conducted, it did not take Donald Sinclair long to realise how enormous the rift between them had become. By the end of the interview, although they were still smiling, the thinness of the smiles barely concealed their teeth. Sinclair had been given two options – to prepare a press communiqué which more or less negated his publicly stated approach to the problems he had been appointed to resolve – or to quit. Even Fortyne, who left a step behind him, had an iciness in his bearing that was almost palpable.

Sir Gerald, who had 'fitted in' Donald at 6.15 p.m., had been affability itself. His own private secretary, a plumpish grey-haired man called Martin Wilson, had poured drinks for all of them, and they had been offered easy chairs. Ashtrays were provided, and Sir Gerald lit a pipe. To Donald, the scene had reeked of insincerity.

'Donald,' said Sir Gerald. 'Gentlemen. I'm sorry I could not organise this meeting earlier, because I understand you feel there are urgent matters to discuss. Of course, there have been some untoward events while you were very unfortunately detained abroad, but we have so far managed to deal with them without too much discomfort. What I'm trying to say is, that I have kept my finger on the pulse. Don't be too anxious, laddie. Everything's in control.'

Sinclair rode the insult with a smile. Pretended, in effect, it had not been offered. Then he outlined the call from Chris Abbey and the one to Pendlebury. Turner's eyes widened slightly at the news that Angus McGregor had been freed, and that he knew about his brother. He sipped whisky.

'Mm,' he said, through clouds of aromatic smoke. 'But he always was a panic merchant, Pendlebury. So what do you propose?'

It was the first real indication Sinclair had of just how stormy were the waters that he faced. It was a response so extraordinary that he was almost rendered speechless. Gerald Turner, it appeared, was going to discount the evidence! Involuntarily, he and

Fortyne exchanged glances. Wilson remained silent, immovable, very like a soft, fat statue.

'My proposal,' he said, 'is to do something about it. Fast. Whatever else one thinks of Pendlebury, he is the man at the centre of the action. I think he must go, largely because he's lost the confidence of his officers, but I think we must take very serious notice of what he's said. Firstly, we must take the pressure off. That means cutting down the numbers in the jail. If we moved the fine defaulters and remand men out alone we'd bring the numbers down below the CNA figure. We should employ more officers, as well. Morale at Bowscar is through the floor, they're prepared to work to rule. We've got to go in fast and sort the place out, root and branch, we've got to be firm but fair.'

Sir Gerald stood and walked over to the drinks table. He splashed some more spirit into his glass and topped it off with mineral water. He did not offer anybody else the bottle. He was deep in thought.

'Donald,' he said at last, 'I am severely disappointed by all this. What you call being fair sounds more like being weak to me. Why sack the governor? He might be a pain, but the POA are far worse, surely? They're greedy, boorish, blinkered. No, Pendlebury shall not go, that would be appeasement, pure and simple. It is a ploy they've used for years now, Fresh Start or no Fresh Start: kowtow to us, or there will be blood and thunder mayhem. I have to say this, Donald, although it pains me. Like all the other ideas you've outlined since I appointed you, this reaction smacks of funk. Not analysis, not thought, not referring back to precedent, but sheer old-fashioned funk. I hoped for better things. Like some solutions.'

Martin Wilson, surprisingly, got heavily to his feet. He went to the small table and brought the whisky bottle over. He refilled Sinclair's glass, his own, and Fortyne's. Then added mineral water. There were many thoughts fighting for superiority in Sinclair's mind. He tried to marshal them. Nobody spoke until Wilson had resumed his seat.

'Sir Gerald,' Sinclair said then. 'I did not actually seek this meeting to talk about the problem in the long-term. But as you know, as we are all agreed, there is more than one reason why the system needs reforming. Firstly and most importantly I believe, because it is morally repugnant. If we cannot do something about the conditions of our jails, at least *start* to bring them up towards the lowest standards of some of our fellow Europeans, it reveals a moral vacuum at the heart of our political system that I can only contemplate with terror. More urgently, however, I believe that if we don't act soon, there will be nothing left to contemplate. This is not the POA's assessment, because they want to earn more overtime, nor any mentally-exhausted governor's, it is my own. The whole thing will go bang, not just one jail, all of them, there'll be a holocaust. And Bowscar, please believe me, Bowscar could be the start of it. We must defuse the situation. We just must.'

Turner was restuffing his pipe now, comfortably, like a man on familiar territory, a man with his feet on terra firma. He struck a match.

'Just as I predicted to the PM,' he said. 'A panic reaction to a local problem, followed by an entirely inappropriate response. Donald, nobody could be more liberal than I. Nobody could have invested more moral capital in sorting out our jails. But this is not the case and it is not the time. Don't you understand? The time's not ripe for "taking off the pressure" as you call it. We're fed up with the whingers and the whiners and the wets. We want action. The crack of firm government for once. Reform's for later, not for now.'

Everybody in the room knew who 'we' was. Sir Gerald had been nobbled. His voice was not his own, but the Prime Minister's. Through the flame of his third Swan Vesta, he appeared completely satisfied with his lot.

'And if you're wrong?' asked Donald Sinclair. 'If the crack of firm government produces an explosion? What then?'

'Thanks to you,' replied Sir Gerald, 'we've had a dummy run at Buckie, haven't we? We'd give fair warning, then we'd go in hard. We'd give them bloody noses and we'd show them where the power lies. Good.'

Sinclair's eyes fell on the digital clock. It occurred to him that Sir Gerald would call a halt to this discussion soon. He was going to the opera, Lady Elizabeth had come up to town by train. *La Traviata*. Nothing should interfere with that.

'I don't think bloody noses would be in it,' he said. 'I think it would be terrible. I think there could be deaths. At the very least it would probably mean losing the building. They'd raze it to the ground.'

'So be it,' said Gerald Turner. He was mocking, there was laughter clearly in his eyes. 'As you know, I think you are over-reacting quite grotesquely. But if we have to lose a building, if it proves absolutely necessary, is that so bad a thing? We sacrifice a prison, but the effect is salutary, is it not? We exercise the dogs of war and we appease the law and order brigade all at a stroke! Good God, if the velvet glove comes off, laddie, no one will ever risk anything like it again, will they? A few million spent, a few lives lost – and catharsis. A sacrifice maybe – but surely a reasonable one?'

'It will be more than just a sacrifice,' said Donald Sinclair. 'It will be a bloodbath. You do not know the evil that will be unleashed, Sir Gerald. It will be like Attica, an appalling, traumatic horror. If it spills outside the confines of the prison, if—'

Sir Gerald was impatient. He stood up, looking pointedly at the time.

'It won't,' he said. 'It won't be allowed to happen. I was proposing at the end of this meeting to prepare a joint communiqué for the press, but I find that I have run out of time, and also out of patience. There is a draft here, which I should like you to work upon alone. You may tinker with the phraseology, naturally, but the sentiments will remain intact.'

He snapped his fingers, and Wilson produced a sheet of paper. It was typewritten, and annotated. At first glance, Sinclair could make little sense of it.

'The gist is,' said Turner, 'that you have promised liberalisation, if it should be appropriate in the light of your researches, but that it must be dependent on a certain quid pro quo, a readiness for the inmates of our prisons to reform themselves, to be deserving of our liberality. In the meantime, the men of violence, the thugs, the bully-boys – they should take note. Any recurrence of indiscipline, any bad behaviour, however slight – and they will be crushed. That's the sort of thing. You'd better work on it tonight. It would be nice if I could clear it in the morning, then you could call the press in. Now I must go.'

He strode to the hat-stand in the corner and took his coat.

'Oh, by the way. This is not a request for consultation, Donald, it is an order. If you don't like it, your office will go immediately to another man. Give my regards to Mary, won't you?'

Later on that evening, Donald had yet another row with Mary. Because things had become so strained between them he found he had a tendency to phone her much more frequently than he ever had before. This time the guilt was compounded by the fact that he planned to stay with Judith, with the communiqué as his excuse. But when he outlined what had happened she was dismissive, unbelieving, and ultimately angry. If what he said of Gerald Turner were true, she said, he should quite simply resign.

'I don't know about that,' responded Sinclair. 'I'm still bowled over. One thing's very clear, though. We were probably doing Cyril Richardson and all my other predecessors a grave injustice. It wasn't them that needed sacking, it was Gerald who was covering his back.'

'It sounds most unlikely is all I can say,' she said. 'But if that's how you see it, go. Good lord, Donald—'

He interrupted her: 'Good lord, Mary! If I just quit, what good would that do? If things are ever going to change, if anything good's ever going to happen, surely I should stay and fight? Politics is the art of the possible, remember.'

'That's the most convenient cliché anybody ever dreamed up,' snapped his wife. 'Politics should be the art of the impossible. The art of taking something difficult, intractable, and kicking it into shape. If politicians can't make things work, can't force them to, they shouldn't be politicians. Don't be so pathetic.'

Donald, who had fought so hard to keep his temper with Sir Gerald, lost it now.

'Listen, you stupid bitch,' he said. 'That's what I'm saying, isn't it? If I just quit . . .'

Mary had slammed the phone down. When he rang back ten seconds later, the number was engaged. For the duration.

'What are you going to do?' asked Judith, as they lay in their bed at the safe house. It was after midnight, and the communiqué was finished. 'Politics isn't really the art of the possible any longer, is it? One thing the PM's taught us is to respect the lie. Politics is the art of lying. We've done quite well tonight, I reckon, considering. But is that what we really want?'

She was referring to the last part of the communiqué, which they both thought was a small gem: 'Liberalisation remains the ultimate goal,' it read. 'But let no one mistake our stance for weakness. For the inmates of our prisons, life will only become more pleasant when the prevailing uncertainties have been removed. Our strength will be their safeguard, our vigilance their freedom.'

Donald Sinclair, lying on his back staring at the ceiling, was not sure what he wanted. But he thought both Gerald Turner and his puppet master had made a grave miscalculation. And he was damned and double-damned if he did not take advantage of it. Whatever that entailed.

* * *

The day Charles Lister brought the pistols back to the cell, the real meaning of what they had agreed to take part in was finally distilled for Masters and Hughes. They had watched him leave, less than an hour before, to meet his contacts, to be 'questioned further about alleged offences' and they had still not really grasped, effectively, what his return would signify. For all the other strands were in place. The phone calls had been made, escape routes for the rich and powerful had been organised, the triggers had been set. When he returned – if he brought the guns – the story, the fantasy, the theory, would suddenly come true. There would be about nine hours left.

For Jerrold, when it came to it, it was too much. As Hughes and Masters tentatively approached the subject, he grunted, and climbed down from his bed. The ironic detachment with which he had bolstered them through many periods of doubt, at last had left him. He stood, large, shoeless and unhappy, facing them.

'Alan,' he said. 'What have we done, guy? This whole damn job's insane. Someone going to die.'

Hughes attempted levity.

'The failure of the academic, Matt. When it comes to cases . . .'

But Jerrold's bony, sculpted face was desolate. He gestured round the yellow, crushing walls.

'Where can I go?' he said. 'Where can I fucking go?'

Where could he go? He could not even pace. He walked, clumsily, having to pick his way past first Masters then past Hughes, his thighs knocking the table. He went back to his bunk and placed his hands palm down upon it, and touched his forehead to the iron frame. Neither of the others spoke.

'We didn't realise, did we? We didn't work it out. Alan, when it comes to it. If it really happens. What . . . ?'

Suddenly, he bounced himself upwards onto his bunk again. He did not roll onto his back, as he usually did, to look sideways at them. He stayed face down and silent. Hughes and Masters, although they both had things they would have liked to say, did not speak. After a few moments, they picked up books. But neither of them opened them.

When Lister at last returned, the cell door was unlocked to let him in and was left unlocked. He took in the situation, but waited until the sounds of boots had faded on the balcony before he broke the silence. Then he pulled his shirt-front open to reveal the dully gleaming butts, a wolfish grin spreading across his face.

There was affection in it, maybe – and certainly contempt. He treated them as aliens.

'You English kill me,' he said. 'You are *weird*. If you could only see the way you looked . . .'

Masters regarded the four pistols, as they were withdrawn and laid on the table one by one, with a mixture of feelings that he could not have expressed. He had spoken to Sarah since she had stolen and delivered them and he knew, he thought he knew, just what it had meant to her. *Cynthia's Beam*, she'd told him, was moored at Bridge 47 and she would be waiting for him. But the happiness and the excitement had been drained completely from her voice. It was as if she did not expect the same man, her Michael Masters, to arrive, as if she saw him through new eyes. Had she known the lengths he was prepared to go to once free of Bowscar, thought Masters, the revenges that he planned, little Sarah Williams would have been appalled.

Before the ammunition had been sorted into piles to match the pistols, Rogers had arrived, followed shortly afterwards by McGregor. Red-haired Billy Ford was the nearest look-out, with Pat Parkinson and Tom Amory strategically placed as early warning. The newcomers eyed the armoury with a hunger that was almost lust. Lister, who understood entirely, stood back to let them closer; while maintaining a proprietorial attitude, a salesman's or curator's eye, as if they might whisk them magically out of sight.

'Sweet Jesus,' said McGregor. 'It's a long time since I saw anything like this inside a jail. You're a wonder, Charlie. And you, Mike. Who's choosing?'

Masters spread his hands.

'They're all good guns,' he said. His voice was flat. 'I got them for the kids, but the local gunshop checks them out for me.'

'The weans? Are you serious? That's irresponsible.'

Lister and Brian Rogers laughed, but McGregor meant it. He picked up the .32 revolver.

'I don't want no automatic,' he said. 'However well it's been looked after. One cost me six years once. And Brian here'll want the howitzer, he's a hardman, eh Bri? Charlie?'

Lister picked up the Ruger.

'It's still warm from rubbing on my pecker.' He kissed the muzzle, theatrically. 'I've gotten used to it. Fine by me, an automatic.'

Rogers pushed the .25 across the table towards Masters, using the business end of the .38 Smith and Wesson. His eyes were full of some obscure pleasure.

'Lady's gun,' he said. 'It wouldn't stop a Pekinese. So how do you feel about that, Mikey? They are yours, after all. You can tuck it in your bodice in case anybody makes a pass at you.'

Lister said: 'It's not a bad little gun, Mike. Close-range. Don't let him put you on.'

'I won't.' He turned to Rogers. 'Close-range,' he said, 'it would turn a scrotum into mist. Think about it, Brian.'

There had never been a question of Alan Hughes desiring a gun. As the men began to load their magazines, he viewed the weaponry with depression and distaste. After a short while he flapped his hands in a kind of pained disgust.

'Look,' he said. 'Do you have to do this now? It brings me out in spots. It reminds me of a family Christmas. Correct me if I'm wrong, but tonight's the night. Correct me if I'm wrong, but that door's unlocked. Correct me if I'm wrong, we ought to talk.'

They took his point. The professionals made their weapons disappear immediately, while Masters took a little longer. As he was thrusting the small, plated pistol into his trouser pocket, Lister leaned across and pulled it out again. With a smile, he engaged the safety catch.

'Talking of scrotums,' he said. 'I hope to Christ you teach your kids better than that.'

Although the talk was detailed and the mood tense, they were all aware that there was nothing new that could be said. Ever since Lister had been sure the guns would actually materialise, the break-out had been timed for the evening they arrived – because if anything went wrong once they were in it could only mean complete disaster. On the time of day, also, there had been no argument – it had to be as close to dark as possible.

Whichever way they tried to cut it, however, there was no getting round the fact that the break-out would occur in daylight. In Bowscar, 8 p.m. marked the end of 'recreation time' and the nightly locking of the cells for most men. In its favour, though, was the atmosphere. For fifteen minutes before the lock-up, the balconies, workshops, TV rooms and corridors were full of inmates, some under escort, others roaming unsupervised. It was characterised by a certain laxness in the officers, as for many of them it meant, to all intents and purposes, that another day was safely over. In a few minutes most of their charges would be banged up, and short of a fire or a suicide they would stay under lock and key until morning slop-out at seven-fifteen. It was illogical, but the screws got demob happy.

The plan was relatively simple, and – they all acknowledged – fraught with dangers and unknowns. The leader of each cadre would not be told until tea-time on the day, and would disseminate the information only to the men who needed to know it. Once the network of trusted people had been teed up, the distribution of the weapons, the knives, the sharpened bodkins, the razor blades in makeshift wooden holders and so on, would begin. Most of them were held centrally, at most in one or two cells to a hall, and they had been earmarked for the stablest and most intelligent. There were bound to be one or two revenge attacks or 'lovers' tiffs', but the hope was that they would be held in check long enough not to precipitate an early crisis. One of the biggest fears was that a minor quarrel could spark off a chain reaction ending in a major lock-up of the sort that had defused the Orchard riot. The weapons would be handed out individually, as far as possible, and the recipients told to keep their mouths shut and to wait. It would not be long . . .

By the time recreation was under way, the task would be to foment rumour and excitement, but still with nothing concrete being said. There would be an hour, roughly, to make the bulk of the prisoners aware that something was in the air, without it getting out of hand. The screws, inevitably, would pick up something, but with luck it would not worry them too much. Tensions and electricity in the atmosphere were almost normal, usually signifying nothing more in prospect than a beating in a sluice or a screaming match over a possession or a sexual partner. Officers often watched such incidents to make sure nobody was killed, almost to see fair play. Sometimes they allowed themselves a kick or two, if the victim was considered vile enough.

At 7.45 p.m. the fires in the cells were due to start. These had been carefully sited to cause maximum disruption at corridor junctions, and to be as far away from fire points as possible. Paper had been stockpiled under mattresses in the chosen places, and woollen clothes were available to make thick smoke. Small amounts of spirit had been provided to make sure the fires took, although Rogers could not guarantee it would not be drunk. Even on pain of death, he said, some things were not possible. The ideal was that the fires should be set at timed intervals, so that the screws would be preoccupied with the first before the second started. That way a disproportionate number of officers could be expected in one place, their minds set on a single, local problem and not a general, preconceived disruptive pattern. When the second cell went up they might assume it was a copy-cat affair, and their resources would be split and stretched. The third, fourth and fifth blazes would confirm a full-scale insurrection, but the officers would be scattered throughout the prison, nowhere in any major strength. By this time, too, the prisoners would know that the balloon was going up. While they exploded indiscriminately, the hostage-taking would begin.

This was carefully planned in theory, but again was bound by its nature to be hit-and-miss, violent, messy. The basic idea was to seize four or five officers on every floor and lock them, immediately and without harm, into cells. Not only would it cut down the numbers available to fight the riot, but the other officers would be cripplingly worried about what was happening to them, and would make their location and rescue top priority. Rogers and Mike Shaw would seize other officers at gun and knife point, and led by Lister would proceed as fast as humanly possible to demand the opening of the gates. If they met any resistance or any refusal, the first hostage officer would be killed after a single warning. At the same time as this frontal assault, Tom Amory and Pat Parkinson would approach the gates with hostages from the laundry side while Billy Ford and a man called Tony Smith took another route. McGregor's role was as a 'roving gun' to watch their backs and flanks and take out dangerous officers as necessary. The Irish contingent, led by a man called Conor Grady, known as the Armagh Wolf, had made their own arrangements, which they had not disclosed in detail. Nobody had any doubt, however, of their ability and determination. It was reckoned that the gates would be open within minutes, and hopefully before a major alarm was raised. They had no concrete knowledge of how information of trouble would be broadcast to the outside world, but they assumed the governor and the deps would be the key. Men had been detailed to cut off the switchboard and all phones immediately the admin block was taken, and to 'immobilise' anyone touching any electronic gear. This part of the operation was in the charge of a fearsome man called Ivan Buckley, who was reckoned to be able to knock down a stout wooden office door with his head alone. Further than that, they could not go. The alarm would be raised somehow, obviously. But for them it was a matter of doing what they could, then getting out – and going.

Michael Masters, although one of the gun holders, was acutely aware that he had been assigned no role. In fact, all three of the original participants had moved into the background, had become irrelevant, almost wraiths. Lister had secured him a gun for self-protection, but mainly because it meant one fewer in hands he did not trust. As to his friends – Alan Hughes, to all intents, was out of it and Jerrold was definitely so. He had refused a weapon, he had refused to make contact with some of the other black inmates, he had made no request to use the phone to contact outside help to get away. Since this final discussion had begun he had not moved. When McGregor, Rogers and Lister left with their pistols to spread the word to their lieutenants, he was still face downwards in his bunk. There were solemn handshakes all round, which included Hughes and Masters. It was the last formal meeting before the riot. But Jerrold did not move.

When the other men had gone, Hughes resumed his seat at the table. Masters took the small pistol from his pocket and held it flat on his palm. He tried to extract the magazine from the butt, possibly to finish loading it. But for the moment, he could not work the catch. He became aware that Jerrold was watching him. He made a face at him, of regret.

'Well,' Masters said. 'It's too late now, brother. Unless you're planning to stay up there and hope nobody sees you.'

Hughes said: 'I'm not going. I'm staying here. There's nowhere that I really want to go, now it comes to it. I'm going to stay and watch. There's a few things I didn't really reckon with, despite the years of thought. It's a bit like studying Shakespeare. You think you've got it sussed, then some first-year student comes along and shows you, quite by accident, that you're insane. I'm bonkers. I've got to be.'

'I'm staying with you,' said Matthew Jerrold. 'It's for savages, all this. A game for savages. First the inmates, then the screws, then the Army, then the government. It's not you who's bonkers, Alan. It's everyone.'

'Where I went wrong,' said Hughes. 'What I left out, was the savages. You're dead right, Matt. To get out, they're going to need the utmost savagery. And that's how they'll be stopped. How did I not notice? How did I spout that balderdash? All we've got to do, I said, is withdraw our consent. Tell them we're not staying any more. Didn't it occur to me that they might disagree? Did I think they'd say OK? How did I overlook the savagery?'

Masters said nothing. He was going to go, he had to. But he understood the intimations, the feeling of disaster and mortality. If he did get out, if he survived the holocaust that was now inevitable, he did not think he would after all pursue his scenario of revenge. At the moment it felt vaguely obscene, and irrelevant. Within a few hours terrible events were going to take place and he would be at the heart of them. He pictured *Cynthia's Beam*, lying easy, moored at the towpath, fringed with trees, near a lovely pub perhaps. He pictured Sarah, whom he strangely imagined as having grown wan and sad with fear, and loneliness, and disillusionment. It would be enough, more than enough, to get to her, and hide, and hold her and be held. To make a new life, to forget the people who had ruined him. For the moment, that would be enough. And more. Fuck the guilty ones, the great betrayer, let it be.

The plan went wrong. Twenty minutes before the first fire was due, a prison officer, looking for Brian Rogers, came to the door of the cell that Angus McGregor shared with Mickie White and the mentally retarded boy. He was already suspicious because Billy Ford, who had directed him, appeared to be slightly merry, and had been concealing something in his hand that could almost have been a knife. The officer, a nervous, gangling man with a perennial money problem, was the bearer, in any case, of bad news. McGregor and Rogers were jovial, but that did not reassure him. He expected Rogers to get angry, fast. Charles Lister was also in the cell.

'Jerry,' said Rogers, smiling. 'What can we do for you? Come into our parlour.'

Jerry Kaye stepped across the threshold. The wet-eyed Englishman and the muscular American reminded him of bears, the smaller Scot some vicious, poison snake. He swallowed. He came straight to the point.

'It's bad news,' he said. 'I'm sorry, Brian. There's a fuck-up going on. A big fuck-up. I've had to pull the phone. It's gone back home. It's finished. There's been appalling trouble.'

Angus McGregor, smoothly, moved round behind him. He stood between him and the door. Kaye felt panic rise.

'What trouble?' Rogers said. 'What d'you mean? Has someone mentioned names?'

'Oh no,' replied the officer. He glanced over his shoulder. 'But there's something going on. Tomorrow, there's going to be changes. There's no more recreation. Everyone's going to be banged up. No privileges. There'll probably be a search.'

He heard a click behind him. The Scot had closed the door.

'Have you been talking?' he said.

'No! Look, McGregor – you shouldn't have done that! The lads are nervous! They know I'm in here! You shouldn't have closed that door!'

As he said it, there was a hammering outside. McGregor sprang forward, spun Kaye round, seized him by the throat.

'You cunt,' he said. 'You fucking stupid cunt.'

'No! They're not here yet! They're on the other landing!'

From outside came a shout: 'McGregor! Let me in, you Scotch prat! What's going on?'

'Fuck!' spat Brian Rogers. 'It's Mickie White! Mac, for fuck's sake let him go!'

McGregor pushed the prison officer away and wrenched the cell door open. Mickie White stood outside, belligerent and stupid. Across the hall, two officers had started to move. There was no doubt of their intention. They were coming round.

Inside the cell behind him, Angus McGregor heard a movement. He spun, and caught Kaye as he tried to barge past him to the balcony. He hit him, hard, in the stomach, and the officer fell back. Then McGregor grabbed Mickie White, hauling him backwards to block the entrance. As he did so, glancing right, he saw the officers speeding up, although still not running. They had the end of the hall to negotiate, then sixty yards of corridor.

'Rogers!' he said. 'Out! They're on their way. It's going up.'

'The fires!' said Lister.

'Too fucking late,' said McGregor. 'For fuck sake go!'

He and Rogers, pushing White before them, moved on to the balcony. They turned the old man towards the officers and propelled him with a shove in their direction. Below them, they could see upturned faces. It was early, but it could still work. If they could spark it before the screws got wise. If they could clear this floor and spread the word, the panic.

In the doorway of the cell, Jerry Kaye appeared, white-faced, his arm pushed up his back. They could not see Lister, but they knew he was there, assessing the situation. As the officers broke into a trot, Rogers shouted.

'Charlie! They're on their way! Do it, Charlie!'

God knows what was in Rogers' mind, but Charlie did it. From the twisted face of Jerry Kaye there came an utterly appalling, bubbling scream. His lanky body abruptly shot across the narrow balcony, and jack-knifed across the iron rail. As it did so, a gush of blood sprayed from his neck, out into the open body of the hall, through the suicide net and down, down, down, catching in the strings, hanging, dripping, splashing on the tiles three floors below. And all the time he screamed, the choking, dreadful scream.

As Mickie White turned back towards his cell, Charles Lister hit him carefully underneath his chin and broke his neck. He then lifted the old man's body and bounced it off the wall into the running prison officers. As one of them fell, his shoulder flipped Mickie onto the iron rail, where he balanced grotesquely for a moment before plunging into the net. Like a child on a trampoline he progressed inelegantly from its outside edge into the middle in four or five short hops.

Then Lister, exhilarated, threw his fists above his head and shouted.

'Come on, you guys! Let's *go*!'

SEVENTEEN

The response to Lister's cry was instantaneous. The split second of shock produced by the sight of the old man's body bouncing absurdly in the net gave way to a release of energy that was almost manic. Prisoners – dozens of them – began to run about, to slam into each other, to shout. In unlocked doors, men in shirt-sleeves appeared, surveyed the chaos, and joined in. For most of them, it was purely automatic. They had sensed the tension, but had known no details. The pandemonium spread in all directions at terrific speed.

As the officers Charlie had knocked over began to clamber to their feet, they were overwhelmed by at least half a dozen prisoners. Despite the bleeding form of Jerry Kaye crumpled by the railing, the excitement was still sufficiently muted for their lives to be safe. At Lister's direction they were stripped of their keys and locked into White's cell. Two other officers, who had rushed out of a corridor onto the same balcony, were similarly trapped. These, also, were lucky.

The speed at which events were moving made the officers' task basically impossible. If Alan Hughes had been watching he could have taken satisfaction from the fact that at least one of his premises was totally correct. While McGregor and Rogers raced to rendezvous with their chosen teams, the sheer weight of aimless numbers meant the officers could not communicate, could not move fast enough, could not, in fact, assess what needed to be done. They did not at first even raise the alarm. The noise level was so high, the disorientation so great, that they were overwhelmed. In the seconds before they could retrench, mentally and physically, it was often too late – they were seized, manhandled, thrown into cells. This aspect was far more successful than had seemed likely in the planning stage. In C-hall alone seventeen officers were locked up. Worse, from the control point of view, was that their keys were put to use immediately. For a short while, the prisoners worked in high spirits and fast. Brutality was not on the agenda.

The spread to other halls and wings was also instantaneous.

The moment the racket signalled a premature blow-up, the cadres of conspirators went into action. Here though, violence quickly became inevitable. The officers realised at the same time as the men that something had gone up, and moved fast and hard to prevent it spreading. A-hall was closed off before a single prisoner escaped into the main body, while in D and F-halls the officers, trying to herd men back along their balconies, were confronted for the first time with knives and other metal weapons. Through extraordinary courage they managed to face the prisoners without bloodshed, but inevitably they dropped back. In F-hall, as the officers gathered all their forces to protect the door and isolate the wing, they were charged from the front, then from the left. In three minutes of hand-to-hand fighting three officers were stabbed and four were badly slashed. All but two of them were taken hostage and locked into a single cell, where one of the stabbed men later bled to death.

It was not until about this point that the first alarm bells began to ring. At the same time, fires were breaking out, and men were going on the rampage. Not only officers were potential targets any more. Some prisoners, when their doors were unlocked, were confronted by snarling men they did not want to see. In the segregation block, the nonces and inadequates, the Rule Forty-Threes who were in constant danger from the 'normal' prisoners, listened to the row in trepidation. The smell of smoke, in some of them, induced incipient panic that would spill easily into terror.

Alan Hughes and Michael Masters were alone when the riot started. As the noise grew they faced each other, at first startled, unbelieving. Jerrold had left them ten minutes before, to see an acquaintance in the kitchen who owed him some big favour, to try and bum a cake or two from the supper batch. He figured they'd never get distributed, and he figured he and Hughes might go hungry when the place went up. He had intended to be back well before the action started.

'It's happening!' said Alan Hughes. 'Something's gone wrong! Christ – Jerrold's out there!'

They hurried to the doorway and looked out. Men were thundering along the balcony and its twin opposite. Below them every balcony was swarming, every open cell disgorging prisoners. The main floor, far below, was a mass of grey and blue.

'Fucking hell!' said Masters. 'There's no fires, nothing! It's anarchy!'

In the doorway at the end of the balcony they saw officers. There was a roar as more inmates raced to tackle them.

'You'd better go the other way,' said Hughes. 'Mike – you'd better get your skates on, feller. Go.'

For one blinding moment, Masters thought he'd stay. The noise was rising by the second. There was madness in it, lunacy.

'It won't work,' he said. 'The skull beneath the skin.'

'You can get out. You can escape. If it fails, you'll be back anyway. It's what you wanted, Mike. For God's sake, go.'

In the main hall there was furious fighting. The number of men involved seemed far higher than they had expected. It seemed impossible that the officers could hold it. Masters felt the pistol in his pocket and nearly gagged. He thrust his hand out and seized Alan Hughes'. They shook hands almost passionately.

'I won't use it, Alan,' he said. 'The pistol.'

'No,' said Alan Hughes. 'Where's Matthew? Where's Matthew Jerrold?'

He was distraught. As Masters began to move along the balcony, expecting to be challenged or seized at any moment, Hughes went to the edge and gripped the rail. The last words Masters heard from him were shouted into the howling void, lost, pathetic: 'Matthew! Jerrold! Matthew!'

Matthew Jerrold was in the servery when Lister's shout set off the riot. He was not precisely welcome, but few prisoners would ever dare to cross him. The officers in the hotplate area, when they realised something was going on, also knew they were especially vulnerable. There were knives, cleavers, pans, skillets, open spaces. There were also gallons of hot water in the boilers, in preparation for the last tea serving of the day. The people in the cooking area were hand-picked for docility, but nothing could be relied upon. Without much thought the officers began to clear the area, driving men before them urgently.

It might have worked. About half the kitchen staff went through the door, and most of the weapons were behind the officers' lines, before disaster struck. It came in the form of a concerted rush of inmates from D-hall, who had finally broken free of the wall of officers trying to contain them. The kitchen and servery were between them and the admin block, which was behind the main gate. D-hall contained some of the most violent and determined men. The kitchen implements would not be left behind.

As the phalanx of furious, excited inmates came sweeping into the servery, Jerrold recognised his danger. D-hall was a 'white wing', with many inmates who attacked or verballed black or Asian prisoners on sight. A whoop went up from ten or fifteen throats when he was spotted, and a chair originally destined to be hurled at the screws clearing the area was redirected at his head. Jerrold ducked and ran towards the officers. But their faces were contorted also, in fear or hatred, and he leapt sideways before he reached them, vaulting through a hot-plate hatchway.

He was in the preparation room. Behind him were three rows of shining, stainless steel tables, flanked by tall, polished cupboards. There were few men left, and they were panicking, blundering among the tables, trying to reach the doors. But to one side officers charged through to cut off Jerrold, and at the cooking end, D-hall men seized pans and steels and heavy trays, and hunted him with joy. As Jerrold ran towards a high cabinet which he hoped to climb and kick off his tormentors, he passed a butcher's cleaver. As he fell, under raining, savage blows, it crossed his mind how appropriate it would have been for him to use it, as he was meant to have done at Buckingham Estate. He died quite philosophically, dazed then dulled by the crashes to his skull. He wished he had not left the company of Hughes.

It was more than four minutes after the riot started that Richard Pendlebury knew with certainty that the disaster had finally occurred. Throughout the afternoon, and especially since tea-time, most officers had been aware that there was trouble not far below the surface, that could erupt. But for many reasons, the men who might have warned the governor did not care to. In some ways, it was a case of getting even, of being able to show him, yet again, as out of touch with the realities. But it was more than that. He and Christopher Abbey were at the point of open enmity, and Abbey could not have borne it if he had warned of trouble, and trouble had not come. When Kaye and White were murdered, when Lister raised his arms and yelled, Abbey and his fellows had been simply swamped. They had also recognised, with horror, that the thing was orchestrated.

Pendlebury heard the growing row within probably half a minute. As he stood, cocking his head to listen, Ian Serple knocked briefly on the connecting door, opening it at the same time. The noise grew louder.

'Sir,' said Serple.

Pendlebury ran past him, through the outer office, and opened that door. There was a long corridor in front of him, carpeted in green. There were stout oak doors at the other end of it, and to the sides. The noise was frightening, reverberant.

'Sir,' repeated Serple, at his elbow now. 'It's a riot. Should I . . . ?'

Other members of the admin staff appeared along the corridor. Pendlebury made a gesture with his hand, a stupid, pointless gesture. He noticed that they were all men, as if he had not noticed it before. He was glad.

'We mustn't over-react,' he said. 'It's not the first one we've had. There are no alarms yet. Go into your offices, please, and— No, forget that. Come into the conference room. There's a fire-escape from there.'

One of the five men said purposefully: 'Sir, we ought at least to check.'

He began to move towards the farthest door, but slowly, as if he would rather be called back.

'Bennett!' snapped Pendlebury. 'There's a procedure! The officers will not thank you to interfere. Come. Now.'

As Serple led the admin staff into the conference room, Pendlebury returned to his office. His mind felt dulled, stupid. Where were the officers? Where were his reports? He reached for the internal telephone, to ring the duty room. Ridiculous. Nobody would be there. Over the noise of shouting, the drumming on cell doors, the alarm bells started, sharp, insistent. Pendlebury reached for another telephone. He began to dial the number of the local police. It was agreed procedure. They would alert the main station, thirteen miles away, and cars would be despatched immediately. But how many were needed? How bad was it? Would the sight of policemen just make things worse? He put the receiver down and pressed the button marked E on his automatic phone pad. E for Emergency. The number of the nearest Army and Royal Air Force bases, and the codeword to activate the responses honed by Sinclair and the Home Secretary, snapped into view. Serple was re-entering the room when they heard the door at the far end of the block crash open, and the sound of running feet.

'Sir! Sir! Mr Pendlebury! It's an emergency!'

The voice was distorted with fear, but both men knew it. Pendlebury was punching buttons on the phone as Arthur Probert burst in, followed by an officer called Les Rix. Both men were an odd, pasty colour, Probert looking old and sick. He had only been back on duty for three days.

'Sir! It's a . . . it's . . .'

Pendlebury, breathing shallowly, flapped his hand to shut Probert up. He began to tell Serple to lock what doors he could, but he was through. A young, efficient-sounding voice announced a name and rank, and asked his business.

'This is Richard Pendlebury. I am the governor of Bowscar Jail, at Bowscar, Staffordshire. Do you know the meaning of the codename Operation Cicero?'

There was the briefest of pauses.

'Yes, sir. Is it go?'

'Thank you,' said Pendlebury. The relief was unbearable. 'Thank you, yes it is. Should I talk to someone else?'

'No, sir, that's unnecessary. Just hang on one moment.'

Pendlebury heard the officer talk to someone else, his hand across the receiver. Pendlebury met Probert's eyes, which were wide and frightened. He looks like death, thought Pendlebury. He tried to smile, to be reassuring, and failed. The voice came back onto the line.

'Are you in a position to give details, sir? It's a matter of knowing what to send. Is it a full alert?'

At the far end of the corridor there were shouts, crashes, screams. Les Rix dashed to the office door and back again, like a caged animal. Probert said: 'For God's sake, sir! There's murder being done! They're killing!'

'I heard that,' said the voice. 'We're go. Don't worry, sir, we'll be . . . twenty minutes.'

'Twenty *minutes*?'

'I'm sorry, sir? We move by road, of course. But—'

Pendlebury cut him off. He began to punch the numbers for the RAF. They could hear fighting in the corridor.

'Serple. Clear the admin staff. Down the fire escape. Arthur, is it safe? Or should we . . . ?'

He abandoned the phone call, knowing it was ridiculous. The air base was sixty miles away. They couldn't even land a helicopter near the prison. What could they do? Bomb the place?

'Lock them in,' said Probert. His colour was alarming, now, pasty with purple blotches. 'Lock us all in. It's our only defence. Are there any weapons? We can't go down the fire escape, we'd be walking into it. Are there any guns?'

'No. Serple, go with the admin staff. Lock the doors and hide or something. Arthur. Rix. Secure this office if you can, please.'

He began to dial the local police, cursing himself for the time he had wasted. The phone rang out for ages, second after second. In the outer office he could hear Probert and Rix shifting furniture, barricading the door. And all the time the noise outside grew louder, wilder, overlaid by the shrill insistence of the bell.

It was a woman's voice, young. She sounded rather bored.

'Inspector Whelan, please. This is Pendlebury, at the prison. The governor. It's an emergency.'

'I'm sorry, the inspector's not here today. Sergeant Thompson is in charge.'

'Put me through to him, then.'

'Well I'll try, but I think he's at supper. Can you hang on for a minute?'

'No!' said Pendlebury. His voice was high, shocked. But it was too late. She had put him onto hold. Agreed procedure! It had all seemed so simple when they'd talked it through, so logical. His instinct was to slam the phone down, to dial another number. Outside, through two thick doors, the noise was less easy to interpret, but no less frightening. Mercifully, the phone clicked into life after only fifteen seconds. But it was the girl again.

'Sir? We can't find Sergeant Thompson. We think he's left the building. Is it a serious matter?'

'It's very serious. Put me onto the constable in charge, please. Anybody.'

'I'm a constable,' she replied. 'I'm not a switchboard girl, you know. What seems to be the trouble?'

In the outer office there was a thunderous crash. Then more, shorter, sharper bangs. They were kicking at the door, charging it, trying to knock it down.

'We have an agreed procedure,' said Pendlebury, hopelessly. 'There's a riot going on. Please inform headquarters, and any cars you have available. Tell them they need arms.'

'Arms?' The girl's voice rose a pitch. 'What, you mean guns?'

Pendlebury snapped.

'I mean guns!' he shouted. 'Get onto HQ immediately! There's a full-scale riot going on here, girl! Look out of your window and you'll probably see smoke! This is an emergency! People might escape! They might be on the streets! Do it now!'

'Oh my God,' she said.

Pendlebury heard a splintering of wood that could only mean the outer door was down. He dropped the telephone receiver and stood. At that moment he heard a pistol shot from the yard, followed shortly by another. For a fraction of an instant he thought it must be the police, or the Army. Then he knew the truth. It was too late.

For Brian Rogers and the other ringleaders, the speed at which the chaos spread was at first more a hindrance than a help. To keep control of the plan, to ensure that there would be enough armed men who knew what they were doing at the gates, they had swiftly to make contact with their teams. Rogers had arranged to rendezvous with Mike Shaw outside the D-hall sluice, but D-hall was the scene of one of the first and biggest battles between officers and inmates. Lister and Rogers, who met up on the blood-splashed tiles below where Kaye had died, were loath to get too close, in case they got involved.

'Shall we go without?' asked Rogers. 'We could grab a screw apiece when we get to the gate. Do we need Mike Shaw?'

Lister thought they did. Taking hostages was messy, and could be time-consuming. He had chosen to be lead gun so that whatever happened he could be outside quickly, not bargaining with men's lives.

'Let's go over there,' he said. 'Stick on the edges. Shaw's a hard guy. He'll get clear.'

As they moved purposefully through the milling crowd, they spotted Billy Ford against a wall. He was laughing, and waved at them with a ten-inch carving knife.

'He's fucking drunk,' said Brian Rogers. 'He's fucking mad, that bloke.'

'Where's Tony?' shouted Billy Ford. 'We'll never get out of this place if people don't keep their appointments!'

They were distracted by a rush of men behind them. It was a gang of about thirty black prisoners chasing Archie Watkins, a militant fascist from Wolverhampton who regularly conspired with a small coterie of like-minded prison officers to torment and humiliate young West Indians. As they reached a corridor, a counter-attack of Archie's men rushed out, and the struggle burst bloodily across the whole tiled area. Out of the ruck, miraculously, Tony Smith appeared.

'Come on, Bill!' he shouted. 'Work to be done, you drunken twat!'

Both of them were in a terrific humour, as if they were going on a pub crawl with transport home laid on. They pushed their way through the mêlée, waving.

'Mad,' said Brian Rogers. 'I hope they remember the idea's to get out. Fucking mad.'

'There's Shaw,' said Lister, tersely. He did not understand the English attitude at all. Some of them treated it like a game. He wanted out.

Shaw was bleeding heavily from a cut above one eye, and he held up a hand with two badly broken fingers. He, too, was grinning.

'I got Chris Abbey,' he said. 'I tore his fucking ear off. Magic.'

'Come on,' said Lister. 'Let's go.'

McGregor was waiting for them on the edge of the hall, and he gestured down a smoke-filled corridor. His eyes were streaming.

'That one's clear,' he said. 'If you can take the fumes. It's going brilliant. The screws don't know what's hit them.'

'Have you seen Pat and Tom?'

'Aye. Tom got hit. I saw him go down with some screws on top, but I didn't hang about. Pat fucked off like a blue-arse fly. He's a good man, he'll be there.'

'What about some hostages?'

'Tell me where they are,' said McGregor. 'You show me a screw, I'll take the bastard. They're busy, Brian, wouldn't you just know it! There'll be plenty near the admin.'

The corridor they were moving down was thick with acrid smoke, but empty of life. They moved fast and carefully, watchful for attack, and when they reached the end of the passage, they stopped. An iron gate hung open, with a blue shirt, for some unfathomable reason, jammed between two upright bars. In two steps, they would be out of the prison-proper, the cell halls, and close to the laundry, the reception hall, the admin. And the gates.

As they hesitated, three prison officers turned a corner twenty feet from them, at a run. They were in riot gear, with helmets, clubs and shields. They were almost past the motionless prisoners before they saw them, and when it registered they were shocked beyond reason. As they stumbled to a halt Lister stepped in front of them, the long Ruger pointing at the nearest stomach. Rogers, beaming with delight, presented his .38 more like a Western gunslinger than a marksman, at eye height and arm's length, the barrel inches from an officer's face. McGregor merely showed his small revolver, in an unassuming, casual gesture that spoke volumes. Shaw, smiling through his blood, waved a thin, honed blade.

'If you drop them,' said Lister, 'you won't get hurt. If you don't, we'll kill you.'

Everyone knew Charles Lister. One of the officers had seen him kill Mickie White and Kaye. They dropped the clubs.

Brian Rogers said: 'We don't need three. It's one too many. Shall I shoot one?'

'Animal,' said Angus McGregor.

He put the .32 in his pocket, and bent to pick up a club. Before he could swing it, Lister shot his stiffened fingers into the neck of the nearest officer, who dropped without opening his mouth. One of the others did, to gasp. The third was deadly silent.

'You Limeys are so goddam crude,' Charles Lister said.

'Right,' said McGregor. 'I'll go round that way, now Pat Parkinson's on his own. Fuck knows if Billy Ford and Tony'll make it, but we'll have to hope they do. Where's Masters?'

'Fucking skulking,' muttered Brian Rogers. 'Bastard.'

As he and Shaw drove the hostages forward flanked by Lister, McGregor moved off to act as fireman and cover. He moved rapidly to his right, checking doors and windows, wondering at the emptiness of the area. Judging from the din behind him in the jail, most of the officers were still trying for containment. It occurred to him that it was probably only a few minutes, five or so, since the thing had started, although it felt much longer. He was very calm, with no anxiety at all. He was enjoying it.

When the three men with their hostages reached the open doorway to the yard, they realised that some attempts had already been made to storm the gate. Without a game-plan or firepower it had been a waste of time, and bloody with it. The yard was littered with debris, and several windows of the gatehouse had been broken. There were four bodies visible – or at least, four immobile men – all of them inmates. They guessed that any injured officers had been moved. Now there were about fifteen officers, all with clubs and some in full gear, ranged across the gate. In the gatehouse one or two were visible, and one was on the phone.

'Shit,' spat Rogers. 'The phones! Whose job was it to do the phones?'

'Ivan Buckley and his mob,' said Shaw. 'Maybe they did, Brian. They were meant to hit admin. They couldn't do all the bleeding phones, could they? Maybe that one's separate from the switchboard. The screws aren't stupid.'

'Not so sure,' Charles Lister said, laconically. 'If they had brains, they'd have cleared that place and thrown away the keys.

They'd have screwed us. Do we show the hostages? Or do we wait for Ford and Smith and Parkinson?'

As if in answer to his own question, he stepped through the doorway into the yard, into full view of the prison officers. He held the Ruger above his right shoulder, pointing upwards as if in salutation.

'We're going out,' he shouted. 'We've got two of your men here. Tell them in there to open the gates.'

The officers did not reply. It was clear that they did not know what to believe, or what to do.

'No shit,' called Lister. 'You better believe me. We're going to shoot one soon.'

He gestured with his left hand to Shaw and Rogers. Rogers jabbed his gun into the kidney area of his man, who jumped forward. Shaw followed. The two hostages stood in the doorway, with Lister between them and their fellows.

'Take your helmets off,' Lister ordered. 'Let your buddies see you sweat.'

Inside the block, as he passed the main stairway to the governor's suite and offices, Angus McGregor heard the roaring mob at Pendlebury's door. He tried, for a moment, to ignore it, to hurry past. More important to get out, to find Parkinson, or Ford and Tony Smith, to check the safety of the flank. Then he pictured Pendlebury, stooped and grey, and listened to the baying of enraged men. In any case, he thought, nothing would go wrong. Lister and Brian Rogers and two guns could handle anything.

Before climbing the stairway, though, he checked all the passageways back into the main jail. There was movement halfway along one. He called out to the men, difficult to see in the rolling smoke, and they stopped. They did not look like screws.

'Who's that? It's McGregor here. I've got a gun. Who are you?'

Two of the men moved forward. They stopped twenty feet from him, underneath a recessed wall lamp. They both held knives.

'Satisfied?'

McGregor did not know Conor Grady, the Armagh Wolf, but the flat Ulster was a fair indicator. There were six or seven men, and they looked like brothers, thin, pale-skinned, black-haired. If killing screws was needed, he thought, they were the boys.

'The Yank's got hostages,' he said. 'He's down that passage there. It's looking good.'

Without waiting for a reply, he bounded up the scrubbed stone stairs, two at a time. A yellow-painted doorway at the top led to an ante-room with polished floor, which gave onto the green-carpeted corridor to Pendlebury's offices. At the farther end there was a mass of men, perhaps fifteen or more, trying to smash their way through the oaken door. Other office doors were open, and he could hear glass smashing, furniture being wrecked. A prisoner emerged as he approached one, carrying a ream of typing paper. He had a concentrated, intent look, as if he had looted the Crown Jewels. He gazed at McGregor sightlessly, then rushed towards the stairway.

McGregor, approaching fast, could see the door begin to give. He shouted, but his voice just added to the row. The weight of men was enormous, and would have knocked a wall down if they had co-ordinated it. Then the door splintered with a crack, from top to bottom. In the confusion of arms, legs and bodies, parts of it fell inwards, against a barricade of filing cabinets. He had an impression of two prison officers trying to escape through an inner doorway, but of one of them, an older man, being pulled down. He also thought he heard two shots outside. Several men had fallen in the doorway, and McGregor, moving furiously fast, ran up and over them.

When he arrived, screeching like a dervish, in Pendlebury's room, the governor had already been knocked backwards from his desk onto the floor. Three men were on him, punching and tearing at his face. Arthur Probert was lying in the doorway, apparently dead from a stroke or heart attack, his face a dull blue-black. Les Rix had grabbed a table lamp and was in a corner, swinging it ferociously at anyone who approached.

McGregor, the Animal of old, took a flying kick at the head of one of Pendlebury's attackers that dislocated his jaw and left him screaming. Another one he seized by the hair and jerked sideways off the governor, then he crashed his foot into the face of the third. As others came at him, their eyes as mad as his, he drew the small revolver.

'Get back! Get back! Get back!'

The men stopped. Even in the outer office the noise diminished.

'Sir,' said McGregor. 'Get to another room. I'll get these bastards out of here.'

'Angus—'

'Shut your fucking mouth and move,' snarled McGregor. 'You'll get me killed, I'm in a hurry! Move!'

He began to herd the prisoners out, back into the ante-room, the corridor. The governor, half-helped by Rix, half-helping him, moved towards the conference suite. They paused by Probert's body until McGregor waved his gun at them.

'He's dead, for Christ's sake. Move.'

Within five seconds, the governor and Rix had gone. Everybody heard the locking of the door.

'You prats!' McGregor shouted at the sullen men. 'You fucking morons. Why waste your time on him? There's bastards galore downstairs! There's gates to open! Just fucking go!'

As he shouted, he moved his head a fraction backwards. It saved his life, as the glancing, downward blow missed his carotid artery by the tiniest possible margin. But the blade still plunged deep into his neck, behind his breast-bone and into the top of his thorax. McGregor staggered, and fell to one knee, and turned, and pulled the trigger. He did not know the knife-man, it was just some prat who did not like to be crossed in anything. The bullet entered just above his Adam's apple and lodged in his brain. McGregor, falling, fired one more shot, that broke an ornamental light fitting in the ceiling. Lying on the floor, he pulled the home-made knife from the hole in his neck, and watched the others run down the passageway and disappear.

Out in the yard, the shots from inside the admin block broke down the last resistance of the officers on the gate. They had watched the shooting of their colleague in the yard in a kind of paralysis, which had frozen, gelled, as time ran on. It had been a matter of timing, of bad luck, inexperience. Even Charles Lister, to whom every sort of violence, in passion or cold blood was commonplace, had never killed a hostage before. He did not wait long enough after the first warning, he did not let the implications sink in fully. When the men were helmetless, and white with terror, he had announced a count of five. When he had finished, the watching officers were still witless, unbelieving. And he had placed the gun against the stomach, and pulled the trigger.

Worse, the man had not died instantly. He was heavily built, and God knows what damage the bullet wrought on his insides. But when he collapsed, he was not still. He writhed, groaning loudly, and his left leg twitched and beat upon the ground. Two of the watching officers, far from giving in, moved forward a pace or two, clubs raised, until Rogers levelled the .38 at them, smiling. Two more threw up, and continued to do so when Lister fired another bullet into the writhing man, which silenced him.

A second or two later, the impasse was compounded. Billy Ford and Tony Smith appeared at one end of the yard, with another hostage. They had torn his tie and shirt off, and criss-crossed his chest with knife-cuts. They held one arm each, and jabbed him playfully with blades. Billy Ford, his pale skin redder than his hair, was roaring, furiously drunk.

'One fucking move, you bastards, that's all it needs!' he shouted. 'I'll stick it in him and out the other fucking side! One fucking move!'

To Lister and to Rogers, it had seemed logical that the officers should be allowed to run. There were too many to take captive, and nobody to keep them under guard. The gates should be opened, the guards should run, and they should go. Now Smith and Billy Ford were blocking off one exit, and threatening another death. To his right, Lister saw another band. Seven men, he counted, moving like shadows along the wall, thin and watchful. They would be the Irish. The men that no one saw.

He shouted to them: 'Clear a passage there, you guys! Let them run! I'm going to shoot the next one!'

He dragged the second hostage away from Brian Rogers by his arm. The man's skin had become translucent, his eyes stretched wide with near-hysteria.

'This time I'll count to ten! So go now, if you want to save him! Run! Brian, go get the fucking gate unlocked. Shoot some bastard. Let's move it!'

As Rogers walked towards the officers, the Irishmen walked with him. Rogers glanced at their leader, so small beside his own bulk, and grinned. The Armagh Wolf did not smile back, but he acknowledged it.

'One!' yelled Charles Lister. 'Two! Three!'

For several seconds, the officers held their ground. Rogers and the Wolf, flanked by six more terrorists with blades, approached to within feet of them. The gatehouse door was closed, and possibly locked. But that was not a problem.

'Open it!' roared Rogers. 'Can't you hear the fucker counting?'

'Five!' yelled Lister. 'Six!'

It was then that McGregor's shots were heard from the governor's suite. The hostage let out a cry, and dropped to his knees, and urinated uncontrollably. Then he began to sob. Charles Lister, leaving go his arm, kicked him violently.

'Seven! Eight!'

The officer facing Rogers' pistol screamed to the gatehouse: 'Open it! Open it!'

And Rogers turned and fired a bullet at the door. The .38 jumped and smoked, and Rogers gave a whoop of pure joy, his ears still ringing from the bang.

Seconds later the officers, their clubs abandoned, were running from the yard, being harried by Billy Ford and Tony Smith at one end, their own bloodied hostage among them. At the other end the Irish watched the officers impassively, while Brian Rogers, delirious, crashed shot after shot at the running figures. He was not aiming, except to please himself, but he caught one man below the shoulder and crippled him for life. More were injured as they met the prisoners McGregor had flushed from the admin block, and more as they were hunted like rats within the smoking corridors. Lister's hostage, who had fainted in a pool of urine, was touched no more.

Electronically, and then with keys, the Bowscar gates were unlocked. And opened.

EIGHTEEN

Alan Hughes, for reasons far more complicated than mere self-preservation, had taken to his bunk long before Angus McGregor returned to the cell. At first the Scot, whose eyes had been misting periodically since he was stabbed, thought that he had gone. But Hughes uncovered his head when he heard movement, and stared at McGregor from underneath the blankets.

'Angus. What's happened to you? Have you seen Matthew Jerrold?'

McGregor stumbled, and lowered himself onto the chair. He was very pale, his skin glistening with sweat, and he held a bloody rag or handkerchief to his neck. In the other hand he had the small revolver.

'Get up, ' he said. 'You're coming with me.'

Hughes did not believe him. He could not imagine why.

'Angus, you're hurt. Have you been shot?'

McGregor lifted the revolver from his side and aimed at Hughes. The aim was not steady.

'Alan, I'm not joking. You're coming too. Move fast. You know I'll shoot you. You know I'm mad.'

'But why?' asked Hughes. He pulled the covers back. He was fully dressed, including shoes.

'Because I want to talk to the Home Secretary. I want to have a word with him before I die. I want to ask him why he did it to my brother.'

'For Christ's sake, Angus! I used to be a neighbour of the man! Years ago! How should I know if he lives there any more?'

He lowered himself to the floor, however. McGregor's face was full of pain, his eyes were bright. Hughes did not want to die.

'It's worth a try. Some bastard's stabbed me in the neck. I'll not be getting far, will I? I'll not be drinking with my pals in the Sarry Heid this fucking Hogmanay. We'll go and have a look. You never know.'

'All right.' Hughes did not want to stay, particularly. The stench of burning and the constant, undiminished noise would drive him insane soon. The whole thing was sickening, the reality so much worse than anything he had foreseen. He guessed that Jerrold – like many more – was dead. 'Will we get out? Did it work?'

'Oh, like a fucking charm,' McGregor said, sarcastically. 'Like clockwork, Alan. The screws unlocked the gates and everyone filed out, in good order. The charabancs were waiting, and the governor dished out sherbet dips. You should've been there.' He gave a snort of laughter. 'I don't know for certain. I went to save the governor from Ivan Buckley. A wee detour. I'm as daft as you are. But I reckon so, it worked. Rumour has it. And there's a constant flow of bodies towards the gates.'

There was, in fact, still chaos in the hall below them when they went onto the balcony. Several pitched battles were being fought, all, as far as Hughes could see, between gangs of inmates. On the higher levels, small groups of men were systematically smashing cells, throwing bedding, tables, anything, into the nets, some of which were piled like Steptoe's cart. If the nets gave way, the fighting men below would probably be killed.

McGregor was still bleeding, and he was at times unsteady on his feet. But the grip he took of Hughes' arm was strong, and the revolver in his right hand jutted forward pugnaciously whenever they met anyone who took an interest in them. It was not often, though. The prison officers, if they were fighting on a front, must have moved it to another part of the jail. Perhaps they had taken a defensive position somewhere. Hughes, despite himself, was fascinated. The fabric of the place was scarred, defaced, as if men had tried desperately to hurt the stone and brick. There were fires everywhere, smashed water pipes gushed from all the sluices, electrical trunking – carrying volts and amps enough to kill the vandalisers – had been torn from walls and ceilings. The damage must run into millions, if parts of Bowscar could be saved at all. That much, he did find satisfying.

The main gates and yard reminded him of newsreel film from Europe in the aftermath of war. There was a refugee air to it, a sense of purposelessness mixed with purpose. Men were moving out through the open gates, not unexpectedly, but men were also moving in. Others were undecided, and just hung about, greeting acquaintances with a hollow jollity that was almost comical. Yet more had taken up the attitude of guards, were holding the officers' discarded clubs in stances of aggression. They were the barons' men, keeping in the biggest debtors. Another small knot of D-hallers were beating blacks and Asians back into the jail, with John Peel cries of satisfaction. And there were the gates themselves, and towers, and the smoke. Berlin, after the surrender.

McGregor, because of his condition and his gun, got some peculiar looks, but no one challenged them. Hughes, to his utter disbelief, quite suddenly found himself outside the gates in a darkening and rather chilly evening, smelling fresh, clean air. He marvelled at the lengthening shadows, the sunshine blazing redly on the west-facing windows of not-too-distant houses, the newly-greening trees, the fields, the clouds, the sky. He was filled with a tremendous excitement, a childlike sense of wonder. Whatever happened next, this moment had made it worth it.

Peculiarly, the world outside Bowscar was still behaving almost normally. The villagers themselves, although not very close, knew that something had gone wrong, but did not know quite what. It was ten minutes or so since the first bells had been heard, and children had been called in just in case, and curtains, oddly, drawn. Many people, in the very recent moments, had realised that it was more serious than most alerts, and become alarmed. A single call to the police had become a trickle, and soon the flood would jam the switchboard. Some people, seeing smoke, had rung the fire brigade, and some, sensing a profit, the newspapers. But so far, there had been no sirens, no fire engines, no Army trucks, no police.

The traffic through the village was hardly affected yet. It was never heavy, but some motorists who knew the jail slowed down when they saw the men outside the main gate, down the access road, until toots from behind hurried them along. Most people guessed there was a fire in the Scar, which would account for the bells and smoke, and assumed some of the inmates, under heavy supervision, had been led out for their safety. Having deduced this, some drivers, for *their* safety, wanted to speed on. Some dawdled, though, despite the tooting. And some stopped.

The car that halted nearest McGregor and Hughes was a Fiat Uno. The driver was a youth of nineteen or so, and his companion was a pretty blonde of seventeen. They watched almost open-mouthed as the two men came towards them. They could see that one was bleeding, although they did not see his gun until it was too late, and they could see that they were inmates. It did not occur to them for many moments that they were in danger.

When they were close, the two men broke into a stumbling run, with McGregor pushing Hughes, while holding on to him for support. Hughes saw the faces through the windscreen change, the girl's mouth opening to scream. Then McGregor flopped forward onto the car and wrenched the passenger door open.

Hughes did not move. He did not know what would happen next. He assumed the people would get out, or— The muzzle flashed and the girl's face, hit just below the cheekbone, tore redly in front of his eyes, a lump of blood springing brightly from her right temple. McGregor seized her by the hair and jerked her towards him, simultaneously firing over her. Both reports reached Alan Hughes' ears like one, and there seemed to be a lot of blood, and the muzzle – how, he did not know – pointed at him. McGregor had moved fast and crabwise round the bonnet, and pulled the other door open. He dragged the driver out backwards, making a circular movement with his pistol at Hughes. Hughes passed the bonnet, stepped over the bleeding youth, and fell into the driving seat. The engine was still running. McGregor, mysteriously, was in the passenger seat, wiping blood from the inside of the windscreen with his sleeve, pointing the revolver at Hughes' head.

'Drive,' he said. He made a small sound of disgust. 'Yeach. Messy wee bitch. Curiosity killed the fucking cat.'

For the first time in seven years, Alan Hughes engaged a gear, switched on his winking indicator, checked over his shoulder and in his mirror, and pulled away. Even on auto-pilot, he hadn't lost the knack.

Michael Masters, by this time, was also in a car, although it was a large and powerful one, unlike the Fiat Uno. He was as disoriented as Hughes, and he was also under guard. A man with a hooked nose and a crew-cut was nestling a large black automatic on his lap on the opposite side of the wide back seat. In the front was another man with a sawn-off shotgun, beside the driver, and nobody was talking. Masters had been kidnapped.

Ever since Charles Lister had warned him of his need to have a gun, Masters had thought about the danger he would be in. It had not taken him long to realise that there was more to it than common envy. If there was a successful break-out, if any of the powerful men got free, one or more of them were bound to see him as a useful bargaining chip. At the very least his wealth and position would make him a better than usual hostage in a sticky situation, and at best he could be a passport to freedom and riches. Although Masters did not discount Lister himself, or McGregor, the most likely candidate was Brian Rogers. Masters had set out from the cell with his hand on the small pistol in his pocket. He had told Hughes he would not use it, and had meant that, then. But as the chaos and the carnage unrolled before his eyes, he knew he would.

Masters was a big man, blond and quite conspicuous. He was moving at the start of the riot, when prison officers had energy and hope, if not coherency. He quickly developed a technique of pushing smaller men aside quite brutally, and of dashing into cells to hide. One officer confronted him inside the entrance to a sluice, and Masters seized his arm, took him off balance, and hurled him backwards into the white-tiled wall. To prisoners who seemed inclined to threaten him, he showed the pistol and assumed a John Wayne look. One aspect or the other did the trick; whichever way, his progress was very rapid.

Of all the ringleaders, Masters could have entered the yard first by probably two minutes. Much good it would have done him, he thought ironically. When he glanced out of a window in the reception hall, men and officers were fighting viciously, and to no set plan. He noted with relief that they were not his men – very few had blades and there were certainly no guns – and he noted also that the battle was attracting fresh waves of officers by the second. Feeling rather like a schoolboy, Masters hid behind the counter of the clothes store. He was invisible, and he could keep watch. With sweating hands, he fiddled with the pistol, tried to imagine firing it. The magazine was full now, and he could remove it and replace it reasonably expertly. But the whole idea was alien.

To a hidden man, the din and panic seemed always on the point of a crescendo which somehow never came. There were occasional clatterings of many feet, and once or twice the sound of a lone man walking carefully through. Masters heard the first two shots, and wondered if it was not time to move. He was halfway across the room, to look into the yard, when the second shots thudded out – then screams and pandemonium. Masters ran out of the reception hall and found a short passage leading to the gate yard. He heard the crashing fusillade of Rogers' shots, and flattened himself into a recess as frightened officers raced past him. Seconds later screeching savages arrived from inside the jail, some chasing officers, some seeking to escape. Masters held the pistol boldly, and was left alone. But he dared wait no longer. Right or wrong, he dared not miss the opening of the gates. Leading with the bright two-five, he pushed through the double-doorway into daylight.

There were perhaps a hundred prisoners in the courtyard, and more were pouring from every exit. The inner gate, an electronic steel device of vertical tubular bars, was almost open, and men were hauling at the great old wooden door. Masters spotted Lister on the fringes of the mass, and searched for a glimpse of Rogers. He felt him before he saw him, though. Or rather, he felt the barrel of the Smith and Wesson jammed just below his ribs. He smelled the big man's breath and heard his voice. It was rich with triumph.

'Oh, there you are, Mr Masters,' he said. 'I wondered where you'd slithered to. Give us the pop-gun, eh?'

Mike Shaw, without a qualm, walked up to the little jutting pistol and closed his good hand over it. Masters could feel the heat from the muzzle of the .38. It was burning him, through his shirt. He dismissed a snap desire to pull the trigger of his pistol and kill Shaw, although the bloody mask of the man's leering face added to his revulsion. Stay calm, he thought, stay calm. At least you're still alive.

'Silly cunt,' mocked Rogers, affectionately, when Masters was safely covered with his own gun. He flipped the chambers of the Smith and Wesson open. 'It was empty.' He pulled a handful of cartridges from his pocket, smiling.

The smile was still on his lips when the high-velocity hunting bullet hit his partner in the eye. It was frozen there as Mike Shaw's brains sprayed out behind him like a dynamic candy floss. It was gone when the Armagh Wolf, pointing the tiny, smoking pistol at his neck now, took the Smith and Wesson from him. Another Irishman picked up the .25 automatic Shaw had dropped.

'A cartoon,' he said. But he turned it on Rogers while his companion relieved him of the .38 shells.

'This is a good little gun,' said the Wolf to Rogers, dropping Peter Smith's small masterpiece into his pocket with the ghost of a smile on his lips. 'It was empty, just like yours was, though. An Englishman made it for me, think of that. Smart, but only single-shot.'

The events had been so quick and startling that Masters had not realised that they concerned him. But the Armagh Wolf, finished with mocking Rogers, jerked his head, unmistakably, for Masters to move. Five more Irishmen materialised, one of them taking gun and shells from Conor Grady. A hundred yards beyond the outer gateway were three big powerful cars, two Granadas and the Mercedes that Masters was bundled into. Each held two men, heavily armed. He saw one submachine-gun and a hand-grenade. Although his brain was almost numb, he had a terrifying sense of loss as they sped away from Bowscar.

Less than two miles from the prison lay *Cynthia's Beam*, and Sarah. She was waiting for him.

The man Charles Lister targeted, before he walked two hundred yards beyond the prison to meet his friends, was Billy Ford. It was something he had thought over often, something that Ford had said that had lodged in his mind. It was a piece of information he thought might come in useful.

The last time Lister had seen Rogers' oafish sidekick was when he had chased after the escaping officers with Tony Smith. Rather than follow them into the building, Lister had positioned himself near the gates and watched. Men surging round the yard and battering at the bars had noted the Ruger balanced in his hand and stayed away. He had briefly spotted Michael Masters looking like a nervous amateur with the tiny automatic, then seen Rogers and Shaw take him from behind. That was a matter of some slight regret, because he liked the rich Englishman. Then he saw Billy Ford's red head emerging from a door a hundred yards away, and went for him.

Ford had a broken billyclub in his left hand and a bloody knife in his right. He had lost his companion somewhere, and seemed in two minds whether to go for the gates with the rest of the growing crowd, or to look for some more mayhem. His eyes lit up with drunken recognition when he saw Charles Lister, who was striding easily with the gun at his side.

'What a good do, eh!' he cried. 'What a brilliant fucking do! We've killed three of the cunts, no danger. Here – we electrocuted one of them. We chucked him on a wire and held him there with sticks. Fucking stink!'

Lister levelled the Ruger at Billy Ford's stomach.

'That farm,' he said. 'World's End or someplace. Where's it at, exactly?'

Billy blinked at the automatic, as if it was a joke.

'Go easy, mate! You're on my side!'

'I'm in a hurry.'

'No sweat,' said Ford. 'No skin off my nose, is it? It's called Pratt's Farm, OK? World's End. Can you remember Denmead?

That's a little village a few miles north of Portsmouth, off the old London Road. Denmead. Ask for World's End there. Well, follow the signs, all right? Pratt's Farm's in a wood, near the pub called the Chairmen, or the Chairmakers, or something like that. Something to do with chairs, you can't miss it. Just past it there's a lane to Pratt's. It's marked. It leads right into this wood, it's brilliant. A fucking foxhole.'

'Pratt's Farm, World's End, Denmead, Portsmouth to London Road,' repeated Lister, to nods. Then he shot him. 'Sorry, Billy. I just don't want no one else to know, OK? See you, feller.'

He shot him a second time, in the head, for luck.

'Hallelujah,' he muttered. 'I ought to get a bounty from the government.'

Lister's team had also got a high-performance car, a big BMW automatic, which was warmed and purring, ready to move off. They all smiled hugely as he walked towards them, even Al Pruchak, who was not given to exercising his face that much. Syvil leapt out of the back seat, and gave him a hug and a light kiss on the mouth.

'Jesus, Chuck,' she said. 'Is it good to see you, babe.'

'One thing wrong,' said Lister, before getting in. 'Sidney, for fuck's sakc get out of that driver's seat. This is England, are you crazy?'

Sidney Gibbin was bemused. He was wearing a cream silk shirt and a tartan golfing cap.

'Huh?'

'This car cost forty thousand bucks. You're a nigger, right? How many times they stopped you so far?'

'You're putting me on, man!'

'We didn't see no cops,' said Pete Delano. 'Are you kidding, Chuck?'

'Unless you've got a chauffeur uniform, the hell I am. Sidney. Out.'

When they were moving, with Gibbin in the back and Syvil Hollis driving, Charles Lister pulled another little stunt. The plan, Pruchak told him, was to head for Manchester, then fly back Stateside via Frankfurt. They had tickets, passports, luggage, everything.

'No,' said Lister. 'We head for London.'

'London! But London'll be crawling! By tonight London'll be Africa, the jungle. Heathrow Airport—'

'Fuck Heathrow. I have a little business first. Something to attend to. So what the hell about Heathrow, anyway? Will Manchester be different? Birmingham? You fool yourselves. We attend to something first, then we hide up for a day or two. Talk to some friends. Cook something up.'

Pruchak and Delano were inclined to argue, almost to sulk. The documents were brilliant, the plan perfection. They could be flying out of England in less than two hours' time. The chances of being picked up so soon, they said, were zilch. Lister was conciliatory.

'OK, OK,' he said. 'You guys may be right. But I got something I must do. Business. Look, for fuck sake! Have I ever let you down? Ever? Ain't I *here*? I just walked out of fucking *jail* to please you guys! Hey, you should see the scars around my asshole! These English hoods are wild!'

They all laughed, and the argument was over. They talked comfortably of the small ship on its way to Florida. Of sixty million bucks.

Twelve miles from the prison, heading for the M6 and London, they were passed by a police car at high speed, going the way they had come.

'Holy shit,' said Sidney. 'They sure in for some fun.'

'Damn good thing you weren't driving,' smiled Chuck Lister.

It was 7.57 p.m. precisely when Donald Sinclair heard that something had happened at Bowscar Prison. Although it was so early, he and Judith were in a small French restaurant that they liked, and they had finished their first course. Sinclair was going home to Mary, and he did not intend to be late. Judith did not know it, but he was hoping to patch up the rift to some extent. In the boot of his car was an expensive bunch of roses, and a quart of mussels which he would cook for her.

The bleeper in his inside pocket went just as the waiter was serving Sinclair's lamb cutlets. He checked the LCD and cursed. Fortyne, from the office. He pushed his chair back.

'I want some left when I come back. Otherwise – no pudding!'

The reason that they liked the restaurant was its anonymity. It was just off Cambridge Circus, and it was anything but high-class. The food was fine, the house wine adequate, and it was dark and full of bustle. No one knew them, it was not a haunt of the rich or trendy. It was the sort of place a rising politician could go with his mistress and feel just like a normal human being. That was good.

The phone, though, was a disaster. It was on the counter next to the till, and it was British hi-tech at its wonderful worst. Fortyne's voice was woolly and disembodied, Sinclair's drowned by the clatter of cash and cutlery.

'Is this really necessary?' he shouted, after failing twice to catch what he was being told. 'I'm in the middle of a meal!'

'Bowscar!' Fortyne shouted back. This time Sinclair heard him, and decoded the exasperation in his voice from the electronic fuzz. 'It's up to you, but—'

The cash-register clanged and the rest was lost. Then he heard: '. . . seems quite sanguine, but I'm not so sure. In fact he's delirious. The Army operation . . .'

His voice was lost again, but Sinclair had heard enough. 'I'm on my way!' he yelled. To the waiter he snapped: 'My bill, please. Quickly.' He went back to the table with both coats and told Judith the news.

At Queen Anne's Gate Fortyne was already fielding phone calls from the press. So far they were non-urgent, and easy. They'd had reports from local residents that there was trouble at the Scar, so was it true? Was it worthwhile going up there? Was there anything to it? No, said Fortyne, it was an exercise, a fire drill. Prisoners on the streets? Ridiculous! People had heard the bell, presumably, and must have panicked. Or, more likely, were hoping for a five pound credit. No, he did not know why the local police station was not answering. Maybe they were all out working! He signalled Judith Parker to his chair.

'Can you take over? You'll only get one call at a time, I've told the switchboard.' To Donald he added: 'I've also rung the MOD and told them to say nothing, absolutely nothing, if some crafty scribe tries them. All calls referred to us, on pain of death. I think they got the message. Actually' – back to Judith – 'I doubt if we'll get many more for a while. The local stringers have been on and I've stone-walled them. I don't think Fleet Street or TV will latch on yet. Unless the Army blows its mouth off.'

He told Sinclair what they knew, which was very little. Operation Cicero had been triggered by the governor, who had then got off the line in something of a panic. The police had been alerted ditto, and everyone had gone racing off to Bowscar. Unlike Fleet Street and the telly, he added drily, they did know where it was, despite it being north of Watford. Nobody had scrambled the RAF, and on balance he thought that was a good thing. It would be almost dark by the time a helicopter got there, and it would just add to the general panic. And it would *really* alert the press.

'But is anybody out?' demanded Sinclair. 'Is it a riot, or is it a break-out? Doesn't anybody know?'

'Sir Gerald,' said Christian Fortyne, pushing his spectacles slyly up his nose, 'is convinced there will not be escapes. The governor's panicking, he assured me, just as you will panic. He's very pleased indeed with the way the Army operation went. Like a well-oiled machine. He was disinclined to even bother you with the situation. It will be all over by the morning. Finished. As will your reputation, if and when the story leaks out.'

As Sinclair pondered that, Judith picked up a buzzing phone.

'Where is Sir Gerald?' he asked.

'He's in his club. Luckily he's a little drunk, early though it be. Euphoria, I expect. A well-oiled machine.'

'Luckily?'

'I didn't say that,' said Christian Fortyne.

'It's for you, Chris,' said Judith. 'Ministry of Defence.'

Fortyne listened for some minutes, nodding and making noises of agreement. 'Thank you,' he said at last. 'That's very clear. I have the minister here with me now. I am sure we will return your call within a few minutes. Keep to hand if possible, please. Yes, thank you.'

When he turned back to Sinclair, his face was impassive, the Eton sang-froid unassailable.

'Donald,' he said, 'it's serious. The Army are inside Bowscar. The parts of it that aren't on fire or being held by prisoners. There are some dead, and many hostages.'

'Escapes?'

'Dozens, maybe more. No one knows. The Army and police are organising roadblocks, and any minute now those phones are going mad. I'll rustle up some staff, and we'll need a joint committee with the MOD. The Home Office is perhaps the best location, we've got the files and plans and things, but you'll need to sort that out with the defence wallahs. Their minister's on his way from Devon.'

'Sir Gerald?'

'I'd say we were a little busy at the moment, wouldn't you? When I called him half an hour ago I told you his response. He also mentioned how good his relations with the military are. They're sure to tell him, aren't they?'

Sinclair let out a little hiss through his nostrils.

'Dangerous game,' he said. 'He'll be expecting updates if the situation gets worse.'

Fortyne looked straight into his eyes.

'I thought you wanted to screw him Donald,' he said. 'There won't be another chance.'

Judith's telephone was ringing. The green one, dedicated to the press.

'What shall I tell them? What's the tactic?'

'The usual one,' said Sinclair. He knew Fortyne was right. If things were as bad as they sounded, he would not get a second chance. He had to take it. To Fortyne he said: 'We've got to cut the village off. We'll need a *cordon sanitaire* of eight or ten miles. Get your staff while I talk to the MOD. Then I want the police chiefs for Staffs and all the bordering counties, plus fire chiefs and medicos. Jesus, Christian. Jumping Jesus.'

'But someone saw it coming, didn't they?' said Christian Fortyne. 'And others didn't.'

Judith Parker, in her most mellifluous voice, was saying: 'Look honestly, if you want to drive all the way to deepest Staffs, you're welcome to. I don't *believe* the natives still practise cannibalism up there! But we've heard nothing here that's causing us alarm. No, I will *not* meet you for a drink!'

She put the phone down.

'Thank God for British journalists,' she said.

The fat man and Paddy Collins were watching Forbes' house when Charles Lister and his friends turned up. They were in a Vauxhall Viva, and they were chilly. The bodywork was mainly rust, and the wind was weeping through it and playing with their feet. About the only parts of it that worked well were the electronics, although the camera-aerial sometimes jammed. The seats, according to the fat man, were even harder on his piles than the Lada's.

'Jesus,' said Paddy Collins, when the BMW limousine nosed down the street. 'Some rich bastard's lost his way. He must think this is Knightsbridge!'

'Probably a fresh delivery of tarts for Forbes. He must be almost sick of fucking the skinny one by now. I'm sick of looking at her.'

'Nah,' said Paddy Collins. 'One thing I've noticed about him. Nobody, no one, ever visits him by car. That's training, that. Surveillance. I bet you've never clocked it.'

The fat man sucked his teeth. Surprisingly, to him, he never had. He cast his mind back, to see if it could be true. He was admitting nothing.

'They're looking for somebody,' said Paddy Collins. 'They're looking for a number. Maybe this will be a first, old son. See if that bleeding camera will point.'

His companion leaned forward and pressed the button. The computer beeped and the aerial whirred and swivelled. The BMW was close to Forbes' door by now, its bonnet level with the bumper of the rusting Porsche. It had almost stopped.

'You can tell they're rich,' said Paddy Collins. 'They think he's in because the light's on! No coons where they come from, eh mate? No burgling swine at every corner.'

'They've brought one with them,' said the fat man. 'They bring their own. Class, eh?'

'Never!'

'Use your eyes. One coon. That's training, that is. Surveillance.'

As the car edged into the kerb, Sidney Gibbin climbed out, followed by Delano. On the nearside, Charles Lister emerged, and Pruchak. The camera whirred and clicked. It was dark, but the fat man knew his gear. They'd come out a funny colour, especially the black man, but they'd come out. As they looked up the steps to the front door, he got a lovely group.

Charles Lister bounded up the steps, and hammered on the door. He waited for perhaps twenty seconds, then stood back a pace. He lifted his left leg and smashed it, flat, into the jamb. The other men moved up with him.

'Fuck!' said Paddy Collins. 'Are they ours?'

'Buggery they are. I checked everybody out today. We're on our own.'

'Check again.'

The door to Andrew Forbes' house was stout, and stouter since the last official burglary. By the time it splintered open HQ had confirmed it: they were alone. What's more, it was not desirable for others to sniff round in Forbes' house. They might find things. Paddy Collins and the fat man, reluctantly, left their draughty sanctuary. They did not glance at the BMW, their minds on other things. When they paused at the top of the steps and drew out pistols, Syvil Hollis, as much to warn the men inside as anything, shot Paddy Collins in the back. The fat man, turning fast for one so bulky, took a nine millimetre bullet in the side, then a .44 from Pruchak in the rib-cage, which threw him clean into the street. The men leapt into the car and Syvil hit the gas.

Rosanna Nixon and Andrew Forbes, returning from the Princess Louise an hour later, saw the activity around their house from three hundred yards away. Police cars, ambulances, arc-lights. They had been planning their next move over Bowscar, and chatting with Jackson's American oppo, John de Sallis, and they were merry. Now they stopped, sobering rapidly.

'Jings,' said Rosanna, uncertainly. 'You know how to show a girl a time, and no mistake. What is it?'

'Am I psychic?' Forbes was thrown. It seemed too much like coincidence, all this going on outside his place. But it could hardly be a raid, it was more like a disaster movie. He turned her round in a smooth movement and headed back the way they'd come, keeping to the shadows.

'Where are we going? There's ambulances. Could it be an accident?'

'I don't know, but we sure as hell can't risk finding out. Look, why don't we go tonight? To Bowscar. Instead of just ringing Pendlebury in the morning? We could try the Fradshawe. See if they'll give us our old room back.'

Now they were moving away again, the threat seemed drastically diminished, the situation almost funny. Rosanna giggled.

'You're pissed,' she said. 'You're running scared. We haven't got a car.'

'You're pissed,' he said. 'I'm the older, more mature party, saving you from impetuous behaviour. And we still haven't got a car!'

They held hands, happily. They'd been complaining in the pub that things were slowing down, that something had to happen. They had not sobered that much.

'Peter's?' suggested Rosanna. 'Then an early start to see our man? We could check the house out in the morning.'

He simulated shock.

'What! Four in a bed? Mouse, that's disgraceful!'

'No!' said Rosanna. 'You don't mean he's sleeping with de Sallis! He's not gay, is he?'

'Hardly. He fancies you something rotten. I've slept with him, many times. And I'm not gay.'

'You're not black, though. John de Sallis is.'

'Oh, you're a racist, too? A racist homophobic.'

'I wouldn't mind a fuck,' said Rosanna. 'With you. What does that make me?'

'A very sensible wee wumman,' said Forbes. 'Let's find a hotel.'

'Done.'

'Oh for God's sake,' said Andrew Forbes. 'Don't be so impatient!'

The disturbance, although not quite forgotten, had dwindled in their minds. Tomorrow would be soon enough for that . . .

The squat black telephone had become a kind of horror to Sarah Williams. It sat beside her, plugged into the double 12-volt socket above the shelf, draining her domestic battery and giving nothing in return. For the last two days, moored, she had started the Sabb and listened to the even thumping as the diesel had brought up the batteries to run the fridge, the TV set, the telephone. For the last two days she had expected it to ring, then willed it, then even pleaded. Michael Masters had given her a date, and a time, and had said he'd probably ring again, but in any case not to worry about anything, he'd be there. By the round brass clock on the after bulkhead he was two hours late, at least. She was frantic.

It was a cold night outside, and very black. The boat was moored round a bend a hundred yards from Bridge 47, which was on a tiny country road leading, roughly, from nowhere to nowhere. The tow-path was fringed with a thick, tall hedge, and the other side of the canal rose steeply from the water, with trees and underbrush. Sarah had been rather proud of her choice of spot. Apart from two anglers and a handful of passing boats, she had seen nobody since she had moored. Now, despite the cheerful fire in the stove, despite the lights to welcome Michael, she felt vulnerable, and afraid. If he did not come, what would she do? How long should she wait? What if . . . ?

Sarah stood, impatient with herself, and went to stir the casserole on the stove. That at least had worked out well. He could turn up at midnight or the early hours and the food would be all right. She was angry, though, at the other preparations she had made, because they pointed up his absence, and the precariousness of the whole awful, frightening, business. She was wearing a long, soft crimson skirt and an Indian cotton top, sheer and beautiful. She had on neither bra nor pants.

Pausing only to take a mouthful of Rioja from the crystal glass on the work-top – there was champagne in the fridge for later – Sarah turned towards the forward cabin. She was going to stop this nonsense, she was going to change. When Michael got here he would be tired, hungry, and probably in a state. He would not be thinking of seduction scenes and candlelight. She was going to put some knickers on, and her jeans, and a shapeless, hairy jumper.

With the thought came a listing of the boat, and a tremendous surge of joy. Somebody had stepped onto the rail by the hatchway, someone heavy. Sarah darted aft and put her hand on the door-latch, almost opening it. She stopped herself, but only just. It was locked, of course, it had to be. At the bedhead, just underneath the pillow, was the four-pound mooring hammer. Should she get it?

Very softly, she called out: 'Hallo? Who's there?'

'Sarah?'

Sarah choked on happiness. She had a twinge of love that she felt from her scalp down through her fingernails and beyond. She slipped the catch and twisted the handle and opened the door. Brian Rogers crashed it back against its hinges as she gaped, and stepped inside, and struck her once across the face before she had time to scream. He locked the door and tore her clothes off and straddled her legs open with his knees inside her thighs while he unbelted his trousers and unzipped. Then he seized two handfuls of her hair and pulled her face to his penis and drove it, urine-stinking, between her teeth. Sarah tried to bite, then vomited. He punched her face until it was bloody, then wiped the sick off both of them with a cover and threw it to the deck. Then he raped her anally, then made her suck, then forced it, limp, into her vagina with three stiff fingers and his thumb. After ten minutes he stood up, his trousers and stained underpants dropped around his knees, and drank the bottle of Rioja, which had been three-quarters full, from the neck. He leered at her.

'That's what you get,' he said.

NINETEEN

By eight o'clock next morning – twelve hours after the Scar exploded – it was clear to Donald Sinclair that the disaster he had predicted, and which Sir Gerald Turner had pooh-poohed, had indeed occurred. It was also clear that the Home Secretary, faced with mounting reports of a human slagheap spreading across the Midlands, of rape, burglary and murder, had gone to pieces. Where Sinclair had been cool-headed in response, Turner had dithered, where Sinclair had been ruthless, he had been woolly. And Sinclair, as he had promised himself he would, had struck.

Sir Gerald, in fact, had not returned to the Home Office until nearly 2 a.m., and he was not sober. At first he seemed unable to grasp quite what was going on, the large number of people in the suite of rooms, the fact of MOD personnel manning telephones. When he had been told of road-blocks, of ports and airports alerted, of troop movements onto no fewer than seven other jails, he had tended to the apoplectic.

'But it cannot be,' he spluttered. 'I've been with two generals. The last we heard . . .'

Sinclair said crisply: 'Things moved very fast, Sir Gerald. We tried to contact you, but the commanders on the ground and the police chiefs in the area were insistent that decisions must be made. We know of five people killed already, two shot, the others stabbed or strangled. There've been rapes. There might be two hundred men free.'

'Good God. If this gets out . . . What about the prison? What about the village?'

'Isolated. All telephones cut, all roads blocked. The Army have completed their preliminary reconnaissance at the prison, and are waiting for the order. Now you're here, of course, that lies in your hands.'

Sir Gerald was becoming increasingly confused.

'What order? How do you mean?'

Fortyne and Sinclair exchanged a glance.

'To go in,' said Sinclair. 'It will be very bloody, unfortunately, but I don't think there's much alternative, do you? There are hostages, and some of them will die. A lot of the men are armed, as well. But at least it's night. No one will see.'

Turner was quite genuinely horrified.

'Hostages! You'd risk their lives like that? How many hostages?'

Fortyne said: 'Quantity unknown, exactly. We think between twenty-five and forty. More than two hundred officers have been identified, and we're sure that several were murdered. We have a hundred and twenty-three in hospital. The governor is being held, we think. An officer called Rix escaped, who was with Pendlebury shortly after the thing blew up. Incidentally, he says that the Animal is probably out.'

'Apparently he saved the governor's life,' put in Sinclair. 'Rather ironic if Pendlebury should lose it being rescued. I suppose it's not entirely without symmetry.'

Sir Gerald Turner went brick red.

'I find your sense of humour filthy! This is not the time for jokes! I countermand the order. It will not be given. We cannot possibly risk so many innocent lives until we have had a proper assessment of the situation. In daylight.'

Sinclair remained unruffled.

'It's an emergency. There could be more casualties if we don't go in. Potentially it's the biggest emergency this country's faced for years.'

'Then let's treat it as such! Let a State of Emergency be declared, if it's necessary. But that, laddie, is not a matter for you, it's a matter for the Cabinet. Until they've met, there'll be no more bloodletting, do you hear? Good God, Sinclair, I thought you were a liberal!'

Sinclair did not argue. He shrugged, and Sir Gerald turned away. Oh no, thought Sinclair, not in this I'm not. I'm a survivor. If we can't end this soon, however much blood gets spilled, if we can't stop the bald truth coming out, we're finished. And I'm bloody sure I'm closer to the PM's pulse on this than you'll ever imagine. Bloody sure.

With this in mind, and despite the Home Secretary's later ruling that there was no need for the Prime Minister to be informed until the morning's 'less hysterical' assessments, Sinclair later called Christian Fortyne into a quiet office for a conference. The upshot was that Fortyne, with Sinclair listening on an extension, rang the PM's press supremo, Velma Goodman, at 5 a.m. and gave her a detailed briefing on the situation. He mentioned Sir Gerald's lofty dismissal of Sinclair's warnings, and said the 'sacrifice' he had accepted as a reasonable idea had become the holocaust he had been promised. His naivety had been compounded by his countermanding of Sinclair's plan to end the siege in darkness before it had time to either become set-in or public, and indeed that he was already mooting a State of Emergency, that would be a complete admission that the government had lost control.

Fortyne ended thus: 'My minister doesn't know I've rung you, Velma, and I'm sure he'd be furious. So far he's handled it superbly. He's imposed a total news ban and set every possible wheel in motion. But Turner's messed things up at every turn, entirely off the record, and I think your boss needs to know. If the fainthearts take over and this gets out the government will fall. I mean it.'

When he had put the phone down, Sinclair asked him: 'Don't you think it was going a bit far, mentioning the sacrifice idea? That was the PM's surely?'

'The PM's what, though? I'd say joke, wouldn't you? Undoubtedly. And that egregious fool took it to be serious, one would swear to it. The man's a menace. Anyway, it's entirely deniable, but we've put Turner on record as originating it. He's stitched.'

'Will Velma tell, though?'

'Everything. It's symbiosis, with those two. They're like Siamese twins. The poison will be leaked into the Royal ear within an hour, is my guess. You'd better catch some sleep, let's find you a couch.'

Before he dozed off, Sinclair had the horrors for a while. The night hours had brought more news from the Scar and elsewhere, much of it deeply disturbing. Two Special Branch men in an unmarked car had been shot outside the home of Andrew Forbes, who had subsequently disappeared with the Scottish woman. Charles Lister the American gangster was free, as well as the fearsome Angus McGregor and several English killers. Michael Masters, whose potential as trouble he did not care to calculate, was out – apparently with a gun. Four more murders and several rapes had been reported. The slagheap was spreading. Despite Fortyne's Machiavellian brilliance, despite his own absolute determination that whoever was brought down by this it would not be him, Sinclair could not quite see how he could escape unscathed. There were too many wild cards, too many sleeping sins.

'I need some luck,' he muttered. 'I need some bastards shooting, quick. I need some good news.'

When he was awoken by Judith Parker, at 7.40, he heard the first. Sir Gerald Turner had been despatched to Bowscar to glean first-hand information for a Commons statement later in the day. If it was anybody's job, it was Sinclair's, and for Turner it was the equivalent of being sent to Siberia for a long weekend.

But Donald Sinclair had been invited to have breakfast. With the Prime Minister.

•

Being a journalist herself, Rosanna Nixon found many of Andrew Forbes' habits that would have driven another woman mad rather endearing. When they woke up in their tatty but expensive hotel bedroom, he switched the radio on. Then, discovering as he often did that his slight hangover had produced a serious erection, he proposed to put it in her while they listened to the news. Rosanna, who was wearing nothing but a tee-shirt, spread her legs luxuriously and enjoyed the sensation of her vulva being nudged delicately open. It was not a serious fuck, but it was very pleasant – and there were the events outside their house to chat about as well.

Bowscar came third or fourth in the running order and just before Andrew, moving lazily, was about to come himself. Rosanna went 'ooh' when she heard the name, and looked automatically over her shoulder at the radio. Andrew, his head buried in her hair, put himself on hold. They lay still, wrapped around each other, listening.

'Overnight reports of escapes from Bowscar Prison, Staffordshire, have been denied by a Home Office spokesman,' the announcer said. 'There was a minor disturbance earlier last night, which has not yet been fully investigated, but nobody is reported to have been hurt. Bowscar, which houses more than one thousand men, some of them in the highest-risk security category, was the scene of another small disturbance last month. It is not thought that the incidents were related.'

'Fuck,' said Andrew Forbes, when the next item had started.

'I thought we were.'

But she was not serious. They were no longer. She moved her body under him, and Andrew rolled to one side. They looked into each other's eyes, both troubled.

'I don't believe those swine,' said Forbes. 'If they say no escapes, it could mean anything. What if McGregor's done a bunk? This could be our story down the tubes.'

'Could he have attacked Pendlebury, maybe? Oh Christ, maybe he's flipped?'

Andrew rolled back over her and grabbed the telephone. He punched off the radio and began to dial a number.

'On the other hand,' he said, 'it could be a coincidence. Peter ought to know, if he's heard the news. He's got Lister to worry about, he'll be shitting bricks.'

While he waited for an answer, he moved back slightly, nestling his body in a curve round hers. Rosanna, with a small and anxious smile, touched his curled-up penis.

'It's like a walnut,' she said, irrelevantly. 'I love that.'

When Peter Jackson answered, he was panting.

'Shit,' he said. 'I've just done three flights back up. I hoped it might be you. Where the hell are you?'

'Hotel. They had the place surrounded when we got back last night. Then we heard—'

'It was Lister,' cut in Jackson. 'He came looking for you and killed two coppers. The Lada Fusiliers. You did well.'

Rosanna's head was close to the receiver, but she did not hear completely. Their heads banged as Andrew stared at her.

'What?' she said. 'Did he say killed?'

'Hang on,' said Peter Jackson. 'I'll close the front door. De Sallis is down below with more of them. We're not exactly on our own, these times.'

Andrew said to her: 'It's lies. The radio. Lister's escaped. That was his mess last night.'

Her eyes were wide.

'Did he say killed?' she said, again. 'Andrew. Who?'

He did not answer. He licked the inside of his mouth. Jesus Christ, he thought.

'Andrew?' said Jackson. 'Look, I'll be brief. You're in the shit, mate. And Rosanna. The men who got blitzed had taken pictures from the spymobile, and they came out well. Lister and some others, going in your house. When they recognised Lister, the coppers went to my lot, in case we knew the other hoods, and ended up with me. De Sallis was the bonus: he knew all of them. It's the mob, the ones we've been waiting for. They screwed us, Andy-boy. They got the bastard out of Bowscar.'

'Yeah,' said Forbes. There was no point in commiseration. 'But why did the spooks ask you? They're in cahoots, aren't they? They're Lister's mates? Do they really want to find him?'

'Mates or no mates, you don't go shooting coppers, do you? Even by mistake. We're buddies now, we're allies, can you believe that? We're on an invite to a manhunt. And Andy. There's a mouse-hunt, too.'

'Go on,' said Andrew Forbes. He flashed a smile at Rosanna, a smile that barely touched his mouth. 'And tell me about Bowscar. Who else is out?'

'Some, I don't know who. These guys are wild for Lister, nobody else. Lister, and you, and the lady. They've got pictures of you going out last night, and they want to know why you never came back. Me and John played it blank, naturally. We don't know you from Adam and Eve, and we don't know what you are to Lister. Could be they believe us, but I wouldn't bank on it. Either way, keep on the move, all right? I'm serious, mate. Look for trouble.'

'Aye,' said Andrew, soberly. 'You too, friend, don't trust the bastards. Look, we'll keep in touch. We'll see you soon, OK? It's your round, as I remember.'

For twenty minutes, afterwards, Forbes and Rosanna Nixon chased all the information that they had round and round in circles. They were both cast down and worried by what they knew, as much for what it meant to Pendlebury as for themselves. They both knew that they would have to find the truth out fast, and they both knew it could only be achieved in person. They would have to buy some clothes, said Rosanna (to a derisive snort from Andrew), and get some cash, and hire a car. They'd go to Bowscar, and see what they could see. If the governor would not talk to them in the jail – and that seemed highly likely – they'd ring him from a nearby phone box, or the Fradshawe. The decision made, they both felt better.

'Are you afraid?' said Andrew. Rosanna, getting out of bed, paused.

'Should I be?'

Andrew considered. The Lister aspect had come as a bad shock. But after all, they had done nothing wrong. They'd have to ride that for a while, see what transpired. He smiled.

'Nah, I suppose not. After all, you've got me to protect you! Here – where you going?'

He pulled her purposefully back, and laid her on her side. Then he lifted her knee onto his thigh and slid his hand between her legs. He began to stroke her properly, as if he meant it this time. Rosanna stretched, and sighed.

'That's unexpected,' she said. 'What have I done to deserve this sort of attention in the middle of a crisis?'

He put his lips into the soft part of her neck.

'Who knows,' he said. 'If the nasties get us, this could be our last. And I'm rather fond of you, my mouse. Didn't you know that?'

Alan Hughes awoke to groans, which for many minutes, so it seemed, had been part of his dreams. The dreams had been of Bowscar, and involved blood and sorrow in about equal proportions. The most vivid image was of Matthew Jerrold, bound in a chair, weeping to be freed. Prison officers, led by Christopher Abbey, were threatening him with staves, and taunting him.

The first thing Hughes saw when he opened his eyes was a woman's face, white and frightened. She was lying on a double bed, and her wrists were tied together so that her hands were rested on her chest as if in prayer. The dream faded instantly and Hughes knew where he was. He turned his head to the left, to the source of the groans. Angus McGregor, looking ghastly, was asleep or unconscious in a small armchair. His right hand was hanging over the arm, and on the floor below it was the pistol.

Hughes was also in an armchair, but he was not free to move. When sleep had become inevitable, at about three o'clock that morning, McGregor had made his arrangements carefully. He had tied a single rope around Hughes' body, high up underneath his armpits, and secured it behind the chair. It was not so very tight, but it was constricting. There was nothing Hughes could do that would not make a racket. McGregor had also locked the door.

The movement of his head alerted the woman, and she turned her eyes to him. Her face wore such a look of incomprehension, such anxiety, that he had a physical twinge of pity for her. Until the night before he had not seen Carole Rochester for ten years or so, but he remembered her as a vivacious, happy girl of about nineteen. She had changed.

'It's all right,' he said, very quietly. 'You'll be all right I think. Just be kind to him. That's the secret.'

Her eyes widened slightly. She turned to stare at McGregor. His neck was wrapped in a thick, bloody cloth and his mouth was open. Then she turned back to Hughes.

'I just don't understand,' she said.

Outside, incongruously, Hughes could hear sheep baaing. They were in a caravan, a static forty-footer, in a small copse at the bottom of a hill farm in North Wales. They had arrived at 2.30 in the morning, in Carole Rochester's camper van, and on the journey down from Leicester there had been little talk. McGregor was too ill to do anything except hold the gun, Hughes had been disinclined to speak, and the woman, forced to drive, had needed all her concentration to overcome her dislocation and terror. When she had opened her front door to two men with a gun, she had been on the point of setting off for Wales, alone. What made it worst for her was that she had quickly realised she had lost her liberty by perhaps two minutes.

The drive from Bowscar had itself been terrible, because of McGregor's state. He had bled intermittently and badly, and had forced a stop once so that he could tear the back out of his shirt to make more bandages. He had rambled almost deliriously from time to time, but had also had flashes of almost gruesome lucidity, in which he had detailed what he intended to do to Gerald Turner. Every time Hughes had repeated his warning that the man had probably left the area years before, McGregor had become silent, introspective. If he was right on that score, Hughes suspected, his life would quickly end. When they passed his own old house, which he saw was now in flats, he found the tension dreadful. The area, on the edge of Stoneygate, was of huge houses and had the air of bedsit land. Gerald Turner must have left.

In the porchway, McGregor had been barely able to stand. Hughes had rung the bell, praying that nobody would answer it. Although the door was opened by a lone woman of thirty or so, she did not put it on the safety chain – she was dressed to leave. McGregor, showing the pistol, stumbled forward into the house, driving the others in front of him. In the hallway, Hughes recognised Gerald Turner's daughter, and she him. But her father no longer lived there, she explained, through shaking lips. She showed McGregor the empty house, to prove it. She had married, was now divorced, and rented it from her father's Trust. She did not know where he lived, they were estranged, they did not speak. Most foolishly, she said she was on her way to Wales, where she had the caravan. McGregor, who knew they could not live undetected in the heart of Leicester, forced a description out of her. With the ghost of gallows humour, he asked to be invited, with his friend. Before leaving, in the camper, they put the Fiat Uno in the garage. Carole Rochester, noticing the bloodstains, had appeared to shrink.

By the time Sir Gerald Turner had been at Bowscar Prison for an hour, his sense of simple outrage had been modified to one he hardly dared to put a name to. Returned to the portable office erected by the military in the night, he excused himself from Colonel Simon Benson, who had conducted him on his tour, and went to the lavatory. For many minutes he sat in the quietly hissing cubicle, studying his hands upon his knees. He was horrified by what he had seen, horrified and ashamed. He had made a great mistake.

Bowscar, in the light of a glorious summer morning, was devastated beyond belief. A low pall of smoke spread over the fields in the fitful easterly breeze, and the roof of one whole wing had collapsed into the burnt-out shell. Fires were still burning in several other places, with fire engines drawn up near them. As far as Sir Gerald could discern, there was not one unbroken window in the place, nor one stretch of roof which had not been smashed outwards. Behind every chimney stack flitted men, with other bolder elements standing at the parapets beside piles of jagged slates, which they threw intermittently at soldiers and firemen in the courts below. From one corner, most horribly, hung the corpse of a prison officer, dressed only in a uniform cap and shirt. Much against his will, Turner had been persuaded to look at him through high-definition binoculars. The face was blackened and contorted from strangulation, and had one ear ripped off.

Colonel Benson, whose slight rawness of manner marked him out as not quite establishment, had expressed some bitterness that his units had not been allowed to storm the jail in the early hours, as had been planned and – they understood – agreed. Since daylight, three hostages had died, including the hanging man. One had been thrown into the courtyard still alive, seriously injuring a sergeant and two corporals who had tried to break his fall. The person who had aborted the attack, said Benson levelly, needed his head examining.

When his sojourn in the cubicle had lasted long enough – he did not use the lavatory – Sir Gerald Turner sought out Colonel Benson and asked for a private telephone. The soldiers, grim-faced and impatient, cleared an office for him and left him on his own.

Out of the window, he could see through the prison gates into the main yard. There were covered bodies there, awaiting photographs and measurement, possibly for the coroner. Everywhere were men in uniform, walking carefully, guns in hand. Sir Gerald dialled, aware that what he had to say would be a climb-down. The delay must end immediately, he would order, the Army must go in. And at all costs, the media must be kept away. In Whitehall, long before he made the call, he had been pre-empted on both counts. Donald Sinclair was sitting in an office with Christian Fortyne and Velma Goodman, and very shortly they would be meeting the press. Not for a simple conference, but for a briefing led by Goodman. An unattributable briefing.

Velma Goodman, at the age of forty-six, was a legend. Originally from the working classes, she had made a lot of money in advertising before deciding, late, to enter politics. Because she wanted power, she had chosen the Civil Service rather than the self-deluded ranks of elected politicians as her route, and propaganda as her field. Privately, many colleagues knew she was a great corrupter, a woman with a rare talent for distorting truth into an instrument of power, savagely misused. Publicly, they admitted that she terrified them, while – naturally – defending her integrity. Within three years she had made herself completely indispensable to the Prime Minister.

The strategy that Velma Goodman was soon to initiate was largely Donald Sinclair's, agreed and polished over breakfast and in the hour afterwards. Basically, the siege of Bowscar, the events at the jail itself, were to be turned into a centrepiece, as only that way could the grim reality of the break-out be contained until the police and security forces had had time to mop up the worst elements. The bottom line, however difficult to maintain, must be that there had been a riot, a bad one admittedly, but that only a very small number of criminals had escaped. Then, when the time was ripe, Bowscar should be disinfected, stormed, purged, lanced, cured.

Velma Goodman stood alone at the briefing, with Sinclair and Fortyne listening through a screened-off door. A stout, grim woman with a turned-down mouth, she handled her audience – people of power in the media, editors, programme controllers, deputies – superbly. She presented the aftermath of Bowscar as a logistic problem essentially, flattering them with references to their understanding of the nature of news in a modern society, and its terrible power to upset the equilibrium of the most democratic State. The government, she added, had absolutely no intention of attempting to gag anybody, and unless it proved absolutely necessary, no actual orders or directives would be issued under the Official Secrets Act. However, much of the information they might unearth would naturally fall under the aegis of the Act – so the onus was on them.

Not unnaturally, even the more right-wing of the professionals were a little disturbed by this preamble, as Velma had intended them to be. When one asked her – his pride in his own bluntness reflected in his very voice – just what the hell they were going to be able to report, she smiled, and lingered over the lighting of a small and mild cigar.

'Gentlemen,' she said. 'And lady. We realise that from your point of view this is a great, a terrific story. It is also a not-inconsiderable event in the life of Britain. What we are proposing is to give you unprecedented access to the actual siege itself. We hope, naturally, that it will be short-lived, and the Prime Minister in particular is utterly determined that there should be no more deaths. But facilities will be laid on from this afternoon for all of you. There will be electricity for your cameras and lights, observation posts set up, catering facilities, and the opportunity to speak to some inhabitants of the village. However the siege is ended, you have our absolute assurance that you will be kept informed and – as far as the military and the police advise is possible – be allowed to record the event and its aftermath. What you are being offered, in fact, is unique. The opportunity to observe what is clearly a really rather serious situation at first hand. In return, we request only restraint. You may hear reports of isolated deaths, of murders, possibly rapes. We would ask you, *please*, not to jump to the conclusion that these are necessarily related to the difficulty at Bowscar, and *always* to check with us before you attempt to stand up such a supposed connection. You will get a quick and truthful answer, and you will also be advised on the security classification of an incident, if any such exists. Any questions?'

There were still one or two men, from the remains of Britain's liberal press, who were unhappy. To them, they said, it sounded like repression by another name. They were being offered a juicy sideshow on condition that they kept their eyes off the main attraction. Was it so bloody? Were such terrible events in reality unfolding? Was not the government's intention, in fact, to hide the truth?

Velma Goodman had a line in physical intimidation that would not have disgraced a bar-room brawler. Her eyes flashed venom, and her body language spoke of barely suppressed violence. She raised her voice to a level just below a shout and modified her tone to the pitch of a bandsaw cutting sheet steel. She spoke rapidly, and never stumbled for an instant. She used words like irresponsible, and dangerous, and downright unpatriotic. Whose side were these so-called 'liberals' on, she demanded? What were their motives for questioning and attacking those whose duty it was to pick up the pieces after problems probably caused by softness in the first place? Were they unaware that the government were spending more than a billion pounds in their current programme of improvement, more than any other government in history? Were they unaware that Donald Sinclair, the junior minister, had recently issued a statement announcing severe new measures to deal with violent and uncontrollable men? It was a farrago of non-sequitur and half-truth, attacking the questioners for things they had neither said nor thought. When she had finished, Goodman fixed them with bitter eyes through a blue cloud of cigar smoke. I know who you are, she seemed to say. I won't forget you.

Finally, she thanked everybody for attending, and announced a standard, attributable press conference for three o'clock, with Sinclair in the chair. Just to show that the motives of the detractors were as idle as she'd thought, it would be announced that a small number of prisoners had indeed escaped, and that most of them had been recaptured. Details, names, et cetera, would be given. There was also another matter, that had nothing to do with Bowscar, but might put it in perspective. Two Special Branch detectives had been murdered in a London street in mysterious circumstances. The security services had been called in, and there appeared to be a Cuban connection. It was a tragedy, she said, and a matter of cold-blooded, ruthless disregard for human, civilised values. She hoped the prison difficulties would not be allowed to overshadow it.

Afterwards, in the company of Sinclair and Fortyne, Velma Goodman was beside herself with contempt.

'Scum,' she said. 'You can tell them anything. We could let them watch us storm the place tomorrow, and kill all the hostages. Most of them would say the cons had done it. We could arm the police, we could send in the battalions, and they'd kowtow. You watch, every shot fired will be in self-defence, every death will be a triumph. Journalists and politicians. It's no damn wonder they're so despised, is it?'

Sinclair began to smile, but Velma clapped him briskly on the back.

'Present company excepted, Donald!' she laughed. 'Present company always excepted!'

They watched her waddle off. Sinclair shook his head.

'Christ. What a woman. Incidentally, what about my speech? "Severe new measures to deal with uncontrollables." I never said that.'

Fortyne flicked his glasses up his nose.

'You will, Oscar, you will!'

He grinned.

'The bigger the lie, eh? Well, we did it over Windscale for thirty years, and that was just for starters! Donald, old son, we're going to get away with it!'

They were drinking bottled Beck's when Sir Gerald Turner came through with his urgent plan. Sinclair agreed, very properly, that he had better put it to the PM personally.

Despite the gravity of what Peter Jackson had told them – or perhaps because of it – Forbes and Rosanna, for a while, played out the trip to Bowscar as a road movie. Once out of the grind of London's traffic in their hired red Sierra they found some country music and acted stupid. The day was fine and Rosanna hitched her skirt up to show her knickers, while Andrew played the horny-handed cowboy with the inside of her thigh. They listened to the news assiduously, however, and channel-hopped from time to time. The news angle changed only slowly, and remained downbeat: by midday it was allowed there'd been a riot, but it was still a minor one, with a fair amount of damage done, but no dangerous men among the small number of escapes. They knew that this was untrue, and it intrigued them. If Lister – who was very dangerous indeed – was out, who else might be? Nearly ten miles from the prison, also, they saw a roadblock up ahead. They pulled into the side of the road.

'God,' said Rosanna. 'This is getting to be a habit. Now what the hell's going on?'

Forbes glanced over his shoulder and did a U-turn.

'Search me. We're miles from the Scar. But if Peter's right, we don't want our papers looking at, do we? Let's try another way.'

It took them half an hour to work out that Bowscar was a no-go area for casual visitors, but they still tried to ignore the implications. They stopped at an AA telephone after turning back from their third block, and rang the prison. There was no tone of any sort. The line was dead, and the operator had no explanation that she was sharing with the world. Rosanna, dubiously, suggested they should try the governor's home.

'Well, we've got the number,' said Andrew. 'But he's not going to be there, is he?'

'Not the number, stupid. We'll go there. This is a road movie, remember? We'll go and talk to Eileen, the lovely, mysterious daughter. You'll be expected to sleep with her, in the genre.' She assumed her Bonnie Parker role, although with noticeably little heart. 'But I'm warning you, bo – I got a real mean little gat tucked down my stocking top . . .'

As they neared Richard Pendlebury's house, which was mock-Tudor and detached in half an acre of ground, the last traces of the mood had gone. Remembering Pendlebury's worry, his grey, anxious air, they had tried to sustain it, lately, more to avoid confronting what might have really happened than anything else. They rang the front-door bell feeling rather hollow, hoping probably that Eileen Pendlebury was not at home. But she opened the door, pale and calm, her eyes red-rimmed from crying, and insisted they come in. Her father had spoken about them, she said, and she wanted to talk. She added, wanly, that she was desperate to.

Rosanna Nixon and Andrew Forbes listened with rising horror to her story. Whatever the radio disseminated, she said, her father was still in the prison with dozens of other hostages, and it was assumed, but only that, that he was still alive. There had been a major break-out, many deaths, and total devastation of the building. She had been told these things, she added bitterly, only because of her insistence, and because she was covered by the Official Secrets Act and could not pass them on. She'd probably go to prison for talking to them.

Eileen cried quietly then, quietly but hopelessly. Forbes put the kettle on, while Rosanna cuddled her. When he returned with three mugs of tea-bag tea he watched them for a while.

'A major break-out,' he said, half to himself. 'That means McGregor's got to be involved. What a carve-up.'

Rosanna's eyes were large over the rim of her mug.

'He probably started it,' she said. 'That bastard Sinclair's got a lot to answer for.' She glanced at Eileen Pendlebury. 'Excuse the language.'

Eileen almost laughed.

'Oh, don't mind me,' she said. 'I know all about Donald Sinclair. I'd call him worse than that. It was so sad when he got the job. Dad was so hopeful that they might have put a good man in at last. I didn't have the heart to tell him, it's a part of my murky past he doesn't really know about.' She made a face. 'Dad warned me off politics not so long ago,' she said. 'If only he knew!'

She wiped her eyes and sniffed, hard. She pulled her shoulders back, and Rosanna moved slightly away, to give her space. Andrew waited.

'Am I allowed to ask what you mean?' he said. 'I'm sorry, I'm a nosy prat.'

'You're a journalist,' she said. Then she shrugged. 'OK. I can't see there's a story in it, so I suppose it doesn't matter, it can't do any harm. It wasn't even me he messed about, it was a friend of mine, one of my circle after college. It was just the usual thing in politics, anyway, very boring and predictable, Carole never made too much of a drama out of it. She hung around a bit, out of interest, and she ended up as Sinclair's mistress, that's all. He dropped her when a younger model came along, but she was in love.' She blew sharply through her nostrils. 'He's just a normal sort of bastard, I suppose, but now he's screwed my Dad as well, hasn't he?' She made the noise again, a kind of laugh. 'The only funny thing about the Carole business was that her father ended up his boss. Sir Gerald Turner. I imagine that was the attraction for Donald, an influential father. She married someone else afterwards, but it didn't last. Carole Rochester.'

It was a little over three hours later that the hired car nosed into the city centre traffic of Leicester. They still did not know exactly what Sinclair was up to, or whether the things that Eileen Pendlebury had told them had any relevance at all. But the tangles in his life that were emerging fascinated them, and they were more and more convinced that he was getting away with murder. At last, they felt – they had him in their sights.

Peter Jackson and John de Sallis – having no official power to take part in the arrest – had been alone and silent in the unmarked vehicle for about ten minutes when they heard the shots. There were ten or twelve of them, but they came in short bursts, rather than one fusillade. There had been no firefight. No flights of rooks rose, cawing, over the Liberty Wood, there were just the normal country sounds through the open windows.

De Sallis, who was smoking, threw his cigarette end onto the gravel driveway leading to Pratt's Farm, which was not visible to them.

'These clever ones,' he said, laconically. 'It makes me wonder, sometimes. Take Chuck. He must have rung these guys, he must have told them where he was, how else would they have found a God-forsaken hole like this? Didn't it occur to him he'd just killed their buddies? Did he think they were really going to fix him a nice flight out?'

'This is England,' replied Peter Jackson. 'Nobody understands our secret services, least of all a foreigner. Lister probably thought he'd killed two muggers.'

'Horseshit. He probably thought his friends'd do anything for money, just like him. Sixty million bucks out there is the buzz. I wonder who plays for it now?'

'He'd given them a lot of trouble, one way and another,' said Jackson. 'It was probably something of a relief. And the Mob or whoever can't really argue, can they? He was cut down in a gunfight, with his team. No one to blame.'

They could hear the crunching of feet on gravel. Two of the detectives came into sight, their faces grave. The first one said, to John de Sallis: 'Look, I'm sorry mate, there's been an accident.'

The second spoke to Peter Jackson.

'What's your angle on capital punishment in the Customs?' he asked. 'Do you agree with it? Because I think it's just come back.'

The two policemen glanced at each other. Their faces split. They both gave shouts of laughter.

TWENTY

Over the next few days Sinclair revelled – both as prime mover and star pupil – in the malleability of the press. The death of Charles Lister and his associates was the break he had prayed for, and with the help of Velma Goodman and Christian Fortyne he managed to knock the details of the siege itself onto the lower half of the front pages, and off some of them altogether. The evening papers and the TV news the night before had been dominated by the 'Mystery Spy Deaths' in a London street, and the morning headlines were even larger and more satisfactory. 'US Drugs Link in Bowscar Breakout' was the general line, the murder of a seventy-three-year-old reclusive farmer in a Hampshire wood provided the gruesome note, and the sex angle was covered by big pictures of Syvil Hollis, whose body had been bared to the waist to reveal both bullet holes and bosom. It was a gutter classic.

The story, for those like Peter Jackson who knew the facts, was even more extraordinary. The explosion at Bowscar, sources close to the Cabinet said, had been plotted and financed almost entirely by the American Mafia, and had nothing to do with bad conditions or alleged overcrowding. Indeed, the story came close to conscious parody in its portrayal of the indigenous inmates as innocent victims whose equilibrium and peace of mind had been upset by the vicious machinations of Lister and his confederates.

'Shit,' said Jackson, handing the *Mail* and the *Sun* across to John de Sallis. 'I should have known it. It's you bloody foreigners leading us astray again.'

The marvel for Sinclair, was how self-contradictory the newspapers could be without either apparently noticing or caring. On the front pages they splashed tales of murderous Yankee mobsters and their evil molls, while on inside pages they quoted unnamed government sources still insisting that only a handful of prisoners had escaped, and those unlikely to be dangerous. True to Velma Goodman's direction – and the straitjacket of the Act – they buried stories on their home news pages of isolated acts of violence in isolated places, without making the obvious link. Members of the public who phoned in were listened to with great sympathy, Sinclair understood, and then forgotten. In return, as promised, the newspapers were allowed to overfly the jail in helicopters and publish brilliant aerial pictures of the smoking ruin with arrowed convicts waving from the roof – although the corpse of Abbey, by general consent, was only ever shown in blurred, long-distance shots. On the second day, when it had served its purpose, it mysteriously disappeared – cut down by a small commando of marines in the night. On top of the pictures and film footage, there were diagrams, endless interviews with the military commanders, shots of armed forces discreetly clustered round other jails 'in case of copy-cat violence', and photo-calls with injured officers in hospitals, who gave pre-digested answers to prearranged questions.

Now that they were confident of the press, Sinclair and his advisers went about the business of clearing up the pockets of bestiality with the utmost ruthlessness. Tom Amory, who with Pat Parkinson and Tony Smith had been holding a middle-aged farmer and his wife and teenage daughter since the night of the outbreak, died in a hail of bullets at three o'clock one morning, although they managed to fire several shots from the farmer's shotguns before they died, one of which killed the girl. Her parents, when they told of the family's ordeal, sadly agreed that it was probably best, given all that they had done to her. Several other men were cut down in the street, and two in bars. Tony Geraghty, the husband of Peter Smith's thin bangler, also died, but not by the hands of authority. The landlord of a pub in Gorton found him bleeding rapidly to death in the outside lavatory at closing time one night. Earlier, he had been talking to two men, one blond, one balding.

There were questions in the House, of course, and naturally lies were told. The Prime Minister, naturally again, kept a careful distance from the centre of the crisis, responding to questioners only when it was possible to excoriate them for lack of patriotism or undermining the security services or police. Mostly, the task fell to Sir Gerald Turner, and he did it rather badly. Sinclair, when he got the opportunity, went in hard and hot. When the question of McGregor was raised – 'the man they rightly call the Animal' – he insisted that the government had no reason to think he had escaped, and he blamed the major part of the riot on 'governor Richard Pendlebury's unilateral decision to release this dreadful man from the cellular confinement I personally deemed necessary'. He also dropped in, presumably without realising the implications for his boss, the fact that he had strongly recommended that Pendlebury be sacked – but had been overruled.

Rumours of the simmering row in Westminster surfaced spectacularly when the *Guardian*, in an exclusive front-page piece, revealed that Sir Gerald Turner, shortly before the Bowscar disaster, had said he would be prepared to sacrifice one of Britain's prisons as a way of demonstrating to the rest of the prison population – and the officers who were so militant and bloody-minded in their duties – just what would happen. The choice of the *Guardian* for the leak was a masterstroke, because it had always tended to back Sir Gerald as the most liberal of Home Secretaries, within his party lights. His cries of anguish were audible throughout Parliament, and of rage throughout Queen Anne's Gate. He in turn leaked his fury to *The Times*, suggesting that it was a pack of lies, and that he knew who was responsible. Sinclair refused to rise to the bait, but next morning's *Guardian* contained the transcript of a tape on which he could be quite clearly heard saying 'It will be more than just a sacrifice, it will be a bloodbath. You do not know the evil that will be unleashed, Sir Gerald.' Sir Gerald, sent a full copy of the mini-tape, could only be thankful that no more had been revealed. Later, in the House, Sinclair said piously that he utterly deplored leaks, from whatever source and for whatever reason. What was more, he had absolutely no recollection of such a conversation with the Secretary of State. Next morning's tabloids, however, followed up the story with allegations that Sir Gerald had been anxious to 'send in the troops' the morning after the riot, 'whatever the consequences in terms of human life'. He merely issued a lame denial.

Velma Goodman reported with some satisfaction to Sinclair, Judith Parker and Fortyne that Turner had sought an audience with the PM and demanded that Sinclair should be sacked or curbed. His line had been that Sinclair had begun to use his reputation as a natural liberal to mount a perverted campaign to undermine his own authority. He had become corrupted, Turner claimed, by his ambition, and was, in fact, taking a ridiculously hard line.

'How did that go down?' asked Sinclair, cautiously. Velma Goodman laughed.

'Tactical suicide,' she said. 'I mean, for God's sake, the boss has got the mentality of a *Sun* leader where liberality's concerned.

Anyway it was Turner who claimed that you were soft in the first place. He called you back from Australia to put some backbone into you! You're doing fine, believe me. Fine.'

That night, however, as Sinclair and his mistress drank champagne, Fortyne rang them at her flat with some news that landed like a hammerblow. Michael Masters was being held hostage by the IRA. They wanted a slice of his fortune – to be precise, one of his many millions. If they did not get it soon . . . he would be dead.

Inside Bowscar Prison, the sense of dislocation and unreality gathered momentum as the siege continued. Its movement was from mass excitement and hysteria, through fear and anticipation of a counter-attack, to anger and puzzlement when nothing happened. At first the hatred and latent violence was directed at the hostages. Several prison officers were taunted and roughed up, and for two or three of them the repressed fear of their taunters turned suddenly to something uncontrollable, as when a bull terrier, programmed by its genes, switches from play to kill. Chris Abbey died thus, under a pile of furious bodies which resolved itself into a howling band that dragged him to the roof and stripped and hanged him.

There were many hundred prisoners still in the Scar – far more than had left – and enough of them had been sufficiently calm and motivated to lock and barricade both some outer and some inner doors and gates before the Army had mounted its first assault. In any case, this was not a serious one, because the chaos in the yard, with bodies and injured men and fighting groups littering the tarmac, had made a charge unthinkable. Later in the night, when the situation had been assessed and an attack was planned, Sir Gerald Turner ruled it out. In terms of casualties, he was almost certainly correct. Few of the thirty or so hostages would have survived.

Over the next hours, the leading elements organised a structure, amid the chaos. While most men fought each other, looted and smashed the offices and the governor's suite, urinated and defecated on every square yard of accessible floor and table space which represented prison hierarchy and made bonfires of their secret files, the stronger, saner ones rounded up the hostages and locked them into individual cells. This, although it was done for vindictive reasons – to give them a taste of the medicine they had happily dished out – was tactically brilliant. The hostages, isolated from each other, could not combine their mental energy or their hope. There was no chance of them building up a relationship with their captors, or reasoning with them, or appealing, as a discrete body of suffering humanity, to the better nature which was inevitably lurking in the souls of some of their tormentors.

It was in the first two days that individuals were dragged from their cells to be tortured and occasionally killed. After that, oddly, they were forgotten by most people, in a way that did genuinely echo the fate of the men they once had charge of. They were given bucket lavatories, and they were intermittently taken, under guard for their own safety, to slop out in the ruined sluices, to throw the contents of their plastic pails into the shattered stumps of lavatory bowls or the cracked urinals. They were even given food – unheated tinned mince or tomato soup, and mashed potato powder mixed with cold water – which the former prisoners ate too, since nobody bothered to light the cookers or the ovens. Occasionally, one or two hostages would be paraded on the roof, but it seemed to make no difference. Horribly, the world was forgetting them as well.

It was this bizarre dislocation with reality, this impression that the Bowscar crisis was slipping away from public imagination or concern, that filled the thinking prisoners with most foreboding and anxiety, and would have done the hostages if they had known of it. The radio bulletins on the disaster were increasingly dominated by political bickerings, interspersed with homilies on the need for maturity and restraint coupled with a dialogue with the men inside the Scar. It was exactly what many of them craved also – but it was not happening. No moves of any sort were made.

Richard Pendlebury, who like the other hostages was not allowed a radio and was told nothing about the situation outside his cell, went through a variety of emotions which at times became so powerful that he thought he would go mad. He had seen Arthur Probert dead in front of him, Ian Serple beaten into a bloody pulp, and many other bodies when he had been dragged out of the admin block. He also suspected that Les Rix, who had made a break for it and been hunted out of his sight, must also have been killed. Strangely, he still found his sympathies as much with the majority of the prisoners as he did for himself and his officers. They were victims of a disaster not entirely of their own making. Its seeds existed in the nature of the system, and had been nurtured by the obstinacy, cynicism and incompetence of the government. At times, lying in his filthy cell on a mattress with its guts entirely torn out, he was almost overwhelmed by his hatred and contempt for the authority he served.

He had fantasies, as well, fantasies which he guessed must be common to all prisoners. He saw his dead wife frequently, and almost physically, and he had unbearable dreams about Eileen. Awake, his thoughts about his daughter were almost worse. He imagined the indifference she would receive when she sought information about him, and the lack of support she would get. At times his blood chilled when he imagined escaped prisoners going to his house, despite the fact that its location was a secret that few even of his deputies or admin staff were privy to. Not infrequently he blessed the agony of his torn and infected face because it made thought on other things impossible.

The segregation unit, in the hours after the prisoners of Bowscar had sealed themselves back inside their little world, had surprisingly escaped the worst of the violence. When the riot had erupted, other targets had been uppermost, different battle lines were drawn. By the time the gates to the unit had been unlocked, only a dozen or so inmates had rampaged inside, and most of them, although they possibly did not realise it, had gone for sex. Unlike the officers, whose exaggerated public fear of Aids was treated with some derision, few of the inmates gave total credence to the horror tales, seeing them firstly as political. Beyond that, sex was necessary – and some of the Forty-Threes, as well as looking as healthy as the next man, had been segregated for their own safety, being very beautiful. In three conjoining cells, with good supplies of alcohol and drugs, they had a party.

Incomprehensibly to many of the men, the electricity to the prison was not cut off. The level of filth rose rapidly, and the stench from the broken sanitary systems was very bad, but they still had water, food and light. The more motivated of the prisoners screamed from the rooftop for negotiations to take place, but nobody responded. On the TV news the sameness of the footage – men on roof, banners, arc lights – quickly pushed the story from lead item to lower and lower down the running order, and the radio had even less to hang it on. As the sense of awful gloom and total isolation grew, it seemed to many that the only contact with the outside world was the growing army of rats and cockroaches moving in. Within three days some prisoners had to be beaten back from trying to 'escape'. One jumped off the roof.

Outside, the Army watched indifferently. And the cameras clicked or whirred less frequently.

Apart from the loss of Sarah, Michael Masters settled into his new form of captivity with little difficulty. In fact, when the ransom demand was phoned through to his wife – not from the place where he was being held, of course – the amount was fixed by Masters, in consultation with the men who held him. Although the line was Barbara's own, and ex-directory, he told them it would be tapped. It amused them all to see how quickly their intelligence in London informed them he was right. To the government, the demand represented a major difficulty. To Masters and the Irishmen, it was a business proposition.

After Bowscar, the place where he was held was wonderfully luxurious. What most surprised him was that it was not some remote cottage in the country or a farm, but a semi-detached council house on a rather grim estate. He was held in an upstairs bedroom which had a window, he was told, of armoured glass. There was a thick net curtain nailed across it, through which he could discern empty, rolling landscape. When he asked if they were not afraid he might not signal, they took it as a joke, wondering who the hell might see it, and if they did, so what? Around here, they said, were not so many people who would give his lot aid, and did he doubt that?

Thinking about it, Masters supposed that he did not. He guessed they must be deep in the heart of the Republic, where to a certain extent the gunmen of the North were seen in a romantic light, as long as they kept the details of the carnage well within the confines of the Six Counties or across the water. He could not imagine, either, that the neighbours knew the semi was a nest of 'terrorists', as the men and women who occupied it on a permanent or floating basis were so positively 'normal'. There was a lot of laughter in the house, and even Conor Grady, who stayed for several days, turned out to have a quick, sardonic sense of humour. In Bowscar, it was said, the Armagh Wolf had not smiled in thirty-seven months.

As far as he could calculate, it had taken Masters about twenty hours to reach the house. The car journey had ended in a small transport yard near a motorway, where he had been given tea and biscuits by a languid fat man with a Liverpool accent and a gun. At around midnight, as he guessed, he and the other escapees had gone into the yard, to where three articulated lorries with refrigerated trailers had been waiting. He and two other men had clambered into one of the trailers and been guided to the front, by torchlight. A section of the corrugated aluminium wall had been swung back, revealing a narrow compartment with three foam-rubber covered shelves. Masters had been told to take the top one, and been shown the pistol that would be pointing at his spine. Although there had been a dim light on throughout the ride, all three of them had slept for many hours. There had been a sea journey, presumably from Stranraer to Larne, then two more hours in the truck. Finally there had been unloading noises for an hour until the compartment was swung open, and the journey continued by van. Despite the crampedness of the compartment in the trailer, Masters had not even thought of claustrophobia, which interested him, afterwards. The last part of the journey was worst, because he had to wear a blindfold, but it was soon over. At the council house, where Grady and another escapee had also finished up, there had been tears, laughter, whiskey and a meal.

From the very start, from the moment he awoke after his first sleep in the not-unpleasant bedroom, Masters was treated with a quiet courtesy that rather shocked him after life in Bowscar Jail. It shocked him because he realised how quickly and completely he had become inured to casual and unthinking brutishness in his captors and conditions. He responded, unthinkingly, by treating the quiet-spoken Irish whom he mingled with as equals. Unless they were talking specific business, they let him join 'the crack'.

When it turned to ransoms, and demands, Masters surprised all of them with his interest in it as a problem to be solved. He talked freely of how much money could be realistically raised on his behalf, and put in a bid to be left relatively solvent, which was only partly done in jest. They joked, for their part, on the trouble he would cause them if the ransom was refused, but here the humour became a little brittle. Everybody knew his death would be the price.

'Dommage,' said Masters, *'mais c'est la commerce!'* And a laughing-eyed Belfast man called Liam said: 'You've got it, Michael. Nothing personal, nothing in the world.' The twinkle in the dark eyes deepened. 'But will they pay the money?'

Privately, Masters had a flicker of doubt, but he crushed it. He had been let down once and had landed up in Bowscar. But this was his life, not just four years of liberty.

'They'll pay,' he said. 'Or rather, I will! I've got friends in high places, although you wouldn't think it, looking at me. Just one thing – for the love of God, don't make it public. You know the rules in England. You know Our Glorious Leader.'

They did. They nodded. To make it public might put a messy execution on their hands. That, they did not want, one million pounds apart.

'These friends,' said Liam. 'Just how high are they? If they were high enough, we might just be able to let you keep your money!'

Everybody laughed, Masters included. They asked him would he like a drink, and did not everybody know it was the racing on the telly? He was also asked, almost shyly, as a further friendly overture, if he'd like to place a bet. Masters, also shyly, but with swooping stomach, asked if he could make a telephone call, instead.

It caused an argument that lasted quite a while, and moved to a different room, excluding him. But they returned at peace together. It could not be for a little while, and it would have to be at night, said Liam. They would drive him out a little way, to a phone box, and somebody would need to be there with him, listening. Was that all right?

Oh Christ, thought Michael Masters. That's all right.

Forbes and Rosanna, who still found it hard to believe that anyone might be actively looking for them, nevertheless approached the job in hand as if they did. They parked the Sierra three streets from the address they had squeezed out of Eileen Pendlebury by dint of much persuasion, and walked to the house from separate directions. Forbes stayed fifty yards away, lounging at a bus stop and watching up and down the road, while Rosanna rang the bell. When he was satisfied that nobody was watching them or the house, and she was sure that nobody was in, they met in the gateway and talked. While they stood there, a white-haired and inquisitive woman appeared at a doorway opposite and waved. They went across.

'She's gone,' she said. 'She went last night with a couple of chaps who turned up. It was ever so funny, because she's usually on her own. There's nothing wrong, is there?'

Rosanna tried to appear slightly put out, but in the know.

'Not as far as we've been told,' she said. 'We were just hoping . . . Well, we're old friends, I was at college with Carole. I tried ringing late last night but I must have missed her. We're just passing through.'

'You're Scotch, aren't you? That's interesting. My cousin's Scotch. Morag Brayfield.'

For one surreal moment, Forbes thought she was going to add: 'Do you know her?' He bit his lip to avoid a stupid smirk.

'Scottish,' said Rosanna. 'I suppose you don't know where she's gone? It would be really nice to see her.'

The upshot was, that Carole Rochester had a caravan in Wales, and she'd probably gone down there because she'd loaded food and stuff into the Dormobile. Well, it was more a mobile home than a caravan, really, except that it had no wheels, so couldn't be that mobile, if you thought about it. Mrs Parkinson was not certain where it was, but it was on the funny bit that stuck out pointing towards Ireland. The something peninsula, did they know it? Near where Butlins was.

'Pwllheli,' said Andrew Forbes. 'The Lleyn Peninsula. Would that be it?'

'Ooh,' said Mrs Parkinson. 'I don't know how you pronounce it. It could be, though. Is the . . . is that quite near Butlins?'

He assured her that it was. Mrs Parkinson also remembered that the caravan was near an old windmill, on a hill. A sort of pepperpot-looking thing. Carole had sent a postcard once, with it on. She could see it from her window. It was a sort of folly.

They thanked her profusely, and said it sounded lovely, but they couldn't go all over Wales could they, they'd better get back home to Birmingham. By the way, Rosanna finished, these men? They'd probably be friends of theirs as well. Did she get a glimpse of them?

Well, it had been dark. They were both quite normal, they weren't coloured or anything like that. One of them seemed to be having trouble with his neck, he held onto it a lot. Oh – and they'd left their car in the garage, and gone off in the Dormobile. Yes, she'd almost forgotten. Would they know their car?

While she and Rosanna chatted on, inanely, about the weather for the time of year and what a lovely place Scotland could be if it wasn't raining, Forbes nipped across the road and had a good peer through the garage window. He returned blithely enough and said he did not know it, so that was that, back to Birmingham, and where was the best bus-stop for the station? When they were a hundred yards away, Rosanna laughed at him.

'Hidden depths!' she crowed. 'Butlins at Pwllheli's an open book! Have you got children tucked away, or something?'

'Well, you're a pedant,' he counter-attacked. 'Scottish indeed!

I expected you to tell her you weren't a bottle of pissing whisky, you stuck-up cat.'

His tone was light, but his face belied it. When they were round the corner he stopped. He put a hand on her arm.

'That car in there,' he said. 'The dashboard's covered in blood. And the seat cover. Blood everywhere.'

'Oh Christ,' said Rosanna. 'But surely . . . why?'

'I don't know. But it can't be a coincidence, can it? Somebody in the Scar must . . . I don't know.'

Later, they rang Peter Jackson from a call box. Before Andrew could mention its location, Jackson had told him not to, just in case. In future, he added, no contact at the flat, they could leave messages at the pub, with Antony the barman. Andrew Forbes' spirits dropped another notch.

'Go on,' he said.

'Your house is boarded up, impenetrable. It's under twenty-four hour watch, so don't bother, OK? If this doesn't sound too melodramatic, keep away from big cities and become a bit nocturnal. And do you know anyone who's good at changing accents? Some regional ones are so easy to place, aren't they?'

'This is not a joke?'

'Is God a woman? Lister's dead. Ditto three Miami drugmen and a lady. They did a bad thing when they killed the fat prat and his buddy, and got punished. You'll read it in the papers in the morning. Better, book a nice hotel, now, and watch the news. Get off the streets. Use false names.'

'It's a thought,' said Andrew. 'But we're rather busy. I've got a hunch. We'll be very careful, though. I'll ring again.'

'Yeah. If you *have* to ring me here, keep it short and mystifying, eh? You never know with defenders of the realm, do you? Look Andrew—'

The pips began, and Forbes deliberately cut the connection. He smiled across the receiver at Rosanna's small, sharp face.

'Cheerful twat,' he said. 'I think he wants to frighten us!'

There were a couple of hours of daylight left, but instead of stopping, they drove. They were on country roads, heading towards the border, and Rosanna listened sombrely to what Jackson had said. Like Forbes, she was beginning to take the warnings seriously. Like him, also, she was resistant.

'The trouble with hiding in the daytime is,' she said, 'we're looking for a disused windmill and a caravan. We sure as hell won't find it in the dark.'

'No. Especially not in Wales. Do you know Wales? The roads tend to be small and dark and twisted, like the people. And the signposts, when you find them, are incomprehensible.'

They booked into a bed and breakfast pub at ten to ten, and watched the news. Sinclair's face, so open and concerned, so plausible, upset them both as he told his lies about the death of Lister and his gang. At 10.30, they went to bed. They lay in each other's arms for some time, listening to the noise of the television rising from the bar. In the intervals, they could hear wind blowing through the trees outside their window. Their mood stayed sombre.

'Andrew?' Rosanna said. 'You don't have any children, do you?'

In the darkness, he shook his head.

'No. After Maggie died, I just got lonely. Drank too much. I had a few things with a few women, you know. Couple of them had kids. I came to Butlins once, down here. They don't call it Butlins any more, but it's the place. No secrets, Rosanna.'

A whoop rose from the bar below, disembodied.

'Andrew? Why do you do all this? I mean, McGregor was my fight really. Now we don't even know what we're looking for, do we? We're sort of on the run, and we don't know why. Why do you write your books, get up people's noses?'

Forbes answered slowly, thinking it.

'The face of corruption,' he said. 'That man on telly. Urbane sincerity, with democracy in his sights. I don't do it because of politics, I do it because of politicians. They're loathsome. I like to rock their boats. I like to bring a bit of mayhem to their lives. It's my substitute for chucking bombs. Call me old-fashioned if you like. I'm a patriot.'

Rosanna did not question him. That seemed all right to her.

'I love you,' she said.

There was a long pause.

'Is that a challenge? Or a statement?'

'I'm sorry. I didn't mean to say it. Well, I did. It just slipped out. You don't have to love me, though. I'm sorry.'

There was another long pause. Below, they heard the landlord shout: 'Please. Finish up your drinks now, please!'

'How very mouselike to apologise,' said Andrew Forbes. 'I don't know how to say this, it's been a long long time. I love you too.'

It took them two more days to locate the caravan, with the

help of an Ordnance Survey map, and a lot of walking. The rains had come, and they bought walking boots and corduroys and bobble hats and anoraks at Betws-y-Coed before driving over the mountains and onto the Lleyn. The hoods, especially, gave them cover, and Rosanna spoke in modulated English.

The pepperpot tower, which was nothing like a windmill when they saw it, was off the road from Llanbedrog to Aberdaron, four miles or so from Pwllheli, and on a fairly pointed hill. From the top they could work out all the likely places, and then they rambled. The mobile home was off a tiny, unmarked road in its own small clump of trees at the bottom of a steep field. It had clearly been a rather useless piece of farmland, sold off years before. Parked near it was a camper van.

'Or like stout fucking Cortez,' said Andrew Forbes, as they looked at it. 'What are we going to find?'

'We could go home.'

'But we haven't got a home to go to.'

Donald Sinclair kept in touch with his home solely by telephone. Since the crisis had started, he explained to Mary, it had been quite impossible to get away. He was very tired, and he probably was not looking after himself too well, but she did understand, didn't she? He missed her terribly, and he was sorry that they'd been at loggerheads, and when all this was over, perhaps they should take a little holiday?

Mary, who had watched his performances and read his statements, was too intelligent to argue, and perhaps no longer sure enough of her ground. Despite their recent differences, she had never really doubted the firmness of his purpose, his beliefs, however strained they might have been by the grim realities of office. But there was something in his eyes these days, even on television, that she did not recognise, and did not like. There was an abrasiveness, an attack, that was more than just the expression of his natural self-confidence, his strength of will. She suspected it was a product of ambition.

So she reassured him, and told him she understood, and went into her garden and worked for many hours every day, and wondered. Perhaps it was just the jail disaster, as he said. It did seem pretty bad, from what she read and saw. It did not occur to her that it was far worse than that, worse beyond belief, and that her husband, to a great extent, was running it.

But she did worry, and she hoped. She could not bear it if her husband really was the type of politician she despised.

Even in the rain, she worked among her flower beds . . .

On *Cynthia's Beam*, the telephone never rang. Sarah Williams, through her one unclosed eye, watched it for hours sometimes, used it as a talisman, used it as an anchor for a reality she did not quite believe in any more. It was plugged into the wall, and at night-time – before or after he had played with her – Brian Rogers played with it. He rang the speaking clock, and fantasised about receiving calls or making them, although he was far too canny to risk giving himself away. Like the boat itself, it appeared to heighten his sense of freedom, they were his own, his things. That delighted him.

When Sarah had awoken the morning after Rogers had arrived, she had found herself naked, and tied closely hand and foot. She found it hard to believe that she was still alive, let alone that she had slept, but she remembered that the man beside her had forced her to drink whisky, at least half a pint. He had abused her so much, both physically and mentally, that she had gone beyond exhaustion, beyond the point of feeling anything, any sort of pain or anguish. When she woke her head was like a split rock, her mouth dry and foul. The back beside her was huge and white, practically hairless, and the man was snoring. With the side of her face, she could feel the lump hammer underneath the pillow, but she could not reach or use it.

Fortunately, she supposed, Brian Rogers awoke before her mind could dwell on the horrors of the night. But she realised she was wrong when he rolled over, and untied her legs, and began the process once again. By now, Sarah had gone numb, was incapable of normal thought or movement, let alone response. But Rogers, hugely interested in her body and its details, and its limp compliance with anything he wanted of it, was too absorbed to notice. Last night, she had felt he was trying to destroy her, that his assaults had little to do with actual sex. Now he was fucking her, and if she was a rag doll, what matter, he was fucking. Over the hours, then the days, the pattern alternated. Sarah felt so detached that she wondered if she had perhaps gone mad. Most of the time, she did not care.

Except for the truly awful things. As when Brian Rogers – he had introduced himself, after beating and raping her, and even shaken hands – had said that Michael Masters had told him all about her, and given him her name, and told him where the boat was. As when he asked her, over and over again, if she was enjoying it while they 'made love', and spat at her, or hit or bit her when she cried, unable to say yes. As when he mentioned casually, with his penis grinding up and down inside her mouth, that he was HIV positive, then said it was a joke.

The hardest thing to take of all, in terms of dislocated actuality, was his attitude to the boat. He made her show him how the engine worked, how the tiller fitted to the rudder head with the shaped brass pin, where the spikes were kept when not in use, and how one drove them into the bank. For this, Sarah went into the cabin and returned with the hammer from underneath the cooker, where she had lately hidden it. Normally, and from then on, it was stowed beside the steps in the small doghouse – a name which pleased Rogers especially. Because the tow-path was so accessible, and escape so easy, he tethered Sarah tightly by the ankle with a length of polypropylene so that she could not get out of it – and called her 'Little Bitch' from then. His theory was that they should move, like all the other boats, in case somebody noticed their immobility. More than that, he wanted to. He thought canal boating was very fine good fun. He allowed Sarah her restricted mobility as if it were a privilege, and told her if she screamed or shouted out, or tried to attract attention, he would come below and kill her with a mooring spike, or better, stick it up her. She did not disbelieve him. When he drove the boat too fast she even told him, automatically, that if he caused a wash that damaged the canal bank, someone might report him, and rightly so. He immediately throttled back, patting the tiller with affection.

'It's about time I became a law-abiding citizen,' he said. 'Magic.'

Sarah killed him with the hammer the night he came back drunk from a canalside pub. He had left her bound and tightly gagged, and tucked his hair inside a woollen bobble cap that also hid his distinctive bald dome, and switched the cabin lights off. When he returned he had to cut her bonds, because his fingers were too clumsy to untie them. As he cut the gag, the knife blade nicked her ear and she bled profusely. While Rogers took his clothes off, falling sideways into things and cursing noisily, she went naked to the lavatory on her ankle-leash to get some paper for her ear. She also got the four-pound hammer.

Rogers was seated on the bed, his trousers round his ankles, his head bent forward to untie his boots. As he looked up to demand some help, the first blow hit him almost on the top of his skull, instead of at the base where she had intended. She had put all her strength into it, though, and the hammer was square, sharp-edged, and very heavy. A fold of scalp tore back towards his neck, and the white bone, exposed, crushed in quite visibly. Sarah, heartened, raised the hammer quickly, before he could respond, and brought it down and sideways into the left temple, having read somewhere that temples were most vulnerable. Rogers fell sideways, then slipped onto the deck, onto his bottom. She noticed that his penis, half-erect, was throbbing. That gave her strength to swing the hammer yet again, this time landing it between the first two strikes. There was a definite crunching, and it sank a good half-inch into his skull. When it came away, there was a plate of bone stuck onto it, with plastered hairs. Sarah's strength was gone. She could hardly hold the hammer any more.

Rogers looked at her. His eyes were like two bubbles filled with smoke. He seized her by the hips and pulled her down towards him. As her face passed close by his skull she saw into it, a broken egg with welling blood rolling curtain-like down the side. He seemed very strong, and the blood was pulsing, a strange bright black and red, with bits of pink stuff in it. He put his hands around her throat and began to strangle her. It was oddly undramatic, prosaic even. She was reminded of Jim Hawkins, in *Treasure Island*. Who was it strangling him? Israel Hands? She was interested to see that Rogers could still stand up, was moving past and over her, their bodies lubricated with his blood, his hands still clamped around her neck. Then the telephone rang.

There was a buzzing in her ears, which was displacing everything. Sarah's interest quickened into panic, though. The telephone! It must be Michael! At last, at last. She tried to speak, to squawk, to scream. But Rogers, reaching for the phone, still had her neck enfolded in one big hand. His thumb was pressed into the front of it, closing her windpipe. Sarah's eyes bulged. She would refuse to die until he'd answered it.

It was Michael Masters, and Brian Rogers, his face invisible, laughed at him.

'Fucking hell, Mikey,' he said. 'You would have been proud of her. I got you at last, mate, didn't I? Fucking hell.'

He dropped the receiver and collapsed sideways along the alleyway. Sarah tried to move, to reach it, but it was too late.

She heard his voice, though. He was calling Sarah.

Sarah.

TWENTY-ONE

The secret row over whether or not to save Michael Masters' life was long drawn out and furious. The Prime Minister, using the unacknowledged schism between Turner and Sinclair as rationale, set up a special Cabinet committee to oversee the question, and let them fight it out. It was a brilliant exercise in dividing and ruling, which ultimately meant that any decision which later proved to be disastrous could be blamed on someone else. For the ransoming of hostages was dynamite – especially rich and famous ones like Masters.

As the senior voice in the first committee, Sir Gerald outlined the problem, and his attitude. Michael Masters, he said, was first a human being, then a criminal. He had been caught up in events far beyond anything he had dabbled in, and was now entirely a victim, whose life was forfeit if the government blocked the ransom which his family were willing and able to pay. There were arguments on both sides, naturally. But to him, the moral line seemed clear – if secrecy could be maintained, the money should be paid.

When the discussion was thrown open, the first and fiercest voice was Donald Sinclair's. With hand on heart (he declared) he would love to see this person saved. It was a dreadful thing to contemplate, that such animals as these terrorists would kill so callously to merely swell their coffers. But in the wider view, in the name of sanity, the government could not give in to blackmail, could not treat with men of violence. Would it not set a precedent? Would it not open the floodgates? Would not they – by being 'kind' in Masters' case – be utterly cruel in general, in the cases that would follow, would inevitably follow?

Sir Gerald, sensing that for the first time in many days he had a truer picture than Sinclair did of the PM's mood, expressed surprise at the starkness of his deputy's position. The high moral tone was most impressive, he said, but a bullet in the head was slightly excessive as a punishment for the sort of crime that Masters had committed! He realised that Sinclair's views on crime and punishment had undergone a sea change recently, but many people might think that Masters had suffered enough. Four years in Bowscar had been a pretty monstrous shock, he guessed, without being involved in a bloody insurrection and taken prisoner by a band of murderous savages. Even public prejudice, which saw him as rich and over-privileged, would surely have been satisfied by now? What did Sinclair lack – humanity? What did he want – blood?

Sinclair was not inclined to pussyfoot. He was playing for high stakes. He fixed Sir Gerald Turner with an eye hot with contempt.

'If I may say so,' he said, 'that attitude is typical. You paint this man as a minor criminal, a fiddler caught out with his hand stuck in the till. How do you know, Sir Gerald? How do you know he was not a major instigator in the Bowscar break-out? How do you know he was not armed? How do you know he did not murder, maim, before he himself was captured by the Irish? Is my memory playing me tricks, or did you not tell me that he had been issuing threats from Bowscar? From the jail, on an illicit telephone? Was that not you, Sir Gerald?'

In later meetings, and in intensive lobbyings, all the angles and all the arguments were rehearsed – while the Prime Minister, sitting on the fence, listened to the blandishments. Sinclair's whisperings – conveyed through Velma Goodman – were passionate. Had not the campaign against terrorism been a personal one, a jewel in the PM's crown, almost a crusade? Could the victims and the victims' mothers, the public soul-searching, the promises, be set aside, forgotten? People would understand the personal grief involved in sacrificing Masters, would deeply sympathise with it, and the agony could be shared. But would they understand a decision to do a 'deal' to save him? In the war on terrorism, people expected integrity, not 'deals', however bitter was the price. Sir Gerald's repeated point was this: no one would ever know. And the Northern Ireland Secretary, and the head of MI5, agreed. As long as it was a deadly secret, as long as it was leakproof, there was no real reason not to save him. Nobody knew that Masters was a captive of the PIRA, the swap of cash for prisoner would be done in total secrecy or not at all, and in any case the media was fettered by the Secrets Act. The Prime Minister, having heard it all, gave them a deadline: a decision must be announced the following afternoon.

Next morning, though, the morning after the last full committee meeting on the subject, the news was splashed in every paper in the land. Michael Masters was a Provo prisoner, and a huge ransom had been demanded. Would the British government give in to monstrous blackmail?

There had been fourteen people at the meeting, and one of them had leaked. The chances for a secret deal were done . . .

The drumming of the rain on the alloy roof of the immobile mobile home was a strangely comforting sound, Rosanna Nixon thought. She was standing by the cooker, staring through the clear patch she had rubbed in the window-condensation, and the whole effect was absurdly domestic – or rather, like the memory of a childhood holiday. Away up the hill, through a gap in the trees, she could just make out the pepperpot tower in the gloom, and closer to there were sodden sheep, their tails turned to the wind. When the kettle boiled she would make some tea and take it into the main section, where a dying gunman lay. She would sit down, and serve, and they would drink, and no one was afraid. It was all quite mad.

When they had finally plucked up their courage and knocked on the caravan door, neither Rosanna nor Andrew Forbes had really had the faintest notion what they should expect. The curtains had been drawn, and no sound had been audible from outside, in the wind and rain. It was possible, they knew, that there were armed convicts inside, but it seemed too unlikely for them quite to credit it. So – with water dripping down their necks and their thick cords getting waterlogged – they had rapped on the small blue door, and waited.

Inside, the knock had caused confusion. By now, Angus McGregor was in the bed, and neither he nor Hughes or Carole Rochester ever expected to see him leave it alive. He still held the pistol, though, and his eyes were still bright. He covered both of them, and told them not to move. But he coughed, and when he coughed, he bled.

'For Christ's sake, Angus,' said Alan Hughes. 'Do yourself a favour, man. Let me open it. The police wouldn't come knocking, would they? And if it was them, who would you shoot?'

'I'm not going back, Alan. Never. No surrender.'

Hughes nodded, with real sympathy. He put his hand out.

'Give us the gun,' he said. 'I won't rat on you. We're in it together, mate. No one's taking you.'

To his surprise, and more to Carole Rochester's, Angus McGregor reversed the revolver. His hand, as he held it out to Hughes, was shaking.

'You're a good man, Al,' he whispered. 'No surrender.'

Hughes rubbed the window with his sleeve and looked at the two bright anoraks outside. He put the revolver in his pocket and opened the door. Forbes, relieved, said casually: 'We're friends of Carole Rochester. Is she at home?' Before Hughes had time properly to respond, he was up the step and in, with Rosanna close behind him.

'I'm sorry,' he apologised, 'I used to be a reporter. It's a habit. Can we come in?' And when Hughes produced the pistol he said, apparently still gaily: 'Oh shit. A Bowscar boy. Oh fuck.'

The weak, Scots voice of McGregor said sternly from the bed: 'Watch your language. There's a lady present.'

Carole Rochester, staring at them, said: 'I don't know you from Adam. Alan. Please. Put that thing away.'

'We're not police,' said Rosanna Nixon. 'It's difficult to explain. Eileen Pendlebury gave us your address in Leicester, then we came down here. It's about a man called Angus McGregor. About his brother. I . . .'

Forbes, watching the sick man, added shrewdly: 'She saw him die. You're Angus, aren't you? We got the governor to let you out. We told him about Jimmy. He was murdered.'

Over the next few hours, the shifting pattern of relationships in the caravan, and their perceptions of them, fascinated Forbes and Rosanna. It was clear at first that in the time they had spent as hostages of the dying and probably unstable McGregor, Alan Hughes and Carole Rochester had formed a bond. They sat close together while they talked, although not touching, and they quite often answered for each other, or filled in gaps of information. Equally, however, it emerged that they had a bond with McGregor, that they no longer feared or hated him, and would protect him. Hughes rinsed the compress on his neck several times, and Carole held a cup of warm weak tea to his mouth so that he could drink.

They explained, almost with concern, how McGregor had come to Leicester not to find Carole but her father, whom he planned to kill because of his brother. Carole, watching their faces carefully, added: 'This may sound shocking, but he probably deserved it, too. Well, something bad. For Angus's brother. Alan has this theory about politicians, and it seems to me spot on. My mother says my father's different, but he's not that different. He may not be exactly evil, but he's an awful hypocrite.'

She was very calm about it. Frank-faced and quite attractive in a strained, exhausted way. Rosanna caught herself wondering if she was slightly mad, then remembered all she'd been through. Maybe she was sane, entirely. She asked Hughes what his theory was. He smiled, self-effacingly.

'It seems rather overblown, somehow. Sitting here so snugly, drinking tea. But back in Bowscar I used to think a lot, worry at the problems. I wanted to understand how jail could be so awful, yet so acceptable. I wanted to understand the psychology, you know, of repression, correction, call it what you will – societal revenge. I read somewhere that Carole's father was a really nice man, deeply civilised and all that guff, and I wondered if it could be true. I mean, he's been in charge for years. He's talked about reforms but jammed more and more of us in single cells, doubled us up, trebled us. He's said he's spent more money than anyone before on improving prisons but he's just built more of them – and filled them with new people. He's said he'd curb the prison officers, and he's just provoked them, he's spat on them, he's laughed behind their backs. And I used to wonder, did he *want* an explosion, maybe? Did he want the whole thing to go mad? Perhaps our politicians just can't lead, they can only stumble blindly on, they're hopeless. It's undoubtedly their fault, but can you blame them? It's not much of a theory, is it? I fancied talking to him, though. Asking him to explain the thought processes. Or acknowledge the great mystery.'

Angus McGregor said: 'He wanted to have a chinwag with him. To convince him he was doing something wrong and had to stop. And when he disagreed – I was going to kill him.'

It was a McGregor joke, presumably. He laughed, a wheezy, crippled sound. He groaned at the agony it caused him. When he had finished, Forbes said to Carole Rochester: 'But it wasn't your father who caused Jimmy McGregor's death. It was Donald Sinclair.' To McGregor he added: 'Did you not know that? Sir Gerald's assistant, his junior minister.'

'Never heard of him,' grunted McGregor. 'Ach, what the hell. I'm killing no one now. My killing days are over, thank God.'

'You know Sinclair, don't you?'

Carole looked at Forbes and smiled.

'Eileen told you. Oh yes, I know Sinclair, he's the real rat. Did you see him on the television? He blamed it all on Eileen's father. He moved "the Animal" without permission. Angus. And that was that. So he killed Jimmy, did he? I'm not surprised. How? You mean he was responsible?'

Andrew said: 'He was in charge at Buckie. He covered himself very well. He took most of the credit, but not the blame.'

'Yes,' she said. 'That sounds like Donald.' To Hughes she added: 'I had an affair with him. Before I got married. Before I sussed out politicians. We had a little flat across the river, his "safe house". I wonder how many more he's had like me. Poor silly cows.'

'What was he like?' asked Rosanna. 'We're interested. We'd still like to talk to him. We think it could do some good. We think – do I sound stupid? – we think it would be nice to . . . rub his nose in something.'

Carole liked the idea.

'He's corrupt,' she said. 'He's very clever, but you might just knock him down. That was the oddest thing about him, really. He's incredibly naive in many ways, especially about himself. He's corrupt, but he really doesn't know it. He used to be a journalist and he made a fair amount of cash, he did all right. Then he married money and became an MP and he's a name at Lloyds and he's got directorships galore, you know, he's paid thousands just to be there, to be a conduit to the government. He's lousy, stinking rich with no more talent than he ever had before, but he can't make the connection, he still thinks he's a good man, he doesn't realise how it's all distorted him. Take me, for instance. He more or less told me – excuse the language, Angus, I'm a big girl now – that he was married to a boring cow, and I was a superb fuck with a brain, and he would marry me. He believed it, I'm sure he did. But what he meant, I guess, was that I was Gerald Turner's daughter and I could help him reach the top, perhaps. It was all so holier than thou, he was always bringing conscience into it. But underneath it all, he was prepared to do anything for power. Every move he made, practically, was done with unconscious calculation.' She laughed. 'That's good, isn't it? "Unconscious calculation"! But it's true. And this was years ago, long before the finance deals, the cash corruption, the Masters thing.'

Andrew Forbes felt a rush of excitement. That old black magic, he thought! His instincts, metaphorically, sat up and begged.

'Masters? Michael Masters? What's he got to do with Sinclair?'

'Oh, I don't know any details,' said Carole, dismissively. 'Anyway, they must have fallen out, it can only have been Sinclair who got him into jail, can't it? Although I suppose my father did the secret business with the judges, like the papers said, that's very much his style. No, they've had something going on between them for years, something crooked. They're quite alike in many ways, although I only met Masters once. Both bastards.'

Rosanna's lips were parted. She was hardly breathing.

'Now Sinclair and my Dad have fallen out,' said Carole. 'That's funny, too. Dad never lost his cool when Donald messed me up. He more or less told me it served me right and I should be ashamed of myself. I don't think he even let on to Donald that he knew, it might have caused embarrassment. I rang up once and threatened to commit suicide. Mum and Dad went sailing.'

Despite an almost wild desire to make something of it, both Rosanna and Forbes crushed their reactions. Rosanna could tell from the way he rubbed his eye how frantic Andrew was, and she had to lick dry lips, she could not stop herself. Their hunch was right. Sinclair was a crook, he was involved in something big, and dirty, and bizarre. With Michael *Masters*? But Carole found the subject less than interesting, it appeared, it was just part of the past to her. She soon began to question them, on Eileen Pendlebury.

When evening came, Forbes and Rosanna – aching to get a crack at Sinclair, to get away and somehow track him down – became uncomfortably aware that they had no idea of their position. McGregor had gone to sleep or become unconscious by late afternoon, and the four of them had little left to say. The pistol had never returned to view, but everyone was aware of it. Alan Hughes broke the deadlock.

'Where will you be heading, then?' he asked. 'Are you booked in somewhere, or are you going back to England?'

'That's what we'd like to do,' said Andrew. 'But it's rather up to you in some ways, isn't it? Will you let us go? I'd like to use the info Carole gave us. Confront Sinclair with it somehow, I don't know.' He smiled at her, trying to hide his nervousness. 'It's a lot more powerful than you think it is, I think,' he said. 'I think we could . . . well, we could get the McGregor story out into the open, at least. That would be worthwhile, wouldn't it? Do you mind if we use it?'

'I don't mind at all,' said Carole. 'As long as you don't tell anyone where we are. We haven't got much longer, have we? Angus is going to die or something soon. We'll call an ambulance when he gets too bad, he won't let us otherwise. Alan will give himself up. They won't find us, will they?'

'They're looking for us, apparently,' Rosanna said. 'But we've seen no sign of them. I think you're pretty safe, considering. Are you sure you don't mind?'

'Look, Donald Sinclair can rot in hell for all I care. They all can. Just don't give us away.'

Andrew Forbes said: 'That flat. Across the river. I don't suppose you could remember . . . ?'

Carole stood and picked a pencil from a shelf. She wrote an address on a piece of paper.

'I'm not likely to forget it.'

'And he's not likely to still be there, I suppose.'

She smiled.

'I wouldn't bank on that,' she said. 'I told you, in some ways he's naive. It would probably never occur to him I wished him anything but well. I bought him a watch once, incredibly expensive, a sort of token. I've seen it on TV a lot of times. He still wears it. He's also exceedingly conceited. Try it.'

The farewells they made were stilted, and emotional. Rosanna and Forbes walked in silence for some while, the warm rain lashing in their faces. They had to squirt the car with WD40 to make it start.

'We should be doing handsprings, shouldn't we?' said the Mouse, as they drove towards Porthmadog. 'We've caught the bastard.'

'We've got to land him yet.'

'I feel so bloody sad,' Rosanna said.

In Leicester, two large men in suits had found the Fiat Uno. Across the road, a lady prepared a pot of tea for them.

Until he had made his phone call to *Cynthia's Beam*, Michael Masters had allowed his confidence, quietly, to grow. With the Irishmen in general, and Liam in particular, he had been prepared to discuss the details, so that no mistakes should be made. Liam had a degree in economics, it transpired, and was one of the fund-raising fraternity. He had carried a gun on active service, but his talents and real interests lay elsewhere. They found each other stimulating company, and talked high finance until the others laughed at them, and told them to give it over. But all of them found Masters – for a man who could coolly raise one million pounds and hardly bat an eyelid – surprisingly congenial. He did not fit their stereotype of a capitalist Brit bastard!

To Liam, Masters confided that he had no intention of paying the cash himself, or at least not all of it. His contacts owed him, and one in particular would not, this time, wriggle out of it. For a start, once the payment of a ransom had been agreed in principle, Masters was insisting on a deal. He would be 'received' by his lawyer and his family in the first instance, and until he was safe with them he would co-operate not at all in any government debriefing. Because of the terrible suffering he had undergone in captivity in Ireland – that would be the line – he would either be released on licence for the rest of his jail sentence, or would serve a short proportion of it only, in an open jail. If the deal was not forthcoming, he would blow the gaffe. Although he utterly refused to name his 'friend', he told Liam that he was very high indeed, and could not afford to be exposed.

The Irishman nodded.

'Point taken, Michael, point taken. But why can't he just double-cross you? When he has you back again, he can slap you in another jail like Bowscar, and look after you properly this time. You could shout until you were black in the face then, and no bastard would hear you. Another thing – you escaped. You were armed. In your mad country carrying a gun carries the same max penalty as killing somebody with one, which is why so many people would rather shoot than get arrested, I guess. You could go to jail for life.'

'Self-interest,' Masters said. 'He's driven by it. The way I figure it, he dropped me in the shit out of necessity in the first place, and I don't think he could really understand my whingeing at it. To him, it was all part of the game. He'd have got me out somehow in the end, I'm sure of it. The prat just didn't realise what he'd done. He probably thought I'd like the rest. Do an Open University degree or something. The point is, we're worth a lot of money to each other. As a unit, we've got earning power. Millions. I don't think he'd risk all that just for a bit of power.'

Liam was impressed by Masters' flair and confidence – which he had recovered visibly since leaving Bowscar – but amused by his trust in politicians.

'That's not our experience of the breed,' he said. 'The British politician has been double-crossing us for years. About eight hundred at the last count, or maybe a wee bit more!'

'Ah,' said Michael Masters, with a smile. 'But you're soft Micks.'

The Irishman accepted the bitter little joke.

'But we're not savages,' he said. 'We'll honour our side of the bargain. You have my word for it.'

The confidence, and the fantasies, and the thoughts and dreams of Sarah Williams were shattered by the phone call. In the telephone box, outside a lonely bar in the damp Irish countryside, Masters shouted and called, wild and oblivious to the embarrassed man beside him. He heard no further sound, though, and in the end, his money spent, hung up. Back at the house, there was sympathy at his unspoken horror, but mainly more embarrassment. Shortly, Masters went to his room.

Next morning, on the radio, the news was broken of his kidnapping and the ransom demand. Liam and his friends grew very grave. For the moment, they agreed, Michael Masters had best be left to sleep.

Donald Sinclair decided to speak to Barbara Masters for several reasons. As a public gesture, he thought, it showed a nice compassion now the kidnap news was out, and officially, it was important that she should be warned not to attempt anything silly, any private ransom deal. His real concern, which even Judith Parker did not suspect, was to make absolutely certain that she knew nothing about his connections with her husband.

The official government position, since the leaking of the news, had been complete denial, coupled with a strict refusal to comment or to speculate. The denial meant nothing, as was widely understood, and in the public mind the fact remained a fact. Many a column inch of newsprint had been expended on precedent and prediction, with the general feeling being that the case was too complex for a simple outcome to be wagered on. Even the gutter press – while implying that they knew the answers – were forced to wait and see.

The approach from Barbara Masters had come, ironically, through Sir Cyril France, her lawyer. She had asked him to arrange a meeting with Sir Gerald Turner, the Home Secretary, although she feared desperately that what she wished to say might fall on stony ground indeed in that quarter. Sir Cyril, who knew that the truth was quite the opposite, gently redirected her to Sinclair, and advised him, clandestinely, to accept a meeting. She was received in a small, quiet office in Queen Anne's Gate, alone. She was dressed in black, her face was pale, and Sinclair found her remarkably attractive. He wished he could have offered her some comfort.

Barbara Masters was direct. She knew the government had

not made up its mind on whether to pay the ransom, and she understood the terrible dilemma the publicity had put them in. She also knew – through further contact with her husband's captors – that a deadline had been set, beyond which he would not live. The family had the money, and while she recognised the principle involved, the government had no right, no moral right, to use an innocent victim as a pawn, however serious they felt the game to be. Her husband was a convicted criminal, but that could not be allowed to reduce his value as an individual. He must be saved.

Sinclair, who did not care to insult her intelligence with parliamentary platitudes, listened with every outward sign of interest and concern. He agreed with her that the deadline was very close, and that a decision must be made and announced extremely speedily. He promised to do everything in his own power to sway the argument, at whatever cost. As far as he was concerned, her husband should be saved. Mrs Masters, when he approached, allowed him to drop a hand upon her shoulder.

She stood. She looked at him.

'There is one other thing, if I may? It's quite difficult to express, but bear with me. There is . . . I believe there is . . . I think there's somebody in the government, somebody with power and influence, somebody high up, who wishes Michael . . . No, who has had dealings with him. Illicit dealings. I think there's somebody who has been involved in his activities, clandestinely. His crookedness . . .'

Sinclair turned back to his desk. He sat on it, picked up a pen. Barbara Masters searched his face, eager for some sign of hope.

'We've had our ups and downs,' she said, impulsively. 'We keep our lives quite separate, in some ways. But I'm horribly afraid for him. I think there's somebody who would like to see him dead. Who wouldn't mind.'

She stopped. Sinclair had shrugged, made a shoulder movement she took to be dismissive. It was, in fact, involuntary.

'It sounds far-fetched,' she said. 'But I'm almost certain of it.'

He rocked forward on his desk and put the pen down in a holder.

'Look,' he said. 'I think you're overwrought. I'm not saying it could not happen, but . . . Look, I promise you this much, Mrs Masters. I'll keep my eyes and ears open, and I'll be on my guard. If anybody appears to be arguing strongly against your husband, if I catch the merest hint . . . I suppose you don't have anyone in mind, do you? A name?'

Barbara Masters had not intended to go so far, but the directness of the question took her off guard. She blushed to the roots of her hair.

'Sir Gerald Turner might . . . No, I don't . . . No.'

Donald Sinclair stood. He scratched his chin, contemplatively. He made a little face, almost regretful.

'Well,' he said. 'That does sound unlikely, doesn't it? No – I'm not mocking. I take it very seriously. But you realise, don't you, if you're right . . . we've very little chance of beating the Home Secretary, have we? Don't give up hope, though, Mrs Masters. Please don't give up hope.'

Some hours later, in yet another meeting of the cabinet committee, Sir Gerald Turner and Sinclair clashed violently and publicly for the third time in as many days. Despite the leaking, the Home Secretary maintained, it was incumbent on them, given all the facts, to advise the Prime Minister in the strongest possible terms that Masters should be ransomed. He had suffered far too much, not just from his capture, but from the uncertainty. The government would lose face, inevitably, but that would be offset by public perception of their attachment to the humane principle. To let the deadline drift ever nearer without a statement, even, was appalling. For him, as an exercise in cold-bloodedness, it was just too much to bear. There was a family to consider, also, a wife, two children. If he could not obtain the agreement of the committee, he would be forced to consider his position.

Sinclair, who had seen the expressions round the table cloud at the thought of loss of face, knew he could now win. The Prime Minister would not suffer that, would die far rather. He launched an immoderate tirade on Turner, accusing him of lack of stomach for the fight, of failure of nerve, of lack of leadership. The only point they were agreed on, he said, was the necessity to speak out, to end the waffling, to put Masters – an unfortunate choice of phrase, he inwardly noted – out of his misery. He proposed that the committee should decide the matter and convey their decision to the PM forthwith. He himself, given Sir Gerald's squeamishness, would undertake the task, and make public the announcement. Without more ado, the motion was carried, with Sir Gerald's the only voice against.

Sinclair wrote the press release with Velma Goodman and

Fortyne, and cleared it with the Premier. It spoke of their collective pain at the terrible decision, but the absolute necessity of standing firm. To save one life would have been to condemn the innocent majority to an ever-increasing spiral of blackmail and violence, et cetera, et cetera. The terrorists must not win. To forestall questioning, Velma Goodman released the statement, with no one at ministerial level available for comment. Sinclair and Judith Parker went to their small French restaurant and had a meal.

As they parked Sinclair's car in the private garage near the safe house afterwards, Judith said to him: 'There's a funny smell in here, it's getting worse. Something going off. You haven't got a body in the boot, have you?'

'I certainly hope not!' laughed Sinclair.

When he opened the boot, the smell was foul. He found the bunch of roses and the mussels he had bought for Mary. They were quite rotten.

'And who were *they* for?' asked Judith Parker, although she knew quite well. *Moules Bonne Femme*, she thought. How bloody quaint.

'You,' he said.

When Andrew Forbes rang the Dog and Partridge on the off-chance, Antony the barman said Peter Jackson was standing at the bar. But Jackson would not talk to him. He took the number of the phone box, told Forbes to wait, and rang back from another. When Andrew laughed, he got an earful: By tomorrow, Jackson said, their pictures and descriptions would probably have been issued. In theory, they should be lifted any time.

'Is this gen, or are you winding me up?' asked Forbes. In the interim, he and Rosanna had absorbed the full potential of what they had been told. They had got their spirits back, they felt invincible, they were on song. He had rung, in fact, to suggest a secret meeting, to talk tactics. And drink beer.

'It's gen,' said Jackson. 'It's from the horse's mouth. I'm getting pure info from the Special Branch since we helped with Charlie's friends. I won't ask where you are, but what's the strength at your end. How's Rosanna?'

Forbes told him everything, grinning in the darkness, unable to break his mood. Of finding McGregor and another Bowscar con called Alan Hughes, of Gerald Turner's daughter and the secret Sinclair flat, of her caravan near Llanbedrog, of the Michael Masters scam. Indeed, his elation grew.

'We've got enough to hang the twat,' he said. 'We'll even be able to spring a confrontation on him, if we're lucky. Carole Rochester thinks he won't have moved. Too big-headed and too idle. He thinks he's fireproof. Otherwise, we'll get him at the House!'

'Christ,' said Jackson. 'You don't half sound confident, old son. Hasn't it occurred to you just what you mean to Sinclair? Apart from Carole Rochester, you and Rosanna are the only threat. You're the only ones with anything at all on him.'

'He doesn't know that, though. He doesn't know we've talked to her. We're just two nuts who disappeared the night the Scar blew up. Anyway—'

Jackson interrupted: 'And the night two spooks got blasted outside your house. And who've been baiting him for weeks about the Animal. Anyway what?'

'There's Masters, too. He's the biggest threat, for Christ's sake. We're just chickenfeed.'

Jackson filled him in on that score, rapidly. Andrew Forbes was shocked. He looked at Rosanna, sitting in the car studying a map by the courtesy light. She glanced up, as if by instinct, and smiled at him.

Jackson said: 'It was a corporate decision, naturally. A Cabinet committee, excluding the Prime Minister. But Donald Sinclair put his name to it. He's not so squeamish. It's a potential death warrant, Andrew.'

'Now who's being squeamish? Why say potential? It's a death warrant.'

Jackson grunted. He said no more. Forbes sighed.

'All right,' he said, 'you win. Playtime over. But I'm going to see the man, Peter. Nothing's going to stop me. And I'm going to keep a smile stuck on my face, OK? Got any good ideas?'

Jackson mentioned an address in Clapham. It was a mutual friend of theirs, who was in Australia. It was a ground-floor flat, and the door key was under the rotten bottom of the gatepost. The phone was not connected, but it was safe.

'That's good,' said Andrew. 'Sinclair's is in Stockwell, ideal. We were thinking of maybe tapping up Rosanna's Clapham contacts, but it didn't seem a very good idea, they wouldn't understand. Any more instructions, Uncle?'

'Get into London quick, and ditch the car. Get to Clapham and don't be seen. Apart from that, you're on your own. How's the Mouse on growing beards?'

'She's got one already, thanks, and I'm in love with it. And her.' He stopped. There was a heaviness around his heart. 'Oh by the way, that's official now, old cock. All sexual fantasies obtainable only on licence from now on. You're excluded. Sorry.'

There was a brief pause. Then Jackson said: 'I'm very happy for you both. Live to enjoy it.'

He rang off before Andrew could reply.

Angus McGregor died quite unexpectedly, after he had made a powerful rally for a while. He had asked for a bowl of soup, and when Hughes brought it to him, he found him dead. Carole came in from the kitchen, and they looked at him. He had looked like a corpse for days, but in death he was different. The lines around his mouth had gone.

'What shall we do?' said Hughes. 'We'd better call the law.'

'We could make love,' said Carole Rochester. 'Angus wouldn't mind. We don't have to use the bed, do we? The floor's all right.'

There was no reason to ask if she was joking. She wasn't. But Alan Hughes did not know what to do.

'I don't know if I can,' he said. 'It's been so many years. I wasn't really very good at it, I don't think. I'd got out of the habit long before they locked me up.'

'This is very sudden, Alan. I apologise. I just wanted to, that's all.'

'It's a normal reaction as I understand it. It's called the Stockholm Syndrome. Captors and captives get confused. Dependent. They sometimes fall in love. I'd like to try. If you can stand a failure?'

They took each other's clothes off and, oblivious to McGregor's sightless stare, they did quite well, they thought. At least, they laughed a lot, and they stroked each other. Then, lying on her back, Carole asked Hughes: 'Did you really kill your wife? Your wives?'

'In my heart of hearts,' said Hughes, 'I like to think I didn't. But I did kill one of them. The other one just disappeared. The one I killed fell down the stairs. I didn't push her, but I didn't try to save her. I'm lying. She was pushed. I pushed her.'

'I'd have liked to have pushed my husband down the stairs. And my father. And Donald Sinclair.'

'No stairs in here,' said Alan Hughes. 'We're safe.'

She turned to him, and put her head on his chest.

'Yes,' she said. 'I feel that. Tonight – let's put old Angus on the floor, shall we? He wouldn't mind.'

If Michael Masters had any thoughts about the setting for his execution, it was the wildly irrelevant one that it should have been in the rain. Everything else about the picture was absolutely right, spot-on. He was driven in a black car through the lovely, lonely countryside, followed by a red Toyota and a Suzuki jeep. He picked his way through soggy bogland to a clump of low trees behind a ruined farmhouse, and a fierce wind whipped the hair into his eyes and drove scudding clouds across the sky. Even the cows seemed hand-picked, bored but curious, a stunning black and white against the opulent green of Ireland. If there only were a little rain.

The occupants of the other vehicles were curiously clumsy, and ill-at-ease. Conor Grady and Liam, who had accompanied him in the black car, stood beside him while they waited, smoking almost in companionship. It was not only rifles that were being readied in the building's lee. A video camera, with built-in sound recording, was taken from its black box and tested on the cows. There were to be four rifles, all expert men they told him comfortingly, and it would be very military, done with precision, for the camera. Liam, picking a frond of tobacco from the lip-end of his hand-rolled cigarette, smiled.

'It will make some impact on the TV news,' he said. 'They won't know what fucking hit them, so they won't.'

When the guns and the two-man film crew were ready, Conor and Liam, apologetically, tied his hands behind his back, and put a blindfold on his eyes. Masters protested, quietly, but they said it had to be. He conceded, with a weary shrug, that it would look far better, for the filming. In reality, he did not care. He did not care for anything any more, not anything. They tried it, adjusted it, and took it off again.

'Time to shake hands,' said Liam. 'Good luck.'

Conor Grady held his other hand. He gripped it tightly.

'You're a good man, Michael,' he said. 'It's a crying shame, all this. A crying shame.'

The last thing Michael Masters saw, before the blindfold was tightened properly, was the line of riflemen, in masks, black berets and black gloves. To their side, two other men in civvies, with the camera. Then he was alone.

Fifteen seconds later he was crumpled on the ground, with Liam bending over him, a pistol in his hand.

'Mother of God,' he said to Conor Grady. 'The things we have to do.'

TWENTY-TWO

It was one of Donald Sinclair's former journalistic colleagues who alerted him to the video that was delivered to ITN in London, and Sinclair moved like lightning. He telephoned the Prime Minister, interrupting a private dinner with the highest possible codeword, he spoke to MI5 in Curzon Street, he summoned Deputy Assistant Commissioner Claud Molyneaux, head of the Metropolitan Police Special Branch, and he alerted the Ministry of Defence. Within twenty minutes news-room staff at ITN and the BBC found themselves in the midst of scenes that could have come from a television thriller. They were moved back from their computer terminals and made to line the walls. Telephones were left unanswered, and the studios and editing suites were invaded by heavy men with humourless faces. The duty editors in both buildings, and the presenters for the night, were conducted to their offices and told to do nothing and to call nobody while the most senior people in both organisations were sought out. All over the country similar swoops were made. It was not known how many tapes had been released, but no risks could be taken. Within forty minutes, legal moves were being made to injunct the contents.

The IRA, who had studied media matters in mainland Britain for many years, in fact had delivered only one tape, to ITN in London. They had little hope of the BBC using such material, suspecting as they did that its news output was virtually under government control, but by timing the delivery at 9.00 p.m., they hoped to give the independent service enough time to assess the tape and do some background research before the News at Ten. If there were a paid mole at ITN it would leave the government very little time to act indeed, and with luck they might barge in on the BBC news in a panic, in case they had the tape, and even pull the plug at ITN while the news was on the air. They also rang all the daily newspapers, giving the IRA codeword, and told them that the government would be raiding television offices later in the evening and to keep a watch.

Donald Sinclair, before any of the undercover squads went in, insisted to the people in control that they should 'remember Zircon'. Any repetitions of blanket trawls by hammer-wielding teams of KGB-type heavies, as had happened not many years before at the BBC offices in Glasgow, would be met with the direst consequences for the perpetrators. 'We are not a police state,' he said, 'nor must we be misrepresented as one. You are looking for one specific tape, and you are looking for one tape only. Ask for it, and it will be given. The only threat you need is the Act. Under no circumstances must the main news bulletins be interrupted.' In the event they were not, although the last five minutes of the BBC's Nine O'Clock News were read with two F5 officers standing just out of camera shot, sweating like pigs in the studio lights.

By the time the operation was over, and the news programmes were off the air, the broadcasters, joined by the more alert newspaper editors, were onto the Home Office like a swarm of furious hornets. Although most of the Special Branch and F5 operations had been restrained, there had inevitably been one or two clumsy spots, and in Manchester and Birmingham freelance photographers had been roughed up. What was worse, an over-enthusiastic deputy at the Ministry of Defence had scrambled special units in several parts of the country, and at least one ITN transmitter mast had acquired a 'perimeter of bayonets', as a reporter put it. The freedom of the press, it seemed, was indeed in jeopardy.

At 10.50, leaving Judith Parker to man the hot-phone, Sinclair, Fortyne and Velma Goodman went into an office for a hurried conference. At 10.56 Velma started ringing her main contacts, with Fortyne handling the less important ones. The first targets were the deputy director general of the BBC, the ITN supremo, all the editors of the national dailies, and anybody else they could contact who had attended Goodman's post-Bowscar gagging conference. The subject, confusingly for the recipients of the calls, was not the 'alleged operations' at the TV stations, on which a statement would be made tomorrow, but Bowscar Prison. Suddenly, appallingly, the situation had become critical and – as promised – they were being given warning in advance. Latest intelligence suggested that random killing of the hostages was taking place, and consequently the government was going to act. Every other avenue had been exhausted, and a military solution was all that was left. The troops would be going in tonight – yes, *tonight*. That in itself – official, from the highest sources – was enough to clear the front pages. But Velma Goodman promised updates throughout the action, and suggested special editions and print-runs into the early hours. They loved it, they were galvanised, they lapped it up like cream.

'The highest sources,' said Christian Fortyne, when Velma had made her last call. 'Should we tell Sir Gerald, do you think!'

'Damn him,' said Sinclair. 'We'll tell the PM, that's enough. He'd only accuse us of a cover up!'

The timing of the last assault was critical. All the intelligence they had gathered over the course of the siege suggested that between 3 and 4 a.m. would be best, as there was very little detectable activity in the jail at that time. It was also desirable from a reportage point of view. Although they did not yet suspect it, the press and TV representatives were going to be moved well out of camera shot – for military reasons – just before the troops went in. And Velma Goodman knew that, realistically, no edition, however 'special', could be put together, printed and distributed if the news broke beyond 3.45.

The main problem they faced in raising the siege remained the hostages. Because they had been put in individual cells, and never herded round or guarded as a group, none of the listening devices or heat-seeking locaters had ever identified them except as part of the Bowscar population. There was no way of knowing where or how they were being kept, or how close they were at any time to the people who might kill them. The simple fact was that the troops would go in blind, and they could provoke a massacre.

'The pity of it is,' said Judith Parker, 'that if we had a few more days, they'd probably all come out anyway, of their own accord. Sod the IRA.'

'What ghouls,' said Velma Goodman, crushing out her small cigar. 'To video it! Appalling.'

Judith's point, according to the government's medical advisers, was an exact one. The strategy of leaving the Bowscar men completely isolated had worked brilliantly. Apart from three hostage deaths and two suicides from the roof-top, there had been little upset. It had been Spaghetti House without negotiation, just a breakdown of morale. The next natural step was to switch off the electricity for a day or two and see what happened. They'd probably wander out.

'It's unfortunate, yes,' said Donald Sinclair. 'But there's no alternative, is there? In any case, if some hostages do get hurt we can hardly accept any blame that I can see. We have to rescue them, don't we? Tonight.'

'If no *prisoners* are killed,' put in Christian Fortyne, positively merrily, 'we'll be in trouble with our public, I should say. It's what they expect, you know.'

Over the next few hours, the logistics kept them fully occupied, although most of it involved going over well-turned ground. The designated hospitals were alerted, the camps where the bulk of the prisoners would go were manned, and the governors who had high-security places waiting were told to expect 'visitors' in the middle of the night. Sinclair, in case of triumph, went up to Bowscar, but kept himself well-hidden until the press – protesting violently – had been moved back. He heard the signal given, and he watched the troops go in. He thought of Buckie, and he crossed his fingers.

It was a magnificent success. The first wave of soldiers, using ingress spots they had reconnoitred exhaustively, flooded the main areas of occupation – charted painstakingly by the boffins – and used disorientation techniques perfected over many years. With stun grenades, bright lights and noise they woke the sleeping prisoners, then terrified them with their camouflage paint and rifles. There were some pockets of resistance, and sporadic shooting was heard by those outside the jail, but only four more people died, and none of those were hostages. Some of the soldiers, indeed, were a little disappointed at how easy it had been. It reminded them of pictures they had seen of surrendering Italians – almost too eager to get out of something they knew to be insane. Sinclair, on a whim that was a PR masterstroke, allowed the pressmen in before most of the prisoners had been evacuated. He was far too busy being filmed and interviewed with the filthy, shuffling men as backdrop to remember, for a while, to go and offer comfort to the freed hostages. Long enough, in fact, for Fortyne to get Pendlebury into an ambulance and away. The man was being a positive embarrassment.

By the time Sir Gerald Turner reached his office in the morning, Donald Sinclair was the hero of the hour. There was no question, this time round, of him being in the shadows. His face was everywhere, and he had been interviewed on all the early TV shows and on Today. The PM, Turner learnt, was absolutely cock-a-hoop.

The Bowscar siege was over.

Throughout the long drive from London to North Wales, Peter Jackson had metaphorically kicked himself quite frequently. It had been a simple buzz along the information network that had set him off, and it had been uncheckable. The real reason he had decided to follow it, he knew, was to get away from London for a while. He feared for Rosanna and for Andrew Forbes and knew he could not help them. From what they had said, though, Carole Rochester seemed worth saving. There was no justification that he could think of for anyone else to suffer.

When he reached Llanbedrog, Jackson traced the static van quite easily by asking at the Post Office. A lone Englishwoman with a Dormobile who had a caravan in a clump of trees at the bottom of a farm sounded easy. Unlike Forbes and Rosanna, Jackson had the name of the village to work on, and no worries about giving any games away. He just needed not to be too late. But as he approached it, ten minutes later, he knew he was. There were two cars parked discreetly behind the camper van, and the curtains were drawn. As he approached the door, one was twitched aside and a face peered out. A police face.

'Peter Jackson,' he said, before anybody asked him. 'Customs and Excise. I worked with your lot on the Charlie Lister shoot-out. With Steve Kelly and Craig Bell.' He showed his ID. 'I was looking for a woman called Carole Rochester. Some money matters.'

The Special Branch man laughed and stood aside.

'Too late, mate. Sorry. Even you bastards can't get blood from a stone, thank Christ.'

Jackson stepped inside. There were three more men in the caravan, one of whom recognised him. He raised a casual hand.

'Shit,' said Jackson. 'What was it? Troilism? Lovers' tiff?'

Carole Rochester's body was in the corner. There was a bullet hole in her cheek, and blood on the wall beside her. A slightly-built man he took to be Alan Hughes was lying on his back on the floor, looking as if the Special Branch men had been dragging him when Jackson had arrived. In an armchair, with a pistol in his hand, sat the smallest corpse. The Animal. There was a black gash and ripped flesh at his throat, as if he had shot himself at very close range – after he was dead. The smell of gunsmoke lingered in the air.

'Something like that. That's Angus McGregor there, that little shite. As far as we can see he shot the other two, then himself. The woman's been fucked. You know, Angus McGregor? The Animal. Escaped from Bowscar.'

'Christ. He got all this way. Poor bitch, I wonder how she copped for this lot?'

'Search us, mate, we're just clearing up. Now, can we help you? Because we're a wee bit busy here, as you can see.'

Jackson could see very well. He guessed that they had shot all three, and were setting up the scene now, for the photograph.

'No,' he said. 'No interest to me now. Oh well. It was a lovely drive.'

'There's a good pub down the road,' said one of the policemen, suddenly quite friendly. 'The Ship. They all speak fucking Welsh there, but they seem quite human. Beer's good.'

'No,' said Jackson. 'I'll get back. Duty calls.'

'Ah. But if you did drop off, like. You haven't seen us, have you? Know what I mean? Nothing official.'

'Not a word, mate. We're only interested in the live ones. Dead men pay no Vat. See you.'

But he did not return to London. Instead, in Llanbedrog, he turned right on the road to Aberdaron, where he had stayed in a hotel as a kid. He'd have a night off, stay out of the pull of trouble, drink some beer. He'd left a message at the Dog to say he'd gone to Wales. What more could he do?

The news of Sir Gerald Turner's resignation was announced officially by Velma Goodman, as Prime Minister's Press Secretary. His letter, which she released, was terse and to the point. As the PM was aware, for some time now he had been undergoing treatment for a pulmonary condition, and his medical advisers had insisted that a period of total rest was essential. After his long service in the post it was a wrench, but he left confident that he had served his government and his country to the best of his abilities. He thanked both his Premier and all his colleagues for the help and support he had always received. The text of the Prime Minister's reply was even shorter. It expressed great shock and deep regret, coupled with a sense of loss after his years of sterling service. The last two sentences were the finest: 'May I thank you in particular for your part in the brilliantly handled affair of Bowscar Prison. It will not be forgotten.'

Donald Sinclair, a glass of ice-cold Beck's in front of him, was still chuckling over the letters with Judith and Chris Fortyne when the telephone rang. It was his wife. Her voice was colder than the beer.

'I suppose you're satisfied now, are you?' she asked. 'Donald, what exactly does this mean? And incidentally, are you intending ever to come home?'

Sinclair frowned, nodding to the other two to leave. That very morning, he had bitten on the bullet. He had told Judith that he must return to his Surrey home, probably that evening, and try to rescue something from the ashes. It was nothing to do with love, he said, nor even plain affection. At this delicate stage, he could not afford a marital scandal, could he? It might blight both their futures . . .

Judith, who had an understanding now, agreed entirely. Sinclair was going to seek a nomination for her, he was going to pull some strings. They may never be free to marry, but that was not everything. They could rise up the parliamentary ladder together, and probably reach the top. That sounded wonderful to her.

'Yes,' said Sinclair, to his wife. 'This evening, if I can get away. I've moved heaven and earth, but you must understand how rushed it's been.'

'Oh I do,' said Mary, icily. 'I've been talking to Elizabeth Turner. We're expecting the announcement at any moment.'

'What announcement?'

'Oh – pick any one from twenty. Your appointment as Home Secretary in Gerald's place. The return of capital punishment, the building of that American prison you were on about, goose-stepping in primary schools, transportation, arming the police. You name it.'

Judith was hovering in the doorway. Sinclair waved her out. He took a nervous sip of beer.

'Mary, have you been drinking? Gerald resigned for health reasons. Listen to th—'

'I've been talking to his *wife*, you fool! He was sacked. You've done very well, my dear, very well indeed. You've made Gerald look like a bumbling idiot over everything, you've made the Prime Minister look like a savage over Michael Masters, and you've turned out Mr Clean. I thought you were a liberal sort of person, Donald, a liberal of the right. But the people you've been playing to are the people of power, aren't they? What will be the next step – depose the Prime Minister? There's a vacuum where your heart should be, are you aware of that? A total vacuum. You're the Vicar of Bray, a hypocrite. You're a moral fascist.'

'Dear dear,' said Donald Sinclair. 'Perhaps I'd better stay away tonight, then. I wouldn't like my jackboots to make the bedclothes dirty. That would never do. I'll be in touch tomorrow.'

He put the receiver down and drank some beer. He buzzed for Judith.

'That was a reprieve. The mad lady I took to wife and bed. Tonight I'll take you to bed again, and a bloody good thing too. Do you think I'm a savage?'

'What, in bed? Try me!'

But Sinclair had become preoccupied.

'Mm,' he said. 'Look, call Christian in again. Let's sort this business out.'

In truth, there was very little left to sort. There were forty-seven people in hospital from Bowscar, and slightly under seven hundred prisoners had been dispersed. Ironically, about fifty of the most dangerous had had to go to prisons, rather than the camps, with the real possibility that they would cause unrest. Secretly, huge extra contingents of prison officers had been drafted in, and more general recruitment was quietly taking place. Pendlebury, although he did not know it yet, had got the sack, losing many of his pension rights. He was in a private hospital room, paid for by the Home Office, in case he was tempted to contact anybody. He did not know that he was effectively incommunicado, having been allowed a visit from his daughter. For the moment, for him, that was enough.

'Is the crisis really over, that's what bothers me,' said Sinclair. 'I feel rather flat about it. How many men are still at large?'

'Only seventeen who might be dangerous,' said Judith. 'But there's been no violence for days. They'll come in, in dribs and drabs. The papers have forgotten them, in any case.'

'Just like Sir Gerald said,' grinned Fortyne. 'These things are never as bad or bloody as you think they'll be. How many dead were there? Sixty, fifty, seventy-five? You see, we don't even know exactly, and we're in charge of it. If it was an air crash it would have been two hundred odd, all in one lump, indigestible. Although they'd still have been forgotten, soon enough. What's more, most of these were prisoners, so it matters even less.'

'You're so bloody cynical, Chris,' laughed Judith. 'Stop it, you're upsetting Donald.'

'Donald should be laughing,' said Fortyne, disapprovingly. 'Look on the bright side, Don. You can bring in any new regime you like now, and nobody will squeak. Marion with knobs on. National ID cards, radio tagging, brand the buggers – anything you like!'

'Shut up,' said Sinclair. 'You sound just like my wife. This is *not* a fascist state!'

'Who said it was? I'll vote for democracy every time. The police, the military, the press, the television, the MP on the ground – we've trained them all up, haven't we? No more chance of civil disorders now, eh – we've got the expertise. No guerilla strife for us! No voices of dissent! Who needs fascism?'

Sinclair looked sour.

'Look, knock it off, please. It's not a joke I relish, OK? You make it sound as if it's all turned out for the best, as if somehow we dreamed up and orchestrated the whole damned thing. It's been a pretty bloody tragedy, one way and another.'

Christian Fortyne studied his face to see how far this line would be taken. Sinclair looked back levelly, no humour in his eyes. Fortyne glinted.

'Donald,' he said, 'one day you *will* be Premier.'

But in the meantime, there was a prior call. That afternoon, Donald Sinclair was conducted to the Prime Minister, and given a small whisky. He emerged as the Home Secretary.

'Well,' he thought.

The bodies of Sarah Williams and Brian Rogers were discovered by a twelve-year-old boy called Sam Hopkins. He had been sitting in the forward cockpit of his family's narrowboat, *Emma*, when she came round a bend in the canal to be confronted with another boat swung out almost bank-to-bank. Sam called back to his father, who was steering, and the engine was reversed.

'Their stern line's come undone,' shouted Sam. 'Spike pulled out, I expect. There can't be anyone on board.'

His father edged *Emma*'s nose into the bank, and Sam jumped onto the towpath. He ran towards the canal boat, *Cynthia's Beam*. It seemed a stupid name to Sam. But he noted with satisfaction that his prediction was correct. There was a jagged mud-hole where the stern spike had pulled from the bank. Someone must have gone past too quickly, and sucked the boat towards the middle.

All the curtains on *Cynthia's Beam* were drawn, and nobody responded to his shouts. After a minute or two, Sam pulled in on the bow line, and jumped on board. He clambered aft along the cabin roof so that he could pull the stern rope in, then throw it to his sister Angela, who had followed him along the bank. He noticed that the after hatch was open, and being twelve, looked in. Even over the sound of *Emma*'s engines, his father heard his screams.

The discovery of two unnamed bodies, both savagely murdered

on one boat, came on the same news bulletin that told the world of Donald Sinclair's elevation. Although the canal boat was identified as the *Cynthia's Beam*, the name of Bowscar Prison figured not at all . . .

Forbes and Rosanna, holed up in the rather poky flat in Stormont Road, listened to all the news they could absorb, and watched the television bulletins almost obsessively. There had been no mention of them, and no pictures on the screen, but they found this unsurprising, in view of the vast amount of information and the tremendous interviews and pictures that the end of the siege provided. They noticed the brief announcement that Masters had been 'executed' with a chill, and wondered what the even briefer reference to Special Branch men seizing a tape under the Official Secrets Act might signify. Without leaving the flat they could not contact Peter Jackson, and they could not get a newspaper. They lived from the fridge and freezer, and they slept a lot, and made love. There was some wine on a wooden rack beside the fridge, but Forbes soon began to have withdrawal symptoms for lack of beer – and action. At ten o'clock on the evening that Sinclair was made Home Secretary, they took a bus to Stockwell and walked to the address that Carole Rochester had given them. They watched the street door for nearly half an hour before they moved. Donald Sinclair might not use it any longer, but it surely was not guarded.

Inside, Sinclair and Judith were talking seriously. The evening was meant to have been a celebration, and they had drunk champagne and eaten some marvellous game pie she had sent out for from Queen Anne's Gate that afternoon. But Sinclair had been quite moody and Judith, attributing it to his wife, had swung between sympathy and irritation. Mary's continued influence, especially when his triumph should have been unalloyed, was galling. He had reluctantly given her the details of Mary's phone call.

'You're mad,' she'd said. 'How can you be bothered with crap like "moral vacuum"? It's like a *Guardian* leader, for God's sake. She doesn't just mean you, she means the system. Politics is compromise, playing the cards you have to win the best you can. Mary doesn't want the real world, she wants Utopia. What she calls hypocrisy, I call common sense. You've beaten Gerald Turner because he had to lose. He's had his day. He was an ineffectual weakling.'

'She thinks I've stabbed him in the back. She thinks that basically he's a good man and I'm not.'

'Then she's *wrong*. Gerald Turner is as much a snake as anyone. He started it, for God's sake! He's charming, he's civilised, he's urbane, he's plausible, and he's a swine. His method was to delegate the no-win situations, always. How many juniors did he use then kick downstairs? How many times did someone carry the can for some disaster while he smiled on, smelling of roses? He used to make snide remarks about how he could never get the man to match the task, how sad it was the way he was let down. Then you came on the scene and screwed him. Your wife is stupid.'

'Maybe.'

'Maybe nothing. You played Turner at his own dirty little game and you wiped the floor with him. You've done an exhausting, demanding, impossible job, and you've done it brilliantly. Ever since Buckie you've run the whole shebang, you've cleared up Turner's mess, and you've managed – for the first time ever – to stop him grabbing all the credit. Well any of it, actually! Christian's right, darling – you're a genius. You've been the voice of sanity, against a Prime Minister with the mind of a caveman, and a duplicitous bastard of a boss. And you've won! Now *cheer up*, damn you!'

'I've won.'

It sounded good. The shades of doubt were lifting.

'You've won.'

Nevertheless, he was very cautious when he went down the stairs to the street door. It was not unknown for somebody to ring the bell, usually looking for another flat. There was no reason not to answer it. Sinclair put the safety chain on first.

'Hallo,' he said, to the man and woman standing on the doorstep. 'Can I help you?'

'My name's Andrew Forbes. This is Rosanna Nixon. We understand you've been looking for us.'

At first, and for several seconds, Sinclair was stunned. The secret services, the police, had been looking for this pair for days. Yet they had found him, at an address the secret services did not even know. Suddenly, it struck him as laughable, ridiculous. Instead of fear or anger, he felt euphoria. He was tempted, for a moment, to ask them in. He did not, though.

'Indeed I have,' he said. 'How nice of you to drop by. What can I do for you?'

The couple appeared to him to be totally unthreatening. The man was scruffy, even seedy, and the woman was small and fragile, like a child. They were nervous.

'There were a few things we wanted to put to you,' said Forbes. 'Miss Nixon, as you know, saw James McGregor murdered on the roof at Buckie. The night you were staying at the Fox Hotel under the name of Swift. Then you had his brother taken to an English prison, and held in solitary confinement. The governor complained, and warned you about the unrest in the prison, and ultimately freed McGregor, against your instructions.'

'Which were probably illegal, anyway,' put in Rosanna, fiercely. 'Then you had the gall to blame Mr Pendlebury for everything. You can't deny that.'

Forbes put his hand out to touch her sleeve. It was a tender gesture.

'There's the question of Michael Masters, too,' he said. 'We know you're in cahoots with him. Were. We've quite a lot of evidence that you were directly responsible for his imprisonment and death. Don't you think you'd better let us in, to talk?'

Donald Sinclair, disconcertingly, began to laugh. Both Rosanna and Forbes experienced fear. They glanced behind them, as if expecting spooks to emerge from the shadows round the cars and railings on the street, spooks with guns. They saw nobody.

'Carole Rochester,' said Sinclair, finally. 'It was her. She knows this place, she knew Masters. Well well, the bitch.' He was quite amused. 'Go on, then,' he said. 'All this juicy information, these so-called facts. What do you propose to do with them? Who do you think's going to believe a word of it? What does it all add up to?' He laughed once more, a bark, almost of delight. 'The ragged trousered philanthropist and his moll!' he said. 'Who do you reckon's going to publish it? How quickly can you persuade the media to put their heads on the chopping block for me, I honestly can't wait. Fuck off, will you, crawl back to your hole.'

At this time, in this place, until they had regrouped, Andrew Forbes and Rosanna Nixon had no shots left, and all three of them knew it. The frontal ploy had failed. Donald Sinclair unclipped the chain and stepped into the doorway. They retreated before him, as if from an attack.

'How far do you think you're going to get?' he asked them. 'Outside this front door? We've almost picked you up before, you know, we've missed by inches. Does that worry you? It ought to. Now go.'

He swept towards them, and they retreated further. They turned, and began to walk away.

Sinclair shouted after them: 'Did you come by car, you idiots? You'd best check underneath it before you drive away. You might just find a bomb!'

Two minutes later, as the bell buzzed yet again, he clattered down the stairs in high good humour to give them another earful. What fresh nonsense had they remembered? What threats to make his blood run cold? He pulled the door back wide.

'Now look, you fools,' he started, and the words froze in his mouth. His mouth hung open, his eyes grew wide, the blood drained from his face. It was Michael Masters. In his hand he carried a heavy automatic, and he was flanked by two stocky men, one blond, one rather bald.

'Sarah Williams is dead,' said Michael Masters. 'You've let me down a bit, Donald. I've come to kill you.'

The automatic leapt like a cannon in Masters' hand. Donald Sinclair was thrown backwards into his safe house, and collapsed onto the stairs. Michael Masters fired twice more into his body, then turned away. A van pulled smoothly to a stop beside the parked cars in front of him.

'Nice one,' said the older of the men. 'He won't be sending any Christmas cards this year.'

Barbara Masters was in front of the television set when her husband walked through the door. She had heard footsteps in the passageway, but she had assumed it was one of the staff. The two boys, whose stiff upper lips were now like tempered steel, whose skins were rhinoceros hide, were still at Eton. She turned when the door opened, because there had been no knock. She stood, then dropped back onto the settee. She was speechless.

Masters, in her eyes, had aged ten years. His face was pale and haggard, his bearing was slack, almost slumped. As she gazed at him, Barbara felt no great surprise that he was not really dead. Her eyes slowly filled with tears.

'Mike,' she said. 'Oh, thank God. Oh Michael.'

He did not move, or protest, when she ran to him and put her arms around him, sobbing. He looked down at the top of her head, dark-brown hair with a small streak of white he did not recognise, and he tried to feel emotion, anything. All that came into his head was the name of Sarah. This head was not the head of Sarah Williams. After a minute, though, he managed to raise his right arm from his side, and put it round the heaving shoulder of his wife. He thought of Sinclair's face, and the way his body had hurtled backwards under the weight of the four-five bullet and crumpled on the stairs.

He did not explain much. He told her that he'd done a deal with the terrorists because the government had refused to, and he told her that the execution had been faked. They had made a video, he said, a sort of parody for the British television, but the government had stopped it. He did not say that he had offered Sinclair's life because of Sarah, the sort of propaganda coup the IRA had dreamed of, and how beautiful it had been when he had been promoted to Home Secretary. He did not tell her Sinclair was dead, in the secret place that he'd promised the Irishmen existed.

'I want you to call Sir Cyril France,' he said. 'I want him over here, tonight. I've escaped from the IRA, single-handed, that's their part of the deal, they'll back the story. I want publicity, quickly, before the government can act. I'm going to be a hero, get the sympathy vote, get a pardon, anything. I'm not going back to prison.'

His wife nodded, eagerly.

'I went to see the minister,' she said. 'Donald Sinclair. And now he's Home Secretary! He seemed very sympathetic.'

'Yes,' said Masters. 'He would have been. Cyril will be, too. When I've told him everything. I think he'll see the point. He'll do his best for me.'

'Would you like a drink?' asked Barbara. 'While I ring him up?'

'No thanks,' said Masters. 'I'm going to my study. I want to think.'

They were well into Wales when they heard the news of Donald Sinclair's death. They had decided to go back to Llanbedrog to try and warn Carole Rochester if that were possible, or to see what had transpired. They expected to run into trouble, but they could think of no alternative – they had blown her cover. They had rung Antony at the Dog and Partridge and learned that Jackson had gone there, too. That puzzled them, but reinforced the view. For lack of alternative again, they had hired a car in Rosanna's name, and on her licence. They were both tired, and miserable.

After the first, terrific, shock, the news had rather cheered them. Ghoulish, they conceded, but why try to hide it? The BBC said only that he had been gunned down in a terrorist attack in South London, and the police were working on several leads. They were relieved, in view of the fact that they had spoken to him on the doorstep, that they were not named as suspects, or at least described. It seemed unlikely that Sinclair's vendetta had died so quickly after him.

As the news rolled on, their faint feeling of relief or pleasure that he had got his comeuppance faded fast. The stark statement of the facts was followed by a panegyric which was the soul and model of obsequiousness. From the Prime Minister downwards, Sinclair's colleagues on both sides of the House vied with each other to condemn the atrocity and extravagantly praise the man. From Buckie to Bowscar, they were told, his star had glittered in the firmament, ever climbing. For Rosanna and Andrew Forbes, who had watched the ascent from the inside, it was a bitter cup to swallow. After a few minutes, Forbes switched off.

'Another hero for democracy,' he said. 'They'll be giving him a State funeral next. The fucking hypocrites.'

'All dressed in black. Andrew – do you think we ought to go on now? Just to get arrested? Shouldn't we try and get away somehow? I've got friends in France, you must have contacts. We can get the story out. There's got to be a way.'

It was starting to rain; they were well into North Wales. Andrew Forbes flicked on the windscreen wipers, and flicked his eyes onto her small and anxious face.

'Oh, there'll be a way,' he said. 'Don't worry, little Mouse. What about your old flame? Dublin Desmond! Ireland's the place for disappearing!'

The Ford Escort, with wet moorland rising to its right and the black and ruffled waters of Llyn Celyn close on the other side, swept round a bend at sixty miles an hour. Rosanna laughed.

'Shut up, oaf!' she said, and rapped the outside of his thigh with hard, sharp knuckles. He felt her eyes on him and glanced at her once more. It was a moment, half a second.

When he looked back, he faced two Army lorries side by side, coming towards them, one overtaking the other in his carriageway. There was vertical rock on one side, the waters on his left. Andrew said 'I love you' and had time to be amazed at how cool he felt. Rosanna, screaming, did not hear him. He dabbed the brake and spun, bouncing sideways off the nearside truck, the lakeside truck, and up into the air. The Escort, with one door burst open, hit the surface boot first and sank immediately. The Army lorries, first one and then the other, pulled into the side and stopped. Ten cars behind them disgorged travellers, many of whom screamed, or cried and shook. Some were sick onto the pebbles of the beach. A helicopter, high above the scene, swung to its right and disappeared behind a curve of mountain.

Two hours later Peter Jackson, driving back to England, used his ID to get within the cordon and watch the mobile crane winching the Escort from the waters of the lake. When he arrived its bonnet was just showing. He had spoken to Antony at the Dog and Partridge and had received no message. The caravan at Llanbedrog, when he'd checked, had been empty and unguarded.

'What happened?' he asked the Army sergeant overseeing operations. 'Anybody know?'

The sergeant sniffed in the chilly drizzle. He had heard the rumour, and this bloke was official, so why not?

'Meant to be an accident,' he said. 'Man and a woman, racing round a bend too fast. One of our lads, in a Bedford, overtaking in a dangerous fashion. Fishy.'

'Fishy? How come?'

'Why should an Army driver overtake? To get to the Naafi first? To get put on a charge? Do us a favour. Anyway, there've been a lot of people hanging round. Oddbods. You know.'

Jackson raised his eyebrows, hoping for more. There was a coldness spreading inside him, a clammy sense of fear. The windscreen of the Escort was at the surface, lapped by small waves. The rain had stopped. The crane's diesel barked as the strain grew greater. Now it had to lift both car and water.

The sergeant said: 'You know the funny ones. The men in macs. The snooty bastards.'

Water was gushing from the rising motor car. Both doors were open. Jackson stared, heartsick.

'Young girl,' said the sergeant. 'Little skinny thing, quite pretty they reckoned. They went off with them, another fishy thing. The men. They were here within two minutes. Amazing, isn't it?'

'Went off with them?' He craned his neck to see inside the car. The front seats were empty. The back, three feet above the surface, was full of opaque water. 'What do you mean?'

'In the ambulance. That was cushty, it came from Bala, very quick, considering. I mean out in the wilds like this, you could wait for ever.'

Peter Jackson's heart began to lift. But he held on to his senses.

The car was swung inwards from the lake, towards the stony beach. There was no longer doubt in his mind as to whose it had been, and why they'd met an accident. But now?

'Were they alive?' he said. They had to be. He could not hold the picture in his heart, alone.

The sergeant was preparing for the next stage. The Escort was about to touch the shore. He smiled, indifferently.

'They'd have to be lucky,' he said. 'It's fucking cold in there.'